NEBULA
AWARDS
29

NEBULA AWARDS

29

SFWA's
Choices for the Best
Science Fiction and
Fantasy of the Year

E D I T E D   B Y

PAMELA SARGENT

A Harvest Original

Harcourt Brace & Company

San Diego   New York   London

The Library of Congress has cataloged this serial as follows:
The Nebula awards.—No. 18—New York [N.Y.]: Arbor House, c1983–
v.; 22cm.
Annual.
Published: San Diego, Calif.: Harcourt Brace & Company, 1984–
Published for: Science-fiction and Fantasy Writers of America, 1983–
Continues: Nebula award stories (New York, N.Y.: 1982)
ISSN 0741-5567 = The Nebula awards
1. Science fiction, American—Periodicals.
1. Science-fiction and Fantasy Writers of America.
PS648.S3N38   83-647399
813'.0876'08—dc19
AACR 2 MARC-S
Library of Congress [8709r84]rev

ISBN 0-15-100107-3
ISBN 0-15-600119-5 (Harvest: pbk.)

Designed by G. B. D. Smith
Printed in the United States of America
First edition
A B C D E

Permissions acknowledgments appear on page 308, which constitutes a continuation of the
copyright page.

In Memory of
Avram Davidson
Lester del Rey
Chad Oliver

Contents

INTRODUCTION

Pamela Sargent

The Nebula Awards, given annually to authors of outstanding works of science fiction and fantasy, have been in existence for almost thirty years. They are voted on by members of the Science-fiction and Fantasy Writers of America, an organization that includes most of the writers in these two closely related genres. This makes the Nebula Award unique in that it is the only award for science fiction given to writers by a popular vote of their peers.

Any awards process has its flaws, and that of the Nebula is no exception. A list of writers who have never received this accolade would include some of the field's most accomplished authors. Bickering over rules, politicking, and other kinds of contentiousness have occasionally afflicted the awards procedure in the past. Even so, past Nebula Awards anthologies still provide a comprehensive record of how the field has grown and changed and serve to highlight many of the distinctive and gifted writers who have contributed to the literature. The winning works are also seen in context among other contenders that are equally deserving of honor. Past Nebula winners and nominees include examples of science fiction and fantasy at its best: They are works that grapple with the issues science and new technologies raise, that reflect the social or psychological changes and dilemmas of the modern (or postmodern) age, or that distance us from our conventional reality through fantasy in ways that illuminate our own world and time.

What has been happening in science fiction and fantasy over the past year? Sadly, an acceleration of trends that seem designed to poison the wellsprings of the genre instead of feeding them. Those writers who have been commercially successful with their past work are encouraged to do more of the same, while less fortunate writers are pushed into writing brand-name fiction. Writers who should be looking ahead, imaginatively exploring the new, estranging us from our own time through their fiction so that we see our world with fresh eyes, are instead being encouraged, even forced, into strip-mining the old or repeating themselves. Talented writers are diverted from their own work to write what publishers think will sell, or they fall silent. We're not immortals; work postponed or delayed can easily become work that is never completed or published.

At exactly the time we need new directions, we're being pushed to look back. Readers unacquainted with science fiction and fantasy may be forgiven for believing that most of it is novels based on television series, novels based on movies, multivolume yarns of medieval fantasy, tales set in one writer's universe that are actually written by another, and books by a very few best-selling writers. One purpose of the Nebula anthology, an ideal to which it should aspire even when that ideal is only imperfectly achieved, is to display excellence, work of a quality often only grudgingly or fortuitously accepted in the wider marketplace.

THE 1993 NEBULA AWARDS
FINAL BALLOT

For Novel

Assemblers of Infinity by Kevin J. Anderson and Doug Beason
(*Analog,* September–December 1992; Bantam Spectra)

Hard Landing by Algis Budrys (*The Magazine of Fantasy & Science Fiction,* November 1992; Warner/Questar)

Beggars in Spain by Nancy Kress (William Morrow/AvoNova)

°*Red Mars* by Kim Stanley Robinson (Bantam Spectra)

Nightside the Long Sun by Gene Wolfe (Tor)

For Novella

"The Beauty Addict" by Ray Aldridge
(*Full Spectrum 4,* Bantam Spectra)

°"The Night We Buried Road Dog" by Jack Cady (*The Magazine of Fantasy & Science Fiction,* January 1993)

"Dancing on Air" by Nancy Kress
(*Asimov's Science Fiction,* July 1993)

°Indicates winner.

"Into the Miranda Rift" by G. David Nordley (*Analog*, July 1993)

"Naming the Flowers" by Kate Wilhelm (Axolotl Press; *The Magazine of Fantasy & Science Fiction*, February 1993)

"Wall, Stone, Craft" by Walter Jon Williams (Axolotl Press; *The Magazine of Fantasy & Science Fiction*, October/November 1993)

For Novelette

"England Underway" by Terry Bisson (*Omni*, July 1993)

"The Nutcracker Coup" by Janet Kagan
(*Asimov's Science Fiction*, December 1992)

"The Franchise" by John Kessel
(*Asimov's Science Fiction*, August 1993)

*"Georgia on My Mind" by Charles Sheffield
(*Analog*, January 1993)

"Things Not Seen" by Martha Soukup
(*Analog*, September 1992; *More Whatdunnits*, DAW)

"Death on the Nile" by Connie Willis
(*Asimov's Science Fiction*, March 1993)

For Short Story

"The Man Who Rowed Christopher Columbus Ashore" by Harlan Ellison (World Fantasy Convention Program Book; *Omni*, July 1992)

"All Vows" by Esther Friesner
(*Asimov's Science Fiction*, November 1992)

"Alfred" by Lisa Goldstein
(*Asimov's Science Fiction*, December 1992)

*"Graves" by Joe Haldeman (*The Magazine of Fantasy & Science Fiction*, October/November 1992)

"The Good Pup" by Bridget McKenna (*The Magazine of Fantasy & Science Fiction*, March 1993)

"The Beggar in the Living Room" by William John Watkins
(*Asimov's Science Fiction*, April 1993)

What do these works demonstrate about the state of science fiction and fantasy? The field has become increasingly diverse—some would say chaotic—with no center and writers going off in all directions. The future seems even more uncertain, and also threatening in new ways that we don't yet understand. It may be no accident that an increasing number of science fiction writers are attempting the alternative history story, "what if" stories that seem, more and more often, to be turning into "if only" stories.

So what one can say about this year's Nebula finalists as a group is only that each displays its particular sort of excellence. Esther Friesner's "All Vows" is a story of faith, promises, and ghosts, while "The Beggar in the Living Room" by William John Watkins deals with the ways in which new communications technologies alienate us. "Naming the Flowers" by Kate Wilhelm is a love story centered around a human mutant, while G. David Nordley's "Into the Miranda Rift" is a realistic and carefully extrapolated story of a possible future expedition to a satellite of Uranus. Nancy Kress, in "Dancing on Air," shows how advances in biological technology might alter the art of ballet, Janet Kagan tells a humorous story with a political point in "The Nutcracker Coup," while Walter Jon Williams, in his splendid alternative history "Wall, Stone, Craft," examines the origins of science fiction itself. Algis Budrys, in a rare and long-awaited appearance as a novelist, contributes a hard-bitten novel of aliens trying to live out their lives on Earth in *Hard Landing*, while Gene Wolfe, in *Nightside the Long Sun*, gives us a story of, as he puts it, "a good man in the service of a bad god."

I urge readers to seek out these works, as well as the other finalists not included in this volume and the works on this year's preliminary Nebula ballot (listed in an appendix in the back), and to appreciate their individual and very different virtues. The ground of science fiction and fantasy is yielding such a varied crop that almost any reader can find works to his or her taste. My hope, in these increasingly ambiguous times, is that this wide variety of stories and novels foreshadows a renewal of the genre's vitality, rather than representing, as writer Norman Spinrad puts it, "the voice of a collective visionary spirit . . . shouting into the gathering darkness."

The Year in Science Fiction and Fantasy: A Symposium

Michael Swanwick

Maureen F. McHugh

Rebecca Ore

Robert J. Sawyer

Paul Di Filippo

Norman Spinrad

Eleanor Arnason

Gregory Benford

At a time when science fiction and fantasy are increasingly fragmented, it seems appropriate to listen to several eloquent voices, rather than one lone commentator, discuss the state of the genre this year.

Michael Swanwick has won a Nebula Award for his novel *Stations of the Tide* and a Theodore Sturgeon Memorial Award for his short story "The Edge of the World." His most recent novel is *The Iron Dragon's Daughter.*

Maureen F. McHugh won the 1992 James Tiptree, Jr., Award and a Locus Award for her first novel, *China Mountain Zhang,* which was also a Nebula and Hugo Award finalist.

Rebecca Ore has been a finalist for the Philip K. Dick Award; her most recent books are *Alien Bootlegger and Other Stories* and the fantasy novel *Slow Funeral.*

Robert J. Sawyer is Canadian Regional Director of the SFWA and the author of the novels *Golden Fleece, Far-Seer, Fossil Hunter, Foreigner,* and *End of an Era.*

Paul Di Filippo's stories have appeared in *Amazing Stories, The Magazine of Fantasy & Science Fiction,* and several past Nebula Awards anthologies; he writes reviews and essays for *Asimov's Science Fiction* and *Science Fiction Age.*

Norman Spinrad is a past president of the SFWA and the author of, most recently, *Pictures at Eleven*. His past novels include *Bug Jack Barron, The Iron Dream, The Void Captain's Tale, Little Heroes,* and *Russian Spring;* he lives in Paris, France.

Eleanor Arnason was honored with a James Tiptree, Jr., Award for her novel *A Woman of the Iron People*. Her latest novel is *Ring of Swords*, and she is also the author of *The Sword Smith, To the Resurrection Station,* and *Daughter of the Bear King*.

Gregory Benford won a 1980 Nebula Award for his novel *Timescape;* his most recent novel is *Furious Gulf,* and his other books include *Against Infinity, In Alien Flesh, Artifact, Great Sky River,* and *Tides of Light.* He is also a professor of physics at the University of California at Irvine.

THE RISE OF AMBITION, THE FALL OF THE FUTURE
Michael Swanwick

I'll have to be careful how I say this. Just so you don't get the wrong idea.

Word on the street was that 1993 was a disappointing year. Oh, like any other disappointing year, there were exceptions—stories like Rebecca Ore's "Alien Bootlegger" or Ian R. MacLeod's "Papa" or Nancy Kress's "Dancing on Air" or Bruce Sterling's "Deep Eddy" or Jack Cady's "The Night We Buried Road Dog" that could hold their own with the best of any year. There were novels like William Gibson's *Virtual Light* and Nancy Kress's *Beggars in Spain* and Nicola Griffith's *Ammonite* and Lucius Shepard's *The Golden* that roused a great deal of excitement. Kim Stanley Robinson and Gene Wolfe both began major novel sequences with *Red Mars* and *Nightside the Long Sun,* respectively, and normally no year containing two such works could be deemed anything less than vintage. But they were all considered to be exceptions, sports, blips on the statistical map that proved nothing. A hundred more such works piled atop the heap would've been considered merely a hundred more exceptions. Not a very interesting year, was the common perception.

Nineteen ninety-three was also the year when many critics joined voices to proclaim that science fiction was in a state of crisis. They were reacting to the wholesale collapse—the genre equivalent of the fall of the Soviet Union—of the consensus futures that science fiction had been assembling for decades. Together we had charted a reasonably plausible spread of possibilities that anyone who wanted to could build stories upon. At one end of the spectrum were O'Neill colonies and lunar dome cities and at the other was the postapocalyptic wasteland with its martyrs and mutants.

Those futures are dead and gone. The world has moved on, and the inherent contradictions in yesterday's extrapolations have piled up to the point where they can't be ignored. It's not that space colonies or mass extinctions can't happen anymore but that if they *do* occur, they'll look nothing at all like what we've been expecting.

That makes this a particularly exciting time for science fiction. All the old furniture has to be swept aside, reimagined, reinvented. Futures have to be built, plausible ones, and they cannot look like anything anybody has ever suggested before. It's a daunting challenge, but ours is a genre built upon imagination. Anyone who doubts the challenge will be met is obviously in the wrong place.

Meanwhile, unheralded, genre fantasy has passed through its own crisis and undergone a quiet revolution. Years of background carping about "derivative fantasies" and "interchangeable trilogies" (there were always exceptions, but, again, we're discussing not truth but perceptions here) combined with the near-limitless potential inherent in the form to create an ideal environment for literary ambition. One in which not only were writers producing innovative work but readers were actively seeking it out.

By my reading, this cycle began with the publication of Greer Ilene Gilman's difficult and remarkable *Moonwise* in 1991 and continued at least into 1993 with Peter S. Beagle's *The Innkeeper's Song* and into 1994 with Rebecca Ore's *Slow Funeral* and Rachel Pollack's stunning *Temporary Agency*. But the phenomenon was not limited to specific books. There was a buzz in the air. Something was going on, and, as a group, the fantasists knew it. You never saw such a confident batch of writers in your life. Their eyes were alight with plans and conspiracies.

Other influences were in play in 1993, but those two—the fall of the future and the rise of ambition—were the two great wheels that ground the finest. The last time the field was this quietly busy was back in the early 1980s, when the first cyberpunks were publishing their now-canonical works. Those were disappointing years, everyone agreed. The outlook was bleak.

But the exceptions then, as now, were no exceptions at all; they were the very heart and soul of the enterprise. Pay close attention! It's going on now, right before us. A decade from now, a new generation of readers will envy our having been here when it all happened. We'll look back and imagine we saw it all from the very start. It was all so clear, we'll think. So obvious.

SEX AND GENDER IN 1993'S SF
Maureen F. McHugh

I was a member of the jury for the James Tiptree, Jr., Award, and my reading last year concentrated on books recommended because of the way they handled issues of sex and sexual identity.

Over the history of the genre, SF writers have created new sexes and aliens that switched sex; have had old men's brains transferred into young women's bodies; have written about male societies and female utopias. While there has been some amazingly sophisticated writing about sex and sex roles, there's been a lot of silly stuff. There's been a lot of wish fulfillment: if we could just get rid of those pesky men and have women run the world, everything would be wonderful; or if men could change into women, wouldn't the sex be just wonderful. The best of this year's crop didn't necessarily come up with any new ideas, but they took old SF ideas and looked at them a little more ruthlessly.

One of the best of the year was Nicola Griffith's *Ammonite*. *Ammonite* takes an old SF trope—the planet of women/the women's utopia—but describes a complex society. There are nurturing women in a community of sharing and art and mysticism, but there are also women tribesmen on horseback and women sailors. They don't all get along. Some of the women are ambitious, some are kind, some interested in their own agendas and willing to sacrifice anything and anybody to avoid facing change. *Glory Season* by David Brin is a story of a world run by women, and although, in my mind, less successful than *Ammonite,* it also presents a vast canvas of women merchants and scientists and pirates. *Glory Season* is about a society where both men and women come into sexual arousal at different times of the year, where most children born are daughter clones, and where there is separation of the sexes. It is an examination of sexual roles changed by changing biology.

"Motherhood, Etc." by L. Timmel Duchamp is about a woman who catches her partner's gender from him/her and becomes both male and female. What complicates and enriches this story is the protagonist, Pat (perhaps an unfortunate choice of name, thanks to "Saturday Night Live"), who is nineteen and as full of anger and naïveté and contradiction as any nineteen-year-old, and who also is suddenly developing male sex organs and feeling the rush of testosterone.

Another way to question certain assumptions about sex and gender identity is to depict gay or bisexual characters, to view an imagined world through their eyes. One of the nice things to notice is that novels like *Crash Course* by Wilhemina Baird, *Burning Bright* by Melissa Scott, *Drawing Blood* by Poppy Z. Brite, *Dancing Jack* by Laurie J. Marks, and *Songs of Chaos* by S. N. Lewitt are not books about being gay, but rather are books in which some of the characters are gay. The relationships between the characters are not all of a type, either. At one time it seemed as if all the gay characters I read about were saints. They died young a lot. In these books some die, some don't, and damn few are saints.

Books about strong women shouldn't be considered gender benders (and that's a good thing—it's a sad commentary when a strong woman is considered a bender of sexual roles). But two exceptional books this year that featured strong female characters were *Parable of the Sower* by Octavia Butler and *Vanishing Point* by Michaela Roessner.

Ring of Swords by Eleanor Arnason and *Coelestis* by Paul Park both take place in space and both are standouts. Both involve aliens who have very different ideas of sex. *Ring of Swords* has male and female aliens who share some of our assumptions about sexual roles but who are just different enough that they find humans perverse. *Coelestis* is the story of a diplomat who falls in love with an alien pianist. "She" is surgically altered to look human and is able to stay that way only with the help of drugs. When she is cut off from the drugs he is unwilling to stop thinking of her in terms he understands. A dark but interesting novel.

Other strong works: "A Defense of Social Contracts" and "The Story So Far" by Martha Soukup, for their examination of social roles; *A Plague of Angels* by Sheri Tepper, for the play of ideas; "Chemistry" by James Patrick Kelly, for a reminder that falling in love is mostly a matter of biochemistry, although that doesn't make it feel any less like love; "Forever, Said the Duck" by Jonathan Lethem, because if virtual reality ever does come about, someone is going to have this party; *Rainbow Man* by M. J. Engh, about a woman who finds that customs vary and who, not incidentally, finds herself categorized as a man; *Passion Play* by Sean Stewart, for his street-smart woman detective; "Shrödinger's Cathouse" by Kij Johnson, about a whorehouse where the staff exists in a state of male/not male (or female/not female), just as Schrödinger's cat is dead/not dead until you open the box.

STATE OF PLAY CIRCA 1993
Rebecca Ore

In 1993, everyone did his or her usual story. Conservatives wrote conservative stories. Whatever form of weirdness the weird writers specialized in, that's what they did this year, too. In Kim Stanley Robinson's case, he did very well indeed, but nobody, on or off the ballot, did anything uncharacteristic.

No "Dori Bangs." Admittedly, a cynic pointed out that Bruce Sterling had just updated the Victorian fable about the more-or-less happy obscure (in Sterling's story, the surviving obscure) compared to the genius damned (the weird intense). Since Sterling isn't generally considered a Victorian moralist, the story of the rock critic and the comic artist who died in our continuum but who moved to the Midwest and survived in the story universe was neat. This year, oh, well. In a year's worth of Preliminary Ballot stories, nobody wrote a story that played against the writer's usual preoccupations, political stance, images, technophobia, or technophilia.

Perhaps the money whip cracked and we all froze? An editor suggested the economy crunched us. But we weren't rushing for the center. We were doing what we did, well, sometimes brilliantly.

I guess I shouldn't expect new ground every year from everyone, but . . .

. . . let's blame this on the global situation. One major organizing myth collapsed, and we all are thoroughly aware that if we have to lead ecologically correct lives it won't be fun. We went to the country or the slums in the sixties and seventies, but now we've moved back to the suburbs or are trying to.

Science fiction at its most pessimistic has an optimism that Louis-Ferdinand Céline would never share: apocalyptic novels assume that having humans around is a good thing; the ecotopias of the 1960s and '70s assumed humans would willingly do stoop labor if the economy or the vibes were changed. (Play enough whale chants, maybe?) Both types and others are as optimistic about humanity as any technophilic wonder boy is.

But the bombs didn't fall, we didn't make it to Mars, and the state didn't wither away. So maybe we're stuck with ourselves, and we might as well see what we can do with what we've got.

Arrgh. . . .

1993: THE DARK SIDE OF THE FORCE
Robert J. Sawyer

Any year that sees new books by such brilliant writers as William F. Wu, Timothy Zahn, K. W. Jeter, Roger MacBride Allen, and Garfield and Judith Reeves-Stevens should be noteworthy. Add to that the long-awaited first collaborative novel by Kristine Kathryn Rusch and Dean Wesley Smith, and 1993 should have been an auspicious year indeed.

(Wu, of course, is known for his wonderful short stories, including "Wong's Curiosity Emporium." Zahn's "Cascade Point" won the 1984 best-novella Hugo. K. W. Jeter's *Dr. Adder* [1984] was an outstanding early cyberpunk work. Roger MacBride Allen's *The Ring of Charon* [1991] was one of the most inventive hard-SF novels in many a year. Gar Reeves-Stevens gave us *Nighteyes* [1989], *Dark Matter* [1990], and several other excellent mainstream SF novels. And multiple-award nominee Rusch and her husband, Smith, are the energetic team responsible for the Pulphouse Publishing empire.)

Yes, a distinguished group of authors indeed—and yet not one of their 1993 books made even the *preliminary* Nebula Award ballot, let alone the list of five finalists.

The reason becomes clear when we mention their 1993 titles: Wu's contributions were *Isaac Asimov's Robots in Time #1, #2,* and *#3,* plus *Mutant Chronicles Volume 1: In Lunacy* (based on material from Target Games). Zahn weighed in with a couple of Star Wars novels. Allen gave us *Isaac Asimov's Caliban.* The Reeves-Stevenses wrote *The Day of Descent,* the first in a series of books based on the TV show "Alien Nation"; Jeter's book was also in that series. And Rusch and Smith served up a frothy "Star Trek: Deep Space Nine" novel called *The Big Game.*

SF used to be about exploring strange new worlds. But 1993 was the year in which it seemed to give up the good fight and finally to admit that it had become devoted to exploiting tired old worlds instead.

The phenomenon of SF's being "product" instead of literature began with the Star Trek novels. When these first started appearing, authors used words like "homage" and "nostalgia" to describe their motives for doing them. But in 1993 that pretense was finally dropped: Pocket announced a forthcoming line of books based on "Voyager," a new Star Trek TV series that will hit the airwaves in 1995. No one outside of the Paramount studios knew the premise of the show, no one had seen even a single frame of it on film, no one could possibly have any sentimental attachment to the material. But the feeding frenzy of authors on GEnie (the computer network on which SFWA has its electronic home) clamoring to sign contracts to do books based on that series was a sight to behold.

I don't (much) blame the writers, of course. We've all got to eat. No, the publishers are the culprits here. They pay less in real dollars now than they ever have before for original SF novels—and they often keep those novels in print for only months, or even weeks.

Not that publishers can't get behind books when they want to: Pocket mounted a campaign in 1993 to get the first Alien Nation novel onto the Nebula ballot, sending out copies to SFWA members in hopes of getting Nebula recommendations. But how does one assess a volume whose characters, premises, and backgrounds were created by other writers working in other media? For that matter, how does one assess the contributions of writers to books that have the possessive form of Isaac Asimov's name as part of the title?

I'd love to say that 1993 was an aberration. But it wasn't: 1994 and future years are shaping up to be more of the same. See, in 1993 Roger MacBride Allen signed a contract to produce a trilogy of Star Wars novels and another couple of books about Asimov's robots. More power to him—but I'd rather have the rest of his saga of *The Hunted Earth*, the ground-breaking original series he began with *Ring of Charon*. Also in 1993, Kevin J. Anderson signed to do a trilogy of Star Wars novels. Good work if you can get it, I suppose—but I'd much rather see another minimasterpiece from him, like this year's Nebula-nominated *Assemblers of Infinity*, which he coauthored with Doug Beason. Dave Wolverton, one of our absolute best authors, has signed on to do a Star Wars trilogy, too, while Barry B. Longyear, whose "Enemy Mine" landed him both a Hugo and a Nebula in 1980, has reappeared on bookstore shelves with an Alien Nation book.

The SF author I feel sorriest for is John E. Stith. He was a Nebula nominee for 1990's brilliant *Redshift Rendezvous*, and he had an even better novel in 1993 called *Manhattan Transfer*. But that book didn't make it to either the Nebula or the Hugo ballot—and I think I know why. Many bookstores have taken to treating the terms Star Trek and Star Wars as authors' names. Stith's work was no doubt lost in the alphabetical limbo after row upon row of media tie-in books.

Indeed, it's getting hard to find any original SF on shelves groaning under the weight of Star Trek, Star Wars, seaQuest, and Quantum Leap novels; of products licensed by Target Games and TSR; of books in the universes of Isaac Asimov, Ray Bradbury, Arthur C. Clarke, Anne McCaffrey, and Larry Niven; of false collaborations between big-name authors and newcomers; of sharecropping, franchise fiction, and packaged books. It used to be that such fare was the province of hack writers, those who needed a quick buck, and Trekkies who got lucky. Now, though, it's where many of the best and brightest of our younger writers are spending most of their time.

Pocket Books failed in its bid to get an Alien Nation novel on the Nebula ballot—but, if things continue, it's inevitable that someday, all too soon, the Nebula Award *will* be won by a media or gaming tie-in product. The year in which that happens will be the year in which SF literature will be said to have truly died—but when literary historians look back they'll mark 1993 as the year in which the field's condition became terminal.

THE SCIENCE FICTION
IN THE YEAR
Paul Di Filippo

Nineteen ninety-three was yet another year when it really helped to have read a lot of science fiction. Nothing gives more comfort and sustenance nowadays to the sensibilities of the beleaguered postmodern citizen than the realization that our whole life was laid out for us in the pages of pulp magazines and Ace Doubles, if we had only had the wit to see it.

In Waco, Texas, the authorities burned Michael Valentine Smith for the umpteenth time in this country's history of religious tolerance. Good as Heinlein was at predicting, he forgot to include in his *Stranger* T-shirt hawkers and live media coverage of the martyrdom. On the other hand, we can certainly hold David Koresh accountable for failing to preach as well as Smith did. Even Manson's theology was better than this guy's. It's easy to imagine Koresh at his postimmolation interview with the Old Ones.

"What happened, son, to the water ceremony and the grokking?"

"Screw that New Age shit! I only wanted sex, drugs, and rock 'n' roll!"

California, meanwhile, had the J. G. Ballard franchise nailed down. While Heidi Fleiss and Michael Jackson upheld the *Vermilion Sands* tradition of decadence, the rest of the state busied itself enacting the Master's simultaneously vigorous and desultory postapocalyptic scenarios. *The Burning World* meets *The Wind from Nowhere*. Is it true that a mysterious aviator rescued a boy named Jim from Sean Penn's burning home? And have you heard the latest party craze? Watching the water drain from cracked swimming pools.

Of course, the American Midwest also chose the year to host Ballard's *The Drowned World*, but the Nebula judges claimed that all the protagonists were too clean-cut to make it a true Ballard infotainment. Hell, even the conscripted *prisoners* tossing sandbags were virtuous.

And how about that Internet? Growing by ten trillion percent a day, until now when you log on you're likely to find E-mail from your grandmother wanting to know how come you haven't visited in so long. Post all replies to "cybergram@cookie.snak." Why, it's, it's like—something out of John Brunner's *The Shockwave Rider!* Too bad John didn't get a nickel for every time some wonk who thought he was unique cited this fine novel.

The incredible success of a new 'zine of high-tech culture named *Wired* in 1993 made the modest good luck and smart management of even the *SF Age* people look like a kid's lemonade stand outside the grounds of Microsoft. *Wired*'s readers were SF's natural audience. Except that they weren't really reading SF anymore, as symbolized in the 1993 demise of Britain's revamped *New Worlds*.

What *were* all of SF's former readers doing for entertainment besides scrolling through "alt.hotpants" and reading 'zines that actually looked graphically like the future they ostensibly cared about? Watching tabloid television, for one thing. Remember Norman Spinrad's "scandalous" *Bug Jack Barron?* Although an asshole, at least the title character went to the wall for his beliefs and did some good. But, in real life, slimy pin-miked, pinheaded hosts of both sexes brought us only seminars on wearing PVC undies and inseminating transsexuals. A new Greenberg anthology (Greenberg's entry in the Clute and Nicholls *Encyclopedia,* a 1993 millstone—sorry, milestone—will soon be issued as a separate volume) tries to marry SF with tabloid topics, proving that the old adage "If you can't beat them, try to do something you're totally unfit for" still holds as much water as it ever did.

And then there were MUDs: multi-user dungeons. These online role-playing games allowed everyone who ever wished to inhabit Roger Zelazny's *Amber* or Phil Farmer's *World of Tiers* books to do so. It was cheaper and less sweaty than the Society for Creative Anachronism, and you didn't have to drink any poorly fermented mead.

On the biological horizon, the scientists at the National Institutes of Health seemed intent on reifying John Varley's familiar Eight Worlds continuum, as they wildly sought to patent everything from

Julia Roberts's cheekbones to Lyle Lovett's hair. Rumor was that you'd be able any day now to check into a clinic where, after a dose of BST-laced milk, you could get a fetal-brain-cell transplant, a fetal-egg donation, and a pair of tits identical to Madonna's.

But America was not the whole story, of course. Although still number one in science-fictional happenings and general life-style, this country was given a run for its dwindling money by other spots across the globe.

Ever the classicists, the English opted to stage *Lord of the Flies* by having two eleven-year-old Liverpool kids murder an abducted two-year-old.

In Bosnia, reluctant but game citizens played along with one of those interminable slide-to-chaos scenarios, perhaps Algis Budrys's *Some Will Not Die* or Octavia Butler's *Parable of the Sower*.

U.S. intervention in Somalia turned out to follow a script from Poul Anderson or Eric Frank Russell (except, in the latter case, without the laughs): self-assured armored giants on a goodwill mission descend on the low-tech runty natives and get their asses whipped.

Russia and its former republics were sold quietly a few years ago to Baen Books. Hence Yeltsin's easy decision to lob a few dozen artillery shells into his own Parliament building. "If it worked for Hammer's Slammers, it'll work for me!"

A couple of rare hopeful notes were sounded in South Africa and Israel, of all places. In the former, a peaceful transition to black majority rule was well under way by year's end. In the latter country, archenemies sat down under PLO and government flags to hash out a treaty. And what could have inspired such radical moves? Why, what else but the sight of Klingons on the bridge of the *Enterprise* in "Star Trek: The Next Generation"! Didn't you know that Arafat always wore his headgear simply to conceal those telltale cranial ridges?

And so it went. Life imitating art—if you grant SF that lofty distinction—wherever you looked.

Life imitating *old* SF, anyhow, as you might have noticed. The new stuff that I read in 1993—the .5 percent of the genre that wasn't fantasy or horror in chromalloy drag—was still too busy with intergalactic empires, generation ships, and terraforming to worry about what was happening in its own backyard.

1993 IN SCIENCE FICTION
Norman Spinrad

Looking back over 1993 in search of a hot trend, I simply can't find one, so perhaps such trendlessness is something of a trend itself. Quite a few interesting first novels were published, quite a few good novels by diverse hands, but nothing that seems to have broken bold new stylistic ground or opened new thematic pathways.

The strongest trend, if you can call it that, is a retro one in a strangely twisted sort of way—the ongoing renewed interest in Mars.

In the past few years, we have had *Red Genesis* by S. C. Sykes, Ben Bova's *Mars,* Greg Bear's *Moving Mars,* and the first two novels of Kim Stanley Robinson's projected Mars trilogy, *Red Mars* and *Green Mars,* as well as any number of novelettes and novellas.

Most of this latter-day Martiana is set not on the romantic old Mars of Burroughs and Bradbury but on the post-Viking realistic Mars of the stark astronomical facts and hard science fiction. Most of it, one way or another, concerns the colonization of Mars, and more of it than not the planet's future terraforming.

So why do I call it retro?

Alas, for the saddest of reasons.

Not that these are negative or depressing works in and of themselves. Far from it. Most of them take the cold facts of Martian planetology and demonstrate the ability of human science and technology to transform the dead red planet into a second living world within the rules of the hard-science game. To one degree or another, most of them are realistic but visionary paeans to the triumph of the human spirit over geophysical adversity. Robinson's two novels may be two-thirds of a visionary masterpiece.

What depresses me is that this literary trend has developed at a time when the collapse of the Soviet Union seems to have eliminated one of the two major players in the dialectic of human exploration of the planets, and when Clintonomics and a general loss of courage and visionary idealism seem to have taken the heart out of the American program.

What awful irony that science fiction has turned to convincing demonstrations of how we can quicken Mars to life, and why we should do it, at a time when it's all the Russians can do to keep *Mir* crewed and NASA hasn't even gotten the funding together to build a pathetic second-rate space station hardly in advance of what the Soviet Union already had in orbit a decade ago!

What's retrograde about this modern science fiction about Mars is certainly not the scientific background or technological extrapolation. Most of it is the rigorous hard stuff designed to depict Martian colonization and terraforming as squarely in the realm of the current technological possible and, indeed, inspire the species to go out there and do it.

What's retrograde about this literarily and technologically admirable stuff is the air of nostalgia that it exudes. What's nostalgic about it is that while the Martian background is usually finely detailed, accurate, and realistic, and the technological means of reaching the planet, colonizing it, and even terraforming it in a fairly short time frame is quite convincing, political and economic realities in the real world have pushed the earliest possible first landing on Mars beyond the life span of most of the writers of these works and the actual colonization of Mars, let alone its terraforming, virtually into the realm of fantasy.

What I find saddening is not this visionary Martian science fiction itself, but the very longing for the actualization of the visionary future it inspires in me, which it is *supposed* to inspire in me, given the realities of the real world and the real time in which it is being published.

It is as if a collective dream were burning brightest at the hour of its demise. It is as if the voice of a collective visionary spirit were shouting into the gathering darkness.

FOUR TRENDS IN RECENT SF
Eleanor Arnason

I. Expansion of vision

To a remarkable extent, the best SF of the eighties was set in the near future and/or in near space. Whether cyberpunk or ecofeminist, the universe it described was a place of limited resources, limited options, and not a lot of room. This was a "reasonable" fiction, appropriate to an era dominated by what might be called "the counterrevolution of falling expectations."

A little of this goes a long way. By the end of the 1980s, a lot of people were ready to break free. The result has been a return to wide-screen, big-idea, proactive SF.

Following Caesar, let's split this category into three parts.

A. Space opera, examples being *Aristoi,* by Walter Jon Williams (1992), and *Against a Dark Background,* by Iain M. Banks (1993). Both books use the conceits of old-time space opera: vast forces are engaged in vast conflicts in the vast arena of interstellar space. But they use these classic shticks in a critical fashion. Power is not the answer. Violent action has serious consequences that the protagonists (unlike the heroes of old-time space opera) cannot avoid.

B. Big-equipment SF, also known as hard SF, examples being *Red Mars,* by Kim Stanley Robinson (1993), and *Moving Mars,* by Greg Bear (1993). As with the writers of contemporary space opera, Robinson and Bear don't see violence as an answer. Robinson's novel ends in a revolution that nearly destroys the Martian colony. Bear avoids a knock-down-drag-out fight by taking his colony where the bad guys can't follow. In both novels, technology is neither demon nor *deus ex machina,* but a tool, which can be used for good or evil and which should be used mindfully.

C. Big-idea biotech SF. Examples of this are *Daughter of Elysium,* by Joan Slonczewski (1993), and *Metaphase,* by Vonda N. McIntyre (1992). Biotech SF differs from hard SF in being (1) often written by women and (2) more interested in biology and biotechnology than in very large pieces of equipment. It's interesting to compare *Daughter of Elysium* with Slonczewski's earlier novel in the same universe, *A Door into Ocean* (1986). *Daughter* has a much wider scope: more cultures, more kinds of people, more kinds of science and technology, more complicated arguments about right and wrong. This opening up is typical of nineties SF, as is the tendency to see human culture and behavior as complex and ambiguous. Science is neither good nor evil. Violent action does not provide easy answers. Power remains a problem, whether embraced or opposed.

II. Expansion of media

Increasingly, SF authors are being published outside the traditional markets. Octavia E. Butler's new novel, *Parable of the Sower* (1993), came out from Four Walls Eight Windows, which is a literary—rather than SF—publisher. Samuel R. Delany's Nevèrÿon books were reprinted by Wesleyan University Press. Pat Cadigan's *Dirty Work* (1993) was published by Mark V. Ziesing, and this is increasingly typical; single-person collections come out from small presses, rather than from the big New York houses. The third novel in P. C. Hodgell's Jame series, *Seeker's Mask* (1993), came out from Hypatia Press, a specialty SF publisher. Due to changes in technology, it's now possible to produce high-quality books at a reasonable (more or less) cost in money and time; this, combined with the contraction of our traditional New York market, makes small-press SF publishing look like a wave of the future.

SF continues to flourish and grow in "nontraditional" media: movies, TV, et cetera.

The computer book seems likely to change the way stories are told and the relationship—artistic and economic—between authors and their work. Imagine books that are distributed via computer network and printed one copy at a time in the bookstore or the reader's home. Imagine multimedia, interactive novels that exist only in electronic form. How does one collect royalties in such works? Who owns the copyright? Who has artistic control? These are questions we ought to be discussing now. The publishers are.

III. Expansion of audience

When I first discovered fandom, it was a small, culturally homogeneous community, self-consciously in opposition to the outside world. The key artifacts of this traditional SF community were made of words on paper: prozines, fanzines, and books.

None of this is true today. The community of people interested in SF is vastly larger than it used to be, much more varied and much less clearly separated from mundania, which has become less mundane. (SF ideas and images are now pervasive in mass culture. The line between SF and the fine-art avant-garde is increasingly hazy.) Like the world in general, SF has become multimedia; and a considerable percentage of the people at cons these days have more interest in movies, TV, gaming, comics, and the like than in traditional words-on-paper SF.

IV. Definition by exclusion

A few years back, straight white male academics of European descent noticed that their rule of high culture was no longer unquestioned. They had a fit. Something similar is apparently happening in the SF community, not for the first time, but repetition does not make this kind of behavior any more attractive. At the moment, a number of fans and pros are attempting to define the field so as to exclude media SF, "literary" SF, fantasy, comic books, gaming, you name it. The result of this, which may not be conscious, is to draw a line between old-time SFers and most of the people who have come into the field in recent decades: women, kids, people of color, gays, lesbians, and so on. All I need to do is look around at Minicon. The new fans—the Trekkers and punkers and so on—are a far more diverse group than old-time fandom. This attempt to define the field by deciding what and who does not belong is ungenerous and may be suicidal. If SF is going to have a future, it needs new fans.

CONVERSATIONS AND CONSTRAINTS
Gregory Benford

Genres are constrained conversations. Constraint is essential, defining the rules and assumptions open to an author. If hard SF occupies the center of science fiction, that is probably because hardness gives the firmest boundary.

Genres are also like immense discussions, with ideas developed, traded, and variations spun down through time. Players ring changes on each other—a steppin'-out jazz band, not a solo concert in a plush auditorium. Contrast "serious" fiction—more accurately described, in my eyes, as merely self-consciously solemn—which proceeds from canonical classics that supposedly stand outside of time, deserving awe, looming great and intact by themselves.

This last year seemed unusually rich to me. Kim Stanley Robinson's *Red Mars* mirrored science itself in the importance of cross talk, as an entire society frets and labors at the resurrection of a world. Scientific decisions in this novel arise from overlapping, complex dialogue. To me, this is a better picture of how the scientist / technology/society gradients actually work than is the oversimplified paradigm-shift model. Genres do this, hard SF even more so.

Genre pleasures are many, but this quality of shared values

within an ongoing discussion may be the most powerful, enlisting lifelong devotion in its fans. In contrast to the Grand Canon view, genre reading satisfactions are a striking facet of modern democratic ("pop") culture.

Greg Bear's *Moving Mars* was probably the best political/hard SF novel of the year, written in evocative prose with a telling eye toward the way actual politics works. Its painterly depiction of how a society responds to a major reality-shifting discovery had an instructive parallel in Nancy Kress's *Beggars in Spain,* which spins an insightful labyrinth of implication from changes in humble human sleep.

World-painting in great colorful swipes, David Brin courageously took on feminist concerns in *Glory Season.* Its intricately supported biology in which males play a minor role unfurls before a picaresque adventure story, convincing in detail. Robinson, Bear, and Brin all seem to stand in a tradition begun by Hal Clement's *Mission of Gravity.*

Closer to the gritty, lived world was William Gibson's stylishly turned *Virtual Light.* As in his best work, plot is secondary and at times implausible, serving up descriptions and carefully nuanced details in lovingly rendered techno-sheen. Its conspicuous stylistic gloss and bleak gaze recall Ballard.

Charles Pellegrino's *Flying to Valhalla,* on the other hand, threw ideas at us by the handfuls—big concepts plainly rendered, not intricate surfaces. Readers who can penetrate the sometimes daunting genre vernacular will find much to think about, as with the weird science of Stephen Baxter's *Timelike Infinity.*

How does such SF, much of the best of the past year, sit in the recent razoring of literature by critics—the tribes of structuralists, postmodernists, deconstructionists, and so on? To many SF writers, "postmodern" is simply a signature of exhaustion. Its typical apparatus—self-reference, heavy dollops of obligatory irony, self-conscious use of older genre devices, pastiche and parody—betrays lack of invention, of the crucial coin of SF, imagination. Some deconstructionists have attacked science itself as mere rhetoric, not an ordering of nature, seeking to reduce it to the status of the ultimately arbitrary humanities. Most SF types find this attack on empiricism a worn old song with new lyrics, quite retro.

At the core of SF lies the experience of science. This makes the genre finally hostile to such fashions in criticism, for it values its empirical ground. Deconstructionism's stress on contradictory or self-contained internal differences in texts, rather than their link to reality, often merely leads to literature seen as empty word games.

SF novels give us worlds that are to be taken not as metaphors but as real. We are asked to participate in wrenchingly strange events, not merely to watch them for clues to what they're really talking about. (Ummm, this must stand for . . . Not a way to gather narrative momentum.) The Mars and stars and digital deserts of our best novels are, finally, to be taken as real, as if to say: life isn't *like* this, it *is* this. Journeys can go to fresh places, not merely return us to ourselves. Fortunately, this past year gave us quite a few great trips.

THE MAN WHO ROWED
CHRISTOPHER COLUMBUS ASHORE

Harlan Ellison

Harlan Ellison is a master of fiction, journalism, and commentary who has been honored with almost too many awards to count. I shall list a few of his honors anyway: the Nebula Award, the Hugo Award, the Mystery Writers of America Edgar Allan Poe Award, the Writers Guild of America Most Outstanding Teleplay Award, the PEN Silver Pen Award for Journalism, the Horror Writers of America Bram Stoker Award, and the prestigious Lifetime Achievement Award of the World Fantasy Convention. (Bear in mind that he has won most of these awards more than once.) His recent works include the short novel *Mefisto in Onyx;* the 33-story collaboration with Polish surrealist Jacek Yerka, *Mind Fields;* and the forthcoming collection *Slippage.*

The story you are about to read, in addition to being a Nebula finalist, was selected for the 1993 edition of *The Best American Short Stories.* About "The Man Who Rowed Christopher Columbus Ashore," Harlan Ellison writes:

"On the day I sit down to write this note, literary ruminations meant to add only a grace note . . . I have just hung up the phone, having been informed that my pal, the most excellent and virtually unremembered master talent, the great Avram Davidson, has died.

"And I am suddenly more concerned with stealing a moment here to honor him, than I am with blowing my own horn about how clever I was to have written 'The Man Who Rowed Christopher Columbus Ashore.' Because, you see, for all the hot air and Monday-morning-quarterback deconstructionist horse puckey that writers and academics like to slather on the subject, there are only a couple of genuine Secrets about writing.

"The first has to do with the *why.* And most of what is said and written is sententious claptrap. . . . Quentin Crisp once observed that 'Artists in any medium are nothing more than a bunch of hooligans who cannot live within their income of admiration.' Oh, how we want that assurance that once we're gone, no matter that we were as specialized a savory as Nathanael West or as common a confection as Clarence Budington Kelland, that we will be read fifty years hence. Because the *why* is as simply put as this: 'I write only because I cannot stop.' Don't credit that one to me, I'm not that smart. It was Heinrich Von Kleist. And he nailed it; what he suggests, in literary terms, is the equivalent of the answer to *most* of the stuff that we do: 'It seemed like a good idea at the time.'

"But West is barely read today, not to mention Shirley Jackson (who was the inspiration for 'The Man Who Rowed—'), or James Agee, or William March, or Jim Tully, or even John O'Hara or Zoë Oldenbourg. Or Avram Davidson, who was one of the most stylish, witty, erudite, and wildly imaginative writers of our time. So, what are these thoughts in aid of? Well . . .

"I have a T-shirt that bears the message NOT TONIGHT, DEAR, I HAVE A DEADLINE.

"Funny, till the last deadline comes; as it did for Avram. And then, like West or Tully or F. Van Wyck Mason, you're no-price. So what was it all about?

"The secret is this: *anyone* can become a writer . . . The trick, the secret, is to *stay* a writer. To produce a body of work that you hope improves and changes with time and the accumulation of skill. To stay a writer day after year after story . . .

"There is no pattern; no pantheon of busybody entities up there in the clouds ordaining our lives; no Grand Scheme. . . . *That's* what 'The Man Who Rowed Christopher Columbus Ashore' is about. Don't listen to the bonehead deconstructionists when they start all that 'basic Apollonian-Dionysian Conflict' hooey. The story is about nothing more difficult or loftier than the admonition that *you* are responsible, that posterity is a snare, that memory is short, and that life is an absolutely unriggable crap shoot, with the stickman a civil servant who works for some department as inept as you are."

This is a story titled
The Man Who Rowed
Christopher Columbus Ashore

LEVENDIS: On Tuesday the 1st of October, improbably dressed as an Explorer Scout, with his great hairy legs protruding from his knee-pants, and his heavily-festooned merit badge sash slantwise across his chest, he helped an old, arthritic black woman across the street at the jammed corner of Wilshire and Western. In fact, she didn't *want* to cross the street, but he half-pulled, half-dragged her, the old woman screaming at him, calling him a khaki-colored motherfucker every step of the way.

LEVENDIS: On Wednesday the 2nd of October, he crossed his legs carefully as he sat in the Boston psychiatrist's office, making certain the creases of his pants—he was wearing the traditional morning coat and ambassadorially-striped pants—remained sharp, and he said to George Aspen Davenport, M.D., Ph.D., FAPA (who had studied with Ernst Kris *and* Anna Freud), "Yes, that's it, now you've got it." And Dr. Davenport made a note on his pad, lightly cleared his throat, and phrased it differently: "Your mouth is . . . vanishing? That is to say, your mouth, the facial feature below your nose, it's uh disappearing?" The prospective patient nodded quickly, with a bright smile. "Exactly." Dr. Davenport made another note, continued to ulcerate the inside of his cheek, then tried a third time: "We're speaking now—heh heh, to maintain the idiom—we're speaking of your lips, or your tongue, or your palate, or your gums, or your teeth, or—" The other man sat forward, looking very serious, and replied, "We're talking *all* of it, Doctor. The whole, entire, complete aperture and everything around, over, under, and within. My *mouth,* the all-ness of my mouth. It's disappearing. What part of that is giving you a problem?" Davenport hmmm'd for a moment, said, "Let me check something," and he rose, went to the teak and glass bookcase against the far wall, beside the window that looked out on crowded, lively Boston Common, and he drew down a capacious volume. He flipped through it for a few minutes, and finally paused at a page on which he poked a finger. He turned to the elegant, gray-haired gentleman in the consultation chair, and he said, "Lipostomy." His prospective patient tilted his head to the side, like a dog listening for a clue, and arched his eyebrows expectantly, as if to ask *yes, and lipostomy is what?* The psychiatrist brought the book to him, leaned down, and pointed to the definition. "Atrophy of the mouth." The gray-haired gentleman, who looked to be in his early sixties, but remarkably well-tended and handsomely turned-out, shook his head slowly as Dr. Davenport walked back around to sit behind his desk. "No, I don't think so. It doesn't seem to be withering, it's just, well, simply, I can't put it any other way, it's very simply disappearing. Like the Cheshire cat's grin. Fading away." Davenport closed the book and laid it on the desktop, folded his hands atop the volume, and smiled condescendingly. "Don't you think this might be a delusion on your part? I'm looking at your mouth right now, and it's right there, just as it was when you came into the office." His prospective patient rose, retrieved his homburg from the sofa, and started toward the door. "It's a good thing I can read lips," he said, placing the hat on his head, "because I certainly don't need to pay your sort of exorbitant fee to be ridiculed." And he moved to the office door, and opened it to leave, pausing for only a moment to readjust his homburg, which had slipped down, due to the absence of ears on his head.

LEVENDIS: On Thursday the 3rd of October, he overloaded his grocery cart with okra and eggplant, giant bags of Kibbles 'n Bits 'n Bits 'n Bits, and jumbo boxes of Huggies. And as he wildly careened through the aisles of the Sentry Market in La Crosse, Wisconsin, he purposely engineered a collision between the carts of Kenneth Kulwin, a 47-year-old homosexual who had lived alone since the passing of his father thirteen years earlier, and Anne Gillen, a 35-year-old legal secretary who had been unable to find an escort to take her to her senior prom and whose social life had not improved in the decades since that death of hope. He began screaming at them, as if it had been *their* fault, thereby making allies of them. He was extremely rude, breathing muscatel breath on them, and finally stormed away, leaving them to sort out their groceries, leaving them to comment on his behavior, leaving them to take notice of each other. He went outside, smelling the Mississippi River, and he let the air out of Anne Gillen's tires. She would need a lift to the gas station. Kenneth Kulwin would tell her to call him "Kenny," and they would discover that their favorite movie was the 1945 romance *The Enchanted Cottage,* starring Dorothy McGuire and Robert Young.

LEVENDIS: On Friday the 4th of October, he found an interstate trucker dumping badly sealed cannisters of phenazine in an isolated picnic area outside Phillipsburg, Kansas; and he shot him three times in the head; and wedged the body into one of the large, nearly empty trash barrels near the picnic benches.

LEVENDIS: On Saturday the 5th of October, he addressed two hundred and forty-four representatives of the country & western music industry in the Chattanooga Room just off the Tennessee Ballroom of the Opryland Hotel in Nashville. He said to them, "What's astonishing is not that there is so much ineptitude, slovenliness, mediocrity, and downright bad taste in the world . . . what *is* unbelievable is that there is so much *good* art in the world. Everywhere." One of the attendees raised her hand and asked, "Are you good, or evil?" He thought about it for less than twenty seconds, smiled, and replied, "Good, of course! There's only one real evil in the world: mediocrity." They applauded sparsely, but politely. Nonetheless, later at the reception, *no one* touched the Swedish meatballs, or the rumaki.

LEVENDIS: On Sunday the 6th of October, he placed the exhumed remains of Noah's ark near the eastern summit of a nameless mountain in Kurdistan, where the next infrared surveillance of a random satellite flyby would reveal them. He was careful to seed the area with a plethora of bones, here and there around the site, as well as within the identifiable hull of the vessel. He made sure to place them two-by-two: every beast after his kind, and all the cattle after their kind, and every creeping thing that creepeth upon the earth after his kind, and every fowl after his kind, and every bird of every sort. Two-by-two. Also the bones of pairs of gryphons, unicorns, stegosaurs, tengus, dragons, orthodontists, and the carbon-dateable 50,000-year-old bones of a relief pitcher for the Boston Red Sox.

LEVENDIS: On Monday the 7th of October, he kicked a cat. He kicked it a far distance. To the passersby who watched, there on Galena Street in Aurora, Colorado, he said: "I am an unlimited person, sadly living in a limited world." When the housewife who planned to call the police yelled at him from her kitchen window, "Who are you? What is your name!?!" he cupped his hands around his mouth so she would hear him, and he yelled back, "Levendis! It's a Greek word." They found the cat imbarked halfway through a tree. The tree was cut down, and the section with the cat was cut in two, the animal tended by a talented taxidermist who tried to quell the poor beast's terrified mewling and vomiting. The cat was later sold as bookends.

LEVENDIS: On Tuesday the 8th of October, he called the office of the District Attorney in Cadillac, Michigan, and reported that the blue 1988 Mercedes that had struck and killed two children playing in a residential street in Hamtramck just after sundown the night before, belonged to a pastry chef whose sole client was a Cosa Nostra *pezzonovante.* He gave detailed information as to the location of the chop shop where the Mercedes had been taken to be banged out, bondo'd, and repainted. He gave the license number. He indicated where, in the left front wheel-well, could be found a piece of the skull of the younger of the two little girls. Not only did the piece fit, like the missing section of a modular woodblock puzzle, but pathologists were able to conduct an accurate test that provided irrefutable evidence that would hold up under any attack in court: the medical examiner got past the basic ABO groups, narrowed the scope of identification with the five Rh tests, the M and N tests (also cap-S and small-s variations), the Duffy blood groups, and the Kidd types, both A and B; and finally he was able to validate the rare absence of Jr a, present in most blood-groups but missing in some Japanese-Hawaiians and Samoans. The little girl's name was Sherry Tualaulelei. When the homicide investigators learned that the pastry chef, his wife, and their three children had gone to New York City on vacation four days before the hit-and-run, and were able to produce ticket stubs that placed them seventh row center of the Martin Beck Theater, enjoying the revival of *Guys and Dolls,* at the precise moment the Mercedes struck the children, the Organized Crime Unit was called in, and the scope of the investigation was broadened. Sherry Tualaulelei was instrumental in the conviction and thirty-three-year imprisonment of the pastry chef's boss, Sinio "Sally Comfort" Conforte, who had "borrowed" a car to sneak out for a visit to his mistress.

LEVENDIS: On Wednesday the 9th of October, he sent a fruit basket to Patricia and Faustino Evangelista, a middle-aged couple in Norwalk, Connecticut, who had given to the surviving son, the gun his beloved older brother had used to kill himself. The accompanying note read: *Way to go, sensitive Mom and Dad!*

LEVENDIS: On Thursday the 10th of October, he created a cure for bone-marrow cancer. Anyone could make it: the juice of fresh lemons, spiderwebs, the scrapings of raw carrots, the opaque and whitish portion of the toenail called the *lunula,* and carbonated water. The pharmaceutical cartel quickly hired a prestigious Philadelphia PR firm to throw its efficacy into question, but the AMA and FDA ran accelerated tests, found it to be potent, with no deleterious effects, and recommended its immediate use. It had no effect on AIDS, however. Nor did it work on the common cold. Remarkably, physicians praised the easing of their workload.

LEVENDIS: On Friday the 11th of October, he lay in his own filth on the sidewalk outside the British Embassy in Rangoon, holding a begging bowl. He was just to the left of the gate, half-hidden by the angle of the high wall from sight of the military guards on post. A woman in her fifties, who had been let out of a jitney just up the street, having paid her fare and having tipped as few rupees as necessary to escape a strident rebuke by the driver, smoothed the peplum of her shantung jacket over her hips, and marched imperially toward the Embassy gates. As she came abaft the derelict, he rose on one elbow and shouted at her ankles, "Hey, lady! I write these pomes, and I sell 'em for a buck inna street, an' it keeps juvenile delinquents offa the streets so's they don't spit on ya! So whaddaya think, y'wanna buy one?" The matron did not pause, striding toward the gates, but she said snappishly, "You're a businessman. Don't talk art."

This is a story titled
The Route of Odysseus

"You will find the scene of Odysseus's wanderings when you find the cobbler who sewed up the bag of the winds."
Eratosthenes, late 3rd century, B.C.E.

LEVENDIS: On Saturday the 12th of October, having taken the sidestep, he came to a place near Weimar in southwest Germany. He did not see the photographer snapping pictures of the scene. He stood among the cordwood bodies. It was cold for the spring; and even though he was heavily clothed, he shivered. He walked down the rows of bony corpses, looking into the black holes that had been eye sockets, seeing an endless chicken dinner, the bones gnawed clean, tossed like jackstraws in heaps. The stretched-taut groins of men and women, flesh tarpaulins where passion had once smoothed the transport from sleep to wakefulness. Entwined so cavalierly that here a woman with three arms, and there a child with the legs of a sprinter three times his age. A woman's face, looking up at him with soot for sight, remarkable cheekbones, high and lovely, she might have been an actress. Xylophones for chests and torsos, violin bows that had waved goodbye and hugged grandchildren and lifted in toasts to the passing of traditions, gourd whistles between eyes and mouths. He stood among the cordwood bodies and could not remain merely an instrument himself. He sank to his haunches, crouched and wept, burying his head in his hands, as the photographer took shot after shot, an opportunity like a gift from the editor. Then he tried to stop crying, and stood, and the cold cut him, and he removed his heavy topcoat and placed it gently over the bodies of two women and a man lying so close and intermixed that it easily served as coverlet for them. He stood among the cordwood bodies, 24 April 1945, Buchenwald, and the photograph would appear in a book published forty-six years later, on Saturday the 12th of October. The photographer's roll ran out just an instant before the slim young man without a topcoat took the sidestep. Nor did he hear the tearful young man say, "Sertsa." In Russian, *sertsa* means soul.

LEVENDIS: On Sunday the 13th of October, he did nothing. He rested. When he thought about it, he grew annoyed. "Time does not become sacred until we have lived it," he said. But he thought: *to hell with it; even God knocked off for a day.*

LEVENDIS: On Monday the 14th of October, he climbed up through the stinking stairwell shaft of a Baltimore tenement, clutching his notebook, breathing through his mouth to block the smell of mildew, garbage, and urine, focusing his mind on the apartment number he was seeking, straining through the evening dimness in the wan light of one bulb hanging high above, barely illuminating the vertical tunnel, as he climbed and climbed, straining to see the numbers on the doors, going up, realizing the tenants had pulled the numbers *off* the doors to foil him and welfare investigators like him, stumbling over something oily and sobbing jammed into a corner of the last step, losing his grip on the rotting bannister and finding it just in time, trapped for a moment in the hopeless beam of washed-out light falling from above, poised in mid-tumble and then regaining his grip, hoping the welfare recipient under scrutiny would not be home, so he could knock off for the day, hurry back downtown and crosstown and take a shower, going up till he had reached the topmost landing, and finding the number scratched on the doorframe, and knocking, getting no answer, knocking again, hearing first the scream, then the sound of someone beating against a wall, or the floor, with a heavy stick, and then the scream again, and then another so closely following the first that it might have been one scream only, and he threw himself against the door, and it was old but never had been well-built, and it came away, off its hinges, in one rotten crack, and he was inside, and the most beautiful young black woman he had ever seen was tearing the rats off her baby. He left the check on the kitchen table, he did not have an affair with her, he did not see her fall from the apartment window, six storeys into a courtyard, and never knew if she came back from the grave to escape the rats that gnawed at her cheap wooden casket. He never loved her, and so was not there when what she became flowed back up through the walls of the tenement to absorb him and meld with him and become one with him as he lay sleeping penitently on the filthy floor of the topmost apartment. He left the check, and none of that happened.

LEVENDIS: On Tuesday the 15th of October, he stood in the Greek theatre at Aspendos, Turkey, a structure built two thousand years earlier, so acoustically perfect that every word spoken on its stage could be heard with clarity in any of its thirteen thousand seats, and he spoke to a little boy sitting high above him. He uttered Count Von Manfred's dying words, Schumann's overture, Byron's poem: "Old man, 'tis not so difficult to die." The child smiled and waved. He waved back, then shrugged. They became friends at a distance. It was the first time someone other than his mother, who was dead, had been kind to the boy. In years to come it would be a reminder that there was a smile out there on the wind. The little boy looked down the rows and concentric rows of seats: the man 'way down there was motioning for him to come to him. The child, whose name was Orhon, hopped and hopped, descending to the center of the ring as quickly as he could. As he came to the core, and walked out across the orchestra ring, he studied the man. This person was very tall, and he needed a shave, and his hat had an extremely wide brim, like the hat of Kül, the man who made weekly trips to Ankara, and he wore a long overcoat far too hot for this day. Orhon could not see the man's eyes because he wore dark glasses that reflected the sky. Orhon thought this man looked like a mountain bandit, only dressed more impressively. Not wisely for a day as torpid as this, but more impressively than Bilge and his men, who raided the farming villages. When he reached the tall man, and they smiled at each other, this person said to Orhon, "I am an unlimited person living in a limited world." The child did not know what to say to that. But he liked the man. "Why do you wear such heavy wool today? I am barefoot." He raised his dusty foot to show the man, and was embarrassed at the dirty cloth tied around his big toe. And the man said, "Because I need a safe place to keep the limited world." And he unbuttoned his overcoat, and held open one side, and showed Orhon what he would inherit one day, if he tried very hard not to be a despot. Pinned to the fabric, each with the face of the planet, were a million and more timepieces, each one the Earth at a different moment, and all of them purring erratically like dozing sphinxes. And Orhon stood there, in the heat, for quite a long while, and listened to the ticking of the limited world.

LEVENDIS: On Wednesday the 16th of October, he chanced upon three skinheads in Doc Martens' and cheap black leatherette, beating the crap out of an interracial couple who had emerged from the late show at the La Salle Theater in Chicago. He stood quietly and watched. For a long while.

LEVENDIS: On Thursday the 17th of October, he chanced upon three skinheads in Doc Martens' and cheap black leatherette, beating the crap out of an interracial couple who had stopped for a bite to eat at a Howard Johnson's near King of Prussia on the Pennsylvania

Turnpike. He removed the inch-and-a-half-thick ironwood dowel he always carried beside his driver's seat and, holding the 2½' long rod at its centerpoint, laid alongside his pants leg so it could not be seen in the semi-darkness of the parking lot, he came up behind the three as they kicked the black woman and the white man lying between parked cars. He tapped the tallest of the trio on his shoulder, and when the boy turned around—he couldn't have been more than seventeen—he dropped back a step, slid the dowel up with his right hand, gripped it tightly with his left, and drove the end of the rod into the eye of the skinhead, punching through behind the socket and pulping the brain. The boy flailed backward, already dead, and struck his partners. As they turned, he was spinning the dowel like a baton, faster and faster, and as the stouter of the two attackers charged him, he whipped it around his head and slashed straight across the boy's throat. The snapping sound ricocheted off the dark hillside beyond the restaurant. He kicked the third boy in the groin, and when he dropped, and fell on his back, he kicked him under the chin, opening the skinhead's mouth; and then he stood over him, and with both hands locked around the pole, as hard as he could, he piledrove the wooden rod into the kid's mouth, shattering his teeth, and turning the back of his skull to flinders. The dowel scraped concrete through the ruined face. Then he helped the man and his wife to their feet, and bullied the manager of the Howard Johnson's into actually letting them lie down in his office till the State Police arrived. He ordered a plate of fried clams and sat there eating pleasurably until the cops had taken his statement.

LEVENDIS: On Friday the 18th of October, he took a busload of Mormon schoolchildren to the shallow waters of the Great Salt Lake in Utah, to pay homage to the great sculptor Smithson by introducing the art-ignorant children to the *Spiral Jetty,* an incongruously gorgeous line of earth and stone that curves out and away like a thought lost in the tide. "The man who made this, who dreamed it up and then *made* it, you know what he once said?" And they ventured that no, they didn't know what this Smithson sculptor had said, and the man who had driven the bus paused for a dramatic moment, and he repeated Smithson's words: "Establish enigmas, not explanations."

They stared at him. "Perhaps you had to be there," he said, shrugging. "Who's for ice cream?" And they went to a Baskin-Robbins.

LEVENDIS: On Saturday the 19th of October, he filed a thirty-million-dollar lawsuit against the major leagues in the name of Alberda Jeannette Chambers, a 19-year-old lefthander with a fadeaway fast ball clocked at better than 96 mph; a dipsy-doodle slider that could do a barrel-roll and clean up after itself; an ERA of 2.10; who could hit from either side of the plate with a batting average of .360; who doubled as a peppery little shortstop working with a trapper's mitt of her own design; who had been refused tryouts with virtually every professional team in the United States (also Japan) from the bigs all the way down to the Pony League. He filed in Federal District Court for the Southern Division of New York State, and told Ted Koppel that Allie Chambers would be the first female player, mulatto or otherwise, in the Baseball Hall of Fame.

LEVENDIS: On Sunday the 20th of October, he drove out and around through the streets of Raleigh and Durham, North Carolina, in a rented van equipped with a public address system, and he endlessly reminded somnambulistic pedestrians and families entering eggs'n'grits restaurants (many of these adults had actually voted for Jesse Helms and thus were in danger of losing their *sertsa*) that perhaps they should ignore their bibles today, and go back and reread Shirley Jackson's short story "One Ordinary Day, with Peanuts."

This is a story titled
The Daffodils That Entertain

LEVENDIS: On Monday the 21st of October, having taken the side-step, he wandered through that section of New York City known as the Tenderloin. It was 1892. Crosstown on 24th Street from Fifth Avenue to Seventh, then he turned uptown and walked slowly on Seventh to 40th. Midtown was rife with brothels, their red lights shining through the shadows, challenging the wan gaslit streetlamps. The Edison and Swan United Electric Light Co., Ltd., had improved business tremendously through the wise solicitations of a salesman with a Greek-sounding name who had canvassed the prostitution

district west of Broadway only five years earlier, urging the installation of Mr. Joseph Wilson Swan and Mr. Thomas Alva Edison's fil-
ament lamps: painted crimson, fixed above the ominously yawning
doorways of the area's many houses of easy virtue. He passed an
alley on 36th Street, and heard a woman's voice in the darkness
complaining, "You said you'd give me two dollars. You have to give
it to me first! Stop! No, *first* you gotta give me the two dollars!" He
stepped into the alley, let his eyes acclimate to the darkness so total,
trying to hold his breath against the stench; and then he saw them.
The man was in his late forties, wearing a bowler and a shin-length
topcoat with an astrakhan collar. The sound of horse-drawn carriages
clopped loudly on the bricks beyond the alley, and the man in the
astrakhan looked up, toward the alley mouth. His face was strained,
as if he expected an accomplice of the girl, a footpad or shoulder-
hitter or bully-boy pimp to charge to her defense. He had his fly
unbuttoned and his thin, pale penis extended; the girl was backed
against the alley wall, the man's left hand at her throat; and he had
hiked up her apron and skirt and petticoats, and was trying to get
his right hand into her drawers. She pushed against him, but to no
avail. He was large and strong. But when he saw the other man
standing down there, near the mouth of the alley, he let her garments
drop, and fished his organ back into his pants, but didn't waste time
buttoning-up. "You there! Like to watch your betters at work, do
you?" The man who had done the sidestep spoke softly: "Let the girl
go. Give her the two dollars, and let her go." The man in the bowler
took a step toward the mouth of the alley, his hands coming up in a
standard pugilist's extension. He gave a tiny laugh that was a snort
that was rude and derisive: "Oh so, fancy yourself something of the
John L. Sullivan, do you, captain? Well, let's see how you and I and
the Marquis Q get along . . ." and he danced forward, hindered
considerably by the bulky overcoat. As he drew within double arm's-
length of his opponent the younger man drew the taser from his coat
pocket, fired at point-blank range, the barbs striking the pugilist in
the cheek and neck, the charge lifting him off his feet and driving him back into the brick wall so hard that the filaments were
wrenched loose, and the potential fornicator fell forward, his eyes
rolled up in his head. Fell forward so hard he smashed three of his
front teeth, broken at the gum-line. The girl tried to run, but the

alley was a dead end. She watched as the man with the strange weapon came to her. She could barely see his face, and there had been all those killings with that Jack the Ripper in London a few years back, and there was talk this Jack had been a Yankee and had come back to New York. She was terrified. Her name was Poppy Skurnik, she was an orphan, and she worked way downtown as a pieceworker in a shirtwaist factory. She made one dollar and sixty-five cents a week, for six days of labor, from seven in the morning until seven at night, and it was barely enough to pay for her lodgings at Baer's Rents. So she "supplemented" her income with a stroll in the Tenderloin, twice a week, never more, and prayed that she could continue to avoid the murderous attentions of gentlemen who liked to cripple girls after they'd topped them, continue to avoid the pressures of pimps and boy friends who wanted her to work for them, continue to avoid the knowledge that she was no longer "decent" but was also a long way from winding up in one of these red-light whorehouses. He took her gently by the hand and started to lead her out of the alley, carefully stepping over the unconscious molester. When they reached the street, and she saw how handsome he was, and how young he was, and how premierely he was dressed, she also smiled. She was extraordinarily attractive, and the young man tipped his hat and spoke to her kindly, inquiring as to her name, and where she lived, and if she would like to accompany him for some dinner. And she accepted, and he hailed a carriage, and took her to Delmonico's for the finest meal she had ever had. And later, much later, when he brought her to his townhouse on upper Fifth Avenue, in the posh section, she was ready to do anything he required of her. But instead, all he asked was that she allow him to give her a hundred dollars in exchange for one second of small pain. And she felt fear, because she knew what these nabobs were like, *but a hundred dollars!* So she said yes, and he asked her to bare her left buttock, and she did it with embarrassment, and there was exactly one second of mosquito bite pain, and then he was wiping the spot where he had injected her with penicillin, with a cool and fragrant wad of cotton batting. "Would you like to sleep the night here, Poppy?" the young man asked. "My room is down the hall, but I think you'll be very comfortable in this one." And she was worried that he had done something awful to her, like inject her with a bad poison, but she didn't *feel* any different, and he seemed so nice, so she said yes, that would be a dear way to spend the evening, and he gave her ten ten-dollar bills, and wished her a pleasant sleep, and left the room, having saved her life, for she had contracted syphilis the week before, though she didn't know it; and within a year she would have been unable, by her appearance alone, to get men in the streets; and would have been let go at the shirtwaist factory; and would have been se-duced and sold into one of the worst of the brothels; and would have been dead within another two years. But this night she slept well, between cool sheets with hand-embroidered lace edging, and when she rose the next day he was gone, and no one told her to leave the townhouse, and so she stayed on from day to day, for years, and eventually married and gave birth to three children, one of whom grew to maturity, married, had a child who became an adult and saved the lives of millions of innocent men, women, and children. But that night in 1892 she slept a deep, sweet, recuperative, and dreamless sleep.

LEVENDIS: On Tuesday the 22nd of October, he visited a plague of asthmatic toads on Iisalmi, a small town in Finland; a rain of handbills left over from World War II urging the SS troops to surrender on Chejudo, an island off the southern coast of Korea; a shock wave of forsythia on Linares in Spain; and a fully restored 1926 Ahrens-Fox model RK fire engine on a mini-mall in Clarksville, Arkansas.

LEVENDIS: On Wednesday the 23rd of October, he corrected every history book in America so that they no longer called it The Battle of Bunker Hill, but rather Breeds Hill where, in fact, the engagement of 17 June 1775 had taken place. He also invested every radio and television commentator with the ability to differentiate between "in a moment" and "momentarily," which were not at all the same thing, and the misuse of which annoyed him greatly. The former was in his job description; the latter was a matter of personal pique.

LEVENDIS: On Thursday the 24th of October, he revealed to the London *Times* and *Paris-Match* the name of the woman who had stood on the grassy knoll, behind the fence, in Dallas that day, and fired the rifle shots that killed John F. Kennedy. But no one believed Marilyn Monroe could have done the deed and gotten away unnoticed. Not even when he provided her suicide note that confessed the entire matter and tragically told in her own words how jealousy and having been jilted had driven her to hire that weasel Lee Harvey Oswald, and that pig Jack Ruby, and how she could no longer live with the guilt, goodbye. No one would run the story, not even the *Star*, not even *The Enquirer*, not even *TV Guide*. But he tried.

LEVENDIS: On Friday the 25th of October, he upped the intelligence of every human being on the planet by forty points.

LEVENDIS: On Saturday the 26th of October, he lowered the intelligence of every human being on the planet by forty-two points.

This is a story titled
*At Least One Good Deed a Day,
Every Single Day*

LEVENDIS: On Sunday the 27th of October, he returned to a family in Kalgoorlie, SW Australia, a five-year-old child who had been kidnapped from their home in Bayonne, New Jersey, fifteen years earlier. The child was no older than before the family had immigrated, but he now spoke only in a dialect of Etruscan, a language that had not been heard on the planet for thousands of years. Having most of the day free, however, he then made it his business to kill the remaining seventeen American GIs being held MIA in an encampment in the heart of Laos. Waste not, want not.

LEVENDIS: On Monday the 28th of October, still exhilarated from the work and labors of the preceding day, he brought out of the highlands of North Viet Nam Capt. Eugene Y. Grasso, USAF, who had gone down under fire twenty-eight years earlier. He returned him to his family in Anchorage, Alaska, where his wife, remarried, refused to see him but his daughter, whom he had never seen, would. They fell in love, and lived together in Anchorage, where their story provided endless confusion to the ministers of several faiths.

LEVENDIS: On Tuesday the 29th of October, he destroyed the last bits of evidence that would have led to answers to the mysteries of the disappearances of Amelia Earhart, Ambrose Bierce, Benjamin

Bathurst, and Jimmy Hoffa. He washed the bones and placed them in a display of early American artifacts.

LEVENDIS: On Wednesday the 30th of October, he traveled to New Orleans, Louisiana, where he waited at a restaurant in Metairie for the former head of the Ku Klux Klan, now running for state office, to show up to meet friends. As the man stepped out of his limousine, wary guards on both sides of him, the traveler fired a Laws rocket from the roof of the eatery. It blew up the former KKK prexy, his guards, and a perfectly good Cadillac Eldorado. Leaving the electoral field open, for the enlightened voters of Louisiana, to a man who, as a child, had assisted Mengele's medical experiments, a second contender who had changed his name to avoid being arrested for child mutilation, and an illiterate swamp cabbage farmer from Baton Rouge whose political philosophy involved cutting the throats of peccary pigs, and thrusting one's face into the boiling blood of the corpse. Waste not, want not.

LEVENDIS: On Thursday the 31st of October, he restored to his throne the Dalai Lama, and closed off the mountain passes that provided land access to Tibet, and caused to blow constantly a cataclysmic snowstorm that did not affect the land below, but made any accessibility by air impossible. The Dalai Lama offered a referendum to the people: should we rename our land Shangri-La?

LEVENDIS: On Friday the 32nd of October, he addressed a convention of readers of cheap fantasy novels, saying, "We invent our lives (and other people's) as we live them; what we call 'life' is itself a fiction. Therefore, we must constantly strive to produce only good art, absolutely entertaining fiction." (He did *not* say to them: "I am an unlimited person, sadly living in a limited world.") They smiled politely, but since he spoke only in Etruscan, they did not understand a word he said.

LEVENDIS: On Saturday the 33rd of October, he did the sidestep and worked the oars of the longboat that brought Christopher Columbus to the shores of the New World, where he was approached by a representative of the native peoples, who laughed at the silly clothing the great navigator wore. They all ordered pizza and the man who had done the rowing made sure that venereal disease was quickly spread so that centuries later he could give a beautiful young woman an inoculation in her left buttock.

LEVENDIS: On Piltic the 34th of October, he gave all dogs the ability to speak in English, French, Mandarin, Urdu, and Esperanto; but all they could say was rhyming poetry of the worst sort, and he called it *doggerel*.

LEVENDIS: On Sqwaybe the 35th of October, he was advised by the Front Office that he had been having too rich a time at the expense of the Master Parameter, and he was removed from his position, and the unit was closed down, and darkness was penciled in as a mid-season replacement. He was reprimanded for having called himself Levendis, which is a Greek word for someone who is full of the pleasure of living. He was reassigned, with censure, but no one higher up noticed that on his new assignment he had taken the name Sertsa.

This has been a story titled
Shagging Fungoes

GRAVES

Joe Haldeman

Joe Haldeman's first science fiction novel, *The Forever War*, won both the Nebula and Hugo awards in the mid seventies. Since then he has become one of the most important writers of science fiction with his novels, short fiction, and poetry, for which he has won multiple Nebula, Hugo, and Rhysling awards. Among his novels are *Mindbridge, All My Sins Remembered, Worlds, Buying Time,* and *The Hemingway Hoax.* His latest books are *Feedback,* a collection of stories, and *1968,* a novel.

Of his short story "Graves," which won both a Nebula Award and a World Fantasy Award, Haldeman writes:

"It's funny where stories come from. I wrote the first four or five pages of 'Graves' because my agent needed a few pages of a horror story to help flog an anthology to somebody. Nothing came of it. The opening sat around for some years. Every now and then I'd take it out and look at it. Eh.

"Then one day there was a strange death about three blocks from where I lived. It was a crowded suburb, but we had a little piece of forest (probably because of a zoning singularity)—a triangle of woods perhaps two hundred meters on a side.

"They found the naked body of an old man in there. He'd been dead about a day. Who was he; what was he doing there? No one could say.

"The scandal, as it turned out, was that he was just an old guy from a local nursing home. He walked out the door naked, wandered a couple of blocks, and set himself down in the woods and died. It was a day before anybody realized he was gone.

"It's the kind of thing that makes a writer think, hey, got to be a story in there. I already had one started.

"The Vietnam part is just war and death, just memory and imagination. I walked by Graves Registration once in Kontum, on my way to a helicopter pad. They were unloading a deuce-and-a-half, a large truck, full of bodies.

"I'd seen a lot of dead people, but this was just too many in one place."

I have this persistent sleep disorder that makes life difficult for me, but still I want to keep it. Boy, do I want to keep it. It goes back twenty years, to Vietnam. To Graves.

Dead bodies turn from bad to worse real fast in the jungle. You've got a few hours before rigor mortis makes them hard to handle, hard to stuff in a bag. By that time they start to turn greenish, if they started out white or yellow, where you can see the skin. It's mostly bugs by then, usually ants. Then they go to black and start to smell.

They swell up and burst.

You'd think the ants and roaches and beetles and millipedes would make short work of them after that, but they don't. Just when they get to looking and smelling the worst, the bugs sort of lose interest, get fastidious, send out for pizza. Except for the flies. Laying eggs.

The funny thing is, unless some big animal got to it and tore it up, even after a week or so you've still got something more than a skeleton, even a sort of a face. No eyes, though. Every now and then we'd get one like that. Not too often, since soldiers usually don't die alone and sit there for that long, but sometimes. We called them "dry ones." Still damp underneath, of course, and inside, but kind of like a sunburned mummy otherwise.

You tell people what you do at Graves Registration, "Graves," and it sounds like about the worst job the army has to offer. It isn't. You just stand there all day and open body bags, figure out which parts maybe belong to which dog tag—not that it's usually that important—sew them up more or less with a big needle, account for all the wallets and jewelry, steal the dope out of their pockets, box them up, seal the casket, do the paperwork. When you have enough boxes, you truck them out to the airfield. The first week maybe is pretty bad. But after a hundred or so, after you get used to the smell and the god-awful feel of them, you get to thinking that opening a body bag is a lot better than ending up inside one. They put Graves in safe places.

Since I'd had a couple years of college, premed, I got some of the more interesting jobs. Captain French, who was the pathologist actually in charge of the outfit, always took me with him out into the field when he had to examine a corpse in situ, which happened only maybe once a month. I got to wear a .45 in a shoulder holster, tough guy. Never fired it, never got shot at, except the one time.

That was a hell of a time. It's funny what gets to you, stays with you.

Usually when we had an in situ, it was a forensic matter, like an officer they suspected had been fragged or otherwise terminated by his own men. We'd take pictures and interview some people, and then Frenchy would bring the stiff back for autopsy, see whether the bullets were American or Vietnamese. (Not that that would be conclusive either way. The Vietcong stole our weapons, and our guys used the North Vietnamese AK-47s, when we could get our hands on them. More reliable than the M-16, and a better cartridge for killing. Both sides proved that over and over.) Usually Frenchy would send a report up to Division, and that would be it. Once he had to testify at a court-martial. The kid was guilty, but just got life. The officer was a real prick.

Anyhow, we got the call to come look at this in situ corpse about five in the afternoon. Frenchy tried to put it off until the next day, since if it got dark we'd have to spend the night. The guy he was talking to was a major, though, and obviously proud of it, so it was no use arguing. I threw some C's and beer and a couple canteens into two rucksacks that already had blankets and air mattresses tied on the bottom. Box of .45 ammo and a couple hand grenades. Went and got a jeep while Frenchy got his stuff together and made sure Doc Carter was sober enough to count the stiffs as they came in. (Doc Carter was the one supposed to be in charge, but he didn't much care for the work.)

Drove us out to the pad, and lo and behold, there was a chopper waiting, blades idling. Should've started to smell a rat then. We don't get real high priority, and it's not easy to get a chopper to go anywhere so close to sundown. They even helped us stow our gear. Up, up, and away.

I never flew enough in helicopters to make it routine. Kontum looked almost pretty in the low sun, golden red. I had to sit between two flamethrowers, though, which didn't make me feel too secure. The door gunner was smoking. The flamethrower tanks were stenciled NO SMOKING.

We went fast and low out toward the mountains to the west. I

was hoping we'd wind up at one of the big fire bases up there, figuring I'd sleep better with a few hundred men around. But no such
luck. When the chopper started to slow down, the blades' whir deep-
ening to a *whuck-whuck-whuck,* there was no clearing as far as
the eye could see. Thick jungle canopy everywhere. Then a wisp of
purple smoke showed us a helicopter-sized hole in the leaves. The
pilot brought us down an inch at a time, nicking twigs. I was very
much aware of the flamethrowers. If he clipped a large branch we'd
be so much pot roast.

When we touched down, four guys in a big hurry unloaded our
gear and the flamethrowers and a couple cases of ammo. They put
two wounded guys and one client on board and shooed the helicopter
away. Yeah, it would sort of broadcast your position. One of them
told us to wait; he'd go get the major.

"I don't like this at all," Frenchy said.

"Me neither," I said. "Let's go home."

"Any outfit that's got a major and two flamethrowers is planning
to fight a real war." He pulled his .45 out and looked at it as if he'd
never seen one before. "Which end of this do you think the bullets
come out of?"

"Shit," I advised, and rummaged through the rucksack for a beer.
I gave Frenchy one, and he put it in his side pocket.

A machine gun opened up off to our right. Frenchy and I
grabbed the dirt. Three grenade blasts. Somebody yelled for them
to cut that out. Guy yelled back he thought he saw something. Machine gun started up again. We tried to get a little lower.

Up walks this old guy, thirties, looking annoyed. The major.

"You men get up. What's wrong with you?" He was playin'
games.

Frenchy got up, dusting himself off. We had the only clean fa-
tigues in twenty miles. "Captain French, Graves Registration."

"Oh," he said, not visibly impressed. "Secure your gear and follow me." He drifted off like a mighty ship of the jungle. Frenchy
rolled his eyes, and we hoisted our rucksacks and followed him. I
wasn't sure whether "secure your gear" meant bring your stuff or
leave it behind, but Budweiser could get to be a real collector's item
in the boonies, and there were a lot of collectors out here.

We walked too far. I mean a couple hundred yards. That meant they were really spread out thin. I didn't look forward to spending the night. The goddamned machine gun started up again. The major looked annoyed and shouted, "Sergeant, will you please control your men?," and the sergeant told the machine gunner to shut the fuck up, and the machine gunner told the sergeant there was a fuckin' gook out there, and then somebody popped a big one, like a Claymore, and then everybody was shooting every which way. Frenchy and I got real horizontal. I heard a bullet whip by over my head. The major was leaning against a tree, looking bored, shouting, "Cease firing, cease firing!" The shooting dwindled down like popcorn getting done. The major looked over at us and said, "Come on. While there's still light." He led us into a small clearing, elephant grass pretty well trampled down. I guess everybody had had his turn to look at the corpse.

It wasn't a real gruesome body, as bodies go, but it was odd-looking, even for a dry one. Moldy, like someone had dusted flour over it. Naked and probably male, though incomplete: all the soft parts were gone. Tall; one of our Montagnard allies rather than an ethnic Vietnamese. Emaciated, dry skin taut over ribs. Probably old, though it doesn't take long for these people to get old. Lying on its back, mouth wide open, a familiar posture. Empty eye sockets staring skyward. Arms flung out in supplication, loosely, long past rigor mortis.

Teeth chipped and filed to points, probably some Montagnard tribal custom. I'd never seen it before, but we didn't "do" many natives.

Frenchy knelt down and reached for it, then stopped. "Checked for booby traps?"

"No," the major said. "Figure that's your job." Frenchy looked at me with an expression that said it was my job.

Both officers stood back a respectful distance while I felt under the corpse. Sometimes they pull the pin on a hand grenade and slip it under the body so that the body's weight keeps the arming lever in place. You turn it over, and *Tomato Surprise!*

I always worry less about a hand grenade than about the various weird serpents and bugs that might enjoy living underneath a decomposing corpse. Vietnam has its share of snakes and scorpions and megapedes.

I was lucky this time; nothing but maggots. I flicked them off
my hand and watched the major turn a little green. People are funny.
What does he think is going to happen to him when he dies? Everything has to eat. And he was sure as hell going to die if he didn't
start keeping his head down. I remember that thought, but didn't
think of it then as a prophecy.

They came over. "What do you make of it, Doctor?"

"I don't think we can cure him." Frenchy was getting annoyed
at this cherry bomb. "What else do you want to know?"

"Isn't it a little . . . *odd* to find something like this in the middle
of nowhere?"

"Naw. Country's full of corpses." He knelt down and studied the
face, wiggling the head by its chin. "We keep it up, you'll be able to
walk from the Mekong to the DMZ without stepping on anything
but corpses."

"But he's been castrated!"

"Birds." He toed the body over, busy white crawlers running
from the light. "Just some old geezer who walked out into the woods
naked and fell over dead. Could happen back in the World. Old
people do funny things."

"I thought maybe he'd been tortured by the VC or something."

"God knows. It could happen." The body eased back into its
original position with a creepy creaking sound, like leather. Its mouth
had closed halfway. "If you want to put 'evidence of VC torture' in
your report, your body count, I'll initial it."

"What do you mean by that, Captain?"

"Exactly what I said." He kept staring at the major while he
flipped a cigarette into his mouth and fired it up. Nonfilter Camels;
you'd think a guy who worked with corpses all day long would be
less anxious to turn into one. "I'm just trying to get along."

"You believe I want you to falsify—"

Now, "falsify" is a strange word for a last word. The enemy had
set up a heavy machine gun on the other side of the clearing, and
we were the closest targets. A round struck the major in the small
of his back, we found on later examination. At the time it was just
an explosion of blood and guts, and he went down with his legs
flopping every which way, barfing, then loud death rattle. Frenchy
was on the ground in a ball, holding his left hand, going, "Shit shit

shit." He'd lost the last joint of his little finger. Painful, but not serious enough, as it turned out, to get him back to the World.

I myself was horizontal and aspiring to be subterranean. I managed to get my pistol out and cocked, but realized I didn't want to do anything that might draw attention to us. The machine gun was spraying back and forth over us at about knee height. Maybe they couldn't see us; maybe they thought we were dead. I was scared shitless.

"Frenchy," I stage-whispered, "we've got to get outa here." He was trying to wrap his finger up in a standard first-aid-pack gauze bandage, much too large. "Get back to the trees."

"After you, asshole. We wouldn't get halfway." He worked his pistol out of the holster but couldn't cock it, his left hand clamping the bandage and slippery with blood. I armed it for him and handed it back. "These are going to do a hell of a lot of good. How are you with grenades?"

"Shit. How you think I wound up in Graves?" In basic training, they'd put me on KP whenever they went out for live grenade practice. In school, I was always the last person when they chose up sides for baseball, for the same reason—though, to my knowledge, a baseball wouldn't kill you if you couldn't throw far enough. "I couldn't get one halfway there." The tree line was about sixty yards away.

"Neither could I, with this hand." He was a lefty.

Behind us came the *poink* sound of a sixty-millimeter mortar, and in a couple of seconds there was a gray smoke explosion between us and the tree line. The machine gun stopped, and somebody behind us yelled, "Add twenty!"

At the tree line, we could hear some shouting in Vietnamese, and a clanking of metal. "They're gonna bug out," Frenchy said. "Let's di-di."

We got up and ran, and somebody did fire a couple of bursts at us, probably an AK-47, but he missed, and then there were a series of *poink*s and a series of explosions pretty close to where the gun had been.

We rushed back to the LZ and found the command group, about the time the firing started up again. There was a first lieutenant in charge, and when things slowed down enough for us to tell him what had happened to the major, he expressed neither surprise nor grief.

The man had been an observer from Battalion and had assumed command when their captain was killed that morning. He'd take our word for it that the guy was dead—that was one thing we were trained observers in—and not send a squad out for him until the fighting had died down and it was light again.

We inherited the major's hole, which was nice and deep, and in his rucksack found a dozen cans and jars of real food and a flask of scotch. So, as the battle raged through the night, we munched pâté on Ritz crackers, pickled herring in sour-cream sauce, little Polish sausages on party rye with real French mustard. We drank all the scotch and saved the beer for breakfast.

For hours the lieutenant called in for artillery and air support, but to no avail. Later we found out that the enemy had launched coordinated attacks on all the local airfields and Special Forces camps, and every camp that held POWs. We were much lower priority.

Then, about three in the morning, Snoopy came over. Snoopy was a big C-130 cargo plane that carried nothing but ammunition and Gatling guns; they said it could fly over a football field and put a round into every square inch. Anyhow, it saturated the perimeter with fire, and the enemy stopped shooting. Frenchy and I went to sleep.

At first light we went out to help round up the KIAs. There were only four dead, counting the major, but the major was an astounding sight, at least in context.

He looked sort of like a cadaver left over from a teaching autopsy. His shirt had been opened and his pants pulled down to his thighs, and the entire thoracic and abdominal cavities had been ripped open and emptied of everything soft, everything from esophagus to testicles, rib cage like blood-streaked fingers sticking rigid out of sagging skin, and there wasn't a sign of any of the guts anywhere, just a lot of dried blood.

Nobody had heard anything. There was a machine-gun position not twenty yards away, and they'd been straining their ears all night. All they'd heard was flies.

Maybe an animal feeding very quietly. The body hadn't been opened with a scalpel or a knife; the skin had been torn by teeth or claws—but seemingly systematically, throat to balls.

And the dry one was gone. Him with the pointed teeth.

There is one rational explanation. Modern warfare is partly mind-fuck, and we aren't the only ones who do it, dropping unlucky cards, invoking magic and superstition. The Vietnamese knew how squeamish Americans were and would mutilate bodies in clever ways. They could also move very quietly. The dry one? They might have spirited him away just to fuck with us. Show what they could do under our noses.

And as for the dry one's odd mummified appearance, the mold, there might be an explanation. I found out that the Montagnards in that area don't bury their dead; they put them in a coffin made from a hollowed-out log and leave them aboveground. So maybe he was just the victim of a grave robber. I thought the nearest village was miles away, like twenty miles, but I could have been wrong. Or the body could have been carried that distance for some obscure purpose—maybe the VC set it out on the trail to make the Americans stop in a good place to be ambushed.

That's probably it. But for twenty years now, several nights a week, I wake up sweating with a terrible image in my mind. I've gone out with a flashlight, and there it is, the dry one, scooping steaming entrails from the major's body, tearing them with its sharp teeth, staring into my light with black empty sockets, unconcerned. I reach for my pistol, and it's never there. The creature stands up, shiny with blood, and takes a step toward me—for a year or so, that was it; I would wake up. Then it was two steps, and then three. After twenty years it has covered half the distance and its dripping hands are raising from its sides.

The doctor gives me tranquilizers. I don't take them. They might help me stay asleep.

FESTIVAL NIGHT
from RED MARS

Kim Stanley Robinson

Kim Stanley Robinson, in a recent letter, commented that "I'm not really comfortable talking about my fiction. I don't have that much to say about it." Happily, his fiction overwhelmingly speaks for itself. In his novels *The Wild Shore, The Gold Coast,* and *Pacific Edge,* known as his Orange County trilogy, he movingly examines three possible southern Californias; in such collections as *The Planet on the Table* and *Remaking History,* he shows himself to be one of science fiction's most thoughtful voices. He has won the Nebula Award, the World Fantasy Award, the John W. Campbell Memorial Award, and most recently the Hugo Award.

Red Mars, the first in an ambitious trilogy of novels depicting the terraforming of Mars, was immediately hailed as a definitive example of realistic science fiction. This novel brought Robinson his second Nebula Award, was listed as a *New York Times* Notable Book of the Year for 1993, and seems destined to become one of those yardsticks with which future science fiction is measured. "Festival Night," reprinted here, is the first part of *Red Mars,* and shows Robinson's gift for detail and his insight into the fascinating, difficult, and often disturbing people who populate his novel.

Robinson has said about this book that "I started *Red Mars* when my son David was five months old, and now a blink later he is five years old." In this brief sentence he has managed to capture a bit of the subjective experience of writing such an ambitious novel.

Mars was empty before we came. That's not to say that nothing had ever happened. The planet had accreted, melted, roiled, and cooled, leaving a surface scarred by enormous geological features: craters, canyons, volcanoes. But all of that happened in mineral unconsciousness, and unobserved. There were no witnesses—except for us, looking from the planet next door, and that only in the last moment of its long history. We are all the consciousness that Mars has ever had.

Now everybody knows the history of Mars in the human mind:

*how for all the generations of prehistory it was one of the chief lights in the sky, because of its redness and fluctuating intensity, and the way it stalled in its wandering course through the stars, and sometimes even reversed direction. It seemed to be saying something with all that. So perhaps it is not surprising that all the oldest names for Mars have a peculiar weight on the tongue—*Nirgal, Mangala, Auqakuh, Harmakhis—*they sound as if they were even older than the ancient languages we find them in, as if they were fossil words from the Ice Age or before. Yes, for thousands of years Mars was a sacred power in human affairs; and its color made it a dangerous power, representing blood, anger, war, and the heart.*

Then the first telescopes gave us a closer look, and we saw the little orange disk, with its white poles and dark patches spreading and shrinking as the long seasons passed. No improvement in the technology of the telescope ever gave us much more than that; but the best Earthbound images gave Lowell enough blurs to inspire a story, the story we all know, of a dying world and a heroic people, desperately building canals to hold off the final deadly encroachment of the desert.

It was a great story. But then Mariner *and* Viking *sent back their photos, and everything changed. Our knowledge of Mars expanded by magnitudes, we literally knew millions of times more about this planet than we had before. And there before us flew a new world, a world unsuspected.*

It seemed, however, to be a world without life. People searched for signs of past or present Martian life, anything from microbes to the doomed canal builders, or even alien visitors. As you know, no evidence for any of these has ever been found. And so stories have naturally blossomed to fill the gap, just as in Lowell's time, or in Homer's, or in the caves or on the savannah—stories of microfossils wrecked by our bio-organisms, of ruins found in dust storms and then lost forever, of Big Man and all his adventures, of the elusive little red people, always glimpsed out of the corner of the eye. And all of these tales are told in an attempt to give Mars life, or to bring it to life. Because we are still those animals who survived the Ice Age, and looked up at the night sky in wonder, and told stories. And Mars has never ceased to be what it was to us from our very beginning— a great sign, a great symbol, a great power.

And so we came here. It had been a power; now it became a place.

". . . And so we came here. But what they didn't realize was that by the time we got to Mars, we would be so changed by the voyage out that nothing we had been told to do mattered anymore. It wasn't like submarining or settling the Wild West—it was *an entirely new experience,* and as the flight of the *Ares* went on, the Earth finally became so distant that it was nothing but a blue star among all the others, its voices so delayed that they seemed to come from a previous century. We were on our own; and so we became *fundamentally different beings.*"

All lies, Frank Chalmers thought irritably. He was sitting in a row of dignitaries, watching his old friend John Boone give the usual Boone Inspirational Address. It made Chalmers weary. The truth was, the trip to Mars had been the functional equivalent of a long train ride. Not only had they not become fundamentally different beings, they had actually become more like themselves than ever, stripped of habits until they were left with nothing but the naked raw material of their selves. But John stood up there waving a forefinger at the crowd, saying, "We came here to make something new, and when we arrived our earthly differences fell away, irrelevant in this new world!" Yes, he meant it all literally. His vision of Mars was a lens that distorted everything he saw, a kind of religion.

Chalmers stopped listening and let his gaze wander over the new city. They were going to call it Nicosia. It was the first town of any size to be built freestanding on the Martian surface; all the buildings were set inside what was in effect an immense clear tent supported by a nearly invisible frame and placed on the rise of Tharsis, west of Noctis Labyrinthus. This location gave it a tremendous view, with a distant western horizon punctuated by the broad peak of Pavonis Mons. For the Mars veterans in the crowd it was giddy stuff: they were on the surface, they were out of the trenches and mesas and craters, they could see forever! Hurrah!

A laugh from the audience drew Frank's attention back to his old friend. John Boone had a slightly hoarse voice and a friendly midwestern accent, and he was by turns (and somehow even all at once) relaxed, intense, sincere, self-mocking, modest, confident, serious, and funny. In short, the perfect public speaker. And the audience was rapt; this was *the First Man on Mars* speaking to them, and judging by the looks on their faces they might as well have been watching Jesus produce their evening meal out of the loaves and fishes. And in fact John almost deserved their adoration, for performing a similar miracle on another plane, transforming their tin-can existence into an astounding spiritual voyage. "On Mars we will come to care for each other more than ever before," John said, which really meant, Chalmers thought, an alarming incidence of the kind of behavior seen in rat overpopulation experiments; "Mars is a sublime, exotic, and dangerous place," said John—meaning a frozen ball of oxidized rock on which they were exposed to about fifteen rem a year; "and with our work," John continued, "we are carving out a new social order and the next step in the human story"—i.e., the latest variant in primate dominance dynamics.

John finished with this flourish, and there was, of course, a huge roar of applause. Maya Toitovna then went to the podium to introduce Chalmers. Frank gave her a private look which meant he was in no mood for any of her jokes; she saw it and said, "Our next speaker has been the fuel in our little rocket ship," which somehow got a laugh. "His vision and energy are what got us to Mars in the first place, so save any complaints you may have for our next speaker, my old friend Frank Chalmers."

At the podium he found himself surprised by how big the town appeared. It covered a long triangle, and they were gathered at its highest point, a park occupying the western apex. Seven paths rayed down through the park to become wide, tree-lined, grassy boulevards. Between the boulevards stood low trapezoidal buildings, each faced with polished stone of a different color. The size and architecture of the buildings gave things a faintly Parisian look, Paris as seen by a drunk Fauvist in spring, sidewalk cafés and all. Four or five kilometers downslope the end of the city was marked by three slender skyscrapers, beyond which lay the low greenery of the farm. The skyscrapers were part of the tent framework, which overhead was an arched network of sky-colored lines. The tent fabric itself was invisible, and so, taken all in all, it appeared that they *stood in the open air*. That was gold. Nicosia was going to be a popular city.

Chalmers said as much to the audience, and enthusiastically they agreed. Apparently he had the crowd, fickle souls that they were, about as securely as John. Chalmers was bulky and dark, and he knew he presented quite a contrast to John's blond good looks; but he knew as well that he had his own rough charisma, and as he warmed up he drew on it, falling into a selection of his own stock phrases.

Then a shaft of sunlight lanced down between the clouds, striking the upturned faces of the crowd, and he felt an odd tightening in his stomach. So many people there, so many *strangers!* People in the mass were a frightening thing—all those wet ceramic eyes encased in pink blobs, looking at him . . . it was nearly too much. Five thousand people in a single Martian town. After all the years in Underhill, it was hard to grasp.

Foolishly he tried to tell the audience something of this. "Looking," he said. "Looking around . . . the strangeness of our presence here is . . . accentuated."

He was losing the crowd. How to say it? How to say that they alone in all that rocky world were alive, their faces glowing like paper lanterns in the light? How to say that even if living creatures were no more than carriers for ruthless genes, this was still, somehow, better than the blank mineral nothingness of everything else?

Of course he could never say it. Not at any time, perhaps, and certainly not in a speech. So he collected himself. "In the Martian desolation," he said, "the human presence is, well, a remarkable thing." (They would care for each other more than ever before, a voice in his mind repeated sardonically.) "The planet, taken in itself, is a dead frozen nightmare" (therefore exotic and sublime) "and so, thrown on our own, we of necessity are in the process of . . . reorganizing a bit" (or forming a new social order)—so that yes, yes, yes, he found himself proclaiming exactly the same lies they had just heard from John!

Thus at the end of his speech he too got a big roar of applause. Irritated, he announced it was time to eat, depriving Maya of her chance for a final remark. Although probably she had known he would do that and so hadn't bothered to think of any. Frank Chalmers liked to have the last word.

People crowded onto the temporary platform to mingle with the celebrities. It was rare to get this many of the first hundred in one spot anymore, and people crowded around John and Maya, Samantha Hoyle, Sax Russell, and Chalmers.

Frank looked over the crowd at John and Maya. He didn't recognize the group of Terrans surrounding them, which made him curious. He made his way across the platform, and as he approached he saw Maya and John give each other a look. "There's no reason this place shouldn't function under normal law," one of the Terrans was saying.

Maya said to him, "Did Olympus Mons really remind you of Mauna Loa?"

"Sure," the man said. "Shield volcanoes all look alike."

Frank stared over this idiot's head at Maya. She didn't acknowledge the look. John was pretending not to have noticed Frank's arrival. Samantha Hoyle was speaking to another man in an undertone, explaining something; he nodded, then glanced involuntarily at Frank. Samantha kept her back turned to him. But it was John who mattered, John and Maya. And both were pretending that nothing was out of the ordinary; but the topic of conversation, whatever it had been, had gone away.

Chalmers left the platform. People were still trooping down through the park, toward tables that had been set in the upper ends of the seven boulevards. Chalmers followed them, walking under young transplanted sycamores; their khaki leaves colored the afternoon light, making the park look like the bottom of an aquarium.

At the banquet tables construction workers were knocking back vodka, getting rowdy, obscurely aware that with the construction finished the heroic age of Nicosia was ended. Perhaps that was true for all of Mars.

The air filled with overlapping conversations. Frank sank beneath the turbulence, wandered out to the northern perimeter. He stopped at a waist-high concrete coping: the city wall. Out of the metal stripping on its top rose four layers of clear plastic. A Swiss man was explaining things to a group of visitors, pointing happily.

"An outer membrane of piezoelectric plastic generates electricity from wind. Then two sheets hold a layer of airgel insulation. Then the inner layer is a radiation-capturing membrane, which turns purple and must be replaced. More clear than a window, isn't it?"

The visitors agreed. Frank reached out and pushed at the inner membrane. It stretched until his fingers were buried to the knuckles. Slightly cool. There was faint white lettering printed on the plastic: ISIDIS PLANITIA POLYMERS. Through the sycamores over his shoulder he could still see the platform at the apex. John and Maya and their cluster of Terran admirers were still there, talking animatedly. Conducting the business of the planet. Deciding the fate of Mars.

He stopped breathing. He felt the pressure of his molars squeezing together. He poked the tent wall so hard that he pushed out the outermost membrane, which meant that some of his anger would be captured and stored as electricity in the town's grid. It was a special polymer in that respect—carbon atoms were linked to hydrogen and fluorine atoms in such a way that the resulting substance was even more piezoelectric than quartz. Change one element of the three, however, and everything shifted; substitute chlorine for fluorine, for instance, and you had Saran Wrap.

Frank stared at his wrapped hand, then up again at the other two elements, still bonded to each other. But without him they were nothing!

Angrily he walked into the narrow streets of the city.

Clustered in a plaza, like mussels on a rock, were a group of Arabs drinking coffee. Arabs had arrived on Mars only ten years before, but already they were a force to be reckoned with. They had a lot of money, and they had teamed up with the Swiss to build a number of towns, including this one. And they liked it on Mars. "It's like a cold day in the Empty Quarter," as the Saudis said. The similarity was such that Arabic words were slipping quickly into English, because Arabic had a larger vocabulary for this landscape: *akaba* for the steep final slopes around volcanoes, *badia* for the great world dunes, *nefuds* for deep sand, *seyl* for the billion-year-old dry river-beds. . . . People were saying they might as well switch over to Arabic and have done with it.

Frank had spent a fair bit of time with Arabs, and the men in the plaza were pleased to see him. "*Salaam aleyk!*" they said to him, and he replied, "*Marhabba!*" White teeth flashed under black mustaches. Only men present, as usual. Some youths led him to a central table where the older men sat, including his friend Zeyk. Zeyk said,

"We are going to call this square *Hajr el-kra Meshab,* 'the red granite open place in town.' " He gestured at the rust-colored flagstones. Frank nodded and asked what kind of stone it was. He spoke Arabic for as long as he could, pushing the edges of his ability and getting some good laughs in response. Then he sat at the central table and relaxed, feeling like he could have been on a street in Damascus or Cairo, comfortable in the wash of Arabic and expensive cologne.

He studied the men's faces as they talked. An alien culture, no doubt about it. They weren't going to change just because they were on Mars, they put the lie to John's vision. Their thinking clashed radically with Western thought; for instance, the separation of church and state was wrong to them, making it impossible for them to agree with Westerners on the very basis of government. And they were so patriarchal that some of their women were said to be illiterate— illiterates, on Mars! That was a sign. And indeed these men had the dangerous look that Frank associated with machismo, the look of men who oppressed their women so cruelly that naturally the women struck back where they could, terrorizing sons who then terrorized wives who terrorized sons and so on and so on, in an endless death spiral of twisted love and sex hatred. So that in that sense they were all madmen.

Which was one reason Frank liked them. And certainly they would come in useful to him, acting as a new locus of power. Defend a weak new neighbor to weaken the old powerful ones, as Machiavelli had said. So he drank coffee, and gradually, politely, they shifted to English.

"How did you like the speeches?" he asked, looking into the black mud at the bottom of his demitasse.

"John Boone is the same as ever," old Zeyk replied. The others laughed angrily. "When he says we will make an indigenous Martian culture, he only means some of the Terran cultures here will be promoted, and others attacked. Those perceived as regressive will be singled out for destruction. It is a form of Ataturkism."

"He thinks everyone on Mars should *become* American," said a man named Nejm.

"Why not?" Zeyk said, smiling. "It's already happened on Earth."

"No," Frank said. "You shouldn't misunderstand Boone. People say he's self-absorbed, but—"

"He is self-absorbed!" Nejm cried. "He lives in a hall of mirrors! He thinks that we have come to Mars to establish a good old American superculture, and that everyone will agree to it because it is the John Boone plan."

Zeyk said, "He doesn't understand that other people have other opinions."

"It's not that," Frank said. "It's just that he knows they don't make as much sense as his."

They laughed at that, but the younger men's hoots had a bitter edge. They all believed that before their arrival Boone had argued in secret against UN approval for Arab settlements. Frank encouraged this belief, which was almost true—John disliked any ideology that might get in his way. He wanted the slate as blank as possible in everybody who came up.

The Arabs, however, believed that John disliked them in particular. Young Selim el-Hayil opened his mouth to speak, and Frank gave him a swift warning glance. Selim froze, then pursed his mouth angrily. Frank said, "Well, he's not as bad as all that. Although to tell the truth I've heard him say it would have been better if the Americans and Russians had been able to claim the planet when they arrived, like explorers in the old days."

Their laughter was brief and grim. Selim's shoulders hunched as if struck. Frank shrugged and smiled, spread his hands wide. "But it's pointless! I mean, what can he do?"

Old Zeyk lifted his eyebrows. "Opinions vary."

Chalmers got up to move on, meeting for one instant Selim's insistent gaze. Then he strode down a side street, one of the narrow lanes that connected the city's seven main boulevards. Most were paved with cobblestones or streetgrass, but this one was rough blond concrete. He slowed by a recessed doorway, looked in the window of a closed boot manufactory. His faint reflection appeared in a pair of bulky walker boots.

Opinions vary. Yes, a lot of people had underestimated John Boone—Chalmers had done it himself many times. An image came to him of John in the White House, pink with conviction, his disobedient blond hair flying wildly, the sun streaming in the Oval Office windows and illuminating him as he waved his hands and paced the room, talking away while the president nodded and his aides watched, pondering how best to co-opt that electrifying charisma. Oh, they had been hot in those days, Chalmers and Boone: Frank with the ideas and John the front man, with a momentum that was practically unstoppable. It would be more a matter of derailment, really.

Selim el-Hayil's reflection appeared among the boots.

"Is it true?" he demanded.

"Is what true?" said Frank crossly.

"Is Boone anti-Arab?"

"What do you think?"

"Was he the one who blocked permission to build the mosque on Phobos?"

"He's a powerful man."

The young Saudi's face twisted. "The most powerful man on Mars, and he only wants more! He wants to be king!" Selim made a fist and struck his other hand. He was slimmer than the other Arabs, weak chinned, his mustache covering a small mouth.

"The treaty comes up for renewal soon," Frank said. "And Boone's coalition is bypassing me." He ground his teeth. "I don't know what their plans are, but I'm going to find out tonight. You can imagine what they'll be, anyway. Western biases, certainly. He may withhold his approval of a new treaty unless it contains guarantees that all settlements will be made only by the original treaty signatories." Selim shivered, and Frank pressed: "It's what he wants, and it's very possible he could get it, because his new coalition makes him more powerful than ever. It could mean an end to settlement by nonsignatories. You'll become guest scientists. Or get sent back."

In the window the reflection of Selim's face appeared a kind of mask, signifying rage. *"Battal, battal,"* he was muttering. Very bad, very bad. His hands twisted as if out of his control, and he muttered about the Koran or Camus, Persepolis or the Peacock Throne, references scattered nervously among non sequiturs. Babbling.

"Talk means nothing," Chalmers said harshly. "When it comes down to it, nothing matters but action."

That gave the young Arab pause. "I can't be sure," he said at last.

Frank poked him in the arm, watched a shock run through the

man. "It's your people we're talking about. It's this planet we're talking about."

Selim's mouth disappeared under his mustache. After a time he said, "It's true."

Frank said nothing. They looked in the window together, as if judging boots.

Finally Frank raised a hand. "I'll talk to Boone again," he said quietly. "Tonight. He leaves tomorrow. I'll try to talk to him, to reason with him. I doubt it will matter. It never has before. But I'll try. Afterward . . . we should meet."

"Yes."

"In the park, then, the southernmost path. Around eleven."

Selim nodded.

Chalmers transfixed him with a stare. "Talk means nothing," he said brusquely, and walked away.

The next boulevard Chalmers came to was crowded with people clumped outside open-front bars or kiosks selling couscous and bratwurst. Arab and Swiss. It seemed an odd combination, but they meshed well.

Tonight some of the Swiss were distributing face masks from the door of an apartment. Apparently they were celebrating this *stadtfest* as a kind of Mardi Gras, *Fassnacht,* as they called it, with masks and music and every manner of social inversion, just as it was back home on those wild February nights in Basel and Zürich and Luzern. . . . On an impulse Frank joined the line. "Around every profound spirit a mask is always growing," he said to two young women in front of him. They nodded politely and then resumed conversation in guttural Schwyzerdüütsch, a dialect never written down, a private code, incomprehensible even to Germans. It was another impenetrable culture, the Swiss, in some ways even more so than the Arabs. That was it, Frank thought; they worked well together because they were both so insular that they never made any real contact. He laughed out loud as he took a mask, a black face studded with red paste gems. He put it on.

A line of masked celebrants snaked down the boulevard, drunk, loose, at the edge of control. At an intersection the boulevard opened up into a small plaza, where a fountain shot sun-colored water into the air. Around the fountain a steel-drum band hammered out a calypso tune. People gathered around, dancing or hopping in time to the low *bong* of the bass drum. A hundred meters overhead a vent in the tent frame poured frigid air down onto the plaza, air so cold that little flakes of snow floated in it, glinting in the light like chips of mica. Then fireworks banged just under the tenting, and colored sparks fell down through the snowflakes.

Sunset, more than any other time of day, made it clear that they stood on an alien planet; something in the slant and redness of the light was fundamentally wrong, upsetting expectations wired into the savannah brain over millions of years. This evening was providing a particularly garish and unsettling example of the phenomenon. Frank wandered in its light, making his way back to the city wall. The plain south of the city was littered with rocks, each one dogged by a long black shadow. Under the concrete arch of the city's south gate he stopped. No one there. The gates were locked during festivals like these, to keep drunks from going out and getting hurt. But Frank had gotten the day's emergency code out of the fire department AI that morning, and when he was sure no one was watching he tapped out the code and hurried into the lock. He put on a walker, boots, and helmet and went through the middle and outer doors.

Outside it was intensely cold as always, and the diamond pattern of the walker's heating element burned through his clothes. He crunched over concrete and then duricrust. Loose sand flowed east, pushed by the wind.

Grimly he looked around. Rocks everywhere. A planet sledge-hammered billions of times. And meteors still falling. Someday one of the towns would take a hit. He turned and looked back. It looked like an aquarium glowing in the dusk. There would be no warning, but everything would suddenly fly apart, walls, vehicles, trees, bodies. The Aztecs had believed the world would end in one of four ways: earthquake, fire, flood, or jaguars falling from the sky. Here there would be no fire. Nor earthquake nor flood, now that he thought of it. Leaving only the jaguars.

The twilight sky was a dark pink over Pavonis Mons. To the east stretched Nicosia's farm, a long low greenhouse running downslope from the city. From this angle one could see that the farm was larger

than the town proper, and jammed with green crops. Frank clumped
to one of its outer locks and entered.

Inside the farm it was hot, a full sixty degrees warmer than outside, and fifteen degrees warmer than in the city. He had to keep
his helmet on, as the farm air was tailored to the plants, heavy on
CO_2 and short on oxygen. He stopped at a work station and fingered
through drawers of small tools and pesticide patches, gloves and bags.
He selected three tiny patches and put them in a plastic bag, then
slipped the bag gently into the walker's pocket. The patches were
clever pesticides, biosaboteurs designed to provide plants with sys-
temic defenses; he had been reading about them, and knew of a
combination that in animals would be deadly to the organism. . . .

He put a pair of shears in the walker's other pocket. Narrow
gravel paths led him up between long beds of barley and wheat, back
toward the city proper. He went in the lock leading into town, un-
clipped his helmet, stripped off the walker and boots, transferred the
contents of the walker pockets to his coat. Then he went back into
the lower end of town.

Here the Arabs had built a medina, insisting that such a neighborhood was crucial to a city's health; the boulevards narrowed, and
between them lay warrens of twisted alleyways taken from the maps
of Tunis or Algiers, or generated randomly. Nowhere could you see
from one boulevard to the next, and the sky overhead was visible
only in plum strips, between buildings that leaned together.

Most of the alleys were empty now, as the party was uptown. A
pair of cats skulked between buildings, investigating their new home.
Frank took the shears from his pocket and scratched into a few plastic windows, in Arabic lettering, *Jew, Jew, Jew, Jew, Jew.* He walked
on, whistling through his teeth. Corner cafés were little caves of light.
Bottles clinked like prospectors' hammers. An Arab sat on a squat
black speaker playing an electric guitar.

He found the central boulevard, walked up it. Boys in the
branches of the lindens and sycamores shouted songs to each other
in Schwyzerdüütsch. One ditty was in English: "John Boone / Went
to the moon / No fast cars / He went to Mars!" Small disorganized
music bands barged through the thickening crowd. Some mustached
men dressed as American cheerleaders flounced expertly through a
complicated can-can routine. Kids banged little plastic drums. It was

loud; the tenting absorbed sound, so there weren't the echoes one heard under crater domes, but it was loud nevertheless.

Up there, where the boulevard opened into the sycamore park— that was John himself, surrounded by a small crowd. He saw Chalmers approaching and waved, recognizing him despite the mask. That was how the first hundred knew each other. . . .

"Hey, Frank," he said. "You look like you're having a good time."

"I am," Frank said through his mask. "I love cities like this, don't you? A mixed-species flock. It shows you what a diverse collection of cultures Mars is."

John's smile was easy. His eyes shifted as he surveyed the boulevard below.

Sharply Frank said, "A place like this is a crimp in your plan, isn't it?"

Boone's gaze returned to him. The surrounding crowd slipped away, sensing the agonistic nature of the exchange. Boone said to Frank, "I don't have a plan."

"Oh, come on! What about your speech?"

Boone shrugged. "Maya wrote it."

A double lie: that Maya wrote it, that John didn't believe it. Even after all these years, it was almost like talking to a stranger. To a politician at work. "Come on, John," Frank snapped. "You believe all that and you know it. But what are you going to do with all these different nationalities? All the ethnic hatreds, the religious manias? Your coalition can't possibly keep a thumb on all this. You can't keep Mars for yourselves, John, it's not a scientific station anymore, and you're not going to get a treaty that makes it one."

"We're not trying to."

"Then why are you trying to cut me out of the talks!"

"I'm not!" John looked injured. "Relax, Frank. We'll hammer it out together just like we always have. Relax."

Frank stared at his old friend, nonplussed. What to believe? He had never known how to think of John—the way he had used Frank as a springboard, the way he was so friendly . . . hadn't they begun as allies, as friends?

It occurred to him that John was looking for Maya. "So where is she?"

"Around somewhere," Boone said shortly.

It had been years since they had been able to talk about Maya. Now Boone gave him a sharp look, as if to say it was none of his business. As if everything of importance to Boone had become, over the years, none of Frank's business.

Frank left him without a word.

The sky was now a deep violet, streaked by yellow cirrus clouds. Frank passed two figures wearing white ceramic dominoes, the old comedy and tragedy personas, handcuffed together. The city's streets had gone dark and windows blazed, silhouettes partying in them. Big eyes darted in every blurry mask, looking to find the source of the tension in the air. Under the tidal sloshing of the crowd there was a low tearing sound.

He shouldn't have been surprised, he shouldn't. He knew John as well as one could know another person, but it had never been any of his business. Into the trees of the park, under the hand-sized leaves of the sycamores. When had it been any different! All that time together, those years of friendship; and none of it had mattered. Diplomacy by other means.

He looked at his watch. Nearly eleven. He had an appointment with Selim. Another appointment. A lifetime of days divided into quarter hours had made him used to running from one appointment to the next, changing masks, dealing with crisis after crisis, managing, manipulating, doing business in a hectic rush that never ended; and here it was a celebration, Mardi Gras, *Fassnacht!* and he was still doing it. He couldn't remember any other way.

He came on a construction site, skeletal magnesium framing surrounded by piles of bricks and sand and paving stones. Careless of them to leave such things around. He stuffed his coat pockets with fragments of brick just big enough to hold. Straightening up, he noticed someone watching him from the other side of the site—a little man with a thin face under spiky black dreadlocks, watching him intently. Something in the look was disconcerting; it was as if the stranger saw through all his masks and was observing him so closely because he was aware of his thoughts, his plans.

Spooked, Chalmers beat a quick retreat into the bottom fringe of the park. When he was sure he had lost the man, and that no one else was watching, he began throwing stones and bricks down into the lower town, hurling them as hard as he could. And one for that stranger, too, right in the face! Overhead the tent framework was visible only as a faint pattern of occluded stars; it seemed they stood free, in a chill night wind. Air circulation was high tonight, of course. Broken glass, shouts. A scream. It really was loud, people were going crazy. One last paving stone, heaved at a big lit picture window across the grass. It missed. He slipped farther into the trees.

Near the southern wall he saw someone under a sycamore—Selim, circling nervously. "Selim," Frank called quietly, sweating. He reached into his jumper pocket, carefully felt in the bag, and palmed the trio of stem patches. Synergy could be so powerful, for good or ill. He walked forward and roughly embraced the young Arab. The patches hit and penetrated Selim's light cotton shirt. Frank pulled back.

Now Selim had about six hours. "Did you speak with Boone?" he asked.

"I tried," Chalmers said. "He didn't listen. He lied to me." It was so easy to feign distress: "Twenty-five years of friendship, and he lied to me!" He struck a tree trunk with his palm, and the patches flew away in the dark. He controlled himself. "His coalition is going to recommend that all Martian settlements originate in the countries that signed the first treaty." It was possible; and it was certainly plausible.

"He hates us!" Selim cried.

"He hates everything that gets in his way. And he can see that Islam is still a real force in people's lives. It shapes the way people think, and he can't stand that."

Selim shuddered. In the gloom the whites of his eyes were bright. "He has to be stopped."

Frank turned aside, leaned against a tree. "I . . . don't know."

"You said it yourself. Talk means nothing."

Frank circled the tree, feeling dizzy. You fool, he thought, talk means everything. We are nothing but information exchange, talk is all we have!

He came on Selim again and said, "How?"

"The planet. It is our way."

"The city gates are locked tonight."

That stopped him. His hands started to twist.

Frank said, "But the gate to the farm is still open."

"But the farm's outer gates will be locked."

Frank shrugged, let him figure it out.

And quickly enough Selim blinked and said, "Ah." Then he was gone.

Frank sat between trees, on the ground. It was a sandy damp brown dirt, product of a great deal of engineering. Nothing in the city was natural, nothing.

After a time he got to his feet. He walked through the park looking at people. If I find one good city I will spare the man. But in an open area masked figures darted together to grapple and fight, surrounded by watchers who smelled blood. Frank went back to the construction site to get more bricks. He threw them, and some people saw him, and he had to run. Into the trees again, into the little tented wilderness, escaping predators while high on adrenaline, the greatest drug of all. He laughed wildly.

Suddenly he caught sight of Maya, standing alone by the temporary platform up at the apex. She wore a white domino, but it was certainly her: the proportions of the figure, the hair, the stance itself, all unmistakably Maya Toitovna. The first hundred, the little band: they were the only ones truly alive to him anymore, the rest were ghosts. Frank hurried toward her, tripping over uneven ground. He squeezed a rock buried deep in one coat pocket, thinking, Come on, you bitch. Say something to save him. Say something that will make me run the length of the city to save him!

She heard his approach and turned. She wore a phosphorescent white domino with metallic blue sequins. It was hard to see her eyes.

"Hello, Frank," she said, as if he wore no mask. He almost turned and ran. Mere recognition was almost enough to do it. . . .

But he stayed. He said, "Hello, Maya. Nice sunset, wasn't it?"

"Spectacular. Nature has no taste. It's just a city inauguration, but it looked like Judgment Day."

They were under a streetlight, standing on their shadows. She said, "Have you enjoyed yourself?"

"Very much. And you?"

"It's getting a little wild."

"It's understandable, don't you think? We're out of our holes, Maya, we're on the surface at last! And what a surface! You only get these kinds of long views on Tharsis."

"It's a good location," she agreed.

"It will be a great city," Frank predicted. "But where do you live these days, Maya?"

"In Underhill, Frank, just as always. You know that."

"But you're never there, are you? I haven't seen you in a year or more."

"Has it been that long? Well, I've been in Hellas. Surely you heard?"

"Who would tell me?"

She shook her head, and blue sequins glittered. "Frank." She turned aside, as if to walk away from the question's implications.

Angrily Frank circled her, stood in her path. "That time on the *Ares*," he said. His voice was tight, and he twisted his neck to loosen his throat, to make speech easier. "What happened, Maya? What happened?"

She shrugged and did not meet his gaze. For a long time she did not speak. Then she looked at him. "The spur of the moment," she said.

And then it was ringing midnight, and they were in the Martian time slip, the thirty-nine-and-a-half-minute gap between 12:00:00 and 12:00:01, when all the clocks went blank or stopped moving. This was how the first hundred had decided to reconcile Mars's slightly longer day with the twenty-four-hour clock, and the solution had proved oddly satisfactory. Every night to step for a while out of the flicking numbers, out of the remorseless sweep of the second hand . . .

And tonight as the bells rang midnight, the whole city went mad. Almost forty minutes outside of time; it was bound to be the peak of the celebration, everyone knew that instinctively. Fireworks were going off, people were cheering; sirens tore through the sound, and the cheering redoubled. Frank and Maya watched the fireworks, listened to the noise.

Then there was a noise that was somehow different: desperate cries, serious screams. "What's that?" Maya said.

"A fight," Frank replied, cocking an ear. "Something done on the spur of the moment, perhaps." She stared at him, and quickly he added, "Maybe we should go have a look."

The cries intensified. Trouble somewhere. They started down through the park, their steps getting longer until they were in the Martian lope. The park seemed bigger to Frank, and for a moment he was scared.

The central boulevard was covered with trash. People darted through the dark in predatory schools. A nerve-grating siren went off, the alarm that signaled a break in the tent. Windows were shattering up and down the boulevard. There on the streetgrass was a man flat on his back, the surrounding grass smeared with black streaks. Chalmers seized the arm of a woman crouched over him. "What happened?" he shouted.

She was weeping. "They fought! They are fighting!"

"Who? Swiss, Arab?"

"Strangers," she said. *"Ausländer."* She looked blindly at Frank. "Get help!"

Frank rejoined Maya, who was talking to a group next to another fallen figure. "What the hell's going on?" he said to her as they took off toward the city's hospital.

"It's a riot," she said. "I don't know why." Her mouth was a straight slash in skin as white as the domino still covering her eyes.

Frank pulled off his mask and threw it away. There was broken glass all over the street. A man rushed at them. "Frank! Maya!"

It was Sax Russell; Frank had never seen the little man so agitated. "It's John—he's been attacked!"

"What?" they exclaimed together.

"He tried to stop a fight, and three or four men jumped him. They knocked him down and dragged him away!"

"You didn't stop them?" Maya cried.

"We tried—a whole bunch of us chased them. But they lost us in the medina."

Maya looked at Frank.

"What's going *on!*" he cried. "Where would anyone take him?"

"The gates," she said.

"But they're locked tonight, aren't they?"

"Maybe not to everyone."

They followed her to the medina. Streetlights were broken, there was glass underfoot. They found a fire marshal and went to the Turkish Gate; he unlocked it, and several of them hurried through, throwing on walkers at emergency speed. Then out into the night to look around, illuminated by the bathysphere glow of the city. Frank's ankles hurt with the night cold, and he could feel the precise configuration of his lungs, as if two globes of ice had been inserted in his chest to cool the rapid beat of his heart.

Nothing out there. Back inside. Over to the northern wall and the Syrian Gate, and out again under the stars. Nothing.

It took them a long time to think of the farm. By then there were about thirty of them in walkers, and they ran down and through the lock and flooded down the farm's aisles, spreading out, running between crops.

They found him among the radishes. His jacket was pulled over his face, in the standard emergency air pocket; he must have done it unconsciously, because when they rolled him carefully onto one side they saw a lump behind his ear.

"Get him inside," Maya said, her voice a bitter croak— "Hurry, get him inside."

Four of them lifted him. Chalmers cradled John's head, and his fingers were intertwined with Maya's. They trotted back up the shallow steps. Through the farm gate they stumbled, back into the city. One of the Swiss led them to the nearest medical center, already crowded with desperate people. They got John onto an empty bench. His unconscious expression was pinched, determined. Frank tore off his helmet and went to work pulling rank, bulling into the emergency rooms and shouting at the doctors and nurses. They ignored him until one doctor said, "Shut up. I'm coming." She went into the hallway and with a nurse's help clipped John into a monitor, then checked him out with the abstracted, absent look doctors have while working: hands at neck and face and head and chest, stethoscope . . .

Maya explained what they knew. The doctor took down an oxygen unit from the wall, looking at the monitor. Her mouth was bunched into a displeased little knot. Maya sat at the end of the bench, face suddenly distraught. Her domino had long since disappeared.

Frank crouched beside her.

"We can keep working on him," the doctor said, "but I'm afraid he's gone. Too long without oxygen, you know."

"Keep working on him," Maya said.

They did, of course. Eventually other medical people arrived, and they carted him off to an emergency room. Frank, Maya, Sax, Samantha, and a number of locals sat outside in the hall. Doctors came and went; their faces had the blank look they took on in the presence of death. Protective masks. One came out and shook his head. "He's dead. Too long out there."

Frank leaned his head back against the wall.

When Reinhold Messner returned from the first solo climb of Everest, he was severely dehydrated and utterly exhausted; he fell down most of the last part of the descent, and collapsed on the Rongbuk glacier, and he was crawling over it on hands and knees when the woman who was his entire support team reached him; and he looked up at her out of a delirium and said, "Where are all my friends?"

It was quiet. No sound but the low hum and whoosh that one never escaped on Mars.

Maya put a hand on Frank's shoulder, and he almost flinched; his throat clamped down to nothing, it really hurt. "I'm sorry," he managed to say.

She shrugged the remark aside, frowned. She had somewhat the air of the medical people. "Well," she said, "you never liked him much anyway."

"True," he said, thinking it would be politic to seem honest with her at that moment. But then he shuddered and said bitterly, "What do you know about what I like or don't like."

He shrugged her hand aside, struggled to his feet. She didn't know; none of them knew. He started to go into the emergency room, changed his mind. Time enough for that at the funeral. He felt hollow; and suddenly it seemed to him that everything good had gone away.

He left the medical center. Impossible not to feel sentimental at such moments. He walked through the strangely hushed darkness into the land of Nod. The streets glinted as if stars had fallen to the pavement. People stood in clumps, silent, stunned by the news. Frank Chalmers made his way through them, feeling their stares, moving without thought toward the platform at the top of town; and as he walked he said to himself, *Now we'll see what I can do with this planet.*

ALFRED

Lisa Goldstein

Lisa Goldstein won an American Book Award in 1983 with her first novel, *The Red Magician,* a fantasy set in Hungary during the Holocaust. Since then, her beautifully written and always varied novels have included *The Dream Years, A Mask for the General, Tourists, Strange Devices of the Sun and Moon,* and *Summer King, Winter Fool.* She has also published a short-story collection, *Travellers in Magic.*

About her Nebula finalist, "Alfred," which was also a finalist for the World Fantasy Award, she writes:

" 'Alfred' is in some ways sheer wish fulfillment. My grandfather's name was Alfred, and he looked like the man in the story; he escaped from Germany to Holland with his family, my grandmother and my father. He was a mechanic, though he didn't have the glamorous profession I gave him in the story. I find on rereading that I even made the character who stands in for me a year younger than I am, though that was mainly to get in the reference to John Lennon glasses.

"So I started the story simply because I'd always wanted to meet my grandfather; I wondered what he was like. When I finished I discovered that there was more to the process than just wish fulfillment, that I'd learned something about the healing power of history and family and imagination."

Alison walked slowly through the park near school. Usually she went to Laura's house after school let out, but on Fridays Laura had a Girl Scout meeting. She passed a few older boys playing basketball, two women pushing baby strollers. Bells from the distant clock tower rang out across the park: five o'clock, still too early to go home.

A leaf fell noiselessly to the path in front of her. The sun broke through the dark edge of the clouds and illuminated a spiderweb on one of the trees, making it shine like a gate of jewels. A spotted dog, loping alone down the path, looked back and grinned at her as if urging her on. She followed after it.

An old man sat on a bench ahead of her, his eyes closed and his face turned toward the sun.

If Laura had been here they'd be whispering together about everyone, laughing over their made-up stories. The two women would have had their babies switched at the hospital, and they would pass each other without ever knowing how close they were to their true children. The old man was a spy, of course.

As Alison walked by the man she saw that his face and hands were pale, almost transparent. At that moment he opened his eyes and said, "I wonder—could you please tell me the time?"

He had a slight accent, like her parents. Her guess had been right after all—he *was* a spy. "Five o'clock," she said.

"Ah. And the year?"

This was much too weird; the man had to be crazy. Alison glanced around, acting casual but at the same time looking for someone to run to if things got out of hand. You weren't supposed to talk to strangers, she knew that. Her mother told her so all the time.

But what could this man do to her here, in front of all these people? And she had to admit that his question intrigued her—most adults asked you if you liked school and didn't seem to know where to go from there. "It's 1967," she said. Somehow his strange question made it all right to ask him one in return. "Why do you want to know?"

"Oh, you know how it is. We old people, we can never remember anything."

She tried to study him without being obvious. She'd been right about his accent: it sounded German, like her parents'. He had a narrow face and high forehead, with thinning black hair brushed back from his face. He wore glasses with John Lennon wire frames—very cool, Alison thought.

But other than the glasses, which he'd probably had forever, there wasn't anything fashionable about him. He had on a thin black tie, and his coat was nearly worn through in places.

He pushed back his sleeves. Nothing up my sleeves, Alison thought. Then she saw the numbers tattooed on his arm, and she looked away. Her parents had numbers like that.

"What is your name?" he asked.

She shook her head; she wasn't going to fall for that one. "My mother told me never to talk to strangers," she said.

"Your mother is a very smart woman. My mother never told

me anything like that. My name is Alfred."

"Aren't you supposed to offer me candy now?" Alison said.

"Candy? Why?"

"That's the other thing my mother said. Strangers would try to give me candy."

He rummaged in his pockets as if searching for something. Alison saw with relief that his coat sleeves had fallen back over his arms, covering the tattoo. "I don't have any candy. All I have here is a pocket watch. What would your mother say to that?"

He brought out a round gold watch. The letter A was engraved on it, the ends of the letter looping and curling around each other. Her initial, his initial. She reached for the watch, but he moved it away from her and pressed the knob on top to open it. It had stopped hours ago.

"Aren't you going to wind it?" she asked.

"It's broken," he said. "I can tell you an interesting story about this watch, if you want to hear it."

She hesitated. She didn't want to hear about concentration camps; people—adults—got too strange when they talked about their experiences. It made her uncomfortable. Terrible things weren't supposed to happen to your parents; your parents were supposed to protect you.

On the other hand, she didn't want to go home just yet. "Okay," she said. She was almost certain now that he was harmless, but just to be safe she wouldn't sit on the bench next to him. She could probably outrun him anyway.

"My parents gave this watch to me a long time ago," he said. "I used to carry it with me wherever I went, and bring it out and look at it." He pried open the back and showed her a photograph of a dark-eyed boy and girl who looked a little like her and her brother Joey. But this back opened as well, revealing a small world of gears and springs and levers, all placed one over the other in careful layers, all unaccountably stopped.

"I took the watch down to the river once. I had my own place there where no one could find me, where I would sit and think and dream. That day I was dreaming that someday I would learn how to make a watch like this. Someday I would find out its secrets."

He fell silent. The sun glinted over the watch in his hand. "And did you?" she asked, to bring him back from wherever he had gone.

He didn't seem to hear her. "And then the angel came," he said. "Do you know, I had thought angels were courteous, kind. This one had a force of some sort, a terrifying energy I could feel even from where I sat. His eyes were fierce as stars. I thought he asked me a question, asked me if I desired anything, anything in the world, but in that confused instant I could not think of a thing I wanted. I was completely content. And so he left me.

"I looked down at the watch, which I still held in my hand, but it had stopped. And no one in the world has ever been able to make it start again."

He looked at her as if expecting a reply. But all she could think of was that her first thought had been correct; he was crazy after all. No one in her family believed in angels. Still, what if—what if his story was true?

"But I think the angel granted my desire," he said. He nodded slowly. "Do you know, I think he did."

The shadows of the trees had grown longer while he'd talked to her; it was later than she'd thought. "I've got to go now," she said reluctantly. "My parents are expecting me."

"Come again," he said. "I'm in the park nearly every day."

The bus was just pulling out when she got to the bus stop; she had to wait for the next one and got home just as her father and Joey were sitting down to dinner. Her mother carried plates filled with chicken and potatoes into the dining room. She frowned as Alison came in; it was a family rule that everyone had to be on time for dinner.

Her mother sat, and her parents began to eat. Joey looked from one parent to the other uncertainly. Finally he said, "What happens to planes when they crash?"

Alison could see that he was trying to be casual, but he had obviously been worrying about the question all day. "What do you mean?" Alison's father said.

"Well, like when they fall. Where do they land?"

Her mother sighed. Joey was six, and afraid of everything. He refused to get on an elevator because he thought the cable would break. When they went walking he tried to stay with their parents at all times and would grow anxious if he couldn't see them. Sometimes at night Alison heard screams coming from his room, his nightmares waking him up.

"I mean, could they land on the house?" he said. "Could they come through my bedroom?"

"No, of course not," Alison's father said. "The pilots try to land where there aren't any people."

"Well, but it could happen, couldn't it? What if—if they just fall?"

"Look," Alison's father said. "Let's say that this piece of chicken is the plane. Okay? And your plate here is where the plane comes down." Speaking carefully, his accent noticeable only as a slight gentleness on the *r* and *th* sounds, he took his son through a pretended plane crash. "Past where all the people live, see?" he said.

Joey nodded, but Alison saw that the answer didn't satisfy him. Their father was a psychologist, and Alison knew that it frustrated him not to be able to cure Joey's nightmares. He had told her once that he had studied to become a rabbi before the war, but that after he had been through the camps he had lost his faith in God and turned to psychology. It had made her uncomfortable to hear that her father didn't believe in God.

"He had another nightmare last night," her mother said softly.

"I don't know what it is," her father said. "We try to make a safe place here for the kids. They're in no danger here. I don't understand why he's so frightened all the time."

"Eat your dinner before it gets cold, Alison," her mother said, noticing for the first time that Alison had not touched her food. "There was a time when I would have given anything to have just one bite of what you're turning down now."

The next day, Saturday, Alison called Laura and told her about the old man in the park. She wanted to go back and talk to him again, but Laura said she was crazy. "He's some kind of pervert or something, I bet," Laura said. "Didn't your parents tell you not to talk to strangers?"

"He's not—"

"Why don't you come over here instead?"

Alison liked going to Laura's house, liked her parents and the rest of the family. They were Jewish, the same as her family, but Laura's grandfather had come to America before the war. To Alison that made them exotic, different. They seemed to laugh more, for one thing. "Okay," she said.

The minute Alison stepped into the house Laura's mother called Laura to the phone, then disappeared on some errand of her own. No one had invited Alison farther in than the living room. She looked around her, hoping the call wouldn't last long. In the next room Laura laughed and said something about the Girl Scout meeting.

The furniture in the living room was massive and overstuffed: a couch, two easy chairs, a coffee table, and several end tables. A grandfather clock ticked noisily in the corner of the room, and opposite it stood a clunky old-fashioned television that Alison knew to be black-and-white.

For the first time she noticed the profusion of photographs, what looked like hundreds of them, spread out over the mantelpiece and several end tables. All of them had heavy, ornate frames, and doilies to protect the surfaces under them. Curious, she went over to the mantelpiece to get a closer look.

Most were black-and-white, groups of children bunched around a stern-looking mother and father. Everyone stared straight ahead, unsmiling. The fathers wore fancy evening clothes Alison had never seen outside of movies, and sometimes a top hat and even a walking cane. The mothers wore dresses covering them from head to foot, yards and yards of flowing, shiny material. In one of the pictures the children were all dressed alike, the girls in dark dresses and bows and the boys in coats and shorts.

A trembling hand came over her shoulder and pointed to a small boy in the front row. She turned quickly. Laura's grandfather stood there, leaning on his cane, his eyes watery behind thick glasses.

"That's me," he said. Alison looked back at the photograph, trying to see this ancient man in the picture of the young boy. The shaking finger moved to another kid in the same picture. "And that's my brother Moishe."

He looked down at her, uncertain. His face was flushed now, suffused with blood, a waxy yellow mixed with red. His eyes were vacant; something had gone out of them.

The clock sounded loud in the room. Finally he said, "Which one are you?"

"What?"

"Which one of these are you? You're one of the cousins, aren't you?"

"No, I'm—I'm Alison—"

"Alice? I don't know an Alice. That's me in that picture there, and that's my brother Moishe. Or did I already tell you that?"

Should she tell him? She was unused to dealing with old people; all her grandparents had died in the war. But just then he seemed to pull himself together, to concentrate; she could see the man he used to be before he got old.

"Moishe played the trombone—it was a way of getting out of the army in Russia. If you played an instrument you could be in the marching band. He played for anyone, Moishe did, any army in the world. He didn't care. The only army he ever quit was the White Russians. You know why?"

Alison shook her head.

"Because they made their band march in front of them in the war," the old man said. He laughed loudly.

Alison laughed too. "What happened to him?"

The old man started to cough.

"Hi, Alison," Laura said. Alison turned; she hadn't heard Laura come in. "Let's go to my room. I got a new record yesterday."

As they walked up the stairs Laura said, "God, he's embarrassing. Sometimes he calls my mother by her maiden name—he thinks she's still a kid. My dad wants to put him in a nursing home, but she won't let him. I hope he didn't bother you too much."

"No," Alison said. She felt something she couldn't name, a feeling like longing. "He's okay."

She didn't get a chance to go back to the park for another week, until Friday. Laura had remained firm about not wanting to meet Alfred. But when she finally got there she couldn't see him anywhere. Her heart sank. Why had she listened to Laura? Why hadn't she insisted?

No, wait—there he was, sitting on the same bench, his head tilted back toward the sun. He looked thin, frail, even more transparent than the first time she'd seen him. She hurried toward him.

He opened his eyes and smiled. "Here she is—the child without a name," he said. "I was afraid you would not come again. I thought your mother might have told you not to talk to me."

"She doesn't know," Alison said.

"Ah. You should not keep secrets from your mother, you know

that. But if you do, you should make sure that they are good ones."

Alison laughed. "Got any candy?"

"No, no candy." He looked around him, seeming to realize only then where he was. "Do you want to take a walk?"

"Sure."

He stood, and they went down a shaded path. Alison shuffled through the fallen leaves; she wondered how Alfred managed to walk so quietly. Ahead of them, where the path came out into the sun, she saw a man with an ice-cream cart, and she thought for a moment that Alfred might have intended to buy her a sweet after all. But they passed the cart without stopping, and she realized, ashamed, that he probably didn't have much money. "Do you want some ice cream?" she asked.

He laughed. "Thank you, no. I eat very little these days."

The path fell back into shade again. At the end of the path stood the old broken carousel, with a chain-link fence around it so that children could not play on it. Alfred stood and looked at it for a long time. "I made something like this once," he said.

"Really? Carousel animals?"

"No, not the animals. The—what do you call it? The mechanism that makes the thing go around." He moved his hand in a slow circle to demonstrate.

"Could you fix this?"

"Could I?" He looked at the carousel for a long time, studying the tilting floor, the cracked and leaning animals, the proud horse on which someone had carved "Freddy & Janet." Dirt and cobwebs had dulled the animals' paint. "How long has it been broken?"

"I don't know. It's been like this since I started coming to the park."

"I think I can fix it, yeah," he said. He pronounced it *yah*, just like her parents. "Yah, probably I could. Mostly I made large figures that moved. A king and a queen who came out like this"—he moved his hands together—"and kissed. And a magician who opened a box, and there was nothing inside it, and then he closed it and opened it again, and there was a dove that flew away. I made that one for the Kaiser. Do you know who the Kaiser was?"

She shook her head.

"He was the king. The king of Germany."

"Did you have any kids?" she asked, thinking how great it would be to have a father like this man, and remembering the photograph of the two children in his watch. But almost immediately she wished she hadn't said anything. What if his children had died in the war, like so many of her parents' relatives?

"I did, yah," he said. "A boy and a girl. I wanted them to take over the business when I retired. It was a funny thing, though—they didn't want to."

"They were nuts," Alison said. "I would have done it in a minute."

"Ah, but you would have needed more than an interest in the figures. You would have had to understand electricity, and how the mechanisms work, and mathematics. . . . Both my children were terrible at mathematics."

She was terrible at mathematics, too. But she thought that if she had been given a chance at the kind of work Alfred did she would have studied until she understood everything there was to know.

She could almost see his workshop in front of her, the gears and chains and hinges, the tall wooden cabinets filled with hands and silver hair, tin stars, carved dogs, and trumpets. The king and queen lay on their sides like fallen wooden angels, wearing robes of silk and gauze, and wooden crowns with gaudy paste jewels. The bird hung from the ceiling, waiting for its place inside the magician's box. All around Alfred apprentices were cutting into wood, or doing something incomprehensible with pieces of machinery. She thought that she could even smell the wood; it had the elusive scent of great trees, like a forest from a childhood fairy tale.

She turned back to Alfred. What had happened? The day had grown cold; she saw the sun set through the trees, dazzling her vision. "I've got to go home," she said. "I'll be late for dinner."

"Oh. I hope I have not bored you terribly. I don't get much of a chance to talk."

"No," she said. "Oh, no."

She hurried down the path, shivering in the first real cold of the year. Once she looked back, but Alfred had vanished among the shadows of the trees and the carousel.

Her parents and Joey were already eating dinner when she got home. "Where do you go on Fridays?" her mother said as she sat down. "Doesn't Laura have her Girl Scout meeting today?"

"I don't go anywhere," Alison said.

"You know you're not supposed to be late for dinner. And what about your homework?"

"Come on, Mom—it's Friday."

"That's right, it's Friday. Remember how long it took you to do your math homework last week? If you start now you'll have it done on time."

"We didn't get very much. I can do the whole thing on Sunday."

"Can you? I want to see it after dinner."

Her father looked at her mother. Sometimes Alison thought her father might be on her side in the frequent arguments she had with her mother but that he didn't feel he had the right to interrupt. Now he laughed and said to her mother, "What would you know about math homework? You told me you didn't understand anything past addition and subtraction."

"Well, then, you look at it," her mother said. "I want to make sure she gets it done this time. And maybe you can ask her where she goes after school. I don't think she's telling me the truth."

Alison looked down at her plate. What did her mother know? Sometimes she made shrewd guesses based on no evidence at all. She said nothing.

"Mrs. Smith says she saw you talking to an old man in the park," her mother said.

Alison didn't look up. Didn't Mrs. Smith have anything better to do than spy on everyone in the neighborhood?

"When I was your age I knew enough not to talk to strangers," her mother said. "The Gestapo came after my father—did I ever tell you that?"

Alison nodded miserably. She didn't want to hear the story again.

"They came to our house in Germany and asked for my father," her mother said. "I was twelve or thirteen then, just about your age. This was before they started sending Jews to the camps without a reason, and someone had overheard my father say something treasonous about Hitler. My mother said my father wasn't home.

"But he was home—he was up in the attic, hiding. What do you think would have happened if I'd talked to the Gestapo the way you talk to this man in the park? If I'd said, 'Oh, yes, officer, he's up in the attic'? I was only twelve, and I knew enough not to say anything. You kids are so stupid, so pampered, living here."

It wasn't the same thing, Alison thought, realizing it for the first time. Germany and the United States weren't the same countries. And Alfred had been in the camps too; he and her mother were on the same side. But she felt the weight of her mother's experience and couldn't say anything. Her mother had seen so much more than she had, after all.

"We escaped to Holland, stayed with relatives," her mother said. "And eight years later the Nazis invaded Holland and took us to concentration camps. My father worked for a while as an electrician, but finally he died of typhus. All of that, and he died anyway."

Her mother's voice held the bitterness Alison had heard all her life. Now she sighed and shook her head. Alison wanted to do something for her, to make everything all right. But what could she do, after all? She was only twelve.

She took the bus back to the park the next day. Alfred sat on his usual bench, his eyes closed and turned toward the sun. She dropped down on the bench next to him.

"Tell me a story," she said.

He opened his eyes slowly, as if uncertain where he was. Then he smiled. "You look sad," he said. "Did something happen?"

"Yeah. My mother doesn't want me to talk to you anymore."

"Why not?"

This was tricky. She couldn't say that her mother had compared him to the Gestapo. She couldn't talk about the camps at all with him; she never wanted to hear that note of bitterness and defeat come into his voice. Alfred was hers, her escape from the fears and sadness she had lived with all her life. He had nothing to do with what went on between Alison and her mother.

He was looking at her with curiosity and concern now, expecting her to say something. "It's not you. She doesn't trust most people," Alison said.

"Do you know why?"

"Yeah." His eyes were deep brown, she noticed, like hers, like her mother's. Why not tell him, after all? "She—she has a number on her arm. Like yours."

He nodded.

"And she—well, she went through a bad time, I guess." It felt strange to think of her mother as a kid. "She said last night the Gestapo came after her father when she was my age. She said he had to hide in the attic."

To her surprise Alfred started to nod. "I bet it was crowded in that attic too. Boxes and boxes of junk—I bet they never threw anything away. Probably hot too. But then who knew that someday someone would have to hide in it?"

At first his words made no sense whatsoever. Then she said, slowly, "You're him, aren't you? You're her father. My—my grandfather." The unfamiliar word felt strange on her tongue.

"What?" He seemed to rouse himself. "Your grandfather? I'm a crazy old man you met in the park."

"She said he died. You died. You're a ghost." She was whispering now. Chills kept coming up her spine, wave after wave of them. The sun looked cold and very far away.

He laughed. "A ghost? Is that what you think I am?"

She nodded reluctantly, not at all certain now.

"Listen to me," he said. "You're right about your mother—she went through a bad time. And it's hard for her to understand you, to understand what you're going through. Sometimes she's jealous of you."

"Jealous?"

"Sure, jealous. You never had to distrust people, or hide from them. You never went hungry, or saw anyone you loved killed. She thinks it's easy for you—she doesn't understand that you have problems too."

"She called me stupid. She said I would have talked to the Gestapo, would have told them where my father was. But I never would have done that."

"No. It was unfair of her to say that. She wants you to think of the world the way she does, as an unsafe place. But you have to make up your own mind about what the world is like."

She was nodding even before he had finished. "Yeah. Yeah, that's what I thought, only I couldn't say it. Because she's been through so much more than I have, so everything she thinks seems so important. I couldn't tell her that what happens to me is important too."

"No, and you might never be able to tell her. But you'll know it, and I'll know it too."

"What was your father's name?" Alison asked her mother that night at dinner. Joey stopped eating and gave her a pleading look; he was old enough to know that she was taking the conversation in a dangerous direction.

"Alfred," her mother said. "Why do you ask?"

There were probably a lot of old men named Alfred running around. Did she only think he was her grandfather because she wanted what Laura had, wanted someone to tell her family stories, to connect her with her past?

"Oh, I don't know," she said, trying to keep her voice casual. "I was wondering about him, that's all. Do you have a picture of him?"

"What do you think—we were allowed to take photographs with us to the camps?" The bitterness was back in her mother's voice. "We lost everything."

"Well, what did he look like?"

"He was—I don't know. A thin man, with black hair. He brushed it back, I remember that."

"Did he wear glasses?"

Her mother looked up at that. "Yah, he did. How did you know?"

"Oh, you know," Alison said quickly. "Laura's grandfather has glasses, so I thought . . . What did he do?"

"I named you after him," her mother said. "I wanted a name that started with A." To Alison's great astonishment, she began to laugh. "He told that story about the attic all the time, when we lived in Holland. How crowded it was. He said my mother never threw anything away." She took a deep breath and wiped her eyes. "He made it sound like the funniest thing that ever happened to him."

Alison walked slowly through the park. It was Sunday, and dozens of families had come out for the last warmth of the year, throwing Frisbees, barbecuing hamburgers in the fire pits. Joey held her hand tightly, afraid to let go.

She began to hurry, pushing her way through the crowds. Had she scared Alfred off by guessing his secret? She knew what he was now. He had drifted the way Laura's grandfather sometimes drifted, had forgotten his own time and had slipped somehow into hers. Or maybe this was the one wish the angel had granted him, the wish he hadn't known he wanted. However it had happened, he had come to her, singled her out. She had a grandfather after all.

But what if she was wrong? What if he was just a lonely old man who needed someone to talk to?

There he was, up ahead. She ran toward him. "Hey," Joey said anxiously. "Hey, wait a minute."

"Hi," Alison said to the old man, a little breathless. "I've decided to tell you my name. My name's Alison, and I was named after my grandfather Alfred. And this is my brother Joey. Joey's afraid of things. I thought you might talk to him."

In Memoriam: Avram Davidson, Lester del Rey, Chad Oliver

Lucius Shepard
Robert Silverberg
Howard Waldrop

In 1993, science fiction and fantasy lost three writers who, in very different ways, changed those literary forms forever.

Avram Davidson was one of the most literate and erudite writers ever to write science fiction and fantasy. He served in the U.S. Navy during World War II, then with Israeli forces in 1948–49, and began writing after that. He won a Hugo Award in 1958 for his story "Or All the Seas with Oysters," and edited *The Magazine of Fantasy & Science Fiction* from 1962 to 1964. His novels included *Joyleg* (written with Ward Moore), *Mutiny in Space, Masters of the Maze, The Kar-Chee Reign, Rogue Dragon, The Phoenix and the Mirror,* and *Virgil in Averno.* His short fiction appeared in the collections *What Strange Stars and Skies, Or All the Seas with Oysters, The Enquiries of Doctor Eszterhazy, The Best of Avram Davidson* (edited by Michael Kurland), and *Avram Davidson: Collected Fantasies* (edited by John Silbersack). To quote from his entry in *The Science Fiction Encyclopedia:* "It is hard to imagine the genre that could encompass him; it is even more difficult to imagine fantasy or sf without him."

Avram Davidson is remembered here by Lucius Shepard, the author of *Life During Wartime* and *The Golden,* a past winner of the Nebula and Hugo awards, and himself one of the most literate of the genre's writers.

Lester del Rey began writing science fiction during the 1930s, becoming known for his story of a self-sacrificing female robot, "Helen O'Loy." Among his novels are *Nerves, The Eleventh Commandment, Police Your Planet,* and *Pstalemate;* he also wrote a number of novels pseudonymously or in collaboration with other writers. His short fiction was collected in *Early del Rey* in 1975 and in *The Best of Lester del Rey* in 1978. He was the editor of several science fiction magazines, was a regular guest on the Long John Nebel radio talk show in New York City throughout the sixties, reviewed books for *Analog* in the seventies, and was honored with a Grand Master Nebula Award in 1990. But he may have had his greatest influence on the field as an editor for Del Rey Books, an imprint of Ballantine Books named in honor of his wife, the editor and publisher Judy-Lynn del Rey. Among the fantasy writers he discovered and published for the first time were Stephen Donaldson and Terry Brooks.

Robert Silverberg, winner of multiple Hugo and Nebula awards, and one of science fiction's most prolific, honored, and elegant writers, pays tribute to Lester del Rey.

Chad Oliver was an accomplished writer both of science fiction and of novels set in America's West. He began writing during the 1950s; his novels include *The Wolf Is My Brother, The Winds of Time, Mists of Dawn, Shadows in the Sun, Unearthly Neighbors, The Shores of Another Sea,* and *Giants in the Dust.* He was a finalist for the Nebula Award and a winner of the Golden Spur Award and the Western Heritage Society Award. He was also a professor of anthropology at the University of Texas. The art of anthropologically based science fiction so ably practiced by such writers as Ursula K. Le Guin, Michael Bishop, and Eleanor Arnason was pioneered by Oliver; his ability to use the scientific discipline in which he was trained as the basis for his fiction won praise from, among others, Gregory Benford, who called *The Shores of Another Sea* "probably the best anthropological SF novel ever written."

Chad Oliver is eulogized here by Howard Waldrop, a past Nebula Award winner and one of the most inventive writers in the genre, whose books include *Howard Who?, Them Bones, A Dozen Tough Jobs, All About Strange Monsters of the Distant Past,* and *Night of the Cooters.*

AVRAM DAVIDSON
1923–1993
Lucius Shepard

On Saturday morning, May 8, one of the finest and most idiosyncratic writers of the twentieth century died in Bremerton, Washington. He died not owning a typewriter, being unable to afford one. He died with three unpublished novels in cardboard boxes in his apartment, a dank basement that aspired to the status of a hovel. And unless the staff of the Resthaven Nursing Home can be counted as intimates, he died alone. According to the medical report, his death was due to a heart attack that struck as he was recovering from a bout of pneumonia incurred while lying helpless for several days on the floor of his apartment. Others, however, will tell you that the heart attack was merely the inevitable conclusion of a more poignant dysfunction, that Avram brought this state of neglect and subsequent fate down upon himself through his unrelenting crankiness and arrogance, his lack of politesse when dealing with members of the publishing community. Indeed, those who claim this have a case, for it's true that Avram could at times be deficient in courtesy and that he was often arrogant and cranky to the point of bellicosity. It is also true that he had the misfortune to be born in those days when writers were frequently cherished for their eccentricities and to survive into a time when the soul of the publishing industry became dominated by those who no longer cared as much for talent and good books as they did for the bottom line.

Now being a writer does not automatically grant one a license to be cranky and arrogant, though if one attends conventions and writers' conferences, one would scarcely think this to be so, for there one will encounter no end of successful folk who manifest these negative qualities in revolting abundance. In the main, the distinction between these writers and Avram was not a difference in degree as to the charm of their personalities, but was related to the fact that they wrote mass-marketable product and he wrote literature (I will admit this to be a generalization, but only a slight one), and thus their publishers allowed them a certain leeway as regards their behavior. Also, I believe it is something of an American tradition to punish genius by isolating and degrading it. It seems that in some nether region of our psyches we are in love with the idea of the starving artist, and therefore we exile those less-than-blockbuster writers of genius whom we can legitimately characterize as "cranky" and "arrogant" to the Bremerton basements of the world and ignore them in their miserable decline. And once all their arrogance and their crankiness have passed from the world, those who have long ignored them may then safely revere their work and say what a shame it was that they had not been able to cope with the realities, and do their best to buy their work dirt cheap and push out so-called memorial editions to help firm up the ol' bottom line. Perhaps, a few may even say, if we had it to do all over again, we might recognize that Avram was something special and throw him a bone now and again, so as to allow him to live in dignity and to continue his work. Work that, if any writing whatsoever can be said to have value, was well worth nurturing.

I first met Avram when he taught at the Clarion Workshop in 1980, and over the ensuing years I carried on a correspondence with him and visited him on occasion. Though I spent a fair amount of time with him and considered him a friend, I can't say I knew him well, at least not in the sense of knowing much about his life. He spoke only anecdotally of the past, and I was never able to sew these disjointed fragments of reminiscence into a whole cloth. But what I did know and what endeared him to me was his passion for writing, a passion that, I submit, lay at the heart of his arrogance. I have never met anyone whose intellectual passion surpassed his, whose love of good writing was more intrinsically intertwined with the workings of his personality. Over a period of long years, with no expectation of return, he supported and encouraged me simply because he hoped that someday I might write something he would care to read. In an age of production-line values, he was an elegant anachronistic ideologue, and I loved him as one might a kind of old-fashioned yet timeless ideal, with his obdurate attitudes, his incessant classical allusion, his rigorous morality—a morality that, for instance, caused him to spurn German purchase of his work because of his ethnic heritage, this despite the fact that he could have sorely used the money. Perhaps if we had it all to do over again, we might understand that his inability to suffer fools was to a great extent involved with this morality, this passion, and cut him a bit more slack.

The last time I saw Avram he was so weak I had to carry him up the short stairway that led down to his apartment. He had a lengthy list of errands he wanted run—Avram never made a secret of the fact that part of his joy in a visit was due to the fact that visitors had their uses—and so I proceeded to push him all over Bremerton in his wheelchair, to stores and a bank and so forth. In return he bought myself and two friends a dinner of beans and rice, a rather exuberant gesture for someone of his limited means. During the meal he was erudite and entertaining in the way of an old-world scholar, happily quoting Virgil, making jokes, as cheerful and lively as I had ever seen him. This is how I would like to remember him, sitting as he might have sat at a café in Vienna or Rome at the turn of the century, holding forth on some curious twist of knowledge or oddment of philosophy, surrounded by respectful students; but time and again I am induced to recall instead the sight of that feeble yet mentally acute old man struggling to walk through the clutter of years in a damp, gloomy wreckage of a dwelling place, his life's work mildewing in cartons around him.

Avram did not want to become a helpless object in the web of the medical system, and thus I suppose it might be said that his death was merciful. Perhaps so, but as should be apparent from the body of this text, I am forced to mourn not only his passing but the indecent circumstances of his later years, and to wonder at the massive indifference that allowed him to suffer alone. If there is one tribute we might give him, one that would have real meaning, it would be to turn our attention upon those of us who have slipped through the cracks, writers of talent, even of genius, who for one reason or another have been banished to some terrible and solitary state, and to focus upon them our nurture and solace so that they, unlike Avram, might have the opportunity to continue their work with a modicum of comfort and dignity. If you need to understand why this is a worthwhile purpose, I urge you to read *The Phoenix and the Mirror,* or the Limekiller tales, or stories such as "Naples" and "The Golem," and to think what more we might have had of Avram had he had the benefit of our concern.

If any of you think I have painted too pitiful a portrait of my friend, I ask you to recognize that I am writing from a sense of outrage and helplessness, and further to realize that I am seeking not to evoke pity but rather to commend a course of activism and tolerance. Avram needs no apologist such as I to justify his failings or to commemorate his triumphs. He was a soldier, a husband, a father, a discriminate lover of beauty. His life was founded upon principles informed by courage and painful experience, and if he tended to exercise those principles with too much harshness, well, that is a reckoning I'll leave to others. His faults no longer matter. His days of joy and suffering are ended. His work will stand.

LESTER DEL REY
1915–1993
Robert Silverberg

"Cantankerous" is the first word that comes to mind, and then "stubborn," closely followed by "feisty," and then maybe "outrageous." He worked hard at distancing people through calculated outbursts of curmudgeonly vehemence. But there was a heart of gold somewhere underneath all the outer gruffness, and he was deeply loved by those who loved him, of whom I was one. A childless man himself, he played the role of second father to a number of science fiction writers of my generation, and I counted myself privileged to have been among that group.

I'm speaking of Lester del Rey, who died in May at the age of seventy-seven—another of science fiction's grand masters leaving us. Those of you who are relatively new to the SF world may think of him as the man for whom Del Rey Books—the publisher of so many science fiction best-sellers by Anne McCaffrey and David Eddings and Stephen Donaldson and Arthur C. Clarke—was named. That is in fact not quite the case. The del Rey of Del Rey Books was *Judy-Lynn* del Rey, Lester's wife from 1971 until her death in 1986, who transformed and expanded the publishing and marketing of SF books in so startling a way, some fifteen years ago, that the science fiction and fantasy division of Ballantine Books was renamed in her honor. Lester himself remained in the background at Del Rey Books, an active but much less visible participant than his wife, devoting himself chiefly to the company's fantasy line. But certainly his passionate and powerfully held opinions on writing were a mighty force in shaping Judy-Lynn's editorial policies.

His name, by the way, wasn't really Lester. I'm not sure what it was. I don't think anyone is. The name he accepted as his actual one was, approximately, Ramon Felipe San Juan Mario Silvio Enrico Smith Heathcourt-Brace Sierra y Alvarez-del Rey y de los Verdes, but whenever some SF reference source printed some version of it Lester could usually be heard to say that they had gotten it wrong, and it may be that he added or dropped names to the string as it pleased him to do so. The official list always seemed to begin with

Ramon Felipe San Juan Mario Silvio Enrico, at any rate, and then got less predictable from there. When and how the monicker Lester was hung on him, I never knew, but he was using it when he began writing fan letters that were published in *Astounding Stories* in the middle 1930s, and that was the byline that appeared on his first published story, "The Faithful," in the April 1938 *Astounding*. (But he carved any number of pseudonyms out of his collection of given names later on: Philip St. John, John Alvarez, Marion Henry, R. Alvarez, etc., etc., etc.)

Lester was a short, slender, untidy-looking man with a wispy beard, a disarming grin, and a strong, commanding voice. He got your attention immediately and knew how to keep it. I was amazed when he told me once that he only stood five feet three; surely he was the biggest five-foot-three human being on this planet. His voice had much to do with that, but so did his sublime self-assurance. (He carried a business card, for a while, that simply said, "Lester del Rey—Expert.") He could offer answers to questions on virtually every subject; sometimes they were even the right answers, but they were always given quickly and confidently. I never saw him at a loss for words, never, not even a moment's faltering.

He was not, I think, a great science fiction writer, and perhaps he knew it, and if he did, it certainly must have pained him; but he let no sign of that pain reach the surface. Very early in his career, in 1938, he wrote a story that became a classic: "Helen O'Loy," a warm-hearted, realistic robot story, head and shoulders over most of the SF of that time in its humanity and compassion. But it would win no awards if it were published for the first time today. A number of fine stories followed in the next few years—"The Day Is Done," "The Wings of Night," "Into Thy Hands," and especially the powerful atomic-energy novella, "Nerves." He was an important figure in the so-called Golden Age days of John Campbell's *Astounding* before World War II. But whereas other Golden Age figures—Robert A. Heinlein, Isaac Asimov, Theodore Sturgeon, A. E. van Vogt, L. Sprague de Camp—went on to produce a string of masterly novels and short stories in the postwar era, Lester wrote little of consequence in the fifties, less in the sixties, and then—writing fiction having become a terrible struggle for him—essentially nothing at all.

The problem was, I suspect, that unlike a lot of us he never felt *driven* to write. Writing was just a mechanical skill he had picked up, along with many others—he could just as readily have earned his living as an electrician, a plumber, a mechanic, a typewriter repairman—and he saw it, always, as a craft rather than an art. He wrote his first story more or less to see if he could do at least as good a job as the people who were getting published in *Astounding,* and when he found that he could, he wrote some more. But in the second half of his life he often went a year or two, and sometimes much more than that, without even thinking about writing fiction. Fiction as a concept—assembling words into effective patterns—mattered a great deal to him. But he seemed to feel little impetus to write the stuff himself except when there were bills that needed to be paid, and he left us a surprisingly short list of science fiction masterpieces for one of such lofty reputation.

Why, then, consider him a grand master?

Partly for the *way* he wrote: his unaffected, down-to-earth style, a valuable corrective to the melodramatic excess that afflicted so much SF of the pulp magazine era. But we value him as much for his influence as an editor and a counsellor to other writers as for the example of his own writing.

Fiercely opinionated, irrevocably convinced of the strength of his grasp of storytelling technique, he imparted his knowledge of narrative technique to a whole generation of writers, myself among them. He edited a significant line of boys' adventure novels in the early 1950s—the famous Winston juveniles—and also, for a little while, a group of outstanding SF magazines. Before that, he was office manager for a major literary agency for many years. And throughout his entire career he functioned as a mentor, a conscience, an irritating voice of inescapable truth, for all those dozens of fellow writers. He knew what a story *ought* to be—Lester was dogmatic the way Mount Everest is a tall mountain—and he painstakingly shared his sense of craft with any writer who would listen, though he had no tolerance for fools, none whatever, and quickly separated himself from their company, emphatically and permanently, in a way that even a fool was likely to comprehend.

He was about twice my age when we met—I was nineteen, I think, and he would have been thirty-eight or thirty-nine. I was a raw novice, and he was a stalwart of the Campbell Golden Age. But there was no hint of patronization in his attitude toward me: we fell into a friendship almost at once, one writer with another, and it stayed that way for the next four decades. I lost my awe of him pretty quickly, and when we disagreed on something we disagreed loudly and longly, but our disputes were always within a context of love, and there was never any doubt about that. (Not that I ever won an argument with him. No one ever did.)

He could be blunt: usually was, in fact. But always in pursuit of the truth. Perhaps the best advice anyone ever gave me as a writer came from Lester, when I was twenty-two, maybe twenty-three, and had discovered that I could make a lot of money fast by cranking out bang-bang pulp adventure fiction at a rate of thirty or forty pages a day. "You claim that what interests you in writing is mainly to make money," Lester told me. "But in that case you're really operating against your own best interests by knocking out all this junk. You write a story as fast as you can type, and you get a penny a word for it, *and that's all the money you're ever going to make from it.* It'll be forgotten five minutes from now. But if you were writing at the level of quality that I know is in you, turning out the kind of fiction people respect instead of simply stuff that will sell, you'd be bringing in an income on those stories from anthology sales and reprint editions forever. So even though you tell me that you're strictly a commercial writer, what you're doing these days doesn't make any sense simply on your own dollars-and-cents basis."

I had never stopped to look at it that way, and his reasoning brought me up short in amazement. In my own way I am just as stubborn as Lester ever was; but within five minutes he succeeded in changing my entire outlook on my work and set me on the path toward writing the books and stories that established me in my real career.

That was his specialty—cutting through somebody's carefully constructed bullshit to reach the carefully concealed realities beneath. I saw him do it again and again. (Nobody ever succeeded in doing it to him.)

His life was full of sorrows. His health was never very good. He outlived two dearly loved wives, both much younger than he was, who died in different but tragic ways. His own writing career was marked by anguish, fruitless effort, and, I suspect, profound dissatisfaction with the work that he did manage to produce, though he would have denied that on his deathbed. But he was tougher than nails, and I never heard him complain about anything. (The closest he came, I think, was after the stroke that took his wife Judy-Lynn away at the age of forty or so. "I don't have very good luck with my wives, do I, Bob?" is what he said.)

Of all the many deaths that have rocked our field in recent years, I think this one hits me the hardest. Some of those who have gone from us were greater writers than Lester—the names of Heinlein, Asimov, and Leiber jump instantly to mind, and I could extend the list—and many of them were my dear friends besides. As I've noted, though, it wasn't Lester's writing, particularly, that won him his place in the SF pantheon, and though he was my friend, I mourn his loss in a way that goes beyond, I guess, the way one mourns a friend's death. *Isaac* was my friend, and I was saddened to see him go. But what I felt on hearing of Lester's death was a sense not of friendship ended but of a family tie sundered. I'm not speaking metaphorically here. Sure, the whole science fiction world is a kind of goofy family, and we all bear a certain kind of kinship for one another. But my feelings for Lester went beyond metaphor. I was one of his sons; he was one of my fathers, with all the complexities and turbulence that such a relationship implies. And I suspect that I won't be the only one who says something like that in the tributes that his death will bring forth.

CHAD OLIVER
1928–1993
Howard Waldrop

People never believed me when I told them that the first real-and-for-true SF book I read was Chad's *Mists of Dawn,* his Winston juvenile in the old Schomberg endpapers. Little did I know then that he would be my buddy, that we would spend the last twenty-odd years of his life driving thousands of miles, talking writing (and everything else), and cleaning nasty fish together.

He was born Symmes Chadwick Oliver in Cincinnati in 1928,

the son, grandson, and great-grandson of doctors. He did all the usual kid stuff—reading, fishing, baseball, football, listening to hot jazz. When he was twelve he was hit with rheumatic fever, which put him flat on his back for a year and a half, with nothing to do but read. His favorites were the air-war pulps, *G-8*, and so on. One day somebody brought him his monthly bunch, but in the middle of them was one of the old fat-ass *Amazings* with Edmond Hamilton's "Treasure on Thunder Moon" in it. When Chad read it, he thought, "This is the greatest piece of literature ever written. Where can I get more like it?" Sick or not, he got on his bike, rode to the newsstand, and bought up every SF magazine there. From then on, the letters page of every genre magazine was filled with stuff from the Loon of Ledgewood, as he called himself.

When World War II started, Chad's father went as medical officer to the combination Japanese-American internment camp/ German POW camp at Crystal City, Texas, where the family lived inside. ("The barbed wire wasn't just to keep the Japanese-Americans and Germans *in*, it was to keep any pissed-off farmers who'd lost someone in the Pacific or Europe out. At Crystal City, the machine guns pointed *out*.") Chad went to Crystal City High School. ("Football saved my scrawny life. I went in looking like the ninety-eight-pound weakling in the ads. I came out as Mighty Joe Young.") Not quite, but he stayed at six feet three and two hundred and thirty pounds for most of the rest of his life.

He went to the University of Texas in 1946 (all the while writing and trying to sell his stories, and publishing, with Garvin D. Berry, the first Texas SF fanzine, *The Moon Puddle*). He got his Plan II (a liberal arts) degree and his master's in anthropology from Texas, and his doctorate in anthropology from UCLA. He taught at the University of Texas from 1954 on, and served three terms as chairman of the anthropology department. He was an authority on the ecology of East Africa, and also on the Plains Indians of America. He spent two years of field study in Africa in the early sixties, working on the population ecology of the Akamba. He published many monographs and wrote the standard textbook, *The Discovery of Humanity: An Introduction to Anthropology*, for Harper & Row in 1981.

Chad's first SF sale was in late 1949, to Anthony Boucher at *The Magazine of Fantasy & Science Fiction*; the first to appear was in

Super-Science Stories in 1950. He wrote more than seventy stories in the next forty years. (The Borgo Press book *Bibliographies of Modern Authors #12: The Work of Chad Oliver* by Hal W. Hall gives the details.) His SF novels began with *Mists of Dawn,* his 1952 Winston book of time travel and Cro-Magnons versus Neanderthals aimed at a juvenile audience (and, boy, did it hit *this* juvenile!). A story of his—"Community Study," later published in *Lone Star Universe*— was rejected by Boucher with a one-line note: "This needs to be a novel"—and it became one. Chad turned it into *Shadows in the Sun* (1954), one of the great first-contact novels. Then came *The Winds of Time* (1957), not only about first contact but also about hard, hard choices and time travel the hard way. Those that followed, *Unearthly Neighbors* (1960), *Shores of Another Sea* (1971), and *Giants in the Dust* (1976), mined just about all the first and second contact and anthropological concerns that were or could be. When other writers stumbled over them, they found Chad had been there first.

His two SF collections, *Another Kind* (1955) and *The Edge of Forever* (1971), covered only a small segment of his short-story output. While he made his reputation with stories on anthropological themes ("Of Course," "Any More at Home like You?," "A Star Above It"), it was his offbeat, one-of-a-kind stories he was proudest of— "Transformer," about the toy people who live in a model-railroad-layout town owned by a mean kid; "Didn't He Ramble?," about the re-creation of 1917 Storyville out in the asteroid belt; "King of the Hill," in *Again, Dangerous Visions,* about letting the raccoons have it all and seeing if they can come up with anything better than we did; and "Old Four Eyes," one of his last stories, a quiet and compassionate piece on interspecies . . . well, love.

Some of Chad's stories through the years had been Westerns, which he'd loved since he was a kid. (He did a fair Gabby Hayes, and said, "Go for your smoke pole" to anything that exasperated him.) His first western novel, *The Wolf Is My Brother,* won the Spur Award from the Western Writers of America in 1967, and went through eight or nine printings. Twenty years later, he wrote his "Custer book" he'd been thinking about for twenty-five years, *Broken Eagle.* Before you could say Yatonkah Totonka, it won the Western Heritage Society Award as best novel of the year (1989). (Both Chad *and* his wife, B. J., danced with James Garner at the awards ceremony.) This past year (1993) he finished his third, *The Cannibal Owl*, which Bantam published in 1994. It's set in central Texas in 1855, when the place was still a sea of grass and cane.

Chad was a fly-fisherman all his life. He never forgot the first time he and his father came over Slumgullion Pass in Colorado and saw Lake City, just after the war. (Like Brigham Young as played by Dean Jagger, he said: "This is the place.") He would spend every summer there for the next forty-six years (except for the two in Africa, and even then he managed to fish for trout on Mount Kenya). He was a charter member of Trout Unlimited and spent three terms as president of the (then) Texas chapter (trying to keep trout alive in any river in this state is a thankless damn job). Trout Unlimited gave him its National Appreciation Award early in 1993.

Besides the readers of his SF and Westerns (and all the trout), Chad left behind twenty to thirty thousand students whose lives he changed. As chairman of the anthropology department, he made it a rule that whoever was chairman had to teach the four-hundred-student introduction-to-anthropology course every year—another thankless damn job. The University of Texas gave him just about every teaching award and fellowship it could. Just to be fair about things, Chad donated all his papers to the Special Collections Library at Texas A&M, the university's chief rival.

Chad went through more illnesses in the last eight years than I care to name. He took surgery, chemotherapy, and radiology in his stride; they were just something to get through so he could get back to what was really important, writing and fishing. When the latest bout started, he had a chapter left on *Cannibal Owl;* he went to the hospital, got worked on, went home. Three or four days later he sat down, wrote the last eighteen pages in one sitting, and sent the whole thing off.

I got him into his waders one last time, in May of 1993, on the San Gabriel, just before another round of *everything.* He said, "This is the same goddamn river my friend Jim caught *his* last fish from. It was a bass." Then Chad caught a bass, kissed it, let it go, and we went home.

From now on, wherever I am, I'll be fishing for two people.

Georgia on My Mind

Charles Sheffield

Charles Sheffield is one of science fiction's scientist-writers, with degrees in mathematics and physics from Cambridge University. He is a past president of the SFWA and a past president of the American Astronautical Society. He began publishing science fiction during the late seventies; his books include *Between the Strokes of Night, Summertide, Divergence, Transcendence, Dancing with Myself, The Mind Pool, Godspeed, One Man's Universe, Sight of Proteus,* and *Proteus Unbound*. His novel *Brother to Dragons* won the John W. Campbell Memorial Award in 1993.

Both Sheffield's intellect and his delight in scientific discoveries are displayed in his Nebula Award–winning novelette "Georgia on My Mind," which also won the Hugo Award. About this work he writes:

"On Tuesday, December 10, 1991, I had lunch in New York with Stan Schmidt and Tina Lee of *Analog*. Stan said he could use a good novelette about ten thousand words long. Since I had eaten lunch at his expense, I sort of promised him one, and gave a title, 'Georgia on My Mind.' Then I had to write the story.

"It came out as a strange mixture of factual autobiography and fiction. I felt as though I was inventing very little. Almost every name is that of a real person. Gene in the story is Professor Gene Golub of Stanford, an old friend and for my money the world's best numerical analyst. Marvin Minsky is the world's top AI authority and personally well known to many SFWA members. Danny Hillis is the chief scientist of Thinking Machines Corporation and the designer of the Connection Machine, and I did meet him in Pasadena at the Neptune flyby, just as the story says. Bill Rigley is a composite of two people, Garry Tee (who discovered bits of Babbage's Difference Machine in Dunedin, New Zealand) and another mathematician, Charles Broyden. The SF writers in the story are of course all real. DEUCE was an early and intractable digital computer, dear to the heart of anyone who programmed it. Although the narrator of a story is not the same as its author, the two in this case are too close for comfort.

"I finished the story on December 31, 1991. It came out as seventeen thousand words, not ten thousand. On the strength of that, I claim that Stan Schmidt still owes me seven-tenths of a lunch."

I first tangled with digital computers late in 1958. That may sound like the dark ages, but we considered ourselves infinitely more advanced than our predecessors of a decade earlier, when programming was done mostly by sticking plugs into plug boards and a card-sequenced programmable calculator was held to be the height of sophistication.

Even so, 1958 was still early enough that the argument between analog and digital computers had not yet been settled, decisively, in favor of the digital. And the first computer that I programmed was, by anyone's standards, a brute.

It was called DEUCE, which stood for Digital Electronic Universal Computing Engine, and it was, reasonably enough to card-players, the next thing after the ACE (for Automatic Computing Engine), developed by the National Physical Laboratory at Teddington. Unlike ACE, DEUCE was a commercial machine; and some idea of its possible shortcomings is provided by one of the designers' comments about ACE itself: "If we had known that it was going to be developed commercially, we would have finished it."

DEUCE was big enough to walk inside. The engineers would do that, tapping at suspect vacuum tubes with a screwdriver when the whole beast was proving balky. Which was often. Machine errors were as common a cause of trouble as programming errors; and programming errors were dreadfully frequent, because we were working at a level so close to basic machine logic that it is hard to imagine it today.

I was about to say that the computer had no compilers or assemblers, but that is not strictly true. There was a floating-point compiler known as ALPHACODE, but it ran a thousand times slower than a machine code program, and no one with any self-respect ever used it. We programmed in absolute, to make the best possible use of the machine's 402 words of high-speed (mercury delay line) memory and its 8,192 words of backup (rotating drum) memory. Anything needing more than that had to use punched cards as intermediate storage, with the programmer standing by to shovel them from the output hopper back into the input hopper.

When I add that binary-to-decimal conversion routines were usually avoided because they wasted space, that all instructions were defined in binary, that programmers therefore had to be very familiar with the binary representation of numbers, that we did our own card punching with hand (not electric) punches, and that the machine itself, for some reason that still remains obscure to me, worked with binary numbers whose most significant digit was on the *right* rather than on the left—so that 13, for example, became 1011 rather than the usual 1101—well, by this time the general flavor of DEUCE programming ought to be coming through.

Now I mention these things not because they are interesting (to the few) or because they are dull (to the many) but to make the point that anyone programming DEUCE in those far-off days was an individual not to be taken lightly. We at least thought so, though I suspect that to high management we were all harebrained children who did incomprehensible things, many of them in the middle of the night (when debug time was more easily to be had).

A few years later more computers became available, the diaspora inevitably took place, and we all went off to other interesting places. Some found their way to university professorships, some into commerce, and many to foreign parts. But we did tend to keep in touch, because those early days had generated a special feeling.

One of the most interesting characters was Bill Rigley. He was a tall, dashing, wavy-haired fellow who wore English tweeds and spoke with the open *a* sound that to most Americans indicates a Boston origin. But Bill was a New Zealander, who had seen at first hand things, like the Great Barrier Reef, that the rest of us had barely heard of. He didn't talk much about his home and family, but he must have pined for them, because after a few years in Europe and America he went back to take a faculty position in the department of mathematics (and later the computer science department, when one was finally created) at the University of Auckland.

Auckland is on the north island, a bit less remote than the bleaker south island, but a long way from the East Coast of the United States, where I had put down my own roots. Even so, Bill and I kept in close contact, because our scientific interests were very similar. We saw each other every few years in Stanford, or London, or wherever else our paths intersected, and we knew each other at the deep level where few people touch. It was Bill who helped me to mourn when my wife, Eileen, died, and I in turn knew (but never talked about) the dark secret that had scarred Bill's own life. No matter how long we had been separated, our conversations, when we met, picked up as though they had never left off.

Bill's interests were encyclopedic, and he had a special fondness for scientific history. So it was no surprise that when he went back to New Zealand he would wander around there, examining its contribution to world science. What was a surprise to me was a letter from him a few months ago stating that in a farmhouse near Dunedin, toward the south end of the south island, he had come across some bits and pieces of Charles Babbage's Analytical Engine.

Even back in the late 1950s, we had known all about Babbage. There was at the time only one decent book about digital computers, Bowden's *Faster Than Thought,* but its first chapter talked all about that eccentric but formidable Englishman, with his hatred of street musicians and his low opinion of the Royal Society (existing only to hold dinners, he said, at which they gave each other medals). Despite these odd views, Babbage was still our patron saint. For, starting in 1834 and continuing for the rest of his life, he tried—unsuccessfully—to build the world's first programmable digital computer. He understood the principles perfectly well, but he was thwarted because he had to work with mechanical parts. Can you imagine a computer built of cogs and toothed cylinders and gears and springs and levers?

Babbage could. And he might have triumphed even over the inadequacy of the available technology but for one fatal problem: he kept thinking of improvements. As soon as a design was half assembled, he would want to tear it apart and start using the bits to build something better. At the time of Babbage's death in 1871, his wonderful Analytical Engine was still a dream. The bits and pieces were carted off to London's Kensington Science Museum, where they remain today.

Given our early exposure to Babbage, my reaction to Bill Rigley's letter was pure skepticism. It was understandable that Bill would *want* to find evidence of parts of the Analytical Engine somewhere on his home stamping ground; but his claim to have done so was surely self-delusion.

I wrote back suggesting this in as tactful a way as I could; and received in prompt reply not recantation but the most extraordinary package of documents I had ever seen in my life (I should say, to that point; there were stranger to come).

The first was a letter from Bill explaining in his usual blunt way that the machinery he had found had survived on the south island of New Zealand because "we don't chuck good stuff away, the way you lot do." He also pointed out, through dozens of examples, that in the nineteenth century there was much more contact between Britain and its antipodes than I had ever dreamed. A visit to Australia and New Zealand was common among educated persons, a kind of expanded version of the European Grand Tour. Charles Darwin was of course a visitor, on the *Beagle,* but so also were scores of less well-known scientists, world travelers, and gentlemen of the leisured class. Two of Charles Babbage's own sons were there in the 1850s.

The second item in the package was a batch of photographs of the machinery that Bill had found. It looked to me like what it was, a bunch of toothed cylinders and gears and wheels. They certainly resembled parts of the Analytical Engine, or the earlier Difference Machine, although I could not see how they might fit together.

Neither the letter nor the photographs were persuasive. Rather the opposite. I started to write in my mind the letter that said as much, but I hesitated for one reason: many historians of science know a lot more history than science, and few are trained computer specialists. But Bill was the other way round, the computer expert who happened to be fascinated by scientific history. It would be awfully hard to fool him—unless he chose to fool himself.

So I had another difficult letter to write. But I was spared the trouble, for what I could not dismiss or misunderstand was the third item in the package. It was a copy of a programming manual, hand-written, for the Babbage Analytical Engine. It was dated July 7, 1854. Bill said that he had the original in his possession. He also told me that I was the only person who knew of his discovery, and he asked me to keep it to myself.

And here, to explain my astonishment, I have to dip again into computer history. Not merely to the late 1950s, where we started, but all the way to 1840. In that year an Italian mathematician, Luigi Federico Menabrea, heard Babbage talk in Turin about the new machine that he was building. After more explanations by letter from Babbage, Menabrea wrote a paper on the Analytical Engine, in French, which was published in 1842. And late that year Ada Lovelace (Lord Byron's daughter; Lady Augusta Ada Byron Lovelace, to give her complete name) translated Menabrea's memoir and added her own lengthy notes. Those notes formed the world's first software manual; Ada Lovelace described how to program the Analytical Engine, including the tricky techniques of recursion, looping, and branching.

So, twelve years before 1854, a programming manual for the Analytical Engine existed; and one could argue that what Bill had found in New Zealand was no more than a copy of the one written in 1842 by Ada Lovelace.

But there were problems. The document that Bill sent me went far beyond the 1842 notes. It tackled the difficult topics of indirect addressing, relocatable programs, and subroutines, and it offered a new language for programming the Analytical Engine—what amounted to a primitive assembler.

Ada Lovelace just might have entertained such advanced ideas and written such a manual. It is possible that she had the talent, although all signs of her own mathematical notebooks have been lost. But she died in 1852, and there was no evidence in any of her surviving works that she ever blazed the astonishing trail defined in the document that I received from Bill. Furthermore, the manual bore on its first page the author's initials, L. D. Ada Lovelace for her published work had used her own initials, A. A. L.

I read the manual, over and over, particularly the final section. It contained a sample program, for the computation of the volume of an irregular solid by numerical integration—and it included a page of *output*, the printed results of the program.

At that point I recognized only three possibilities. First, that someone in the past few years had carefully planted a deliberate forgery down near Dunedin and led Bill Rigley to "discover" it. Second, that Bill himself was involved in attempting an elaborate hoax, for reasons I could not fathom.

I had problems with both these explanations. Bill was perhaps the most cautious, thorough, and conservative researcher that I had ever met. He was painstaking to a fault, and he did not fool easily.

He was also the last man in the world to think that devising a hoax could be in any way amusing.

Which left the third possibility. Someone in New Zealand had built a version of the Analytical Engine, made it work, and taken it well beyond the place where Charles Babbage had left off.

I call that the third possibility, but it seemed at the time much more like the third *impossibility*. No wonder that Bill had asked for secrecy. He didn't want to become the laughingstock of the computer historians.

Nor did I. I took a step that was unusual in my relationship with Bill: I picked up the phone and called him in New Zealand.

"Well, what do you think?" he said, as soon as he recognized my voice on the line.

"I'm afraid to think at all. How much checking have you done?"

"I sent paper samples to five places, one in Japan, two in Europe, and two in the United States. The dates they assign to the paper and the ink range from 1840 to 1875, with 1850 as the average. The machinery that I found had been protected by wrapping in sacking soaked in linseed oil. Dates for that ranged from 1830 to 1880." There was a pause at the other end of the line. "There's more. Things I didn't have until two weeks ago."

"Tell me."

"I'd rather not. Not like this." There was another, longer silence. "You *are* coming out, aren't you?"

"Why do you think I'm on the telephone? Where should I fly to?"

"Christchurch. South Island. We'll be going farther south, past Dunedin. Bring warm clothes. It's winter here."

"I know. I'll call as soon as I have my arrival time."

And that was the beginning.

The wavy mop of fair hair had turned to gray, and Bill Rigley now favored a pepper-and-salt beard, which with his weather-beaten face turned him into an approximation of the Ancient Mariner. But nothing else had changed, except perhaps for the strange tension in his eyes.

We didn't shake hands when he met me at Christchurch airport, or exchange one word of conventional greeting. Bill just said, as soon as we were within speaking range. "If this wasn't happening to me, I'd insist it couldn't happen to anybody," and led me to his car.

Bill was South Island born, so the long drive from Christchurch to Dunedin was home territory to him. I, in that odd but pleasant daze that comes after long air travel—after you deplane, and before the jet lag hits you—stared out at the scenery from what I thought of as the driver's seat (they still drive on the left, like the British).

We were crossing the flat Canterbury Plains, on a straight road across a level and empty expanse of muddy fields. It was almost three months after harvest—wheat or barley, from the look of the stubble—and there was nothing much to see until at Timaru when we came to the coast road, with dull gray sea to the left and empty brown coastal plain on the right. I had visited South Island once before, but that had been a lightning trip, little more than a tour of Christchurch. Now for the first time I began to appreciate Bill's grumbling about "overcrowded" Auckland on the north island. We saw cars and people, but in terms of what I was used to it was a thin sprinkle of both. It was late afternoon, and as we drove farther south it became colder and began to rain. The sea faded from view behind a curtain of fog and drizzle.

We had been chatting about nothing from the time we climbed into the car. It was talk designed to avoid talking, and we both knew it. But at last Bill, after a few seconds in which the only sounds were the engine and the *whump-whump-whump* of windshield wipers, said, "I'm glad to have you here. There's been times in the past few weeks when I've seriously wondered if I was going off my head. What I want to do is this. Tomorrow morning, after you've had a good sleep, I'm going to show you *everything*, just as I found it. Most of it just *where* I found it. And then I want you to tell me what *you* think is going on."

I nodded. "What's the population of New Zealand?"

Without turning my head, I saw Bill's quick glance. "Total? Four million, tops."

"And what was it in 1850?"

"That's a hell of a good question. I don't know if anyone can really tell you. I'd say a couple of hundred thousand. But the vast majority of those were native Maori. I know where you're going, and I agree totally. There's no way that anyone could have built a version of the Analytical Engine in New Zealand in the middle of the last century. The manufacturing industry just didn't exist here. The final assembly could be done, but the subunits would have to be built and shipped in big chunks from Europe."

"From Babbage?"

"Absolutely not. He was still alive in 1854. He didn't die until 1871, and if he had learned that a version of the Analytical Engine was being built *anywhere,* he'd have talked about it nonstop all over Europe."

"But if it wasn't Babbage—"

"Then who was it? I know. Be patient for a few more hours. Don't try to think it through until you've rested and had a chance to see the whole thing for yourself."

He was right. I had been traveling nonstop around the clock, and my brain was going on strike. I pulled my overcoat collar up around my ears and sagged lower in my seat. In the past few days I had absorbed as much information about Babbage and the Analytical Engine as my head could handle. Now I needed to let it sort itself out, along with what Bill was going to show me. Then we would see if I could come up with a more plausible explanation for what he had found.

As I drifted into half-consciousness I flashed on to the biggest puzzle of all. Until that moment I had been telling myself, subconsciously, that Bill was just plain wrong. It was my way of avoiding the logical consequences of his being *right.* But suppose he *were* right. Then the biggest puzzle was not the appearance of an Analytical Engine, with its advanced programming tools, in New Zealand. It was the *disappearance* of those things from the face of the Earth.

Where the devil had they gone?

Our destination was a farmhouse about fifteen miles south of Dunedin. I didn't see much of it when we arrived, because it was raining and pitch-black and I was three-quarters asleep. If I had any thoughts at all as I was shown to a small, narrow room and collapsed into bed, it was that in the morning, bright and early, Bill would show me everything and my perplexity would end.

It didn't work out that way. For one thing, I overslept and felt terrible when I got up. I had forgotten what a long, sleepless journey can do to your system. For the past five years I had done less and less traveling, and I was getting soft. For another thing, the rain had changed to sleet during the night and was driving down in freezing gusts. The wind was blowing briskly from the east, in off the sea. Bill and I sat at the battered wooden table in the farm kitchen while Mrs. Trevelyan pushed bacon, eggs, homemade sausage, bread, and hot sweet tea into me until I showed signs of life. She was a spry, red-cheeked lady in her middle sixties, and if she was surprised that Bill had finally brought someone else with him to explore Little House, she hid it well.

"Well, then," she said, when I was stuffed. "If you're stepping up the hill you'll be needing a mac. Jim put the one on when he went out, but we have plenty of spares."

Jim Trevelyan was apparently off somewhere tending the farm animals, and had been since dawn. Bill grinned sadistically at the look on my face. "You don't want a little rain to stop work, do you?"

I wanted to go back to bed. But I hadn't come ten thousand miles to lie around. The "step up the hill" to Little House turned out to be about half a mile, through squelching mud covered with a thin layer of sour turf.

"How did you ever find this place?" I asked Bill.

"By asking and looking. I've been into a thousand like this before, and found nothing."

We were approaching a solidly built square house made out of mortared limestone blocks. It had a weathered look, but the slate roof and chimney were intact. To me it did not seem much smaller than the main farmhouse.

"It's not called Little House because it's *small*," Bill explained. "It's Little House because that's where the little ones are supposed to live when they first marry. You're seeing a twentieth-century tragedy here. Jim and Annie Trevelyan are fourth-generation farmers. They have five children. Everyone went off to college, and not a one has come back to live in Little House and wait their turn to run the farm. Jim and Annie hang on at Big House, waiting and hoping."

As we went inside, the heavy wooden door was snug-fitting and moved easily on oiled hinges.

"Jim Trevelyan keeps the place up, and I think they're glad to have me here to give it a lived-in feel," said Bill. "I suspect that they both think I'm mad as a hatter, but they never say a word. Hold tight to this, while I get myself organized."

He had been carrying a square box lantern. When he passed it to me I was astonished by the weight—and he had carried it for half a mile.

"Batteries, mostly," Bill explained. "Little House has oil lamps, but of course there's no electricity. After a year or two wandering around out-of-the-way places I decided there was no point in driving two hundred miles to look at something if you can't see it when you get there. I can recharge this from the car if we have to."

As Bill closed the door the sound of the wind dropped to nothing. We went through a washhouse to a kitchen furnished with solid wooden chairs, table, and dresser. The room was freezing cold, and I looked longingly at the scuttle of coal and the dry kindling standing by the fireplace.

"Go ahead," said Bill, "while I sort us out here. Keep your coat on, though—you can sit and toast yourself later."

He lit two big oil lamps that stood on the table, while I placed layers of rolled paper, sticks, and small pieces of coal in the grate. It was thirty years since I had built a coal fire, but it's not much of an art. In a couple of minutes I could stand up, keep one eye on the fire to make sure it was catching properly, and take a much better look at the room. There were no rugs, but over by the door leading through to the bedrooms was a long strip of coconut matting. Bill rolled it back to reveal a square wooden trapdoor. He slipped his belt through the iron ring and lifted, grunting with effort, until the trap finally came free and turned upward on brass hinges.

"Storage space," he said. "Now we'll need the lantern. Turn it on, and pass it down to me."

He lowered himself into the darkness, but not far. His chest and head still showed when he was standing on the lower surface. I switched on the electric lantern and handed it down to Bill.

"Just a second," I said. I went across to the fireplace, added half a dozen larger lumps of coal, then hurried back to the trapdoor. Bill had already disappeared when I lowered myself into the opening.

The storage space was no more than waist high, with a hard dirt floor. I followed the lantern light to where a wooden section at the far end was raised a few inches off the ground on thick beams. On that raised floor stood three big tea chests. The lantern threw a steady, powerful light on them.

"I told you you'd see just what I saw," said Bill. "These have all been out and examined, of course, but everything is very much the way it was when I found it. All right, hardware first."

He carefully lifted the lid off the right-hand tea chest. It was half full of old sacks. Bill lifted one, unfolded it, and handed me the contents. I was holding a solid metal cylinder, lightly oiled and apparently made of brass. The digits from 0 through 9 ran around its upper part, and at the lower end was a cogwheel of slightly greater size.

I examined it carefully, taking my time. "It could be," I said. "It's certainly the way the pictures look."

I didn't need to tell him which pictures. He knew that I had thought of little but Charles Babbage and his Analytical Engines for the past few weeks, just as he had.

"I don't think it was made in England," said Bill. "I've been all over it with a lens, and I can't see a manufacturer's mark. My guess is that it was made in France."

"Any particular reason?"

"The numerals. Same style as some of the best French clock-makers—see, I've been working, too." He took the cylinder and wrapped it again, with infinite care, in the oiled sacking. I stared all around us, from the dirt floor to the dusty rafters. "This isn't the best place for valuable property."

"It's done all right for a hundred and forty years. I don't think you can say as much of most other places." There was something else that Bill did not need to say. This was a perfect place for valuable property—so long as no one thought that it had any value.

"There's nowhere near enough pieces here to make an Analytical Engine, of course," he went on. "These must have just been spares. I've taken a few of them to Auckland. I don't have the original of the programming manual here, either. That's back in Auckland, too, locked up in a safe at the university. I brought a copy, if we need it."

"So did I." We grinned at each other. Underneath my calm I was almost too excited to speak, and I could tell that he felt the same. "Any clue as to who 'L. D.' might be, on the title page?"

"Not a glimmer." The lid was back on the first tea chest, and Bill was removing the cover of the second. "But I've got another L. D. mystery for you. That's next."

He was wearing thin gloves and opening, very carefully, a folder of stained cardboard, tied with a ribbon like a legal brief. When it was untied he laid it on the lid of the third chest.

"I'd rather you didn't touch this at all," he said. "It may be pretty fragile. Let me know whenever you want to see the next sheet. And here's a lens."

They were drawings. One to a sheet, India ink on fine white paper, and done with a fine-nibbed pen. And they had nothing whatsoever to do with Charles Babbage, programming manuals, or Analytical Engines. What they did have, so small that first I had to peer, then use the lens, was a tiny, neat "L. D." at the upper right-hand corner of each sheet.

They were drawings of *animals*, the sort of multilegged, random animals that you find scuttling around in tidal pools, or hidden away in rotting tree bark. Or rather, as I realized when I examined them more closely, the sheets in the folder were drawings of *one* animal, seen from top, bottom, and all sides.

"Well?" said Bill expectantly.

But I was back to my examination of the tiny artist's mark. "It's not the same, is it. That's a different 'L. D.' from the software manual."

"You're a lot sharper than I am," said Bill. "I had to look fifty times before I saw that. But I agree completely, the 'L' is different, and so is the 'D.' What about the animal?"

"I've never seen anything like it. Beautiful drawings, but I'm no zoologist. You ought to photograph these and take them to your biology department."

"I did. You don't know Ray Weddle, but he's a top man. He says they have to be just drawings, made-up things, because there's nothing like them, and there never has been." He was carefully retying the folder and placing it back in the chest. "I've got photographs of these with me, too, but I wanted you to see the originals, exactly as I first saw them. We'll come back to these, but meanwhile: next exhibit."

He was into the third tea chest, removing more wrapped pieces of machinery, then a thick layer of straw, and now his hands were trembling. I hated to think how Bill must have sweated and agonized over this before telling anyone. The urge to publish such a discovery had to be overwhelming; but the fear of being derided as part of the scientific lunatic fringe had to be just as strong.

If what he had produced so far was complex and mystifying, what came next was almost laughably simple—if it were genuine. Bill was lifting, with a good deal of effort, a bar, about six inches by two inches by three. It gleamed hypnotically in the light of the lantern.

"It is, you know," he said, in answer to my shocked expression. "Twenty-four-carat gold, solid. There are thirteen more of them."

"But the Trevelyans, and the people who farmed here before that—"

"Never bothered to look. These were stowed at the bottom of a chest, underneath bits of the Analytical Engine and old sacks. I guess nobody ever got past the top layer until I came along." He smiled at me. "Tempted? If I were twenty years younger, I'd take the money and run."

"How much?"

"What's gold worth these days? U.S. currency?"

"God knows. Maybe three hundred and fifty dollars an ounce?"

"You're the calculating boy wonder, not me. So you do the arithmetic. Fourteen bars, each one weighs twenty-five pounds—I'm using avoirdupois, not troy, even though it's gold."

"One point nine six million. Say two million dollars, in round numbers. How long has it been here?"

"Who knows? But since it was *under* the parts of the Analytical Engine, I'd say it's been there as long as the rest."

"And who owns it?"

"If you asked the government, I bet they'd say that they do. If you ask me, it's whoever found it. Me. And now maybe me and thee." He grinned, diabolical in the lantern light. "Ready for the next exhibit?"

I wasn't. "For somebody to bring a fortune in gold here and just *leave* it . . ."

Underneath his raincoat Bill was wearing an old sports jacket and jeans. He owned, to my knowledge, three suits, none less than ten years old. His vices were beer, travel to museums, and about four cigars a year. I could not see him as the Two Million Dollar Man, and I didn't believe he could see himself that way. His next words confirmed it.

"So far as I'm concerned," he said, "this all belongs to the Trevelyans. But I'll have to explain to them that gold may be the least valuable thing here." He was back into the second tea chest, the one that held the drawings, and his hands were trembling again.

"These are what I *really* wanted you to see," he went on, in a husky voice. "I've not had the chance to have them dated yet, but my bet is that they're all genuine. You can touch them, but be gentle."

He was holding three slim volumes, as large as accounting ledgers. Each one was about twenty inches by ten, and bound in a shiny black material like thin sandpapery leather. I took the top one when he held it out, and opened it.

I saw neat tables of numbers, column after column of them. They were definitely not the product of any Analytical Engine, because they were handwritten and had occasional crossings out and corrections.

I flipped on through the pages. Numbers. Nothing else, no notes, no signature. Dates on each page. They were all in October 1855. The handwriting was that of the programming manual.

The second book had no dates at all. It was a series of exquisitely detailed machine drawings, with elaborately interlocking cogs and gears. There was writing, in the form of terse explanatory notes and dimensions, but it was in an unfamiliar hand.

"I'll save you the effort," said Bill as I reached for the lens. "These are definitely not by L. D. They are exact copies of some of Babbage's own plans for his calculating engines. I'll show you other reproductions if you like, back in Auckland, but you'll notice that these aren't *photographs*. I don't know what copying process was used. My bet is that all these things were placed here at the same time—whenever that was."

I wouldn't take Bill's word for it. After all, I had come to New Zealand to provide an independent check on his ideas. But five minutes were enough to make me agree, for the moment, with what he was saying.

"I'd like to take this and the other books up to the kitchen," I said, as I handed the second ledger back to him. "I want to have a really good look at them."

"Of course." Bill nodded. "That's exactly what I expected. I told the Trevelyans that we might be here in Little House for up to a week. We can cook for ourselves, or Annie says she'd be more than happy to expect us at mealtimes. I think she likes the company."

I wasn't sure of that. I'm not an elitist, but my own guess was that the conversation between Bill and me in the next few days was likely to be incomprehensible to Annie Trevelyan or almost anyone else.

I held out my hand for the third book. This was all handwritten, without a single drawing. It appeared to be a series of letters, running on one after the other, with the ledger turned sideways to provide a writing area ten inches across and twenty deep. There were no paragraphs within the letters. The writing was beautiful and uniform, by a different hand than had penned the numerical tables of the first book, and an exact half-inch space separated the end of one letter from the beginning of the next.

The first was dated 12th October, 1850. It began:

My dear J. G., The native people continue to be as friendly and as kind in nature as one could wish, though they, alas, cling to their paganism. As our ability to understand them increases, we learn that their dispersion is far wider than we at first suspected. I formerly mentioned the northern islands, ranging from Taheete to Raratonga. However, it appears that there has been a southern spread of the Maori people also, to lands far from here. I wonder if they may extend their settlements all the way to the great Southern Continent, explored by James Cook and more recently by Captain Ross. I am myself contemplating a journey to a more southerly island, with native assistance. Truly, a whole life's work is awaiting us. We both feel that, despite the absence of well-loved friends such as yourself, Europe and finance is "a world well lost." Louisa has recovered completely from the ailment that so worried me two years ago, and I must believe that the main reason for that improvement is a strengthening of spirit. She has begun her scientific work again, more productively, I believe, than ever before. My own efforts in the biological sciences prove ever more fascinating. When you write again tell us, I beg you, not of the transitory social or political events of London, but of the progress of science. It is in this area that L. and I are most starved of new knowledge. With affection, and with the assurance that we think of you and talk of you constantly, L. D.

The next letter was dated 14 December, 1850. Two months after the first. Was that time enough for a letter to reach England and a reply to return? The initials at the end were again L. D.

I turned to the back of the volume. The final twenty pages or so were blank, and in the last few entries the beautiful regular handwriting had degenerated to a more hasty scribble. The latest date that I saw was October 1855.

Bill was watching me intently. "Just the one book of letters?" I said.

He nodded. "But it doesn't mean they stopped. Only that we don't have them."

"If they didn't stop, why leave the last pages blank? Let's go back upstairs. With the books."

I wanted to read every letter and examine every page. But if I tried to do it in the chilly crawl space beneath the kitchen, I would have pneumonia before I finished. Already I was beginning to shiver.

"First impressions?" asked Bill, as he set the three ledgers carefully on the table and went back to close the trapdoor and replace the coconut matting. "I know you haven't had a chance to read, but I can't wait to hear what you're thinking."

I pulled a couple of the chairs over close to the fireplace. The coal fire was blazing, and the chill was already off the air in the room.

"There are *two* L. D.s," I said. "Husband and wife?"

"Agreed. Or maybe brother and sister."

"One of them—the woman—wrote the programming manual for the Analytical Engine. The other one, the man—if it is a man, and we can't be sure of that—did the animal drawings, and he wrote letters. He kept fair copies of what he sent off to Europe, in that third ledger. No sign of the replies, I suppose?"

"You've now seen everything that I've seen." Bill leaned forward and held chilled hands out to the fire. "I knew there were two, from the letters. But I didn't make the division of labor right away, the way you did. I bet you're right, though. Anything else?"

"Give me a chance. I need to *read*." I took the third book, the one of letters, from the table and returned with it to the fireside. "But they sound like missionaries."

"Missionaries and scientists. The old nineteenth-century mixture." Bill watched me reading for two minutes, then his urge to be up and doing something—or interrupt me with more questions—took over. His desire to talk was burning him up, while at the same time he didn't want to stop me from working.

"I'm going back to Big House," he said abruptly. "Shall I tell Annie we'll be there for a late lunch?"

I thought of the old farmhouse, generation after generation of life and children. Now there were just the two old folks, and the empty future. I nodded. "If I try to talk about this to them, make me stop."

"I will. If I can. And if I don't start doing it myself." He buttoned his raincoat and paused in the doorway. "About the gold. I considered telling Jim and Annie when I first found it, because I'm sure that legally they have the best claim to it. But I'd hate their kids to come hurrying home for all the wrong reasons. I'd appreciate your advice on timing. I hate to play God."

"So you want me to. Tell me one thing. What reason could there be for somebody to come down here to South Island in the 1850s, *in secret,* and never tell a soul what they were doing? That's what we are assuming."

"I'm tempted to say, maybe they found pieces of an Analytical Engine, one that had been left untouched here for a century and a half. But that gets a shade too recursive for my taste. And they did say what they were doing. Read the letters."

And then he was gone, and I was sitting in front of the warm fire. I stewed comfortably in wet pants and shoes, and read. Soon the words and the heat carried me away one hundred and forty years into the past, working my way systematically through the book's entries.

Most of the letters concerned religious or business matters and went to friends in England, France, and Ireland. Each person was identified only by initials. It became obvious that the female L. D. had kept her own active correspondence, not recorded in this ledger, and casual references to the spending of large sums of money made Bill's discovery of the gold bars much less surprising. The L. D.s, whoever they were, had great wealth in Europe. They had not traveled to New Zealand because of financial problems back home.

But not all the correspondence was of mundane matters back in England. Scattered in among the normal chat to friends were the surprises, as sudden and as unpredictable as lightning from a clear sky. The first of them was a short note dated January 1851:

> Dear J. G., L. has heard via A. v. H. that C. B. despairs of completing his grand design. In his own words, "There is no chance of the machine ever being executed during my own life and I am even doubtful of how to dispose of the drawings after its termination." This is a great tragedy, and L. is beside herself at the possible loss. Can we do anything about this? If it should happen to be no more than a matter of money . . .

And then, more than two years later, in April 1853:

> Dear J. G., Many thanks for the shipped materials, but apparently there was rough weather on the journey, and inadequate packing, and three of the cylinders arrived with one or more broken teeth. I am enclosing identification for these items. It is possible that repair can be done here, although our few skilled workmen are a far cry from the machinists of Bologna or Paris. However, you would do me a great favor if you could determine whether this shipment was in fact insured, as we requested. Yours etc. L. D.

Cylinders, with toothed gear wheels. It was the first hint of the Analytical Engine, but certainly not the last. I could deduce, from other letters to J. G., that three or four earlier shipments had been made to New Zealand in 1852, although apparently these had all survived the journey in good condition.

In the interests of brevity, L. D. in copying the letters had made numerous abbreviations; w. did service for both "which" and "with," "for" was shortened to f., and so on. Most of the time it did not hinder comprehension at all, and reconstruction of the original was easy; but I cursed when people were reduced to initials. It was impossible to expand those back to discover their identity. A. v. H. was probably the great world traveler and writer Alexander von Humboldt, whose fingerprint appears all across the natural science of Europe in the first half of the last century; and C. B. ought surely to be Charles Babbage. But who the devil was J. G.? Was it a man, or could it be a woman?

About a third of the way through the book, I learned that this was not just copies of letters sent to Europe. It probably began that way, but at some point L. D. started to use it also as a private diary. So by February 1854, after a gap of almost four months, I came across this entry:

22 February. Home at last, and thanks be to God that L. did not accompany me, for the seas to the south are more fierce than I ever dreamed, although the natives on the crew make nothing of them. They laugh in the teeth of the gale, and leap from ship to dinghy with impunity, in the highest sea. However, the prospect of a similar voyage during the winter months would deter the boldest soul, and defies my own imagination.

L. has made the most remarkable progress in her researches since my departure. She now believes that the design of the great engine is susceptible to considerable improvement, and that it could become capable of much more variation and power than ever A. L. suspected. The latter, dear lady, struggles to escape the grasp of her tyrannical mother, but scarce seems destined to succeed. At her request, L. keeps her silence, and allows no word of her own efforts to be fed back to England. Were this work to become known, however, I feel sure that many throughout Europe would be astounded by such an effort—so ambitious, so noble, and carried through, in its entirety, by a woman!

So the news of Ada Lovelace's tragic death, in 1852, had apparently not been received in New Zealand. I wondered, and read on:

Meanwhile, what of the success of my own efforts? It has been modest at best. We sailed to the island, named Rormaurma by the natives, which my charts show as Macwherry or Macquarie. It is a great spear of land, fifteen miles long but very narrow, and abundantly supplied with penguins and other seabirds. However, of the "cold-loving people" that the natives had described to me, if I have interpreted their language correctly, there was no sign, nor did we find any of the artifacts, which the natives insist these people are able to make for speech and for motion across the water. It is important that the reason for their veneration of these supposedly "superior men" be understood fully by me, before the way of our Lord can be explained to and accepted by the natives.

On my first time through the book I skimmed the second half of the letter. I was more interested in the "remarkable progress" that L. D. was reporting. It was only later that I went back and pondered that last paragraph for a long time.

The letters offered an irregular and infuriating series of snapshots of the work that Louisa was performing. Apparently she was busy with other things, too, and could squeeze in research only when conscience permitted. But by early 1855, L. D. was able to write, in a letter to the same unknown correspondent:

Dear J. G., It is finished, and it is working! And truth to tell, no one is more surprised than I. I imagine you now, shaking your head when you read those words, and I cannot deny what you told me, long ago, that our clever dear is the brains of the family—a thesis I will never again attempt to dispute.

It is finished, and it is working! I was reading that first sentence again, with a shiver in my spine, when the door opened. I looked up in annoyance. Then I realized the room was chilly, the fire was almost out, and when I glanced at my watch it was almost three o'clock.

It was Bill. "Done reading?" he asked, with an urgency that made me sure he would not like my answer.

"I've got about ten pages to go on the letters. But I haven't even glanced at the tables and the drawings." I stood up, stiffly, and used the tongs to add half a dozen pieces of coal to the fire. "If you want to talk now, I'm game."

The internal struggle was obvious on his face, but after a few seconds he shook his head. "No. It might point you down the same mental path that I took, without either of us trying to do that. We both know how natural it is for us to prompt one another. I'll wait. Let's go on down to Big House. Annie told me to come and get you, and by the time we get there she'll have tea on the table."

My stomach growled at the thought. "What about these?"

"Leave them just where they are. You can pick up where you left off, and everything's safe enough here." But I noticed that after Bill said that, he carefully pulled the fireguard around the fender so there was no possibility of stray sparks.

The weather outside had cleared, and the walk down the hill was just what I needed. We were at latitude 46 degrees south, it was close to the middle of winter, and already the sun was sloping down to the hills in the west. The wind still blew, hard and cold. If I took a beeline south, there was no land between me and the "great Southern Continent" that L. D. had written about. Head east or west, and I would find only open water until I came to Chile and Argentina. No wonder the winds blew so strongly. They had an unbroken run around half the world to pick up speed.

Mrs. Trevelyan's "tea" was a farmer's tea, the main cooked meal of the day. Jim Trevelyan was already sitting, knife and fork in hand, when we arrived. He was a man in his early seventies, but thin, wiry, and alert. His only real sign of age was his deafness, which he handled by leaning forward with his hand cupped around his right ear while he stared with an intense expression at any speaker.

The main course was squab pie, a thick crusted delicacy made with mutton, onions, apples, and cloves. I found it absolutely delicious, and delighted Annie Trevelyan by eating three helpings. Jim Trevelyan served us a homemade dark beer. He said little, but nodded his approval when Bill and I did as well with the drink as with the food.

After the third tankard I was drifting off into a pleasant dream state. I didn't feel like talking, and fortunately I didn't need to. I did my part by imitating Jim Trevelyan, listening to Annie as she told us about Big House and about her family and nodding at the right places.

When the plates were cleared away she dragged out an old suitcase full of photographs. She knew every person, and how each was related to each, across four generations. About halfway through the pile she stopped and glanced up self-consciously at me and Bill. "I must be boring you."

"Not a bit," I said. She wasn't, because her enthusiasm for the past was so great. In her own way she was as much a historian as Bill or me.

"Go on, please," added Bill. "It's really very interesting."

"All right." She blushed. "I get carried away, you know. But it's so good to have *youngsters* in the house again."

Bill caught my eye. Youngsters? Us? His grizzled beard and my receding hairline. But Annie was moving on, backward into the past. We went all the way to the time of the first Trevelyan and the building of Big House itself. At the very bottom of the case sat two framed pictures.

"And now you've got me," Annie said, laughing. "I don't know a thing about these two, though they're probably the oldest thing here."

She passed them across the table for our inspection, giving one to each of us. Mine was a painting, not a photograph. It was of a plump man with a full beard and clear gray eyes. He held a churchwarden pipe in one hand, and he patted the head of a dog with the other. There was no hint as to who he might be.

Bill had taken the other and was still staring at it. I held out my hand. Finally, after a long pause, he passed it across.

It was another painting. The man was in half-profile, as though torn between looking at the painter and the woman. He was dark haired and wore a long, drooping mustache. She stood by his side, a bouquet of flowers in her hands and her chin slightly lifted in what could have been an expression of resolution or defiance. Her eyes gazed straight out of the picture, into me and through my heart. Across the bottom, just above the frame, were four words in black ink: "Luke and Louisa Derwent."

I could not speak. It was Bill who broke the silence. "How do you come to have these two, if they're not family?"

His voice was gruff and wavering, but Annie did not seem to notice.

"Didn't I ever tell you? The first Trevelyan built Big House, but there were others here before that. They lived in Little House—it was built first, years and years back, I'm not sure when. These pictures have to be from that family, near as I can tell."

Bill turned to glance at me. His mouth was hanging half-open, but at last he managed to close it and say, "Did you—I mean, are there *other* things? Things here, I mean, things that used to be in Little House."

Annie shook her head. "There used to be, but Grandad, Jim's dad, one day not long after we were married he did a big clear out. He didn't bother with the things you've been finding, because none of us ever used the crawl space under the kitchen. And I saved those two because I like pictures. But everything else went."

She must have seen Bill and me subside in our chairs, because she shook her head and said, "Now then, I've been talking my fool head off, and never given you any afters. It's apple pie and cheese."

As she rose from her place and went to the pantry, and Jim Trevelyan followed her out of the kitchen, Bill turned to me. "Can you believe it, I never thought to *ask?* I mean, I did ask Jim Trevelyan about things that used to be in Little House, and he said his father threw everything out but what's there now. But I left it at that. I never asked Annie."

"No harm done. We know now, don't we? Luke Derwent, he's the artist, and Louisa, she's the mathematician and engineer."

"And the *programmer*—a century before computer programming was supposed to exist." Bill stopped. We were not supposed to be discussing this until I had examined the rest of the materials. But we were saved from more talk by the return of Jim Trevelyan. He was holding a huge book, the size of a small suitcase, with a black embossed cover and brass-bound corners.

"I told you Dad chucked everything," he said. "And he did, near enough, threw it out or burned it. But he were a religious man, and he knew better than to destroy a Bible." He dropped it on the table with a thump that shook the solid wood. "This comes from Little House. If you want to take a look at it, even take it on back there with you, you're very welcome."

I pulled the book across to me and unhooked the thick metal clasp that held it shut. I knew, from the way that some of the pages did not lie fully closed at their edges, that there must be inserts. The room went silent as I nervously leafed through to find them.

The disappointment that followed left me as hollow as though I had eaten nothing all day. There were inserts, sure enough: dried wildflowers, gathered long, long ago and pressed between the pages of the Bible. I examined every one, and riffled through the rest of the book to make sure nothing else lay between the pages. At last I took a deep breath and pushed the Bible away from me.

Bill reached out and pulled it in front of him. "There's one other possibility," he said. "If their family happened to be anything like mine . . ."

He turned to the very last page of the Bible. The flyleaf was of thick, yellowed paper. On it, in faded multicolored inks, a careful hand had traced the Derwent family tree.

Apple pie and cheese were forgotten while Bill and I, with the willing assistance of Jim and Annie Trevelyan, examined every name of the generations shown, and made a more readable copy as we went.

At the time it finally seemed like more disappointment. Not one of us recognized a single name, except for those of Luke and Louisa Derwent, and those we already knew. The one fact added by the family tree was that they were half brother and sister, with a common father. There were no dates, and Luke and Louisa were the last generation shown.

Bill and I admitted that we were at a dead end. Annie served a belated dessert, and after it the two of us wrapped the two pictures in waterproof covers (though it was not raining) and headed back up the hill to Little House, promising Annie that we would certainly be back for breakfast.

We were walking in silence, until halfway up the hill Bill said suddenly, "I'm sorry. I saw it, too, the resemblance to Eileen. I knew it would hit you. But I couldn't do anything about it."

"It was the expression, more than anything," I said. "That tilt to the chin, and the look in her eyes. But it was just coincidence, they're not really alike. That sort of thing is bound to happen."

"Hard on you, though."

"I'm fine."

"Great." Bill's voice showed his relief. "I wasn't going to say anything, but I had to be sure you were all right."

"I'm fine."

Fine, except that no more than a month ago a well-meaning friend of many years had asked me, "Do you think of Eileen as the love of your life?"

And my heart had dropped through a hole in the middle of my chest and lodged like a cold rock in the pit of my belly.

When we reached Little House I pleaded residual travel fatigue and went straight to bed. With so much of Jim Trevelyan's powerful home brew inside me, my sleep should have been deep and dreamless. But the dead, once roused, do not lie still so easy.

Images of Eileen and the happy past rose before me, to mingle and merge with the Derwent picture. Even in sleep I felt a terrible sadness. And the old impotence came back, telling me that I had been unable to change in any way the only event in my life that really mattered.

With my head still half a world away in a different time zone, I woke long before dawn. The fire, well damped by Bill before he went to bed, was still glowing under the ash, and a handful of firewood and more coal were all it needed to bring it back to full life.

Bill was still asleep when I turned on the two oil lamps, pulled the three books within easy reach, and settled down to read. I was determined to be in a position to talk to him by the time we went down to Big House for breakfast, but it was harder than I expected. Yesterday I had been overtired; now I had to go back and reread some of the letters before I was ready to press on.

I had been in the spring of 1855, with some sort of Analytical Engine finished and working. But now, when I was desperate to hear more details, Luke Derwent frustrated me. He vanished for four months from the ledger, and returned at last not to report on Louisa's doings but brimming over with wonder at his own.

21 September, 1855. Glory to Almighty God, and let me pray that I never again have doubts. L. and I have wondered, so many times, about our decision to come here. We have never regretted it, but we have asked if it was done for selfish reasons. Now, at last, it is clear that we are fulfilling a higher purpose.

Yesterday I returned from my latest journey to Macquarie Island. They were there! The "cold-loving people," just as my native friends assured me. In truth, they find the weather of the island too warm in all but the southern winter months of May to August, and were almost ready to depart again when our ship made landfall. For they are migrant visitors, and spend the bulk of the year in a more remote location.

The natives term them "people," and I must do the same, for although they do not hold the remotest outward aspect of humans, they are without doubt intelligent. They are able to speak to the natives, with the aid of a box that they carry from place to place. They possess amazing tools, able to fabricate the necessities of life with great speed. According to my native translators, although they have their more permanent base elsewhere in this hemisphere, they come originally from "far, far off." This to the Maori natives means from far across the seas, although I am less sure of this conclusion.

And they have wonderful powers in medical matters. The Maori natives swear that one of their own number, so close to death from gangrenous wounds that death was no more than a day away, was brought to full recovery within hours. Another woman was held, frozen but alive, for a whole winter, until she could be treated and restored to health by the wonderful medical treatment brought from their permanent home by the "cold-loving people" (for whom in truth it is now incumbent upon me to find a better name). I should add that they are friendly, and readily humored me in my desire to make detailed drawings of their form. They asked me through my Maori interpreter to speak English, and assured me that upon my next visit they would be able to talk to me in my own language.

All this is fascinating. But it pales to nothing beside the one central question: Do these beings possess immortal souls? We are in no position to make a final decision on such a matter, but L. and I agree that in our actions we must assume that the answer is yes. For if we are in a position to bring to Christ even one of these beings who would otherwise have died unblessed, then it is our clear duty to do so.

It was a digression from the whole subject of the Analytical Engine, one so odd that I sat and stared at the page for a long time. And the next entry, with its great outburst of emotion, seemed to take me even further afield.

> *Dear J. G., I have the worst news in the world. How can I tell you this— L.'s old disease is returned, and, alas, much worse than before. She said nothing to me, but yesterday I discovered bright blood on her handkerchief, and such evidence she could not deny. At my insistence she has visited a physician, and the prognosis is desperate indeed. She is amazingly calm about the future, but I cannot remain so sanguine. Pray for her, my dear friend, as I pray constantly.*

The letter was dated 25 September, just a few days after his return from his travels. Immediately following, as though Luke could not contain his thoughts, the diary ran on:

> *Louisa insists what I cannot believe: that her disease is no more than God's just punishment, paid for the sin of both of us. Her calm and courage are beyond belief. She is delighted that I remain well, and she seems resigned to the prospect of her death, as I can never be resigned. But what can I do? What? I cannot sit idly, and watch her slowly decline. Except that it will not be slow. Six months, no more.*

His travels among the colony of the "cold-loving people" were forgotten. The Analytical Engine was of no interest to him. But that brief diary entry told me a great deal. I pulled out the picture of Luke and Louisa Derwent and was staring at it when Bill emerged rumple-haired from the bedroom.

This time I was the one desperate to talk. "I know! I know why they came all the way to New Zealand."

He stared, at me and at the picture I was holding. "How can you?"

"We ought to have seen it last night. Remember the family tree in the Bible? It showed they're half brother and half sister. And *this*." I held the painting out toward him.

He rubbed his eyes and peered at it. "I saw. What about it?"

"Bill, it's a *wedding picture*. See the bouquet, and the ring on her finger? They couldn't possibly have married back in England, the scandal would have been too great. But here, where nobody knew them, they could make a fresh start and live as man and wife."

He was glancing across to the open ledger and nodding. "Damn it, you're right. It explains everything. Their sin, he said. You got to that?"

"I was just there."

"Then you're almost at the end. Read the last few pages, then let's head down to Big House for breakfast. We can talk on the way."

He turned and disappeared back into the bedroom. I riffled through the ledger. As he said, I was close to the place where the entries gave way to blank pages.

There was just one more letter, to the same far-off friend. It was dated 6 October, 1855, and it was calm, even clinical.

Dear J. G., L. and I will in a few days be embarking upon a long journey to a distant island, where dwell a certain pagan native people; these are the Heteromorphs (to employ L.'s preferred term for them, since they are very different in appearance from other men, although apparently sharing our rational powers). To these beings we greatly wish to carry the blessings of Our Lord, Jesus Christ. It will be a dangerous voyage. Therefore, if you hear nothing from us within four years, please dispose of our estate according to my earlier instructions. I hope that this is not my last letter to you; however, should that prove to be the case, be assured that we talk of you constantly, and you are always in our thoughts. In the shared love of our savior, L. D.

It was followed by the scribbled personal notes.

I may be able to deceive Louisa, and the world, but I do not deceive myself. God forgive me, when I confess that the conversion of the Heteromorphs is not my main goal. For while the message of Christ might wait until they return to their winter base on Macquarie Island, other matters cannot wait. My poor Louisa. Six months, at most. Already she is weakening, and the hectic blush sits on her cheek. Next May would be too late. I must take Louisa now, and pray that the Maori report of powerful Heteromorph medical skills is not mere fable.

We will carry with us the word of Christ. Louisa is filled with confidence that this is enough for every purpose, while I, rank apostate, am possessed by doubts. Suppose that they remain, rejecting divine truth, a nation of traders? I know exactly what I want from them. But what do I have to offer in return?

Perhaps this is truly a miracle of God's bounty. For I can provide what no man has ever seen before, a marvel for this and every age: Louisa's great Engine, which, in insensate mechanic operation, appears to mimic the thought of rational, breathing beings. This, surely, must be of inestimable value and interest, to any beings, no matter how advanced.

Then came a final entry, the writing of a man in frantic haste.

Louisa has at last completed the transformations of the information that I received from the Heteromorphs. We finally have the precise destination, and leave tomorrow on the morning tide. We are amply provisioned, and our native crew is ready and far more confident than I. Like Rabelais, "Je m'en vais chercher un grand peut-être." God grant that I find it.

I go to seek a "great perhaps." I shivered, stood up, and went through to the bedroom, where Bill was pulling on a sweater.

"The Analytical Engine. They took it with them when they left."

"I agree." His expression was a strange blend of satisfaction and frustration. "But now tell me this. *Where did they go?*"

"I can't answer that."

"We have to. Take a look at this." Bill headed past me to the kitchen, his arms still halfway into the sleeves. He picked up the folder of drawings that we had brought from the crawl space. "You've hardly glanced at these, but I've spent as much time on them as on the letters. Here."

He passed me a pen-and-ink drawing that showed one of the creatures seen from the front. There was an abundance of spindly legs—I counted fourteen, plus four thin, whiskery antennae—and what I took to be two pairs of eyes and delicate protruding eyestalks.

Those were the obvious features. What took the closer second look were the little pouches on each side of the body, not part of the animal and apparently strapped in position. Held in four of the legs was a straight object with numbers marked along its length.

"That's a scale bar," said Bill, when I touched a finger to it. "If it's accurate, and I've no reason to think Luke Derwent would have drawn it wrong, his 'Heteromorphs' were about three feet tall."

"And those side pouches are for tools."

"Tools, food, communications equipment—they could be anything. See, now, why I told you I thought for the past couple of weeks I was going mad? To have this hanging in front of me, and have no idea how to handle it."

"That place he mentioned. Macquarie Island?"

"Real enough. About seven hundred miles south and west of

here. But I can promise you, there's nothing there relating to this. It's too small, it's been visited too often. Anything like the Hetero-morphs would have been reported, over and over. And it's not where Derwent said he was going. He was heading somewhere else, to their more permanent base. Wherever that was." Bill's eyes were gleam-ing, and his mouth was quivering. He had been living with this for too long, and now he was walking the edge. "What are we going to *do?*"

"We're heading down to Big House, so Annie can feed us. And we're going to talk this through." I took his arm. "Come on."

The cold morning air cut into us as soon as we stepped outside the door. As I had hoped, it braced Bill and brought him down.

"Maybe we've gone as far as we can go," he said, in a quieter voice. "Maybe we ought to go public with everything, and just tell the world what we've found."

"We could. But it wouldn't work."

"Why not?"

"Because when you get right down to it, we haven't found *any-thing*. Bill, if it hadn't been you who sent me that letter and package of stuff, do you know what I would have said?"

"Yeah. Here's another damned kook."

"Or a fraud. I realized something else when I was reading those letters. If Jim and Annie Trevelyan had found everything in the crawl space and shipped it to Christchurch, it would have been plausible. You can tell in a minute they know nothing about Babbage, or com-puters, or programming. But if you wanted two people who could have engineered a big fat hoax, you'd have to go a long way to find someone better qualified than the two of us. People would say, ah, they're computer nuts, and they're science history nuts, and they planned a fake to fool everybody."

"But we didn't!"

"Who knows that, Bill, other than me and you? We have nothing to *show*. What do we do, stand up and say, oh, yes, there really was an Analytical Engine, but it was taken away to show to these aliens? And unfortunately we don't know where they are, either."

Bill sighed. "Right on. We'd be better off saying it was stolen by fairies."

We had reached Big House. When we went inside, Annie Tre-velyan took one look at our faces and said, "Ay, you've had bad news then." And as we sat down at the table and she began to serve hot-cakes and sausage, "Well, no matter what it is, remember this: you are both young, and you've got your health. Whatever it is, it's not the end of the world."

It only seemed like it. But I think we both realized that Annie Trevelyan was smarter than both of us.

"I'll say it again," said Bill, after a moment or two. "What do we do now?"

"We have breakfast, and then we go back to Little House, and we go over *everything,* together. Maybe we're missing something."

"Yeah. So far, it's a month of my life." But Bill was starting to dig into a pile of beef sausage, and that was a good sign. He and I are both normally what Annie called "good eaters" and others, less kind, would call gluttons.

She fed us until we refused another morsel of food, then ushered us out. "Go and get on with it," she said cheerfully. "You'll sort it out. I know you will."

It was good to have the confidence of at least one person in the world. Stuffed with food, we trudged back up the hill. I felt good, and optimistic. But I think that was because the materials were so new to me. Bill must have stared at them already until his eyes popped out.

Up at Little House once more, the real work started. We went over the letters and diary again, page by page, date by date, phrase by phrase. Nothing new there, although now that we had seen it once, we could see the evidence again and again of the brother-sister/ husband-wife ambivalence.

The drawings came next. The Heteromorphs were so alien in appearance that we were often guessing as to the function of organs or the small objects that on close inspection appeared to be slung around their bodies or held in one of the numerous claws, but at the end of our analysis we had seen nothing to change our opinions or add to our knowledge.

We were left with one more item: the ledger of tables of num-bers, written in the hand of Louisa Derwent. Bill opened it at ran-dom, and we stared at the page in silence.

"It's dated October 1855, like all the others," I said at last. "That's when they left."

"Right. And Luke wrote 'Louisa has completed the necessary

calculations.' " Bill was scowling down at a list of numbers, accusing it of failing to reveal to us its secrets. "Necessary for what?"

I leaned over his shoulder. There were twenty-odd entries in the table, each a two- or three-digit number. "Nothing obvious. But it's reasonable to assume that this has something to do with the journey, because of the date. What else would Louisa have been working on in the last few weeks?"

"It doesn't look anything like a navigation guide. But it could be intermediate results. Work sheets." Bill went back to the first page of the ledger, and the first table. "These could be distances to places they would reach on the way."

"They could. Or they could be times, or weights, or angles, or a hundred other things. Even if they are distances, we have no idea what *units* they are in. They could be miles, or nautical miles, or kilometers, or anything."

It sounds as though I was offering destructive criticism, but Bill knew better. Each of us had to play devil's advocate, cross-checking the other every step of the way, if we were to avoid sloppy thinking and unwarranted assumptions.

"I'll accept all that," he said calmly. "We may have to try and abandon a dozen hypotheses before we're done. But let's start making them, and see where they lead. There's one main assumption, though, that we'll *have* to make: these tables were somehow used by Luke and Louisa Derwent, to decide how to reach the Heteromorphs. Let's take it from there, and let's not lose sight of the only goal we have: we want to find the location of the Heteromorph base."

He didn't need to spell out to me the implications. If we could find the base, maybe the Analytical Engine would still be there. And I didn't need to spell out to him the other, overwhelming probability: chances were, the Derwents had perished on the journey, and their long-dead bodies lay somewhere on the ocean floor.

We began to work on the tables, proposing and rejecting interpretations for each one. The work was tedious, time-consuming, and full of blind alleys, but we did not consider giving up. From our point of view, progress of sorts was being made as long as we could think of and test new working assumptions. Real failure came only if we ran out of ideas.

We stopped for just two things: sleep and meals at Big House.

I think it was the walk up and down the hill, and the hours spent with Jim and Annie Trevelyan, that kept us relatively sane and balanced.

Five days fled by. We did not have a solution; the information in the ledger was not enough for that. But we finally, about noon on the sixth day, had a problem.

A *mathematical* problem. We had managed, with a frighteningly long list of assumptions and a great deal of work, to reduce our thoughts and calculations to a very unpleasant-looking nonlinear optimization. If it possessed a global maximum, and could be solved for that maximum, it might yield, at least in principle, the location on Earth whose probability of being a destination for the Derwents was maximized.

Lots of "ifs." But worse than that, having come this far neither Bill nor I could see a systematic approach to finding a solution. Trial-and-error, even with the fastest computer, would take the rest of our lives. We had been hoping that modern computing skills and vastly increased raw computational power could somehow compensate for all the extra information that Louisa Derwent had available to her and we were lacking. So far, the contest wasn't even close.

We finally admitted that and sat in the kitchen staring at each other.

"Where's the nearest phone?" I asked.

"Dunedin, probably. Why?"

"We've gone as far as we can alone. Now we need expert help."

"I hate to agree with you." Bill stood up. "But I have to. We're out of our depth. We need the best numerical analyst we can find."

"That's who I'm going to call."

"But what will you tell him? What do we tell *anyone?*"

"Bits and pieces. As little as I can get away with." I was pulling on my coat and picking up the results of our labors. "For the moment, they'll have to trust us."

"They'll have to be as crazy as we are," he said.

The good news was that the people we needed tended to be just that. Bill followed me out.

We didn't stop at Dunedin. We went all the way to Christchurch, where Bill could hitch a free ride on the university phone system.

We found a quiet room, and I called Stanford's computer science department. I had an old extension, but I reached the man I wanted after a couple of hops—I was a little surprised at that, because as a peripatetic and sociable bachelor he was as often as not in some other continent.

"Where are you?" Gene said, as soon as he knew who was on the line.

That may sound like an odd opening for a conversation with someone you have not spoken to for a year, but usually when one of us called the other it meant that we were within dinner-eating distance. Then we would have a meal together, discuss life, death, and mathematics, and go our separate ways oddly comforted.

"I'm in Christchurch. Christchurch, New Zealand."

"Right." There was a barely perceptible pause at the other end of the line, then he said, "Well, you've got my attention. Are you all right?"

"I'm fine. But I need an algorithm."

I sketched out the nature of the problem, and after I was finished he said, "It sounds a bit like an under-determined version of the Traveling Salesman problem, where you have incomplete information about the nodes."

"That's pretty much what we decided. We know a number of distances, and we know that some of the locations and the end point have to be on land. Also, the land boundaries place other constraints on the paths that can be taken. Trouble is, we've no idea how to solve the whole thing."

"This is really great," Gene said—and meant it. I could almost hear him rubbing his hands at the prospect of a neat new problem. "The way you describe it, it's definitely nonpolynomial unless you can provide more information. I don't know how to solve it either, but I do have ideas. You have to give me *all* the details."

"I was planning to. This was just to get you started thinking. I'll be on a midnight flight out of here, and I'll land at San Francisco about eight in the morning. I can be at your place by eleven-thirty. I'll have the written details."

"That urgent?"

"It feels that way. Maybe you can talk me out of it over dinner."

After I rang off, Bill Rigley gave me a worried shake of his head. "Are you sure you know what you're doing? You'll have to tell him quite a bit."

"Less than you think. Gene will help, I promise." I had just realized what I *was* doing. I was cashing intellectual chips that I had been collecting for a quarter of a century.

"Come on," I said. "Let's go over everything one more time. Then I have to get out of here."

The final division of labor had been an easy one to perform. Bill had to go back to Little House and make absolutely sure that we had not missed one scrap of information that might help us. I must head for the United States and try to crack our computational problem. Bill's preliminary estimate, of two thousand hours on a Cray-YMP, was not encouraging.

I arrived in San Francisco one hour behind schedule, jet lagged to the gills. But I made up for lost time on the way to Palo Alto, and was sitting in the living room of Gene's house on Constanza by midday.

True to form, he had not waited for my arrival. He had already been in touch with half a dozen people scattered around the United States and Canada to see if there was anything new and exciting in the problem area we were working. I gave him a restricted version of the story of Louisa Derwent and the vanished Analytical Engine, omitting all suggestion of aliens, and then showed him my copy of our analyses and the raw data from which we had drawn it. While he started work on that, I borrowed his telephone and wearily tackled the next phase.

Gene would give us an algorithm, I was sure of that, and it would be the best that today's numerical analysis could provide. But even with that best, I was convinced that we would face a most formidable computational problem.

I did not wait to learn just how formidable. Assuming that Bill and I were right, there would be other certainties. We would need a digital data base of the whole world, or at least the southern hemisphere, with the land/sea boundaries defined. This time my phone call gave a less satisfactory answer. The Defense Mapping Agency might have what I needed, but it was almost certainly not generally available. My friend (with a guarantee of anonymity) promised to do some digging, and either finagle me a loaner data set or point me to the best commercial sources.

I had one more call to make, to Marvin Minsky at the MIT

Media Lab. I looked at the clock as I dialed. One forty-five. On the East Coast it was approaching quitting time for the day. Personally, I felt long past quitting time.

I was lucky again. He came to the phone sounding slightly surprised. We knew each other, but not all that well—not the way that I knew Bill, or Gene.

"Do you still have a good working relationship with Thinking Machines Corporation?" I asked.

"Yes." If a declarative word can also be a question, that was it.

"And Danny Hillis is still chief scientist, right?"

"He is."

"Good. Do you remember in Pasadena a few years ago you introduced us?"

"At the *Voyager Neptune* flyby. I remember it very well." Now his voice sounded more and more puzzled. No wonder. I was tired beyond belief, and struggling to stop my thoughts spinning off into non sequiturs.

"I think I'm going to need a couple of hundred hours of time," I said, "on the fastest Connection Machine there is."

"You're talking to the wrong person."

"I may need some high-priority access." I continued as though I had not heard him. "Do you have a few minutes while I tell you *why* I need it?"

"It's your nickel." Now the voice sounded a little bit skeptical, but I could tell he was intrigued.

"This has to be done in person. Maybe tomorrow morning?"

"Friday? Hold on a moment."

"Anywhere you like," I said, while a muttered conversation took place at the other end of the line. "It won't take long. Did you say tomorrow is *Friday?*"

I seemed to have lost a day somewhere. But that didn't matter. By tomorrow afternoon I would be ready and able to sleep for the whole weekend.

Everything had been rushing along, faster and faster, toward an inevitable conclusion. And at that point, just where Bill and I wanted the speed to be at a maximum, events slowed to a crawl.

In retrospect, the change of pace was only in our minds. By any normal standards progress was spectacularly fast.

For example, Gene produced an algorithm in less than a week. He still wanted to do final polishing, especially to make it optimal for parallel processing, but there was no point in waiting before programming began. Bill had by this time flown in from New Zealand, and we were both up in Massachusetts. In ten days we had a working program and the geographic data base was on-line.

Our first Connection Machine run was performed that same evening. It was a success, if by "success" you mean that it did not bomb. But it failed to produce a well-defined maximum of any kind.

So then the tedious time began. The input parameters that we judged to be uncertain had to be run over their full permitted ranges, in every possible variation. Naturally we had set up the program to perform that parametric variation automatically, and to proceed to the next case whenever the form of solution was not satisfactory. And just as naturally we could hardly bear to leave the computer. We wanted to see the results of each run, to be there when—or if—the result we wanted finally popped out.

For four whole days nothing emerged that was even encouraging. Any computed maxima were hopelessly broad and unacceptably poorly defined. We went on haunting the machine room, disappearing only for naps and hurried meals. It resembled the time of our youth, when hands-on program debugging was the only sort known. In the late night hours I felt a strange confluence of computer generations. Here we were, working as we had worked many years ago, but now we were employing today's most advanced machine in a strange quest for its own earliest ancestor.

We must have been a terrible nuisance to the operators, as we brooded over input and fretted over output, but no one said an unkind word. They must have sensed, from vague rumors, or from the more direct evidence of our behavior, that something very important to us was involved in these computations. They encouraged us to eat and rest; and it seemed almost inevitable that when at last the result that Bill and I had been waiting for so long emerged from the electronic blizzard of activity within the Connection Machine, neither of us would be there to see it.

The call came at eight-thirty in the morning. We had left an hour earlier, and were eating a weary breakfast in the Royal Sonesta motel, not far from the installation.

"I have something I think you should see," said the hesitant voice of the shift operator. He had watched us sit dejected over a thousand outputs, and he was reluctant now to raise our hopes. "One of the runs shows a sharp peak. Really narrow and tight."

They had deduced what we were looking for. "We're on our way," said Bill. Breakfast was left half-eaten—a rare event for either of us—and in the car neither of us could think of anything to say.

The run results were everything that the operator had suggested. The two-dimensional probability density function was a set of beautiful concentric ellipses, surrounding a single land location. We could have checked coordinates with the geographic data base, but we were in too much of a hurry. Bill had lugged a *Times* atlas with him all the way from Auckland and parked it in the computer room. Now he riffled through it, seeking the latitude and longitude defined by the run output.

"My God!" he said after a few seconds. "It's South Georgia."

After my first bizarre reaction—South Georgia! How could the Derwents have undertaken a journey to so preposterous a destination, in the southeastern United States?—I saw where Bill's finger lay.

South Georgia *Island*. I had hardly heard of it, but it was a lonely smear of land in the far south of the Atlantic Ocean.

Bill, of course, knew a good deal about the place. I have noticed this odd fact before; people who live *south* of the equator seem to know far more about the geography of their hemisphere than we do about ours. Bill's explanation, that there is a lot less southern land to know about, is true but not completely convincing.

It did not matter, however, because within forty-eight hours I, too, knew almost all there was to know about South Georgia. It was not very much. The Holy Grail that Bill and I had been seeking so hard was a desolate island about a hundred miles long and twenty miles wide. The highest mountains were substantial, rising almost to ten thousand feet, and their fall to the sea was a dreadful chaos of rocks and glaciers. It would not be fair to say that the interior held nothing of interest, because no one had ever bothered to explore it.

South Georgia had enjoyed its brief moment of glory at the end of the last century, when it had been a base for Antarctic whalers, and even then only the coastal area had been inhabited. In 1916, Shackleton and a handful of his men made a desperate and successful crossing of the island's mountains, to obtain help for the rest of his stranded trans-Antarctic expedition. The next interior crossing was not until 1955, by a British survey team.

That is the end of South Georgia history. Whaling was the only industry. With its decline, the towns of Husvik and Grytviken dwindled and died. The island returned to its former role, as an outpost beyond civilization.

None of these facts was the reason, though, for Bill Rigley's shocked "My God!" when his finger came to rest on South Georgia. He was amazed by the *location*. The island lies in the Atlantic Ocean, at 54 degrees south. It is six thousand miles away from New Zealand or from the Heteromorph winter outpost on Macquarie Island.

And those are no ordinary six thousand miles, of mild winds and easy trade routes.

"Look at the choice Derwent had to make," said Bill. "Either he went *west,* south of Africa and the Cape of Good Hope. That's the long way, nine or ten thousand miles, and all the way against the prevailing winds. Or he could sail *east.* That way would be shorter, maybe six thousand miles, and mostly with the winds. But he would have to go across the South Pacific, and then through the Drake Passage between Cape Horn and the Antarctic Peninsula."

His words meant more to me after I had done some reading. The southern seas of the Roaring Forties cause no shivers today, but a hundred years ago they were a legend to all sailing men, a region of cruel storms, monstrous waves, and deadly winds. They were worst of all in the Drake Passage, but that wild easterly route had been Luke Derwent's choice. It was quicker, and he was a man for whom time was running out.

While I did my reading, Bill was making travel plans.

Were we going to South Georgia? Of course we were, although any rational process in my brain told me, more strongly than ever, that we would find nothing there. Luke and Louisa Derwent never reached the island. They had died, as so many others had died, in attempting that terrible southern passage below Cape Horn.

There was surely nothing to be found. We knew that. But still we drained our savings, and Bill completed our travel plans. We would fly to Buenos Aires, then on to the Falkland Islands. After that came the final eight hundred miles to South Georgia, by boat, carrying the tiny two-person survey aircraft whose final assembly must be done on the island itself.

Already we knew the terrain of South Georgia as well as anyone had ever known it. I had ordered a couple of SPOT satellite images of the island, good cloud-free pictures with ten-meter resolution. I went over them again and again, marking anomalies that we wanted to investigate.

Bill did the same. But at that point, oddly enough, our individual agendas diverged. His objective was the Analytical Engine, which had dominated his life for the past few months. He had written out, in full, the sequence of events that led to his discoveries in New Zealand and to our activities afterward. He described the location and nature of all the materials at Little House. He sent copies of everything, dated, signed, and sealed, to the library of his own university, to the British Museum, to the Library of Congress, and to the Reed Collection of rare books and manuscripts in the Dunedin Public Library. The discovery of the Analytical Engine—or of any part of it—somewhere on South Georgia Island would validate and render undeniable everything in the written record.

And I? I wanted to find evidence of Louisa Derwent's Analytical Engine, and even more so of the Heteromorphs. But beyond that, my thoughts turned again and again to Luke Derwent, in his search for the "great perhaps."

He had told Louisa that their journey was undertaken to bring Christianity to the cold-loving people; but I knew better. Deep in his heart he had another, more selfish motive. He cared less about the conversion of the Heteromorphs than about access to their great medical powers. Why else would he carry with him, for trading purposes, Louisa's wondrous construct, the "marvel for this and every age"—a clanking mechanical computer—to beings who possessed machines small and powerful enough to serve as portable language translators?

I understood Luke Derwent completely, in those final days before he sailed east. The love of his life was dying, and he was desperate. Would he, for a chance to save her, have risked death on the wild southern ocean? Would he have sacrificed himself, his whole crew, and his own immortal soul for the one-in-a-thousand chance of restoring her to health? Would *anyone* take such a risk?

I can answer that. Anyone would take the risk, and count himself blessed by the gods to be given the opportunity.

I want to find the Analytical Engine on South Georgia, and I want to find the Heteromorphs. But more than either of those, I want to find evidence that Luke Derwent *succeeded* in his final, reckless gamble. I want him to have beaten the odds. I want to find Louisa Derwent, frozen but alive in the still glaciers of the island, awaiting her resurrection and restoration to health.

I have a chance to test the kindness of reality. For in just two days Bill and I fly south and seek our evidence, our own "great perhaps." Then I will know.

But now, at the last moment, when we are all prepared, events have taken a more complex turn. And I am not sure if what is happening will help us or hinder us.

Back in Christchurch, Bill had worried about what I would tell people when we looked for help in the States. I told him that I would say as little as we could get away with, and I kept my word. No one was given more than a small part of the whole story, and the main groups involved were separated by the width of the continent.

But we were dealing with some of the world's smartest people. And today physical distance means nothing. People talk constantly across the computer nets. Somewhere, in the swirling depths of GEnie, or across the invisible web of an Ethernet, a critical connection was made. And then the inevitable cross talk began.

Bill learned of this almost by accident, discussing with a travel agent the flights to Buenos Aires. Since then I have followed it systematically.

We are not the only people heading for South Georgia Island. I know of at least three other groups, and I will bet that there are more.

Half the MIT Artificial Intelligence lab seems to be flying south. So is a substantial fraction of the Stanford Computer Science Department, with additions from Lawrence Berkeley and Lawrence Livermore. And from southern California, predictably, comes an active group centered on Los Angeles. Niven, Pournelle, Forward, Benford, and Brin cannot be reached. A number of JPL staff members are mysteriously missing. Certain other scientists and writers from all over the country do not return telephone calls.

What are they all doing? It is not difficult to guess. We are talking about individuals with endless curiosity and lots of disposable income. Knowing their style, I would not be surprised if the *Queen Mary* were refurbished in her home at Long Beach and headed south.

Except that they, like everyone else, will be in a hurry, and go by air. No one wants to miss the party. These are the people, remember, who did not hesitate to fly to Pasadena for the *Voyager* close flybys of the outer planets, or to Hawaii and Mexico to see a total solar eclipse. Can you imagine them missing a chance to be in on the discovery of the century, of any century? Not only to *observe* it, but maybe to become part of the discovery process itself. They will converge on South Georgia in their dozens—their scores—their hundreds, with their powerful laptop computers and GPS terminals and their private planes and advanced sensing equipment.

Logic must tell them, as it tells me, that we will find absolutely nothing. Luke and Louisa Derwent are a century dead, deep beneath the icy waters of the Drake Passage. With them, if the machine ever existed, lie the rusting remnants of Louisa's Analytical Engine. The Heteromorphs, if they were ever on South Georgia Island, are long gone.

I know all that. So does Bill. But win or lose, Bill and I are going. So are all the others.

And win or lose, I know one other thing. After we, and our converging, energetic, curious, ingenious, sympathetic horde, are finished, South Georgia will never be the same.

This is for Garry Tee—who is a professor of computer science at the University of Auckland;

—who is a mathematician, computer specialist, and historian of science;

—who discovered parts of Babbage's Difference Machine in Dunedin, New Zealand;

—who programmed the DEUCE computer in the late 1950s, and has been a colleague and friend since that time;

—who is no more Bill Rigley than I am the narrator of this story.

Rhysling Award Winners

William J. Daciuk
Jane Yolen

The Rhysling Awards, named after the Blind Singer of the Spaceways featured in Robert A. Heinlein's "The Green Hills of Earth," are given each year by the members of the Science Fiction Poetry Association in two categories, Best Long Poem and Best Short Poem. Poets honored in the past with these awards include some of science fiction's most distinguished names: Gene Wolfe, Michael Bishop, Thomas M. Disch, Ursula K. Le Guin, Joe Haldeman, Lucius Shepard, John M. Ford, and Suzette Haden Elgin (who founded the Science Fiction Poetry Association in 1978) have all won the Rhysling Award.

This year's Rhysling Award for Best Long Poem went to William J. Daciuk. Until recently, he was the associate editor of *Star°Line*, the bimonthly newsletter and poetry showcase of the Science Fiction Poetry Association. He works in the field of environmental litigation, and spends much of his time advising emerging poets. His latest project is editing and producing *From a Safe Place: Poems and Commentary About Adoption*, an "ongoing anthology—how many different ways can you alter the size and content of a published anthology and still have it be essentially the same body of work? Next year it'll be twice as big!"

About his poem "To Be from Earth," he writes:

" 'To Be from Earth'—what to say about it? It's terribly Eastern in outlook, but then again so am I. I wrote it just before Christmas. It's a celebration—not of that holiday, but just in general. We as a race don't celebrate enough, and then we wonder why we're unhappy. Gestures, moments, and rememberings—these are what make up the very texture of our lives. Not the mountaintop experiences. But the mindfulness of the everyday instead. This, to me, is much more important. How could we ever, when or if someday we are asked, convey that to another, totally alien race if we don't understand it ourselves yet? I could just picture them going away in disappointment, shaking their heads over us, over what we are wasting! I hope it doesn't turn out this way, when that day comes . . ."

The Rhysling Award for Best Short Poem was won by Jane Yolen, a past president of SFWA, a frequent Nebula Award finalist, and a distinguished fantasy writer and editor. She has her own imprint, Jane Yolen Books, at Harcourt Brace & Company, for which she edits children's books; she has also been honored with the World Fantasy Award. Among her many novels are *White Jenna, Cards of Grief, The Devil's Arithmetic, Briar Rose,* and *Sister Light, Sister Dark.*

About her poem "Will," she writes:

"My father was a difficult, charming man who needed all the applause and attention in the family. His name was Will Yolen, 'not William,' he insisted. The day after his funeral I was talking to his younger brother, marveling how—when I opened my father's safety deposit box—I'd discovered his naturalization papers. They were in the name of William Yolen. 'And he'd signed them as *William,*' I said.

" 'His name wasn't William or Will,' my uncle told me. 'In the old country it was Velvul—Wolf!'

"I was forty-five years old and just learning who my father was.

"But of course the poem is about more than his name. It's just that name and nature, for the first time, came together in what was—for me—a powerful combination. Thus was 'Will,' which is part shapeshifter poem, part fairytale poem, and all father-daughter poem, born."

TO BE FROM EARTH
William J. Daciuk

(From *The Journeys of the Night-children,* leaves XXIV–XXX, translated into the modern tongue by the scholars)

. . . and after many, many cycles of trying to reach out to the running, frightened creatures who lived so wastefully and unaware amid the blessings of that incredible blue treasure of a world, our missioners gathered themselves back into the great ship, and for one last time soared silently in long, looping arcs above the land, a final angry world-grazing flight born of bitterness, even of a not-unworthy jealousy.

And in one last gesture, they settled the great silver craft, idling quietly, in the wildest of that world's high places, in winds of cold, dry air, thin and sharp as fangs. There, in the rocks and the ice, they found the last of the great snow leopards, who looked back at them

with the level eyes of a Watcher. On a whim, they granted her the
gifts they had reserved for the others, not only that of True Speech,
but also of Synthesis, and even Understanding.

And then they gathered around her, and sat right there on the
snow, drawing their thin knees up to their chests, sheltering in the
leeward curve of the still-warm acceleration hull.

And knowing what was wanted of her, the snow cat sat down
as calmly as she could in their midst, and she wrapped her grand
dappled tail once about, so ladylike, so Earth-like, she took the hunter's bite from her amber gaze, remembering that she too had once
been a mother, and finding her new speech, she told them what she
once told her long-ago cubs. . . .

To be from Earth means

that you live in a one-day world
where the darkness divides the light, and somehow
you must find that a blessing.

To be from Earth means
that you will walk
wherever you want to go,
even if the ice is sharp and it clings
to your pads, and it burns too cold on your tongue
to even think of licking it off,
and you know that your whole life long
no matter how fast you can go,
you will measure the times of all your days and paces
in the speed of that cold slow walk.

To be from Earth means
that even if you do not believe,
even if you rage and howl and bare your claws,
still you will one day, every day, go down
as far as you can
that long tunnel of prayer
until its adamant walls will narrow and press in against you,
and you know you are trapped and caught,
and yet you go back there for every tomorrow.

Above all,
to be from Earth means to know
that one day you must leave.
So you find your comfort in the wind,
you lose your anger in the hunt, you take your pain
right there in your arms
and you fold it
as many times as you can until
it becomes as light and meaningless as the north wind,
until you can balance it
like a feather on your paws,
and your friend, your wind, blows it away
and makes all your goodbyes for you.

And in this there is madness,
but also much wisdom, the best of which says
that the moment is worth it.

And tired by the burden she had had to bear, the weight of sudden understanding, the sights and smells of that company so alien to her, the long and hard life in the mountains so soon to come to an end, her strength began to fail her, the great eyes closed, her head drooped and fell on her paws.

They wrapped a vapor of blue power around her, enough to sustain and comfort until she would wake. With a gesture they lifted their gifts from her; they carried her to the shelter of an outcrop of the hard blue rock that had defined her life in these hills. There they laid her down, and smoothed out her fur with their cold bare hands.

They returned here to the homeworld, on a pillar of fire forged from the quantum weaving among the thin keening spaces that separate the days of the weeks and the seasons of the years.

A good crew they were, but none ever voyaged again, strange to say. To a one, they retired to the brown wastelands below the Dry Ranges. Some say they practiced strange arts there, but the Father tells us No, they simply wanted to think by themselves, a skill our people had not yet developed.

In time, the great hives that had nurtured our race through its long and hard birth broke up, we abandoned the missioning voyages of our earlier cycles, we turned inward for many generations. . . .

WILL
Jane Yolen

The past will not lie buried.
Little bones and teeth
harrowed from grave's soil,
tell different tales.
My father's bank box told me,
in a paper signed by his own hand,
the name quite clearly: *William.*
All the years he denied it,
that name, that place of birth,
that compound near Kiev,
and I so eager for the variants
with which he lived his life.
In the middle of my listening,
death,
that old interrupter,
with the unkindness of all coroners,
revealed his third name to me.
Not William, not Will, but Wolf.
Wolf.
And so at last I know the story,
my old wolf, white against the Russian Snows,
the cracking of his bones,
the stretching sinews,
the coarse hair growing boldly
on the belly, below the eye.
Why grandfather, my children cry,
what great teeth you have,
before he devours them
as he devoured me,
all of me, bones and blood,
all of my life.

DEATH ON THE NILE

Connie Willis

Connie Willis is the only writer ever to have won Nebula Awards in all four categories of fiction. She has in addition won five Hugo Awards, including one for her novel *Doomsday Book*, which was also honored with the Nebula Award and the Locus Award, and one for this story. Her other honors include the John W. Campbell Memorial Award for her first novel, *Lincoln's Dreams*. *Impossible Things*, a recent collection of her short fiction, and *Uncharted Territory*, a new novella, display this compulsively readable writer at her best.

Of her Nebula Award nominee "Death on the Nile," she writes:

"Stories of wonder often have their beginnings in noticing some magic everyone else has missed, in making some connection no one else has seen, or in illuminating some ordinary thing with skill and style so that it seems extraordinary.

"I don't claim any of that for 'Death on the Nile.' It is, after all, about Egypt, that place of 'wonders more in number than those of any other land,' as Herodotus said, and I never met anyone who wasn't immediately drawn to (and troubled by) its magic and mystery. Even Napoleon's army, arriving at Luxor, 'at the site of its scattered ruins, halted of itself, and by one spontaneous impulse, grounded its arms.' How could they not be awed by its wonders— its pyramids and sphinxes and pharoahs? Its curses and treasures and kings?

"I can't even claim credit for the connections. They are all right there in plain sight: the torchlit tombs and the tarry linen bandages, the jackals and snakes and silence. And the stone steps, drifted with sand, leading down and down. And down."

CHAPTER ONE:
PREPARING FOR YOUR TRIP—
WHAT TO TAKE

" 'To the ancient Egyptians,' " Zoe reads, " 'Death was a separate country to the west—' " The plane lurches. " '—the west to which the deceased person journeyed.' "

We are on the plane to Egypt. The flight is so rough the flight attendants have strapped themselves into the nearest empty seats, looking scared, and the rest of us have subsided into a nervous window-watching silence. Except Zoe, across the aisle, who is reading aloud from a travel guide.

This one is Somebody or Other's *Egypt Made Easy.* In the seat pocket in front of her are Fodor's *Cairo* and Cooke's *Touring Guide to Egypt's Antiquities,* and there are half a dozen others in her luggage. Not to mention Frommer's *Greece on $35 a Day* and the Savvy Traveler's *Guide to Austria* and the three or four hundred other guidebooks she's already read out loud to us on this trip. I toy briefly with the idea that it's their combined weight that's causing the plane to yaw and careen and will shortly send us plummeting to our deaths.

" 'Food, furniture, and weapons were placed in the tomb,' " Zoe reads, " 'as provi—' " The plane pitches sideways. " '—sions for the journey.' "

The plane lurches again, so violently Zoe nearly drops the book, but she doesn't miss a beat. " 'When King Tutankhamun's tomb was opened,' " she reads, " 'it contained trunks full of clothing, jars of wine, a golden boat, and a pair of sandals for walking in the sands of the afterworld.' "

My husband Neil leans over me to look out the window, but there is nothing to see. The sky is clear and cloudless, and below us there aren't even any waves on the water.

" 'In the afterworld the deceased was judged by Anubis, a god with the head of a jackal,' " Zoe reads, " 'and his soul was weighed on a pair of golden scales.' "

I am the only one listening to her. Lissa, on the aisle, is whispering to Neil, her hand almost touching his on the armrest. Across the aisle, next to Zoe and *Egypt Made Easy,* Zoe's husband is asleep and Lissa's husband is staring out the other window and trying to keep his drink from spilling.

"Are you doing all right?" Neil asks Lissa solicitously.

"It'll be exciting going with two other couples," Neil said when he came up with the idea of our all going to Europe together. "Lissa and her husband are lots of fun, and Zoe knows everything. It'll be like having our own tour guide."

It is. Zoe herds us from country to country, reciting historical facts and exchange rates. In the Louvre, a French tourist asked her where the Mona Lisa was. She was thrilled. "He thought we were a tour group!" she said. "Imagine that!"

Imagine that.

" 'Before being judged, the deceased recited his confession,' " Zoe reads, " 'a list of sins he had not committed, such as, I have not snared the birds of the gods, I have not told lies, I have not committed adultery.' "

Neil pats Lissa's hand and leans over to me. "Can you trade places with Lissa?" Neil whispers to me.

I already have, I think. "We're not supposed to," I say, pointing at the lights above the seats. "The seat-belt sign is on."

He looks at her anxiously. "She's feeling nauseated."

So am I, I want to say, but I am afraid that's what this trip is all about, to get me to say something. "Okay," I say, and unbuckle my seat belt and change places with her. While she is crawling over Neil, the plane pitches again, and she half-falls into his arms. He steadies her. Their eyes lock.

" 'I have not taken another's belongings,' " Zoe reads. " 'I have not murdered another.' "

I can't take any more of this. I reach for my bag, which is still under the window seat, and pull out my paperback of Agatha Christie's *Death on the Nile*. I bought it in Athens.

"About like death anywhere," Zoe's husband said when I got back to our hotel in Athens with it.

"What?" I said.

"Your book," he said, pointing at the paperback and smiling as if he'd made a joke. "The title. I'd imagine death on the Nile is the same as death anywhere."

"Which is what?" I asked.

"The Egyptians believed death was very similar to life," Zoe cut in. She had bought *Egypt Made Easy* at the same bookstore. "To the ancient Egyptians the afterworld was a place much like the world they inhabited. It was presided over by Anubis, who judged the deceased and determined their fates. Our concepts of heaven and hell and of the Day of Judgment are nothing more than modern refinements of Egyptian ideas," she said, and began reading out loud from *Egypt Made Easy*, which pretty much put an end to our conversation, and I still don't know what Zoe's husband thought death would be like, on the Nile or elsewhere.

I open *Death on the Nile* and try to read, thinking maybe Hercule Poirot knows, but the flight is too bumpy. I feel almost immediately queasy, and after half a page and three more lurches I put it in the seat pocket, close my eyes, and toy with the idea of murdering another. It's a perfect Agatha Christie setting. She always has a few people in a country house or on an island. In *Death on the Nile* they were on a Nile steamer, but the plane is even better. The only other people on it are the flight attendants and a Japanese tour group who apparently do not speak English or they would be clustered around Zoe, asking directions to the Sphinx.

The turbulence lessens a little, and I open my eyes and reach for my book again. Lissa has it.

She's holding it open, but she isn't reading it. She is watching me, waiting for me to notice, waiting for me to say something. Neil looks nervous.

"You were done with this, weren't you?" she says, smiling. "You weren't reading it."

Everyone has a motive for murder in an Agatha Christie. And Lissa's husband has been drinking steadily since Paris, and Zoe's husband never gets to finish a sentence. The police might think he had snapped suddenly. Or that it was Zoe he had tried to kill and shot Lissa by mistake. And there is no Hercule Poirot on board to tell them who really committed the murder, to solve the mystery and explain all the strange happenings.

The plane pitches suddenly, so hard Zoe drops her guidebook, and we plunge a good five thousand feet before it recovers. The guidebook has slid forward several rows, and Zoe tries to reach for it with her foot, fails, and looks up at the seat-belt sign as if she expects it to go off so she can get out of her seat to retrieve it.

Not after that drop, I think, but the seat-belt sign pings almost immediately and goes off.

Lissa's husband instantly calls for the flight attendant and demands another drink, but they have already gone scurrying back to the rear of the plane, still looking pale and scared, as if they expected the turbulence to start up again before they make it. Zoe's husband wakes up at the noise and then goes back to sleep. Zoe retrieves

Egypt Made Easy from the floor, reads a few more riveting facts from it, then puts it facedown on the seat and goes back to the rear of the plane.

I lean across Neil and look out the window, wondering what's happened, but I can't see anything. We are flying through a flat whiteness.

Lissa is rubbing her head. "I cracked my head on the window," she says to Neil. "Is it bleeding?"

He leans over her solicitously to see.

I unsnap my seat belt and start to the back of the plane, but both bathrooms are occupied, and Zoe is perched on the arm of an aisle seat, enlightening the Japanese tour group. "The currency is in Egyptian pounds," she says. "There are one hundred piasters in a pound." I sit back down.

Neil is gently massaging Lissa's temple. "Is that better?" he asks.

I reach across the aisle for Zoe's guidebook. "Must-See Attractions," the chapter is headed, and the first one on the list is the Pyramids.

"Giza, Pyramids of. West bank of Nile, 9 mi. (15 km.) SW of Cairo. Accessible by taxi, bus, rental car. Admission L.E.3. Comments: You can't skip the Pyramids, but be prepared to be disappointed. They don't look at all like you expect, the traffic's terrible, and the view's completely ruined by the hordes of tourists, refreshment stands, and souvenir vendors. Open daily."

I wonder how Zoe stands this stuff. I turn the page to Attraction Number Two. It's King Tut's tomb, and whoever wrote the guidebook wasn't thrilled with it either. "Tutankhamun, Tomb of. Valley of the Kings, Luxor, 400 mi. (668 km.) south of Cairo. Three unimpressive rooms. Inferior wall paintings."

There is a map showing a long, straight corridor (labeled Corridor) and the three unimpressive rooms opening one onto the other in a row—Anteroom, Burial Chamber, Hall of Judgment.

I close the book and put it back on Zoe's seat. Zoe's husband is still asleep. Lissa's is peering back over his seat. "Where'd the flight attendants go?" he asks. "I want another drink."

"Are you sure it's not bleeding? I can feel a bump," Lissa says to Neil, rubbing her head. "Do you think I have a concussion?"

"No," Neil says, turning her face toward his. "Your pupils aren't dilated." He gazes deeply into her eyes.

"Stewardess!" Lissa's husband shouts. "What do you have to do to get a drink around here?"

Zoe comes back, elated. "They thought I was a professional guide," she says, sitting down and fastening her seat belt. "They asked if they could join our tour." She opens the guidebook. " 'The afterworld was full of monsters and demigods in the form of crocodiles and baboons and snakes. These monsters could destroy the deceased before he reached the Hall of Judgment.' "

Neil touches my hand. "Do you have any aspirin?" he asks. "Lissa's head hurts."

I fish in my bag for it, and Neil gets up and goes back to get her a glass of water.

"Neil's so thoughtful," Lissa says, watching me, her eyes bright.

" 'To protect against these monsters and demigods, the deceased was given *The Book of the Dead*,' " Zoe reads. " 'More properly translated as *The Book of What Is in the Afterworld*, *The Book of the Dead* was a collection of directions for the journey and magic spells to protect the deceased.' "

I think about how I am going to get through the rest of the trip without magic spells to protect me. Six days in Egypt and then three in Israel, and there is still the trip home on a plane like this and nothing to do for fifteen hours but watch Lissa and Neil and listen to Zoe.

I consider cheerier possibilities. "What if we're not going to Cairo?" I say. "What if we're dead?"

Zoe looks up from her guidebook, irritated.

"There've been a lot of terrorist bombings lately, and this is the Middle East," I go on. "What if that last air pocket was really a bomb? What if it blew us apart, and right now we're drifting down over the Aegean Sea in little pieces?"

"Mediterranean," Zoe says. "We've already flown over Crete."

"How do you know that?" I ask. "Look out the window." I point out Lissa's window at the white flatness beyond. "You can't see the water. We could be anywhere. Or nowhere."

Neil comes back with the water. He hands it and my aspirin to Lissa.

"They check the planes for bombs, don't they?" Lissa asks him. "Don't they use metal detectors and things?"

"I saw this movie once," I say, "where the people were all dead, only they didn't know it. They were on a ship, and they thought they were going to America. There was so much fog they couldn't see the water."

Lissa looks anxiously out the window.

"It looked just like a real ship, but little by little they began to notice little things that weren't quite right. There were hardly any people on board, and no crew at all."

"Stewardess!" Lissa's husband calls, leaning over Zoe into the aisle. "I need another ouzo."

His shouting wakes Zoe's husband up. He blinks at Zoe, confused that she is not reading from her guidebook. "What's going on?" he asks.

"We're all dead," I say. "We were killed by Arab terrorists. We think we're going to Cairo, but we're really going to heaven. Or hell."

Lissa, looking out the window, says, "There's so much fog I can't see the wing." She looks frightenedly at Neil. "What if something's happened to the wing?"

"We're just going through a cloud," Neil says. "We're probably beginning our descent into Cairo."

"The sky was perfectly clear," I say, "and then all of a sudden we were in the fog. The people on the ship noticed the fog, too. They noticed there weren't any running lights. And they couldn't find the crew." I smile at Lissa. "Have you noticed how the turbulence stopped all of a sudden? Right after we hit that air pocket. And why—"

A flight attendant comes out of the cockpit and down the aisle to us, carrying a drink. Everyone looks relieved, and Zoe opens her guidebook and begins thumbing through it, looking for fascinating facts.

"Did someone here want an ouzo?" the flight attendant asks.

"Here," Lissa's husband says, reaching for it.

"How long before we get to Cairo?" I say.

She starts toward the back of the plane without answering. I unbuckle my seat belt and follow her. "When will we get to Cairo?" I ask her.

She turns, smiling, but she is still pale and scared looking. "Did you want another drink, ma'am? Ouzo? Coffee?"

"Why did the turbulence stop?" I say. "How long till we get to Cairo?"

"You need to take your seat," she says, pointing to the seat-belt sign. "We're beginning our descent. We'll be at our destination in another twenty minutes." She bends over the Japanese tour group and tells them to bring their seat backs to an upright position.

"What destination? Our descent to where? We aren't beginning any descent. The seat-belt sign is still off," I say, and it bings on.

I go back to my seat. Zoe's husband is already asleep again. Zoe is reading out loud from *Egypt Made Easy*. " 'The visitor should take precautions before traveling in Egypt. A map is essential, and a flashlight is needed for many of the sites.' "

Lissa has gotten her bag out from under the seat. She puts my *Death on the Nile* in it and gets out her sunglasses. I look past her and out the window at the white flatness where the wing should be. We should be able to see the lights on the wing even in the fog. That's what they're there for, so you can see the plane in the fog. The people on the ship didn't realize they were dead at first. It was only when they started noticing little things that weren't quite right that they began to wonder.

" 'A guide is recommended,' " Zoe reads.

I have meant to frighten Lissa, but I have only managed to frighten myself. We are beginning our descent, that's all, I tell myself, and flying through a cloud. And that must be right.

Because here we are in Cairo.

CHAPTER TWO:
ARRIVING AT THE AIRPORT

"So this is Cairo?" Zoe's husband says, looking around. The plane has stopped at the end of the runway and deplaned us onto the asphalt by means of a metal stairway.

The terminal is off to the east, a low building with palm trees around it, and the Japanese tour group sets off toward it immediately, shouldering their carry-on bags and camera cases.

We do not have any carry-ons. Since we always have to wait at the baggage claim for Zoe's guidebooks anyway, we check our carry-ons, too. Every time we do it, I am convinced they will go to Tokyo or disappear altogether, but now I'm glad we don't have to lug them all the way to the terminal. It looks like it is miles away, and the Japanese are already slowing.

Zoe is reading the guidebook. The rest of us stand around her, looking impatient. Lissa has caught the heel of her sandal in one of the metal steps coming down and is leaning against Neil.

"Did you twist it?" Neil asks anxiously.

The flight attendants clatter down the steps with their navy blue overnight cases. They still look nervous. At the bottom of the stairs they unfold wheeled metal carriers and strap the overnight cases to them and set off for the terminal. After a few steps they stop, and one of them takes off her jacket and drapes it over the wheeled carrier, and they start off again, walking rapidly in their high heels.

It is not as hot as I expected, even though the distant terminal shimmers in the heated air rising from the asphalt. There is no sign of the clouds we flew through, just a thin white haze that disperses the sun's light into an even glare. We are all squinting. Lissa lets go of Neil's arm for a second to get her sunglasses out of her bag.

"What do they drink around here?" Lissa's husband asks, squinting over Zoe's shoulder at the guidebook. "I want a drink."

"The local drink is zibib," Zoe says. "It's like ouzo." She looks up from the guidebook. "I think we should go see the Pyramids."

The professional tour guide strikes again. "Don't you think we'd better take care of first things first?" I say. "Like customs? And picking up our luggage?"

"And finding a drink of . . . what did you call it? Zibab?" Lissa's husband says.

"No," Zoe says. "I think we should do the Pyramids first. It'll take an hour to do the baggage claim and customs, and we can't take our luggage with us to the Pyramids. We'll have to go to the hotel, and by that time everyone will be out there. I think we should go right now." She gestures at the terminal. "We can run out and see them and be back before the Japanese tour group's even through customs."

She turns and starts walking in the opposite direction from the terminal, and the others straggle obediently after her.

I look back at the terminal. The flight attendants have passed the Japanese tour group and are nearly to the palm trees.

"You're going the wrong way," I say to Zoe. "We've got to go to the terminal to get a taxi."

Zoe stops. "A taxi?" she says. "What for? They aren't far. We can walk it in fifteen minutes."

"Fifteen minutes?" I say. "Giza's nine miles west of Cairo. You have to cross the Nile to get there."

"Don't be silly," she says, "they're right there," and points in the direction she was walking, and there, beyond the asphalt in an expanse of sand, so close they do not shimmer at all, are the Pyramids.

CHAPTER THREE:
GETTING AROUND

It takes us longer than fifteen minutes. The Pyramids are farther away than they look, and the sand is deep and hard to walk in. We have to stop every few feet so Lissa can empty out her sandals, leaning against Neil.

"We should have taken a taxi," Zoe's husband says, but there are no roads, and no sign of the refreshment stands and souvenir vendors the guidebook complained about, only the unbroken expanse of deep sand and the white, even sky, and in the distance the three yellow pyramids, standing in a row.

" 'The tallest of the three is the Pyramid of Cheops, built in 2690 B.C.,' " Zoe says, reading as she walks. " 'It took thirty years to complete.' "

"You have to take a taxi to get to the Pyramids," I say. "There's a lot of traffic."

" 'It was built on the west bank of the Nile, which the ancient Egyptians believed was the land of the dead.' "

There is a flicker of movement ahead, between the pyramids, and I stop and shade my eyes against the glare to look at it, hoping it is a souvenir vendor, but I can't see anything.

We start walking again.

It flickers again, and this time I catch sight of it running, hunched over, its hands nearly touching the ground. It disappears behind the middle pyramid.

"I saw something," I say, catching up to Zoe. "Some kind of animal. It looked like a baboon."

Zoe leafs through the guidebook and then says, "Monkeys. They're found frequently near Giza. They beg for food from the tourists."

"There aren't any tourists," I say.

"I know," Zoe says happily. "I told you we'd avoid the rush."

"You have to go through customs, even in Egypt," I say. "You can't just leave the airport."

"'The pyramid on the left is Kheophren,'" Zoe says, "'built in 2650 B.C.'"

"In the movie, they wouldn't believe they were dead even when somebody told them," I say. "Giza is *nine* miles from Cairo."

"What are you talking about?" Neil says. Lissa has stopped again and is leaning against him, standing on one foot and shaking her sandal out. "That mystery of Lissa's, *Death on the Nile?*"

"This was a *movie*," I say. "They were on this ship, and they were all dead."

"We saw that movie, didn't we, Zoe?" Zoe's husband says. "Mia Farrow was in it, and Bette Davis. And the detective guy, what was his name—"

"Hercule Poirot," Zoe says. "Played by Peter Ustinov. 'The Pyramids are open daily from 8 A.M. to 5 P.M. Evenings there is a *Son et Lumière* show with colored floodlights and a narration in English and Japanese.'"

"There were all sorts of clues," I say, "but they just ignored them."

"I don't like Agatha Christie," Lissa says. "Murder and trying to find out who killed who. I'm never able to figure out what's going on. All those people on the train together."

"You're thinking of *Murder on the Orient Express*," Neil says. "I saw that."

"Is that the one where they got killed off one by one?" Lissa's husband says.

"I saw that one," Zoe's husband says. "They got what they deserved, as far as I'm concerned, going off on their own like that when they knew they should keep together."

"Giza is nine miles west of Cairo," I say. "You have to take a taxi to get there. There is all this traffic."

"Peter Ustinov was in that one, too, wasn't he?" Neil says. "The one with the train?"

"No," Zoe's husband says. "It was the other one. What's his name—"

"Albert Finney," Zoe says.

CHAPTER FOUR:
PLACES OF INTEREST

The Pyramids are closed. Fifty yards (45.7 m.) from the base of Cheops there is a chain barring our way. A metal sign hangs from it that says "Closed" in English and Japanese.

"Prepare to be disappointed," I say.

"I thought you said they were open daily," Lissa says, knocking sand out of her sandals.

"It must be a holiday," Zoe says, leafing through her guidebook. "Here it is. 'Egyptian holidays.'" She begins reading. "'Antiquities sites are closed during Ramadan, the Muslim month of fasting in March. On Fridays the sites are closed from eleven to one P.M.'"

It is not March, or Friday, and even if it were, it is after one P.M. The shadow of Cheops stretches well past where we stand. I look up, trying to see the sun where it must be behind the pyramid, and catch a flicker of movement, high up. It is too large to be a monkey.

"Well, what do we do now?" Zoe's husband says.

"We could go see the Sphinx," Zoe muses, looking through the guidebook. "Or we could wait for the *Son et Lumière* show."

"No," I say, thinking of being out here in the dark.

"How do you know that won't be closed, too?" Lissa asks.

Zoe consults the book. "There are two shows daily, seven-thirty and nine P.M."

"That's what you said about the Pyramids," Lissa says. "*I* think we should go back to the airport and get our luggage. I want to get my other shoes."

"*I* think we should go back to the hotel," Lissa's husband says, "and have a long, cool drink."

"We'll go to Tutankhamun's tomb," Zoe says. "'It's open every day, including holidays.'" She looks up expectantly.

"King Tut's tomb?" I say. "In the Valley of the Kings?"

"Yes," she says, and starts to read. "'It was found intact in 1922 by Howard Carter. It contained—'"

All the belongings necessary for the deceased's journey to the afterworld, I think. Sandals and clothes and *Egypt Made Easy.*

"I'd rather have a drink," Lissa's husband says.

"And a nap," Zoe's husband says. "You go on, and we'll meet you at the hotel."

"I don't think you should go off on your own," I say. "I think we should keep together."

"It will be crowded if we wait," Zoe says. "I'm going now. Are you coming, Lissa?"

Lissa looks appealingly up at Neil. "I don't think I'd better walk that far. My ankle's starting to hurt again."

Neil looks helplessly at Zoe. "I guess we'd better pass."

"What about you?" Zoe's husband says to me. "Are you going with Zoe or do you want to come with us?"

"In Athens, you said death was the same everywhere," I say to him, "and I said, 'Which is what?' and then Zoe interrupted us and you never did answer me. What were you going to say?"

"I've forgotten," he says, looking at Zoe as if he hopes she will interrupt us again, but she is intent on the guidebook.

"You said, 'Death is the same everywhere,'" I persist, "and I said, 'Which is what?' What did you think death would be like?"

"I don't know . . . unexpected, I guess. And probably pretty damn unpleasant." He laughs nervously. "If we're going to the hotel, we'd better get started. Who else is coming?"

I toy with the idea of going with them, of sitting safely in the hotel bar with ceiling fans and palms, drinking zibib while we wait. That's what the people on the ship did. And in spite of Lissa, I want to stay with Neil.

I look at the expanse of sand back toward the east. There is no sign of Cairo from here, or of the terminal, and far off there is a flicker of movement, like something running.

I shake my head. "I want to see King Tut's tomb." I go over to Neil. "I think we should go with Zoe," I say, and put my hand on his arm. "After all, she's our guide."

Neil looks helplessly at Lissa and then back at me. "I don't know. . . ."

"The three of you can go back to the hotel," I say to Lissa, gesturing to include the other men, "and Zoe and Neil and I can meet you there after we've been to the tomb."

Neil moves away from Lissa. "Why can't you and Zoe just go?" he whispers at me.

"I think we should keep together," I say. "It would be so easy to get separated."

"How come you're so stuck on going with Zoe anyway?" Neil says. "I thought you said you hated being led around by the nose all the time."

I want to say, Because she has the book, but Lissa has come over and is watching us, her eyes bright behind her sunglasses. "I've always wanted to see the inside of a tomb," I say.

"King Tut?" Lissa says. "Is that the one with the treasure, the necklaces and the gold coffin and stuff?" She puts her hand on Neil's arm. "I've always wanted to see that."

"Okay," Neil says, relieved. "I guess we'll go with you, Zoe."

Zoe looks expectantly at her husband.

"Not me," he says. "We'll meet you in the bar."

"We'll order drinks for you," Lissa's husband says. He waves good-bye, and they set off as if they know where they are going, even though Zoe hasn't told them the name of the hotel.

" 'The Valley of the Kings is located in the hills west of Luxor,' " Zoe says, and starts off across the sand the way she did at the airport. We follow her.

I wait until Lissa gets a shoeful of sand and she and Neil fall behind while she empties it.

"Zoe," I say quietly. "There's something wrong."

"Umm," she says, looking up something in the guidebook's index.

"The Valley of the Kings is four hundred miles south of Cairo," I say. "You can't walk there from the Pyramids."

She finds the page. "Of course not. We have to take a boat."

She points, and I see we have reached a stand of reeds, and beyond it is the Nile.

Nosing out from the rushes is a boat, and I am afraid it will be made of gold, but it is only one of the Nile cruisers. And I am so relieved that the Valley of the Kings is not within walking distance that I do not recognize the boat until we have climbed on board and are standing on the canopied deck next to the wooden paddle wheel. It is the steamer from *Death on the Nile*.

CHAPTER FIVE:
CRUISES, DAY TRIPS, AND
GUIDED TOURS

Lissa is sick on the boat. Neil offers to take her below, and I expect her to say yes, but she shakes her head. "My ankle hurts," she says, and sinks down in one of the deck chairs. Neil kneels by her feet and examines a bruise no bigger than a piaster.

"Is it swollen?" she asks anxiously. There is no sign of swelling, but Neil eases her sandal off and takes her foot tenderly, caressingly, in both hands. Lissa closes her eyes and leans back against the deck chair, sighing.

I toy with the idea that Lissa's husband couldn't take any more of this either, and that he murdered us all and then killed himself.

"Here we are on a ship," I say, "like the dead people in that movie."

"It's not a ship, it's a steamboat," Zoe says. " 'The Nile steamer is the most pleasant way to travel in Egypt and one of the least expensive. Costs range from $180 to $360 per person for a four-day cruise.' "

Or maybe it was Zoe's husband, finally determined to shut Zoe up so he could finish a conversation, and then he had to murder the rest of us one after the other to keep from being caught.

"We're all alone on the ship," I say, "just like they were."

"How far is it to the Valley of the Kings?" Lissa asks.

" 'Three-and-a-half miles (5 km.) west of Luxor,' " Zoe says, reading. " 'Luxor is four hundred miles south of Cairo.' "

"If it's that far, I might as well read my book," Lissa says, pushing her sunglasses up on top of her head. "Neil, hand me my bag."

He fishes *Death on the Nile* out of her bag and hands it to her, and she flips through it for a moment, like Zoe looking for exchange rates, and then begins to read.

"The wife did it," I say. "She found out her husband was being unfaithful."

Lissa glares at me. "I already knew that," she says carelessly. "I saw the movie," but after another half page she lays the open book facedown on the empty deck chair next to her.

"I can't read," she says to Neil. "The sun's too bright." She squints up at the sky, which is still hidden by its gauzelike haze.

" 'The Valley of the Kings is the site of the tombs of sixty-four pharoahs,' " Zoe says. " 'Of these, the most famous is Tutankhamun's.' "

I go over to the railing and watch the Pyramids recede, slipping slowly out of sight behind the rushes that line the shore. They look flat, like yellow triangles stuck up in the sand, and I remember how in Paris Zoe's husband wouldn't believe the Mona Lisa was the real thing. "It's a fake," he insisted before Zoe interrupted. "The real one's much larger."

And the guidebook said, Prepare to be disappointed, and the Valley of the Kings is four hundred miles from the Pyramids like it's supposed to be, and Middle Eastern airports are notorious for their lack of security. That's how all those bombs get on planes in the first place, because they don't make people go through customs. I shouldn't watch so many movies.

" 'Among its treasures, Tutankhamun's tomb contained a golden boat, by which the soul would travel to the world of the dead,' " Zoe says.

I lean over the railing and look into the water. It is not muddy, like I thought it would be, but a clear waveless blue, and in its depths the sun is shining brightly.

" 'The boat was carved with passages from *The Book of the Dead*,' " Zoe reads, " 'to protect the deceased from monsters and demigods who might try to destroy him before he reached the Hall of Judgment.' "

There is something in the water. Not a ripple, not even enough of a movement to shudder the image of the sun, but I know there is something there.

" 'Spells were also written on papyruses buried with the body,' " Zoe says.

It is long and dark, like a crocodile. I lean over farther, gripping the rail, trying to see into the transparent water, and catch a glint of scales. It is swimming straight toward the boat.

" 'These spells took the form of commands,' " Zoe reads. " 'Get back, you evil one! Stay away! I adjure you in the name of Anubis and Osiris.' "

The water glitters, hesitating.

" 'Do not come against me,' " Zoe says. " 'My spells protect me. I know the way.' "

The thing in the water turns and swims away. The boat follows it, nosing slowly in toward the shore.

"There it is," Zoe says, pointing past the reeds at a distant row of cliffs. "The Valley of the Kings."

"I suppose this'll be closed, too," Lissa says, letting Neil help her off the boat.

"Tombs are never closed," I say, and look north, across the sand, at the distant Pyramids.

CHAPTER SIX:
ACCOMMODATIONS

The Valley of the Kings is not closed. The tombs stretch along a sandstone cliff, black openings in the yellow rock, and there are no chains across the stone steps that lead down to them. At the south end of the valley a Japanese tour group is going into the last one.

"Why aren't the tombs marked?" Lissa asks. "Which one is King Tut's?" and Zoe leads us to the north end of the valley, where the cliff dwindles into a low wall. Beyond it, across the sand, I can see the Pyramids, sharp against the sky.

Zoe stops at the very edge of a slanting hole dug into the base of the rocks. There are steps leading down into it. "Tutankhamun's tomb was found when a workman accidentally uncovered the top step," she says.

Lissa looks down into the stairwell. All but the top two steps are in shadow, and it is too dark to see the bottom. "Are there snakes?" she asks.

"No," Zoe, who knows everything, says. "Tutankhamun's tomb is the smallest of the pharaohs' tombs in the Valley." She fumbles in her bag for her flashlight. "The tomb consists of three rooms—an antechamber, the burial chamber containing Tutankhamun's coffin, and the Hall of Judgment."

There is a slither of movement in the darkness below us, like a slow uncoiling, and Lissa steps back from the edge. "Which room is the stuff in?"

"Stuff?" Zoe says uncertainly, still fumbling for her flashlight. She opens her guidebook. "Stuff?" she says again, and flips to the back of it, as if she is going to look "stuff" up in the index.

"*Stuff*," Lissa says, and there is an edge of fear in her voice. "All the furniture and vases and stuff they take with them. You said the Egyptians buried their belongings with them."

"King Tut's treasure," Neil says helpfully.

"Oh, the *treasure*," Zoe says, relieved. "The belongings buried with Tutankhamun for his journey into the afterworld. They're not here. They're in Cairo in the museum."

"In Cairo?" Lissa says. "They're in Cairo? Then what are we doing here?"

"We're dead," I say. "Arab terrorists blew up our plane and killed us all."

"I *came* all the way out here because I wanted to see the treasure," Lissa says.

"The coffin is here," Zoe says placatingly, "and there are wall paintings in the antechamber," but Lissa has already led Neil away from the steps, talking earnestly to him.

"The wall paintings depict the stages in the judgment of the soul, the weighing of the soul, the recital of the deceased's confession," Zoe says.

The deceased's confession. I have not taken that which belongs to another. I have not caused any pain. I have not committed adultery.

Lissa and Neil come back, Lissa leaning heavily on Neil's arm. "I think we'll pass on this tomb thing," Neil says apologetically. "We want to get to the museum before it closes. Lissa had her heart set on seeing the treasure."

" 'The Egyptian Museum is open from 9 A.M. to 4 P.M. daily, 9 to 11:15 A.M. and 1:30 to 4 P.M. Fridays,' " Zoe says, reading from the guidebook. " 'Admission is three Egyptian pounds.' "

"It's already four o'clock," I say, looking at my watch. "It will be closed before you get there." I look up.

Neil and Lissa have already started back, not toward the boat but across the sand in the direction of the Pyramids. The light behind the Pyramids is beginning to fade, the sky going from white to gray blue.

"Wait," I say, and run across the sand to catch up with them. "Why don't you wait and we'll all go back together? It won't take us very long to see the tomb. You heard Zoe, there's nothing inside."

They both look at me.

"I think we should stay together," I finish lamely.

Lissa looks up alertly, and I realize she thinks I am talking about divorce, that I have finally said what she has been waiting for.

"I think we should all keep together," I say hastily. "This is Egypt. There are all sorts of dangers, crocodiles and snakes and . . . it won't take us very long to see the tomb. You heard Zoe, there's nothing inside."

"We'd better not," Neil says, looking at me. "Lissa's ankle is starting to swell. I'd better get some ice on it."

I look down at her ankle. Where the bruise was there are two little puncture marks, close together, like a snake bite, and around them the ankle is starting to swell.

"I don't think Lissa's up to the Hall of Judgment," he says, still looking at me.

"You could wait at the top of the steps," I say. "You wouldn't have to go in."

Lissa takes hold of his arm, as if anxious to go, but he hesitates. "Those people on the ship," he says to me. "What happened to them?"

"I was just trying to frighten you," I say. "I'm sure there's a logical explanation. It's too bad Hercule Poirot isn't here—he'd be able to explain everything. The Pyramids were probably closed for some Muslim holiday Zoe didn't know about, and that's why we didn't have to go through customs either, because it was a holiday."

"What happened to the people on the ship?" Neil says again.

"They got judged," I say, "but it wasn't nearly as bad as they'd thought. They were all afraid of what was going to happen, even the clergyman, who hadn't committed any sins, but the judge turned out to be somebody he knew. A bishop. He wore a white suit, and he was very kind, and most of them came out fine."

"Most of them," Neil says.

"Let's go," Lissa says, pulling on his arm.

"The people on the ship," Neil says, ignoring her. "Had any of them committed some horrible sin?"

"My ankle hurts," Lissa says. "Come on."

"I have to go," Neil says, almost reluctantly. "Why don't you come with us?"

I glance at Lissa, expecting her to be looking daggers at Neil, but she is watching me with bright, lidless eyes.

"Yes. Come with us," she says, and waits for my answer.

I lied to Lissa about the ending of *Death on the Nile*. It was the wife they killed. I toy with the idea that they have committed some horrible sin, that I am lying in my hotel room in Athens, my temple black with blood and powder burns. I would be the only one here then, and Lissa and Neil would be demigods disguised to look like them. Or monsters.

"I'd better not," I say, and back away from them.

"Let's go then," Lissa says to Neil, and they start off across the sand. Lissa is limping badly, and before they have gone very far, Neil stops and takes off his shoes.

The sky behind the Pyramids is purple blue, and the Pyramids stand out flat and black against it.

"Come on," Zoe calls from the top of the steps. She is holding the flashlight and looking at the guidebook. "I want to see the Weighing of the Soul."

CHAPTER SEVEN:
OFF THE BEATEN TRACK

Zoe is already halfway down the steps when I get back, shining her flashlight on the door below her. "When the tomb was discovered, the door was plastered over and stamped with the seals bearing the cartouche of Tutankhamun," she says.

"It'll be dark soon," I call down to her. "Maybe we should go back to the hotel with Lissa and Neil." I look back across the desert, but they are already out of sight.

Zoe is gone, too. When I look back down the steps, there is nothing but darkness. "Zoe!" I shout, and run down the sand-drifted steps after her. "Wait!"

The door to the tomb is open, and I can see the light from her flashlight bobbing on rock walls and ceiling far down a narrow corridor.

"Zoe!" I shout, and start after her. The floor is uneven, and I trip and put my hand on the wall to steady myself. "Come back! You have the book!"

The light flashes on a section of carved-out wall, far ahead, and then vanishes, as if she has turned a corner.

"Wait for me!" I shout, and stop because I cannot see my hand in front of my face.

There is no answering light, no answering voice, no sound at all. I stand very still, one hand still on the wall, listening for footsteps, for quiet padding, for the sound of slithering, but I can't hear anything, not even my own heart beating.

"Zoe," I call out, "I'm going to wait for you outside," and turn around, holding onto the wall so I don't get disoriented in the dark, and go back the way I came.

The corridor seems longer than it did coming in, and I toy with the idea that it will go on forever in the dark, or that the door will be locked, the opening plastered over and the ancient seals affixed, but there is a line of light under the door, and it opens easily when I push on it.

I am at the top of a stone staircase leading down into a long wide hall. On either side the hall is lined with stone pillars, and between the pillars I can see that the walls are painted with scenes in sienna and yellow and bright blue.

It must be the anteroom because Zoe said its walls were painted with scenes from the soul's journey into death, and there is Anubis weighing the soul, and, beyond it, a baboon devouring something, and, opposite where I am standing on the stairs, a painting of a boat crossing the blue Nile. It is made of gold, and in it four souls squat in a line, their kohl-outlined eyes looking ahead at the shore. Beside them, in the transparent water, Sebek, the crocodile demigod, swims.

I start down the steps. There is a doorway at the far end of the hall, and if this is the anteroom, then the door must lead to the burial chamber.

Zoe said the tomb consists of only three rooms, and I saw the map myself on the plane, the steps and straight corridor and then the unimpressive rooms leading one into another, anteroom and burial chamber and Hall of Judgment, one after another.

So this is the anteroom, even if it is larger than it was on the map, and Zoe has obviously gone ahead to the burial chamber and is standing by Tutankhamun's coffin, reading aloud from the travel guide. When I come in, she will look up and say, " 'The quartzite sarcophagus is carved with passages from *The Book of the Dead.*' "

I have come halfway down the stairs, and from here I can see the painting of the weighing of the soul. Anubis, with his jackal's head, standing on one side of the yellow scales, and the deceased on the other, reading his confession from a papyrus.

I go down two more steps, till I am even with the scales, and sit down.

Surely Zoe won't be long—there's nothing in the burial chamber except the coffin—and even if she has gone on ahead to the Hall of Judgment, she'll have to come back this way. There's only one entrance to the tomb. And she can't get turned around because she has a flashlight. And the book. I clasp my hands around my knees and wait.

I think about the people on the ship, waiting for judgment. "It wasn't as bad as they thought," I'd told Neil, but now, sitting here on the steps, I remember that the bishop, smiling kindly in his white suit, gave them sentences appropriate to their sins. One of the women was sentenced to being alone forever.

The deceased in the painting looks frightened, standing by the scale, and I wonder what sentence Anubis will give him, what sins he has committed.

Maybe he has not committed any sins at all, like the clergyman, and is worried over nothing, or maybe he is merely frightened at finding himself in this strange place, alone. Was death what he expected?

"Death is the same everywhere," Zoe's husband said. "Unexpected." And nothing is the way you thought it would be. Look at the Mona Lisa. And Neil. The people on the ship had planned on something else altogether, pearly gates and angels and clouds, all the modern refinements. Prepare to be disappointed.

And what about the Egyptians, packing their clothes and wine and sandals for their trip? Was death, even on the Nile, what they expected? Or was it not the way it had been described in the travel guide at all? Did they keep thinking they were alive, in spite of all the clues?

The deceased clutches his papyrus, and I wonder if he has committed some horrible sin. Adultery. Or murder. I wonder how he died.

The people on the ship were killed by a bomb, like we were. I try to remember the moment it went off—Zoe reading out loud and then the sudden shock of light and decompression, the travel guide blown out of Zoe's hands and Lissa falling through the blue air, but I can't. Maybe it didn't happen on the plane. Maybe the terrorists blew us up in the airport in Athens, while we were checking our luggage.

I toy with the idea that it wasn't a bomb at all, that I murdered Lissa and then killed myself, like in *Death on the Nile*. Maybe I reached into my bag, not for my paperback but for the gun I bought in Athens, and shot Lissa while she was looking out the window. And Neil bent over her, solicitous, concerned, and I raised the gun again, and Zoe's husband tried to wrestle it out of my hand, and the shot went wide and hit the gas tank on the wing.

I am still frightening myself. If I'd murdered Lissa, I would remember it, and even Athens, notorious for its lack of security, wouldn't have let me on board a plane with a gun. And you could hardly commit some horrible crime without remembering it, could you?

The people on the ship didn't remember dying, even when someone told them, but that was because the ship was so much like a real one, the railings and the water and the deck. And because of the bomb. People never remember being blown up. It's the concussion or something, it knocks the memory out of you. But I would surely have remembered murdering someone. Or being murdered.

I sit on the steps a long time, watching for the splash of Zoe's flashlight in the doorway. Outside it will be dark, time for the *Son et Lumière* show at the pyramids.

It seems darker in here, too. I have to squint to see Anubis and the yellow scales and the deceased awaiting judgment. The papyrus he is holding is covered with long, bordered columns of hieroglyphics and I hope they are magic spells to protect him and not a list of all the sins he has committed.

I have not murdered another, I think. I have not committed adultery. But there are other sins.

It will be dark soon, and I do not have a flashlight. I stand up. "Zoe!" I call, and go down the stairs and between the pillars. They are carved with animals—cobras and baboons and crocodiles.

"It's getting dark," I call, and my voice echoes hollowly among the pillars. "They'll be wondering what happened to us."

The last pair of pillars is carved with a bird, its sandstone wings outstretched. A bird of the gods. Or a plane.

"Zoe?" I say, and stoop to go through the low door. "Are you in here?"

CHAPTER EIGHT:
SPECIAL EVENTS

Zoe isn't in the burial chamber. It is much smaller than the anteroom, and there are no paintings on the rough walls or above the door that leads to the Hall of Judgment. The ceiling is scarcely higher than the door, and I have to hunch down to keep from scraping my head against it.

It is darker in here than in the anteroom, but even in the dimness I can see that Zoe isn't here. Neither is Tutankhamun's sarcophagus, carved with *The Book of the Dead.* There is nothing in the room at all, except for a pile of suitcases in the corner by the door to the Hall of Judgment.

It is our luggage. I recognize my battered Samsonite and the carry-on bags of the Japanese tour group. The flight attendants' navy blue overnight cases are in front of the pile, strapped like victims to their wheeled carriers.

On top of my suitcase is a book, and I think, "It's the travel guide," even though I know Zoe would never have left it behind, and I hurry over to pick it up.

It is not *Egypt Made Easy.* It is my *Death on the Nile,* lying open and facedown the way Lissa left it on the boat, but I pick it up anyway and open it to the last pages, searching for the place where Hercule Poirot explains all the strange things that have been happening, where he solves the mystery.

I cannot find it. I thumb back through the book, looking for a map. There is always a map in Agatha Christie, showing who had what stateroom on the ship, showing the stairways and the doors and the unimpressive rooms leading one into another, but I cannot find that either. The pages are covered with long unreadable columns of hieroglyphics.

I close the book. "There's no point in waiting for Zoe," I say, looking past the luggage at the door to the next room. It is lower than the one I came through, and dark beyond. "She's obviously gone on to the Hall of Judgment."

I walk over to the door, holding the book against my chest. There are stone steps leading down. I can see the top one in the dim light from the burial chamber. It is steep and very narrow.

I toy briefly with the idea that it will not be so bad after all, that I am dreading it like the clergyman, and it will turn out to be not judgment but someone I know, a smiling bishop in a white suit, and mercy is not a modern refinement after all.

"I have not murdered another," I say, and my voice does not echo. "I have not committed adultery."

I take hold of the doorjamb with one hand so I won't fall on the stairs. With the other I hold the book against me. "Get back, you evil ones," I say. "Stay away. I adjure you in the name of Osiris and Poirot. My spells protect me. I know the way."

I begin my descent.

Big Teeth
and Small Magic:
SF and Fantasy Films of 1993

Kathi Maio

Although there is no Nebula Award for science fiction on film or
television, it has become customary to include a survey of the year's
most important science fiction and fantasy films in this volume.
Science fiction exists in many media, and it's fair to say that, for
most people, movies or television programs are their primary en-
counters with science fiction and fantasy. In the spring of 1994,
while speaking to an audience in Spain and trying to explain what
cyberpunk science fiction was, I said, "It's something like the movie
Blade Runner," and everyone got the point immediately. Our culture's archetypes are, more often than not, drawn from movies.

Kathi Maio is the author of *Feminist in the Dark* and *Popcorn
and Sexual Politics;* her columns on film appear regularly in *The
Magazine of Fantasy & Science Fiction.* She is a lover of movies
who looks for more than well-scripted entertainments or technically
sophisticated visual spectacles. As she wrote in one of her *F&SF*
columns:

"Science fiction films should always 'be ahead of their time.'
But, it pains me to say, this is not always the case. While speculative
movies have consistently pushed out the envelope of FX and the
other technologies of moviemaking, they haven't always furthered
social progress. ('Why should they?' you might ask. But if you *do,*
please read no further.)"

Which seems an appropriate introduction to the comments of
a viewer who loves movies enough to demand the best from them.

You didn't have to have the size and subtlety of a bulldozer to be a
big movie star in 1993, but it didn't hurt. At least if you were a
prehistoric critter, instead of a macho humanoid. The dinosaurs of
Steven Spielberg were a huge success. That surprised no one. What
did raise a few eyebrows was how well several low-budget fantasy
movies, with little to no special effects, did throughout the year.

But first things first: *Jurassic Park*'s mighty dinosaurs trampled the competition at the world box office, taking first place not only for the year but for the history of moviedom. Even without the phenomenal merchandising bonanza, the film enjoyed worldwide grosses in excess of $877 million, making it a global record breaker. (Yet the more sentimental among us will be pleased to know that in the United States little *E. T.* remained the domestic champ.)

Jurassic Park is not a great movie. It's not even a particularly good one, if you consider plot or theme and character development. But moviegoers certainly got what they wanted from this tale of a zoological theme park gone very, very wrong, and that was a bloody stomp fest. Mr. Spielberg learned how to elicit wonder and dread from an audience years ago, when he unleashed another toothy monster, dubbed *Jaws*. Neither his talents nor the demon teeth have dulled over the years.

Spielberg wisely put a sizable chunk of his hefty budget into special effects, hiring some of the best in the business to create his Tyrannosaurus rex, Velociraptor, Brachiosaurus, Gallimimus, Dilophosaurus, and Triceratops characters. And fully realized characters they are. (Much more compelling than any of the human figures in the movie!)

The dinos of *Jurassic Park* show none of those herky-jerky movements of the old monster movies. Stan Winston's team created the live-action dinosaurs, souping up traditional puppetry techniques with space-age hydraulics. In some scenes, a velociraptor might be played by both a guy in a rubber suit and a full-scale robotic puppet operated by up to fourteen technicians.

For the big chomper-stomper, T. rex, puppeteers would create movements on a fifth-scale model and then record the movements into a computer program that would allow them to smoothly re-create the action on a much larger scale. In many cases, shots of articulated figures would blend, in the final product, with computerized creatures created by Dennis Muren's Full Motion team at Industrial Light & Magic (under the guidance of Dinosaur Supervisor and Go-Motion animator Phil Tippett), while Michael Lantieri's FX engineers created the impact a dino might have on her physical environment.

The special effects of *Jurassic Park* are indeed eye-popping. Which may explain why the human characters of the story are given little to do besides slack-jawed gawking followed by blubbering, wide-eyed terror. It's hard to say much about performances—even by the likes of Richard Attenborough, Sam Neill, and Laura Dern— that consist almost entirely of reaction shots. And it is difficult to say anything intelligent about a story that has lost almost all of its intelligence in the wake of an elaborate hunt-and-devour ballet.

Who can blame Spielberg for wanting to create the ultimate creature feature? (He did it, and he did it well.) But the moral and ethical issues of corporate biotechnology raised by Michael Crichton's novel should have found a place in the film adaptation by Crichton and David Koepp, and they did not.

The foolish, egotistical captain of industry, John Hammond, who unleashes all the death and destruction, is transformed from the novel's villain to the film's doddering but sweet old gramps. And he gets off scot-free in the film, instead of being nibbled to death by his creations, as he is in the book. Hammond survives, along with the quasi-nuclear-family unit the filmmakers rather pointedly (and preposterously) concoct from the two scientists, Grant and Sattler, and Hammond's two grandkids.

In Crichton's book, there is a real sense of nature's retribution being meted out to guilty parties. In the movie, there is no guilt and retribution. If you are an attractive, fair-haired, pale-skinned character, chances are good that you'll get off bloodbath island alive. If you are a black man or another expendable type, you'd better say your prayers.

It's hard to believe this film was made by the same director in the same year as he released *Schindler's List*.

But it was a busy year for Mr. Spielberg. His name was also attached to another dinosaur movie of 1993: the animated feature he "present"ed at year's end, *We're Back! A Dinosaur's Story*. If only it *were* a dinosaur story. Unfortunately, the wisdom of America's most successful director—who knew that the key to the success of *Jurassic Park* lay in making the dinos the stars—is sorely lacking in this rather vapid full-length cartoon.

Hudson Talbott's children's picture book, on which the film is based, focuses on a group of dinosaurs experiencing severe culture shock when they are fed a megavitamin called Brain Grain and then are transported to the wilds of twentieth-century New York City. But the screen version, written by John Patrick Shanley and directed by

Dick and Ralph Zondag, Phil Nibbelink, and Simon Wells, blows it big time.

Instead of making a lovable lug of a tyrannosaur named Rex (voiced by John Goodman) and his band of prehistoric pals the cartoon's undisputed leads, the story spends most of its time with two kids (one from each side of the tracks) who are experiencing parental angst. Then there's the near-theological struggle between two elderly brothers, the satanic Professor ScrewEyes (Kenneth Mars) and the saintly Captain NewEyes (Walter Cronkite).

Okay, so we've always suspected that Uncle Walty was America's newscast Buddha. It was therefore a cute touch to have him voice the divine. It was also a delightful idea to cast Julia Child in the voice of the captain's absentminded ally, a paleontologist from the Museum of Natural History. But these are the kinds of bits that appeal to adults. Kids watching the movie want *more dinos,* and they had every right to be disappointed by *We're Back!*

More 'saurs could be found in a few low-cost also-rans as well. In the kiddies' straight-to-tape category, there was *Prehysteria,* an innocuous if loony tale of some ancient dinosaur eggs stolen from a Mayan temple. The eggs end up being incubated by a dog belonging to a raisin farmer/amateur archaeologist (Brett Cullen) and his two kids (Samantha Mills, Austin O'Brien).

Luckily, the hatchlings turn out to be pygmy dinosaurs. Which makes them as cuddly as Barney dolls—and, in this case, just about as fake looking. But these wee ones must have been snorting some of Rex's Brain Grain, because not only can they understand English, but they can even vocalize the words they hear. It's no wonder a trio of bungling (ethnic-stereotyped) bad guys want to steal the dinos from their raisin-farm family.

With its plastic dinosaurs and wooden acting performances, *Prehysteria* is only for very young, extremely forgiving viewers. Likewise, only those who enjoy something considerably less than state-of-the-art FX could love Roger Corman's latest rip-off of the big boys, *Carnosaur.* In keeping with the drive-in mentality behind it, this is a film that substitutes gore for believable monsters.

Most of the budget went into red dye and corn syrup, from the looks of it. Yet *Carnosaur,* written and directed by Adam Simon, is not without its good points. It deals with the same issues as *Jurassic*

Park and has the courage to give them a more hard-edged, downbeat spin.

Dr. Jane Tiptree (!), played with a sad, mad charm by Diane Ladd, is working for an agribusiness conglomerate when she starts filling in the blank pieces of old dinosaur DNA with that of chickens. I think it would have been fun if she had ended up with a rooster rex with fangs and white feathers, but what she hatches looks at first like a lizard and later takes on the appearance of a petite Godzilla.

Not content merely to rip off *Jurassic Park,* however, the film also takes a swipe at the *Aliens* movies by having the dinos start to incubate inside human hosts. I'm not quite sure how the film's virus plague—ah, an AIDS reference!—ends up causing dinosaurs to pop out of human female abdomens, but you're not supposed to think about the finer points of plot in this kind of a movie. It's enough to be able to exclaim, "Oh, gross!" every couple of minutes. And on that expectation *Carnosaur* surely delivers.

Yes, dinosaurs were huge in 1993. But human superheroes did not have the best of years. An animated Batman deserved to do much better than it did. *Batman: Mask of the Phantasm,* a big-screen spin-off of the TV cartoon series, was coproduced by the show's Alan Burnett, Eric Radomski, and Bruce W. Timm. Using both traditional and computer animation, the film has a very handsome "Dark Deco" look (as directors Radomski and Timm call it).

Although truer to the old comic, it was perhaps a mistake to make Bruce Wayne look so much like a forties-style linebacker, on the order of Jack Carson. A bit too stolid, perhaps. But he's a likable fellow, as voiced by Kevin Conroy. And Dana Delany has a nice melancholy vibe as Bruce's long-lost love, Andrea. Efrem Zimbalist, Jr. is surprisingly good as wise old Alfred. But the real shocker is Mark Hamill as the Joker. Who needs Jack Nicholson when the former Luke Skywalker's around!

This *Batman* did not pack them in at the box office, and neither did a breakthrough African-American superhero played by Robert Townsend, in a feature he wrote and directed. *Meteor Man* has a lovely message about a man's responsibility to his community (which is made up of individuals, each of whom is endowed with dignity and importance).

The problem is that Townsend's schoolteacher/jazz musician is *too* reluctant a superhero. He's less a man on a mission than a poor schlemiel who's been fried by a meteor and would rather forgo the superpowers attached. There's just not enough zip in Townsend's tale, so *Meteor Man* never really takes off.

But even those films practically pumping with high-octane testosterone and high-voltage action had a rough year. Just ask the heretofore invincible Arnold Schwarzenegger, whose *The Last Action Hero* was considered the bomb of the year.

It's a bum rap, of course. By the end of 1993, the film had grossed more than $140 million worldwide, and that does not constitute a flop. But the expense and hype-to-success ratio for this one make it a disappointment of major proportions.

And yet, in its attempt (halfhearted and confusing as it turned out to be) to challenge its formula and its audience, *The Last Action Hero* is a better film than *Jurassic Park*. But that doesn't make it a good picture.

This unwieldy hodgepodge of a movie tries to shove the excesses of the ultra-action down our throats at the same time as it expects us to repudiate them. Not that story-within-a-story satire can't work. This particular fable, of a boy (Austin O'Brien) who uses a magic ticket to burst through the big screen into the latest adventure of his favorite hero, had great potential. And Mr. Schwarzenegger, whose entire career has been based on self-parody, is better equipped than most actors to put the right double spin on a character like Jack Slater.

But a certain clarity of vision is required in the writing of such a complicated story, and the screenplay by Shane Black and David Arnott probably exhibited no such lucidity even before it was towed into the chop shop of doctoring, last-minute rewrites, and editing. Director John McTiernan (*Predator, Die Hard*) might have wanted to inject a tad more subtlety in this particular tale as well.

'Tis a pity. For there are some dandy bits—like the Hamlet scene—in *The Last Action Hero*. The same cannot be said for Sly Stallone's film about a macho time-traveler cop, *Demolition Man*. This overly simplistic and extremely derivative story pits Stallone's violent cop against an even more violent psychopathic criminal (played by Wesley Snipes). They were frozen for their sins in 1996 but are thawed out to do battle anew in the L.A. of 2032. It is (what the filmmakers would probably call) a "politically correct," monotonous future. No crime to speak of, but what's the use if you can't smoke, drink, or curse other people out? The worst of the bad guys are ascetic homosexual vegetarians, it appears. The noble rebels are graffiti-spraying guys (led by Dennis Leary) who champion all the vices and eat only red meat (when they eat at all).

Mr. Stallone's John Spartan is not heroic or particularly likable. He looks like a hopeless anachronism in 2032. And his brand of righteous violence was looking more and more like a pop-culture anachronism in 1993, too. Some theorists have tied the hypermasculinity of the eighties action flick to the politics of the Reagan years. There may be something to it. As the Reagan era ended, the macho action fantasy started to show signs of imminent collapse as well.

Could it be that *The Last Action Hero* and *Demolition Man,* with their lukewarm response from the viewing public, indicate the approaching end of an era? Could the muscle-bound macho man be a dying breed . . . the cinematic dinosaur of the nineties? As I write this, it is far too soon to tell. No-talk action certainly translates very easily in the world marketplace, so there is little chance that such films will disappear completely. And even if they do, for a time, die away, dinosaurs can defy nature. They can return from the dead, bigger and badder than ever. Just ask the she-monsters of *Jurassic Park.*

But what of those viewers who *were* sick of ultra-action and dinosaurs of all descriptions? For them, the most exciting trend in fantasy film for 1993 was the rise to prominence of magic realism. Although some such movies (from the totally strange *Dark at Noon* to the sweetly, oddly spiritual *Household Saints*) came and went with nary a ripple of interest, several believable stories touched with enchantment found a sizable audience. None more so than a modest little Mexican film directed by an actor-filmmaker, Alfonso Arau, from a screenplay by his wife, Laura Esquivel (based on her own first novel).

That movie was *Like Water for Chocolate,* and although it opened to limited release in the United States in February, it went wider and gained momentum throughout the summer, providing an art-house alternative to monster mashes and explosive action. It was still playing a year later, eventually surpassing the censor-shocking Swedish hit, *I Am Curious (Yellow)* (1967), as "the most successful foreign language film of all time."

Like Water for Chocolate is a peculiar little historical soap opera, with most of its action occurring during the years of the Mexican Revolution. A young woman named Tita is kept from marrying the boy she loves by her dictatorial mother. Tita's thickheaded suitor then decides that the next best thing to the woman you love is her sister. And Tita, banished to the ranch kitchen, releases her emotions through her meals.

What follows is an hour and a half of culinary passive-aggressive behavior, starting with a tear-tainted wedding cake that sends all the guests to vomit in the Rio Grande. Tita cooks meals that drive one sister to such sexual heat that she burns down a shower stall, and she drives her other rival sibling to gastrointestinal upsets that even a case of Mylanta couldn't touch.

What's the appeal of this low-tech fantasy of star-crossed love? It's hard to say. (I found it awkward and thoroughly depressing, myself.) It was, at least, unlike anything American audiences had seen before. And it was a film that honored the power of food. A simple but radical concept, that.

Food is something we all love and in which we all indulge. Yet it is hardly even *seen* in movies. To have a film celebrate the sensual (yes, mystical) power of victuals is more than a little unusual. Only *Babette's Feast,* six years earlier (and another surprise art-house success), came close.

Whatever the reason, *Like Water for Chocolate,* springing from the Latin American tradition of magic realism, was a box-office triumph. And it wasn't the only such film released in 1993. Sally Potter's adaptation of Virginia Woolf's satiric love letter to Vita Sackville-West, *Orlando,* also did better than expected with American viewers.

Orlando (Tilda Swinton) is a British lord who falls under the spell of the aging Queen Elizabeth I (played, in drag splendor, by Quentin Crisp), who orders him not to "fade" or "wither." And so Orlando goes through the ages without aging a day. However, a funny thing happens on the battlements in the early eighteenth century; he becomes a she and then continues on to the modern day.

Considering its modest budget (of about $4 million), *Orlando* is an exceedingly handsome movie. Unfortunately, its good looks aren't accompanied by much in the way of warmth and spirit. *Orlando* is a rather cold, sterile cinematic exercise.

Much better in every way is a film that never did find a following.

Too tough for many children and too much about a couple of kids to please most adults, *Into the West* is nonetheless an exquisite treasure from the writer of *My Left Foot*, Jim Sheridan, and the director of *Enchanted April*, Mike Newell.

It is the story of a family of "travelers" (gypsies) in urban Ireland. Papa (Gabriel Byrne) is a lost man, mired in alcohol and grief since the death of his wife. He has no stamina for the wandering life anymore and can offer little comfort or support to his two young sons. Then, suddenly, a white horse adopts the two boys and joins their household—despite the fact that they live on the upper floor of a public-housing high-rise.

When the neighbors complain, complications set in. And soon the boys are tearing across country, into the west of their homeland (and of their cowboy imaginings), with the police (and Papa) in hot pursuit.

The beauty of the Irish countryside and the bite of social commentary to this little fable add greatly to the film's delights. But *Into the West* is, above all, a poignant fantasy of love and healing.

Another film on the restorative power of love, with the smallest touch of magic, is the latest screen adaptation of Frances Hodgson Burnett's 1911 classic, *The Secret Garden*. Scripted by Caroline Thompson (*Edward Scissorhands*) and directed by the Polish director Agnieszka Holland, it doesn't try to make too sweet and cuddly with the harsher aspects of its story. And that makes the blooming of an abandoned garden and a neglected child all the more wondrous.

All of the quiet fantasies I've mentioned so far have, on one level or another, been non-Hollywood movies. It is easy, therefore, to wag one's head in dismay and assume that Hollywood just doesn't get a concept like magic realism. But when truly talented people work together, even in the name of a major studio in the U.S. of A., they can still produce a gentle, high-quality, truly entertaining Hollywood picture show.

Groundhog Day is the kind of movie that renews your faith in Tinseltown. The quirky story of a cynical weatherman and how he grew—while stuck in a time warp on special assignment in Punxsutawney—is warm, romantic, and absolutely hilarious. Would the film have worked as well without the comic genius of Bill Murray? It's doubtful. The screenplay by Danny Rubin and director Harold Ramis is nice work, but this *is* Murray's movie. And what a wonderful movie it is.

Original it isn't, however. It bears close resemblance to several science fiction stories of the past, most recently to an Oscar-nominated Showtime "30-Minute Movie" called *12:01 P.M.* In that film (by Jonathan Heap, based on a short story by Richard Lupoff), a law clerk is doomed to repeat the same lunch hour over and over again. Plans to make a full-length film out of *12:01* began soon after the short was made. Too bad, really, that *Groundhog Day* so completely stole its thunder.

12:01 also came out in 1993, but ended up as a summer movie on the Fox TV network. Where, I am sure, many viewers wondered why someone was ripping off Murray's film. The expanded *12:01* does not have the star power of a Bill Murray to make it memorable, but it is a genuinely entertaining film just the same. (And, unlike *Groundhog Day,* it actually offers a scientific—if farfetched—explanation for its repeating day.)

Jonathan Silverman stars as Barry, an easygoing but undirected young man who works in the personnel department of a major high-tech firm. He is the only one who realizes that his firm's superaccelerator experiments have created a time bump. But Barry isn't complaining. The repeating day gives him a chance, he hopes, to accomplish a crucial task: to save the life of a young research scientist (Helen Slater) he silently loves.

Okay, so *12:01* never would have been destined to become a classic. It's still a nice little film that deserved better. Which is more than you can say for some of the TV movies and miniseries that were broadcast throughout 1993.

Frankenstein, starring Patrick Bergin as the doctor and Randy Quaid as the monster, had possibilities. The TNT film certainly came closer to the original story than earlier treatments had. The problem was that writer-director David Wickes didn't seem to understand about pacing. His story was often awkward and always turgid—rather like a Masterpiece Theatre series done by a clinically depressed Oxford don.

But it could have been worse. It could have been *Wild Palms* or *The Tommyknockers,* miniseries that proved that ABC should stay away from speculative programming. Much better was an original movie for HBO called *Daybreak,* a Romeo and Juliet tale (starring Cuba Gooding, Jr., and Moira Kelly) set in a dystopic future in which those who test positive for an unidentified disease are banished to certain death in a filthy, negligent quarantine system.

Daybreak was certainly a timely piece of science fiction, touching on issues of biological human rights. And there were several other films in 1993 that delved into similar thematic material. The most significant of these was a film very few people were able to see.

Rain Without Thunder is a small movie that played film festivals and had short runs in a few cities but never went into wide release. That's a shame, because it is the most thought-provoking science fiction film of the year. Set in the year 2042 and filmed in the style of a news documentary, it tells the story of a mother and daughter (Betty Buckley, Ali Thomas) who are the first women convicted under a new anti-abortion statute called the Unborn Child Kidnapping Act.

Although it is unquestionably a cautionary tale about how easily, in the space of two generations, civil rights can be eroded away by incremental changes in law and public attitude, you don't have to be a pro-choice activist to appreciate this movie.

It is an amazingly evenhanded treatment of a complex issue. Those prosecuting the women are not portrayed as Nazis. They are merely enforcing a law whose aim is to put some racial and economic equity in anti-abortion policy. (For the first time, well-to-do white women who are financially able to travel to Europe for a termination face the same kind of strict consequences as the poor women of color who must struggle to locate back-alley remedies at home.)

Some may find the pseudo-documentary style too static, but those who are interested in the future of reproductive rights will likely find this compelling viewing—worth seeking out.

Not all reproductive rights have to do with avoiding reproductions, however. *Fortress,* a futuristic adventure story starring Christopher Lambert, is better than *Demolition Man,* even if its more modest budget shows in every scene. In it, the hero and his wife have been imprisoned for defying the law forbidding couples to have more than one child. It is a rather predictable prison-breakout film, but enjoyable.

A foreign (Belgian-French-Spanish) movie with a concept more interesting than the finished film also dealt with a hero who *wanted* to have a baby. But in the case of the TV reporter played by Carmen Maura in *Between Heaven and Earth,* it's not the law keeping her from having a child; it's the fetus himself who refuses to be born.

As I say, it's a most intriguing concept—this worldwide conspiracy of unborn babes who collectively refuse to come into the world of their parents. The catch is that the movie doesn't show enough of what's wrong with society and the planet. (I guess we're automatically supposed to assume that this is indeed a world unfit for new citizens.) Nor does the film offer any attempts at a solution to global ills. In the end, the baby decides to be born because his mother loves him enough to die for him—nothing new about that.

Carmen Maura's baby boy should probably count his blessings. At least he doesn't face the same level of danger as the infant Pubert in *Addams Family Values*. The new mustachioed tyke issuing from the undying love of the macabre Morticia and Gomez is facing serious death threats from his two older siblings.

Addams Family Values is that rare cinematic event, a sequel that is better made, better written, and more lively than the original. Regrettably, though, the public had had its fill of the ooky Addams clan, and even the charms of Joan Cusack as a black-widow nanny and the delightful high jinks of Christina Ricci's Wednesday—her revisionist Thanksgiving skit is alone worth the price of admission—were not enough to make this agreeably ghoulish farce a hit.

It was a bad year all around for sequels and tie-ins. *Teen-Age Mutant Ninja Turtles* seemed about due to crawl back into their shells after their third adventure, this time in feudal Japan. And although we all consumed mass quantities of the Coneheads during the salad days of "Saturday Night Live," the lackluster feature film about the family from Remulak—I mean France—(about twenty years too late) had little going for it besides better cone prosthetics and makeup. The problem with these aliens was that they weren't alien enough. They were successful suburbanites who fit in too well with their bland neighbors.

The Coneheads were boring without the shock value of their otherness. And *Robocop 3* proved that without the satiric humor—and the star—of the first two films, Robo is just a tedious tin man. But even the poor folks versus the police–industrial-conglomerate plot of *Robocop 3* was a good deal more enjoyable than the miserable mess of a feature film called *Super Mario Brothers*.

Good video games do not good movies make, it appears. But fantasies based on history are even more of a danger to themselves and their audience. They can end up being not only a dismal failure but also an insult and an outrage. Such a film was *Hocus Pocus,* a Disney product starring Bette Midler as the eldest of three diabolic witches summoned up from the dead by a trio of unsuspecting kids, three hundred years after the good people of Salem, Massachusetts, lynched them for murdering a little girl.

Now, some people view the Salem witch persecution of the early 1690s as nothing short of a holocaust. Others see it, at the very least, as a shameful example of social hysteria with tragic consequences. The women (and men) who were hanged or tortured to death or who died in prison were *not* evil, satanic trolls who sucked the life out of small, innocent children. They were victims of the most grievous sort of social injustice.

So *what*, in heaven's name, would inspire Mick Garris and Neil Cuthbert to write a screenplay that seems to imply that the witch hangings of Salem were a crackerjack (public safety) idea? And what would cause a star of the caliber of Bette Midler (with Sarah Jessica Parker and Kathy Najimy) to film such a wretched story in the same year as a memorial to the Salem victims was being dedicated?

Who can say? Many moviegoers are willing to forgive anything of a film as long as it's fun to watch. But, alas, *Hocus Pocus* is stupid and uninteresting, as well as disgusting. Viewers in the mood for a little satanic witchcraft were much better served by the utterly eerie make-believe of *Warlock: The Armageddon*.

Blond, effete-looking Julian Sands reprises his role as the son of Satan as he tries to summon his devil-dad into the world during an eclipse. Those who resent the fact that Julian is a wicked witch can comfort themselves with the fact that the good guys (and gals) are witches, too—druid warriors and healers who must beat Beelzebub to save the world.

I like to see a pagan hero (even in a story laden with Christian symbolism). I also like to see ghoulish good guys. So I was delighted by the success of *Tim Burton's Nightmare Before Christmas*. Done in state-of-the-art stop-motion by Henry Selick and his band of magicians, Tim's *Nightmare* was the best animation feature of the year, and a grotesque gem of a movie.

In it, Jack Skellington, the pumpkin king of Halloweentown, becomes disenchanted with the same old terrors and is enchanted, instead, with the new sugarplum Christmas world he discovers. He'd like to claim it—or at least inhabit it with his own brand of merriment. But trying to be something you're not is always a chancy proposition. And the skeletal Jack trying to substitute for Jolly Saint Nick is a plan with disaster written all over it.

Burton's fright-night fable is a charmer, sure to gladden the hearts of kids of all ages. It is wonderfully weird, but never too scary for even the youngest viewer. And what if it were? Being frightened at your neighborhood movie house isn't the worst thing that can happen to a kid. That's the message of my personal favorite of all the science fiction films of 1993.

Well, actually, *Matinee* isn't a science fiction film; it's a film *about* the SF horror films of the fifties and sixties and what they meant to the youth of America.

Directed by Joe Dante—himself a modern master of science fiction and horror for films like *The Howling* and the *Gremlins* movies—from a screenplay by Charlie Haas, *Matinee* is a homage to men like William Castle, who made the B movies that scared the pants off the kids from that more innocent time.

Innocent? Maybe. But terrifying, too. It was the dawn of the nuclear age, when stories about atomic mutants helped us exorcise our fears. And there *was* a lot of fear. Especially during that week in October of 1962 that we call the Cuban Missile Crisis. That is the time of *Matinee*.

Into a Florida community wondering whether it'll see tomorrow comes a corpulent impresario of gimmicky horror, Lawrence Woolsey (John Goodman), with his bag of con-man tricks and his latest SF shock fest, the half-man, half-ant, All Terror *Mant!*

One of the greatest pleasures of *Matinee* is this lovingly created movie-within-a-movie, which tells the story of Bill, a man who is bitten by an ant while having dental X rays taken. Lucky for him he had no cavities. Unfortunately, he shortly thereafter metamorphoses into a monstrous insect. *Mant!* features several cameos by actors (like Kevin McCarthy) who were stars of the old SF classics.

The spoof is hilarious, yet filled with real celebratory affection. And the larger story, involving the young boys of Key West, who are coping with their anxieties about annihilation (as well as first love), is also warmly humorous.

Matinee is about a real time and a real terror. And it's about how make-believe horror in a darkened theater helped us to get through those dark days.

Times have changed. But not that much. We still count on the comfort of science fiction and fantasy films to get us through. And they still do.

ENGLAND UNDERWAY

Terry Bisson

Terry Bisson is the author of the novels *Wyrldmaker, Talking Man, Fire on the Mountain,* and *Voyage to the Red Planet.* The title story in his recent collection, *Bears Discover Fire and Other Stories,* won the Nebula, the Hugo, the Theodore Sturgeon Memorial Award, and the Locus Award. His highly original stories are not only unlike anyone else's, but also unlike one another; this is a writer who doesn't repeat himself. Several of his stories have been optioned for the screen, and stage adaptations were produced at New York's West Bank Theater in 1992 and 1993.

Of his Nebula nominee "England Underway," he writes:

" 'England Underway' is my attempt to explain, once and for all, those mysterious crop circles that keep appearing in Sussex. Film rights have been optioned by Merchant Marine Ivory. Sir Anthony Hopkins has the script and has promised to get around to reading it pretty soon. The dog is based on a character from *Reservoir Dogs.* There actually was a Victorian novelist named Trollope, and England did anchor off the south shore of Long Island for a few days in the autumn of 19–. The rest is made up."

Mr. Fox was, he realized afterward, with a shudder of sudden recognition like that of the man who gives a cup of water to a stranger and finds out hours, or even years, later, that it was Napoleon, perhaps the first to notice. Perhaps. At least no one else in Brighton seemed to be looking at the sea that day. He was taking his constitutional on the Boardwalk, thinking of Lizzie Eustace and her diamonds, the people in novels becoming increasingly more real to him as the people in the everyday (or "real") world grew more remote, when he noticed that the waves seemed funny.

"Look," he said to Anthony, who accompanied him everywhere, which was not far, his customary world being circumscribed by the Boardwalk to the south, Mrs. Oldenshield's to the east, the cricket grounds to the north, and the Pig & Thistle, where he kept a room—or, more precisely, a room kept him, and had since 1956—to the west.

"Woof?" said Anthony, in what might have been a quizzical tone.

"The waves," said Mr. Fox. "They seem—well, odd, don't they? Closer together?"

"Woof."

"Well, perhaps not. Could be just my imagination."

Fact is, waves had always looked odd to Mr. Fox. Odd and tiresome and sinister. He enjoyed the Boardwalk, but he never walked on the beach proper, not only because he disliked the shifty quality of the sand but because of the waves with their ceaseless back and forth. He didn't understand why the sea had to toss about so. Rivers didn't make all that fuss, and they were actually going somewhere. The movement of the waves seemed to suggest that something was stirring things up, just beyond the horizon. Which was what Mr. Fox had always suspected in his heart, which was why he had never visited his sister in America.

"Perhaps the waves have always looked funny and I have just never noticed," said Mr. Fox. If indeed *funny* was the word for something so odd.

At any rate, it was almost half past four. Mr. Fox went to Mrs. Oldenshield's, and with a pot of tea and a plate of shortbread biscuits placed in front of him, read his daily Trollope—he had long ago decided to read all forty-seven novels in exactly the order, and at about the rate, in which they had been written—then fell asleep for twenty minutes. When he awoke (and no one but he knew he was sleeping) and closed the book, Mrs. Oldenshield put it away for him, on the high shelf where the complete set, bound in morocco, resided in state. Then Mr. Fox walked to the cricket ground, so that Anthony might run with the boys and their kites until dinner was served at the Pig & Thistle. A whiskey at nine with Harrison ended what seemed at the time to be an ordinary day.

The next day it all began in earnest.

Mr. Fox awoke to a hubbub of traffic—footsteps, and unintelligible shouts. There was, as usual, no one but himself and Anthony (and of course the Finn, who cooked) at breakfast; but outside, he found the streets remarkably lively for the time of year. He saw more and more people as he headed downtown, until he was immersed in a virtual sea of humanity. People of all sorts, even Pakistanis and foreigners, not ordinarily much in evidence in Brighton off season.

"What in the world can it be?" Mr. Fox wondered aloud. "I simply can't imagine."

"Woof," said Anthony, who couldn't imagine either but who was never called upon to do so.

With Anthony in his arms, Mr. Fox picked his way through the crowd along the King's Esplanade until he came to the entrance to the Boardwalk. He mounted the twelve steps briskly. It was irritating to have one's customary way blocked by strangers. The Boardwalk was half-filled with strollers who, instead of strolling, were holding onto the rail and looking out to sea. It was mysterious, but then the habits of everyday people had always been mysterious to Mr. Fox; they were much less likely to stay in character than the people in novels.

The waves were even closer together than they had been the day before; they were piling up as if pulled toward the shore by a magnet. The surf where it broke had the odd appearance of a single continuous wave about one and a half feet high. Though it no longer seemed to be rising, the water had risen during the night. It covered half the beach, coming almost up to the seawall just below the Boardwalk.

The wind was quite stout for the season. Off to the left (the east) a dark line was seen on the horizon. It might have been clouds, but it looked more solid, like land. Mr. Fox could not remember ever having seen it before, even though he had walked here daily for the past forty-two years.

"Dog?"

Mr. Fox looked to his left. Standing beside him at the rail of the Boardwalk was a large, one might even say portly, African man with an alarming hairdo. He was wearing a tweed coat. An English girl clinging to his arm had asked the question. She was pale, with dark, stringy hair, and she wore an oilskin cape that looked wet even though it wasn't raining.

"Beg your pardon?" said Mr. Fox.

"That's a dog?" The girl was pointing toward Anthony.

"Woof."

"Well, of course it's a dog."

"Can't he walk?"

"Of course he can walk. He just doesn't always choose to."

"You bloody wish," said the girl, snorting unattractively and look-ing away. She wasn't exactly a girl. She could have been twenty.

"Don't mind her," said the African. "Look at that chop, would you."

"Indeed," Mr. Fox said. He didn't know what to make of the girl, but he was grateful to the African for starting a conversation. It was often difficult these days; it had become increasingly difficult over the years. "A storm off shore, perhaps?" he ventured.

"A storm?" the African said. "I guess you haven't heard. It was on the telly hours ago. We're making close to two knots now, south and east. Heading around Ireland and out to sea."

"Out to sea?" Mr. Fox looked over his shoulder at the King's Esplanade and the buildings beyond, which seemed as stationary as ever. "Brighton is heading out to sea?"

"You bloody wish," the girl said.

"Not just Brighton, man," the African said. For the first time, Mr. Fox could hear a faint Caribbean lilt in his voice. "England herself is underway."

England underway? How extraordinary. Mr. Fox could see what he supposed was excitement in the faces of the other strollers on the Boardwalk all that day. The wind smelled somehow saltier as he went to take his tea. He almost told Mrs. Oldenshield the news when she brought him his pot and platter; but the affairs of the day, which had never intruded far into her tearoom, receded entirely when he took down his book and began to read. This was (as it turned out) the very day that Lizzie finally read the letter from Mr. Camperdown, the Eustace family lawyer, which she had carried unopened for three days. As Mr. Fox had expected, it demanded that the diamonds be returned to her late husband's family. In response, Lizzie bought a strongbox. That evening, England's peregrinations were all the news on BBC. The kingdom was heading south into the Atlantic at 1.8 knots, according to the newsmen on the telly over the bar at the Pig & Thistle, where Mr. Fox was accustomed to taking a glass of whiskey with Harrison, the barkeep, before retiring. In the sixteen hours since the phenomenon had first been detected, England had gone some thirty-five miles, beginning a long turn around Ireland which would carry it into the open sea.

"Ireland is not going?" asked Mr. Fox.

"Ireland has been independent since 19 and 21," said Harrison, who often hinted darkly at having relatives with the IRA. "Ireland is hardly about to be chasing England around the seven seas."

"Well, what about, you know?"

"The Six Counties? The Six Counties have always been a part of Ireland and always will be," said Harrison. Mr. Fox nodded politely and finished his whiskey. It was not his custom to argue politics, particularly not with barkeeps, and certainly not with the Irish.

"So I suppose you'll be going home?"

"And lose me job?"

For the next several days, the wave got no higher but it seemed steadier. It was not a chop but a continual smooth wake, streaming across the shore to the east as England began its turn to the west. The cricket ground grew deserted as the boys laid aside their kites and joined the rest of the town at the shore, watching the waves. There was such a crowd on the Boardwalk that several of the shops, which had closed for the season, reopened. Mrs. Oldenshield's was no busier than usual, however, and Mr. Fox was able to forge ahead as steadily in his reading as Mr. Trollope had in his writing. It was not long before Lord Fawn, with something almost of dignity in his gesture and demeanour, declared himself to the young widow Eustace and asked for her hand. Mr. Fox knew Lizzie's diamonds would be trouble, though. He knew something of heirlooms himself. His tiny attic room in the Pig & Thistle had been left to him *in perpetuity* by the innkeeper, whose life had been saved by Mr. Fox's father during an air raid. A life saved (said the innkeeper, an East Indian, but a Christian, not a Hindu) was a debt never fully paid. Mr. Fox had often wondered where he would have lived if he'd been forced to go out and find a place, like so many in novels did. Indeed, in real life as well. That evening on the telly there was panic in Belfast as the headlands of Scotland slid by, south. Were the Loyalists to be left behind? Everyone was waiting to hear from the King, who was closeted with his advisors.

The next morning there was a letter on the little table in the downstairs hallway at the Pig & Thistle. Mr. Fox knew as soon as he saw the letter that it was the fifth of the month. His niece, Emily, always mailed her letters from America on the first, and they always arrived on the morning of the fifth.

Mr. Fox opened it, as always, just after tea at Mrs. Oldenshield's. He read the ending first, as always, to make sure there were no surprises. "Wish you could see your great-niece before she's grown," Emily wrote; she wrote the same thing every month. When her mother, Mr. Fox's sister, Clare, had visited after moving to America, it had been his niece she had wanted him to meet. Emily had taken up the same refrain since her mother's death. "Your great-niece will be a young lady soon," she wrote, as if this were somehow Mr. Fox's doing. His only regret was that Emily, in asking him to come to America when her mother died, had asked him to do the one thing he couldn't even contemplate; and so he had been unable to grant her even the courtesy of a refusal. He read all the way back to the opening ("Dear Uncle Anthony"), then folded the letter very small and put it into the box with the others when he got back to his room that evening.

The bar seemed crowded when he came downstairs at nine. The King, in a brown suit with a green and gold tie, was on the telly, sitting in front of a clock in a BBC studio. Even Harrison, never one for royalty, set aside the glasses he was polishing and listened while Charles confirmed that England was indeed underway. His words made it official, and there was a polite "hip, hip, hooray" from the three men (two of them strangers) at the end of the bar. The King and his advisors weren't exactly sure when England would arrive, or, for that matter, where it was going. Scotland and Wales were, of course, coming right along. Parliament would announce time-zone adjustments as necessary. While His Majesty was aware that there was cause for *concern* about Northern Ireland and the Isle of Man, there was as yet no cause for *alarm*.

His Majesty, King Charles, spoke for almost half an hour, but Mr. Fox missed much of what he said. His eye had been caught by the date under the clock on the wall behind the King's head. It was the fourth of the month, not the fifth; his niece's letter had arrived a day early! This, even more than the funny waves or the King's speech, seemed to announce that the world was changing. Mr. Fox had a sudden, but not unpleasant, feeling almost of dizziness. After it had passed, and the bar had cleared out, he suggested to Harrison, as he always did at closing time, "Perhaps you'll join me in a whiskey"; and as always, Harrison replied, "Don't mind if I do."

He poured two Bells'. Mr. Fox had noticed that when other patrons "bought" Harrison a drink, and the barkeep passed his hand across the bottle and pocketed the tab, the whiskey was Bushmills. It was only with Mr. Fox, at closing, that he actually took a drink, and then it was always scotch.

"To your King," said Harrison. "And to plate tectonics."

"Beg your pardon?"

"Plate tectonics, Fox. Weren't you listening when your precious Charles explained why all this was happening? All having to do with movement of the Earth's crust, and such."

"To plate tectonics," said Mr. Fox. He raised his glass to hide his embarrassment. He had in fact heard the words, but had assumed they had to do with plans to protect the household treasures at Buckingham Palace.

Mr. Fox never bought the papers, but the next morning he slowed down to read the headlines as he passed the news stalls. King Charles's picture was on all the front pages, looking confidently into the future.

ENGLAND UNDERWAY AT 2.9 KNOTS; SCOTLAND, WALES COMING ALONG PEACEFULLY; CHARLES FIRM AT 'HELM' OF UNITED KINGDOM

read the *Daily Alarm*. The *Economist* took a less sanguine view:

CHUNNEL COMPLETION DELAYED; EEC CALLS EMERGENCY MEETING

Although Northern Ireland was legally and without question part of the United Kingdom, the BBC explained that night, it was for some inexplicable reason apparently remaining with Ireland. The King urged his subjects in Belfast and Londonderry not to panic; arrangements were being made for the evacuation of all who wished it.

The King's address seemed to have a calming effect over the

next few days. The streets of Brighton grew quiet once again. The Esplanade and the Boardwalk still saw a few video crews, which kept the fish-and-chips stalls busy; but they bought no souvenirs, and the gift shops all closed again one by one.

"Woof," said Anthony, delighted to find the boys back on the cricket ground with their kites. "Things are getting back to normal," said Mr. Fox. But were they really? The smudge on the eastern horizon was Brittany, according to the newsmen on the telly; next would be the open sea. One shuddered to think of it. Fortunately, there was familiarity and warmth at Mrs. Oldenshield's, where Lizzie was avoiding the Eustace family lawyer, Mr. Camperdown, by retreating to her castle in Ayr. Lord Fawn (urged on by his family) was insisting he couldn't marry her unless she gave up the diamonds. Lizzie's answer was to carry the diamonds with her to Scotland in a strongbox. Later that week, Mr. Fox saw the African again. There was a crowd on the old West Pier, and even though it was beginning to rain Mr. Fox walked out to the end, where a boat was unloading. It was a sleek hydrofoil, with the Royal Family's crest upon its bow. Two video crews were filming as sailors in slickers passed an old lady in a wheelchair from the boat to the pier. She was handed an umbrella and a tiny white dog. The handsome young captain of the hydrofoil waved his braided hat as he gunned the motors and pulled away from the pier; the crowd cried "hurrah" as the boat rose on its spidery legs and blasted off into the rain.

"Woof," said Anthony. No one else paid any attention to the old lady, sitting in the wheelchair with a wet, shivering dog on her lap. She had fallen asleep (or perhaps even died!) and dropped her umbrella. Fortunately it wasn't raining. "That would be the young Prince of Wales," said a familiar voice to Mr. Fox's left. It was the African. According to him (and he seemed to know such things), the Channel Islands, and most of the islanders, had been left behind. The hydrofoil had been sent to Guernsey at the Royal Family's private expense to rescue the old lady, who'd had a last-minute change of heart; perhaps she'd wanted to die in England. "He'll be in Portsmouth by five," said the African, pointing to an already far-off plume of spray.

"Is it past four already?" Mr. Fox asked. He realized he had lost track of the time.

"Don't have a watch?" asked the girl, sticking her head around the African's bulk.

Mr. Fox hadn't seen her lurking there. "Haven't really needed one," he said.

"You bloody wish," she said.

"Twenty past, precisely," said the African. "Don't mind her, mate." Mr. Fox had never been called "mate" before. He was pleased that even with all the excitement he hadn't missed his tea. He hurried to Mrs. Oldenshield's, where he found a fox hunt just getting underway at Portray, Lizzie's castle in Scotland. He settled down eagerly to read about it. A fox hunt! Mr. Fox was a believer in the power of names.

The weather began to change, to get, at the same time, warmer and rougher. In the satellite pictures on the telly over the bar at the Pig & Thistle, England was a cloud-dimmed outline that could just as easily have been a drawing as a photo. After squeezing between Ireland and Brittany, like a restless child slipping from the arms of its ancient Celtic parents, it was headed south and west, into the open Atlantic. The waves came no longer at a slant but straight in at the seawall. Somewhat to his surprise, Mr. Fox enjoyed his constitutional more than ever, knowing that he was looking at a different stretch of sea every day, even though it always looked the same. The wind was strong and steady in his face, and the Boardwalk was empty. Even the newsmen were gone—to Scotland, where it had only just been noticed that the Hebrides were being left behind with the Orkneys and the Shetlands. "Arctic islands with their own traditions, languages, and monuments, all mysteriously made of stone," explained the reporter, live from Uig, by remote. The video showed a postman shouting incomprehensibly into the wind and rain.

"What's he saying?" Mr. Fox asked. "Would that be Gaelic?"

"How would I be expected to know?" said Harrison.

A few evenings later, a BBC crew in the Highlands provided the last view of the continent: the receding headlands of Brittany, seen from the 3,504-foot summit of Ben Hope, on a bright, clear day. "It's a good thing," Mr. Fox joked to Anthony the next day, "that Mrs. Oldenshield has laid in plenty of hyson." This was the green tea Mr. Fox preferred. She had laid in dog biscuits for Anthony as well. Lizzie herself was leaving Scotland, following the last of her guests back to London, when her hotel room was robbed and her strongbox was stolen, just as Mr. Fox had always feared it would be. For a week it rained. Great swells pounded at the seawall. Brighton was almost deserted. The faint-hearted had left for Portsmouth, where they were protected by the Isle of Wight from the winds and waves that struck what might now be properly called the *bow* of Britain.

On the Boardwalk, Mr. Fox strolled as deliberate and proud as a captain on his bridge. The wind was almost a gale, but a steady gale, and he soon grew used to it; it simply meant walking and standing at a tilt. The rail seemed to thrum with energy under his hand. Even though he knew that they were hundreds of miles at sea, Mr. Fox felt secure with all of England at his back. He began to almost enjoy the fulminations of the water as it threw itself against the Brighton seawall. Which plowed on west, into the Atlantic.

With the south coast from Penzance to Dover in the lead (or perhaps it should be said, at the bow) and the Highlands of Scotland at the stern, the United Kingdom was making almost four knots, 3.8 to be precise.

"A modest and appropriate speed," the King told his subjects, speaking from his chambers in Buckingham Palace, which had been decked out with nautical maps and charts, a lighted globe, and a silver sextant. "Approximately equal to that of the great ships-of-the-line of Nelson's day."

In actual fact, the BBC commentator corrected (for they will correct even a king), 3.8 knots was considerably slower than an eighteenth-century warship. But it was good that this was so, Britain being, at best, blunt; indeed, it was estimated that with even a half knot more speed, the seas piling up the Plymouth and Exeter channels would have devastated the docks. Oddly enough, it was London, far from the head winds and bow wave, that was hardest hit. The wake past Margate, along what used to be the English Channel, had sucked the Thames down almost two feet, leaving broad mud flats along the Victoria Embankment and under the Waterloo Bridge. The news showed treasure seekers with gum boots tracking mud all over the city, "a mud as foulsmelling as the ancient crimes they unearth daily," said the BBC. Not a very patriotic report, thought Mr. Fox, who turned from the telly to Harrison to remark, "I believe you have family there."

"In London? Not hardly," said Harrison. "They've all gone to America."

By the time the Scottish mountaintops should have been enduring (or perhaps "enjoying" is the word, being mountains, and Scottish at that) the first snow flurries of the winter, they were enjoying (or perhaps "enduring") subtropical rains as the United Kingdom passed just to the north of the Azores. The weather in the south (now west) of England was springlike and fine. The boys at the cricket ground, who had usually put away their kites by this time of year, were out every day, affording endless delight to Anthony, who accepted, with the simple, unquestioning joy of a dog, the fact of a world well supplied with running boys. "Our Day's Log," the popular new BBC evening show, which began and ended with shots of the bow wave breaking on the rocks of Cornwall, showed hobbyists with telescopes and camcorders on the cliffs at Dover, cheering "Land ho!" on sighting the distant peaks of the Azores. Things were getting back to normal. The public (according to the news) was finding that even the mid-Atlantic held no terrors. The wave of urban seasickness that had been predicted never materialized. At a steady 3.8 knots, Great Britain was unaffected by the motion of the waves, even during the fiercest storms: it was almost as if she had been designed for travel, and built for comfort, not for speed. A few of the smaller Scottish islands had been stripped away and had, alarmingly, sunk; but the only real damage was on the east (now south) coast, where the slipstream was washing away house-sized chunks of the soft Norfolk banks. The King was seen on the news, in muddy hip boots, helping to dike the fens against the wake. Taking a break from digging, he reassured his subjects that the United Kingdom, wherever it might be headed, would remain sovereign. When a reporter, with shocking impertinence, asked if that meant that His Majesty *didn't know* where his Kingdom was headed, King Charles answered coolly that he hoped his subjects were satisfied with his performance in a role that was, after all, designed to content them with *what was,* rather than to shape or even predict *what might be.* Then, without excusing himself, he picked up his silver shovel with the royal crest and began to dig again.

Meanwhile, at Mrs. Oldenshield's, all of London was abuzz with Lizzie's loss. Or supposed loss. Only Lizzie (and Messrs. Fox and Trollope) knew that the diamonds had been not in her strongbox but under her pillow. Mr. Fox's letter from his niece arrived a day earlier still, on the third of the month, underscoring in its own quiet manner that England was indeed underway. The letter, which Mr. Fox read in reverse, as usual, ended alarmingly with the words "looking forward to seeing you." Forward? He read on backward and found "underway toward America." America? It had never occurred to Mr. Fox. He looked at the return address on the envelope. It was from a town called, rather ominously, Babylon.

Lizzie was one for holding on. Even though the police (and half of London society) suspected that she had engineered the theft of the diamonds in order to avoid returning them to the Eustace family, she wasn't about to admit that they had never been stolen at all. Indeed, why should she? As the book was placed back up on the shelf day after day, Mr. Fox marveled at the strength of character of one so able to convince herself that what was in her interest was in the right. The next morning there was a small crowd on the West Pier, waving Union Jacks and pointing toward a smudge on the horizon. Mr. Fox was not surprised to see a familiar face (and hairdo) among them.

"Bermuda," said the African. Mr. Fox only nodded, not wanting to provoke the girl, who he suspected was waiting on the other side of the African, waiting to strike. Was it only his imagination, that the smudge on the horizon was pink? That night and the two nights following, he watched the highlights of the Bermuda Passage on the telly over the bar. The island, which had barely been visible from Brighton, passed within a mile of Dover, and thousands turned out to see the colonial policemen in their red coats lined up atop the coral cliffs, saluting the Mother Country as she passed. Even where no crowds turned out, the low broads of Norfolk, the shaley cliffs of Yorkshire, the rocky headlands of Scotland's (former) North Sea coast, all received the same salute. The passage took nearly a week, and Mr. Fox thought it was quite a tribute to the Bermudans' stamina, as well as their patriotism.

Over the next few days the wind shifted and began to drop. Anthony was pleased, noticing only that the boys had to run harder to lift their kites, and seemed to need a dog yipping along beside them more than ever. But Mr. Fox knew that if the wind dropped much further they would lose interest altogether. The Bermudans were satisfied with their glimpse of the Mother Country, according to BBC; but the rest of the Commonwealth members were outraged as the United Kingdom turned sharply north after the Bermuda Passage, and headed north on a course that appeared to be carrying it toward the U.S.A. Mr. Fox, meanwhile, was embroiled in a hardly unexpected but no less devastating crisis of a more domestic nature: for Lizzie had had her diamonds stolen—for real this time! She had been keeping them in a locked drawer in her room at the loathsome Mrs. Carbuncle's. If she reported the theft, she would be admitting that they hadn't been in the strongbox stolen in Scotland. Her only hope was that they, and the thieves, were never found.

COMMONWEALTH IN UPROAR. CARIBBEAN MEMBERS REGISTER SHARP PROTEST. BRITS TO BASH BIG APPLE?

The British and American papers were held up side by side on BBC. Navigation experts were produced, with pointers and maps, who estimated that, on its current course, the south (now north) of England would nose into the crook of New York Harbor, where Long Island meets New Jersey, so that Dover would be in sight of the New York City skyline. Plymouth was expected to end up off Montauk and Brighton somewhere in the middle, where there were no place-names on the satellite pictures. Harrison kept a map under the bar for settling bets, and when he pulled it out after "Our Daily Log," Mr. Fox was alarmed (but not surprised) to see that the area where Brighton was headed was dominated by a city whose name evoked images too lurid to visualize.

Babylon.

On the day that Lizzie got her first visit from Scotland Yard, Mr. Fox saw a charter fishing boat holding steady off the shore, making about three knots. It was the *Judy J* out of Islip, and the rails were packed with people waving. Mr. Fox waved back, and waved Anthony's paw for him. An airplane flew low over the beach towing a sign. On the telly that night, Mr. Fox could see on the satellite picture that Brighton was already in the lee of Long Island; that was why the wind was dropping. The BBC showed clips from *King Kong*.

"New York City is preparing to evacuate," said the announcer, "fearing that the shock of collision with ancient England will cause the fabled skyscrapers of Manhattan to tumble." He seemed pleased by the prospect, as did the Canadian earthquake expert he interviewed, as, indeed, did Harrison. New York City officials were gloomier; they feared the panic more than the actual collision. The next morning there were two boats off the shore, and in the afternoon, five. The waves, coming in at an angle, looked tentative after the bold swells of the mid-Atlantic. At tea, Lizzie was visited for the second time by Scotland Yard. Something seemed to have gone out of her, some of her fight, her spunk. Something in the air outside the tearoom was different, too, but it wasn't until he and Anthony approached the cricket ground that Mr. Fox realized what it was. It was the wind. It was gone altogether. The boys were struggling to raise the same kites that had flown so eagerly only a few days before. As soon as they stopped running, the kites came down. Anthony ran and barked wildly, as if calling on Heaven for assistance, but the boys went home before dark, disgusted.

That night Mr. Fox stepped outside the Pig & Thistle for a moment after supper. The street was as still as he had always imagined a graveyard might be. Had everyone left Brighton, or were they just staying indoors? According to "Our Daily Log," the feared panic in New York City had failed to materialize. Video clips showed horrendous traffic jams, but they were apparently normal. The King was . . . but just as the BBC was about to cut to Buckingham Palace, the picture began to flicker, and an American game show came on. "Who were the Beatles," said a young woman standing in a sort of bright pulpit. It was a statement and not a question.

"The telly has arrived before us," said Harrison, turning off the sound but leaving the picture. "Shall we celebrate with a whiskey? My treat tonight."

Mr. Fox's room, left to him by Mr. Singh, the original owner of the Pig & Thistle, was on the top floor under a gable. It was small; he and Anthony shared a bed. That night they were awakened by a mysterious, musical scraping sound. "Woof," said Anthony, in his sleep. Mr. Fox listened with trepidation; he thought at first that someone, a thief certainly, was moving the piano out of the public room downstairs. Then he remembered that the piano had been sold twenty years before. There came a deeper rumble from far away—and then silence. A bell rang across town. A horn honked; a door slammed. Mr. Fox looked at the time on the branch bank across the street (he had positioned his bed to save the cost of a clock): it was 4:36 A.M., Eastern Standard Time. There were no more unusual sounds, and the bell stopped ringing. Anthony had already drifted back to sleep, but Mr. Fox lay awake, with his eyes open. The anxiety he had felt for the past several days (indeed, years) was mysteriously gone, and he was enjoying a pleasant feeling of anticipation that was entirely new to him.

"Hold still," Mr. Fox told Anthony, as he brushed him and snapped on his little tweed suit. The weather was getting colder. Was it his imagination, or was the light through the window over the breakfast table different as the Finn served him his boiled egg and toast and marmalade and tea with milk? There was a fog, the first in weeks. The street outside the inn was deserted, and as he crossed the King's Esplanade and climbed the twelve steps, Mr. Fox saw that the Boardwalk was almost empty, too. There were only two or three small groups, standing at the railing, staring at the fog as if at a blank screen.

There were no waves, no wake; the water lapped at the sand with nervous, pointless motions like an old lady's fingers on a shawl. Mr. Fox took a place at the rail. Soon the fog began to lift; and emerging in the near distance, across a gray expanse of water, like the image on the telly when it has first been turned on, Mr. Fox saw a wide, flat beach. Near the center was a cement bathhouse. Knots of people stood on the sand, some of them by parked cars. One of them shot a gun into the air; another waved a striped flag. Mr. Fox waved Anthony's paw for him.

America (and this could only be America) didn't seem very developed. Mr. Fox had expected, if not skyscrapers, at least more buildings. A white lorry pulled up beside the bathhouse. A man in uniform got out, lit a cigarette, looked through binoculars. The lorry said GOYA on the side.

"Welcome to Long Island," said a familiar voice. It was the African. Mr. Fox nodded but didn't say anything. He could see the girl on the African's other side, looking through binoculars. He wondered if she and the GOYA man were watching each other. "If you expected skyscrapers, they're fifty miles west of here, in Dover," said the African.

"West?"

"Dover's west now, since England's upside down. That's why the sun rises over Upper Beeding."

Mr. Fox nodded. Of course. He had never seen the sun rising, though he felt no need to say so.

"Everyone's gone to Dover. You can see Manhattan, the Statue of Liberty, the Empire State Building, all from Dover."

Mr. Fox nodded. Reassured by the girl's silence so far, he asked in a whisper, "So what place is this; where are we now?"

"Jones Beach."

"Not Babylon?"

"You bloody wish," said the girl.

Mr. Fox was exhausted. Lizzie was being harried like the fox she herself had hunted with such bloodthirsty glee in Scotland. As Major Mackintosh closed in, she seemed to take a perverse pleasure in the hopelessness of her situation, as if it bestowed on her a vulnerability she had never before possessed, a treasure more precious to her than the Eustace family diamonds. "Mr. Fox?" asked Mrs. Oldenshield.

"Mr. Fox?" She was shaking his shoulder. "Oh, I'm quite all right," he said. The book had fallen off his lap, and she had caught him sleeping. Mrs. Oldenshield had a letter for him. (A letter for him!) It was from his niece, even though it was only the tenth of the month. There was nothing to do but open it. Mr. Fox began, as usual, at the ending, to make sure there were no surprises, but this time there were. "Until then," he read. As he scanned back through, he saw mention of "two ferries a day," and he couldn't read on. How had she gotten Mrs. Oldenshield's address? Did she expect him to come to America? He folded the letter and put it into his pocket. He couldn't read on.

That evening the BBC was back on the air. The lights of Manhattan could be seen on live video from atop the cliffs of Dover, shimmering in the distance through the rain (for England had brought rain). One-day passes were being issued by both governments, and queues were already six blocks long. The East (now West)

Kent ferry from Folkestone to Coney Island was booked solid for the next three weeks. There was talk of service to Eastbourne and Brighton as well. The next morning after breakfast, Mr. Fox lingered over his tea, examining a photograph of his niece which he had discovered in his letter box while putting her most recent (and most alarming) letter away. She was a serious-looking nine-year-old with a yellow ribbon in her light brown hair. Her mother, Mr. Fox's sister, Clare, held an open raincoat around them both. All this was thirty years ago, but already her hair was streaked with gray. The Finn cleared the plates, which was the signal for Mr. Fox and Anthony to leave. There was quite a crowd on the Boardwalk, near the West Pier, watching the first ferry from America steaming across the narrow sound. Or was "steaming" the word? It was probably powered by some new type of engine. Immigration officers stood idly by, with their clipboards closed against the remnants of the fog (for England had brought fog). Mr. Fox was surprised to see Harrison at the end of the pier, wearing a windbreaker and carrying a paper bag that was greasy, as if it contained food. Mr. Fox had never seen Harrison in the day, or outside, before; in fact, he had never seen his legs. Harrison was wearing striped pants, and before Mr. Fox could speak to him he sidled away like a crab into the crowd. There was a jolt as the ferry struck the pier. Mr. Fox stepped back just as Americans started up the ramp like an invading army. In the front were teenagers, talking among themselves as if no one else could hear; older people, almost as loud, followed behind them. They seemed no worse than the Americans who came to Brighton every summer, only not as well dressed.

"Woof, woof!"

Anthony was yipping over his shoulder, and Mr. Fox turned and saw a little girl with light brown hair and a familiar yellow ribbon. "Emily?" he said, recognizing his niece from the picture. Or so he thought. "Uncle Anthony?" The voice came from behind him again. He turned and saw a lady in a faded Burberry. The fog was blowing away, and behind her he could see, for the first time that day, the drab American shore.

"You haven't changed a bit," the woman said. At first Mr. Fox thought she was his sister, Clare, just as she had been thirty years before, when she had brought her daughter to Brighton to meet him.

But of course Clare had been dead for twenty years; and the woman was Emily, who had then been almost ten, and was now almost forty; and the girl was her own child (the great-niece who had been growing up inexorably), who was almost ten. Children, it seemed, were almost always almost something.

"Uncle Anthony?" The child was holding out her arms. Mr. Fox was startled, thinking she was about to hug him; then he saw what she wanted and handed her the dog. "You can pet him," he said. "His name is Anthony, too."

"Really?"

"Since no one ever calls us both at the same time, it creates no confusion," said Mr. Fox.

"Can he walk?"

"Certainly he can walk. He just doesn't often choose to."

A whistle blew, and the ferry left with its load of Britons for America. Mr. Fox saw Harrison at the bow, holding his greasy bag with one hand and the rail with the other, looking a little sick, or perhaps apprehensive. Then he took his niece and great-niece for a stroll along the Boardwalk. The girl, Clare—she was named after her grandmother—walked ahead with Anthony, while Mr. Fox and his niece, Emily, followed behind. The other Americans had all drifted into the city looking for restaurants, except for the male teenagers, who were crowding into the amusement parlors along the Esplanade, which had opened for the day.

"If the mountain won't come to Mahomet, and so forth," said Emily, mysteriously, when Mr. Fox asked if she'd had a nice crossing. Her brown hair was streaked with gray. He recognized the coat now; it had been her mother's, his sister's, Clare's. He was trying to think of where to take them for lunch. The Finn at the Pig & Thistle served a pretty fair shepherd's pie, but he didn't want them to see where he lived. They were content, however, with fish and chips on the Boardwalk; certainly Anthony seemed pleased to have chips fed to him, one by one, by the little girl named for the sister Mr. Fox had met only twice: once when she had been a student at Cambridge (or was it Oxford? he got them confused) about to marry an American; and once when she had returned with her daughter for a visit.

"Her father, your grandfather, was an air-raid warden," Mr. Fox told Emily. "He was killed in action, as it were, when a house collapsed during a rescue; and when his wife (well, she wasn't exactly his wife) died giving birth to twins a week later, they were each taken in by one of those whose life he had saved. It was a boardinghouse, all single people, so there was no way to keep the two together, you see—the children, I mean. Oh dear, I'm afraid I'm talking all in a heap."

"That's okay," said Emily.

"At any rate, when Mr. Singh died and his inn was sold, my room was reserved for me, in accordance with his will, *in perpetuity,* which means as long as I remain in it. But if I were to move, you see, I would lose my patrimony entire."

"I see," said Emily. "And where is this place you go for tea?"

And so they spent the afternoon, and a rainy and an English afternoon it was, in the cozy tearoom with the faded purple drapes at the west (formerly east) end of Moncton Street where Mrs. Oldenshield kept Mr. Fox's complete set of Trollope on a high shelf, so he wouldn't have to carry them back and forth in all kinds of weather. While Clare shared her cake with Anthony, and then let him doze on her lap, Mr. Fox took down the handsome leather-bound volumes, one by one, and showed them to his niece and great-niece. "They are, I believe, the first complete edition," he said. "Chapman and Hall."

"And were they your father's?" asked Emily. "My grandfather's?"

"Oh no!" said Mr. Fox. "They belonged to Mr. Singh. His grandmother was English, and her own great-uncle had been, I believe, in the postal service in Ireland with the author, for whom I was, if I am not mistaken, named." He showed Emily the place in *The Eustace Diamonds* where he would have been reading that very afternoon, "were it not," he said, "for this rather surprisingly delightful family occasion."

"Mother, is he blushing," said Clare. It was a statement and not a question.

It was almost six when Emily looked at her watch—a man's watch, Mr. Fox noted—and said, "We had better get back to the pier, or we'll miss the ferry." The rain had diminished to a misty drizzle as they hurried along the Boardwalk. "I must apologize for our English weather," said Mr. Fox, but his niece stopped him with a hand on his sleeve. "Don't brag," she said, smiling. She saw Mr.

Fox looking at her big steel watch and explained that it had been found among her mother's things; she had always assumed it had been her grandfather's. Indeed, it had several dials, and across the face it said: "Civil Defense, Brighton." Across the bay, through the drizzle as through a lace curtain, they could see the sun shining on the sand and parked cars.

"Do you still live in, you know . . ." Mr. Fox hardly knew how to say the name of the place without sounding vulgar, but his niece came to his rescue. "Babylon? Only for another month. We're moving to Deer Park as soon as my divorce is final."

"I'm so glad," said Mr. Fox. "Deer Park sounds much nicer for the child."

"Can I buy Anthony a good-bye present?" Clare asked. Mr. Fox gave her some English money (even though the shops were all taking American), and she bought a paper of chips and fed them to the dog one by one. Mr. Fox knew Anthony would be flatulent for days, but it seemed hardly the sort of thing one mentioned. The ferry had pulled in, and the tourists who had visited America for the day were streaming off, loaded with cheap gifts. Mr. Fox looked for Harrison, but if he was among them he missed him. The whistle blew two warning toots. "It was kind of you to come," he said.

Emily smiled. "No big deal," she said. "It was mostly your doing anyway. I could never have made it all the way to England if England hadn't come here first. I don't fly."

"Nor do I." Mr. Fox held out his hand, but Emily gave him a hug, and then a kiss, and insisted that Clare give him both as well. When that was over, she pulled off the watch (it was fitted with an expandable band) and slipped it over his thin, sticklike wrist. "It has a compass built in," she said. "I'm sure it was your father's. And Mother always . . ."

The final boarding whistle swallowed her last words. "You can be certain I'll take good care of it," Mr. Fox called out. He couldn't think of anything else to say. "Mother, is he crying," said Clare. It was a statement and not a question. "Let's you and me watch our steps," said Emily.

"Woof," said Anthony, and mother and daughter ran down (for the pier was high, and the boat was low) the gangplank. Mr. Fox waved until the ferry had backed out and turned and everyone on board had gone inside, out of the rain, for it had started to rain in earnest. That night after dinner he was disappointed to find the bar unattended. "Anyone seen Harrison?" he asked. He had been looking forward to showing him the watch.

"I can get you a drink as well as him," said the Finn. She carried her broom with her and leaned it against the bar. She poured a whiskey and said, "Just indicate if you need another." She thought indicate meant ask. The King was on the telly, getting into a long car with the President. Armed men stood all around them. Mr. Fox went to bed.

The next morning Mr. Fox got up before Anthony. The family visit had been pleasant—indeed, wonderful—but he felt a need to get back to normal. While taking his constitutional, he watched the first ferry come in, hoping (somewhat to his surprise) that he might see Harrison in it; but no such luck. There were no English, and few Americans. The fog rolled in and out, like the same page on a book being turned over and over. At tea, Mr. Fox found Lizzie confessing (just as he had known she someday must) that the jewels had been in her possession all along. Now that they were truly gone, everyone seemed relieved, even the Eustace family lawyer. It seemed a better world without the diamonds.

"Did you hear that?"

"Beg your pardon?" Mr. Fox looked up from his book. Mrs. Oldenshield pointed at his teacup, which was rattling in its saucer. Outside, in the distance, a bell was ringing. Mr. Fox wiped off the book himself and put it on the high shelf, then pulled on his coat, picked up his dog, and ducked through the low door into the street. Somewhere across town a horn was honking. "Woof," said Anthony. There was a breeze for the first time in days. Knowing, or at least suspecting, what he would find, Mr. Fox hurried to the Boardwalk. The waves on the beach were flattened, as if the water were being sucked away from the shore. The ferry was just pulling out with the last of the Americans who had come to spend the day. They looked irritated. On the way back to the Pig & Thistle Mr. Fox stopped by the cricket ground, but the boys were nowhere to be seen, the breeze being still too light for kiting, he supposed. "Perhaps tomorrow," he said to Anthony. The dog was silent, lacking the capacity for looking ahead.

That evening, Mr. Fox had his whiskey alone again. He had hoped that Harrison might have shown up, but there was no one behind the bar but the Finn and her broom. King Charles came on the telly, breathless, having just landed in a helicopter direct from the Autumn White House. He promised to send for anyone who had been left behind, then commanded (or, rather, urged) his subjects to secure the kingdom for the Atlantic. England was underway again. The next morning the breeze was brisk. When Mr. Fox and Anthony arrived at the Boardwalk, he checked the compass on his watch and saw that England had turned during the night, and Brighton had assumed its proper position, at the bow. A stout headwind was blowing, and the seawall was washed by a steady two-foot curl. Long Island was a low, dark blur to the north, far off the port (or left).

"Nice chop."

"Beg pardon?" Mr. Fox turned and was glad to see a big man in a tweed coat standing at the rail. He realized he had feared the African might have jumped ship like Harrison.

"Looks like we're making our four knots and more, this time."

Mr. Fox nodded. He didn't want to seem rude, but he knew if he said anything the girl would chime in. It was a dilemma.

"Trade winds," said the African. His collar was turned up, and his dreadlocks spilled over and around it like vines. "We'll make better time going back. If indeed we're going back. I say, is that a new watch?"

"Civil Defense chronometer," Mr. Fox said. "Has a compass built in. My father left it to me when he died."

"You bloody wish," said the girl.

"Should prove useful," said the African.

"I should think so," said Mr. Fox, smiling into the fresh salt wind; then, saluting the African (and the girl), he tucked Anthony under his arm and left the Boardwalk in their command. England was steady, heading south by southeast, and it was twenty past four, almost time for tea.

THE FRANCHISE

John Kessel

John Kessel writes a regular column on books for *The Magazine of Fantasy & Science Fiction* and teaches American literature and fiction writing at North Carolina State University. His inventive and erudite short fiction has won him a Nebula Award, a Theodore Sturgeon Memorial Award, and a Locus Award. He is the author of two novels, *Freedom Beach* (written with James Patrick Kelly) and *Good News from Outer Space;* he has also published a short-story collection, *Meeting in Infinity.*

About his Nebula Award finalist "The Franchise," he writes:

"I had the idea for 'The Franchise' years ago, when I first heard that Fidel Castro was scouted as a pitcher by several major-league baseball teams in 1948. But it didn't get written until I discovered that George Bush was also a superior baseball player, captain of the 1948 Yale squad that made the finals of the college World Series. The resemblance between the Senators and Giants of my story and the real ones of 1959 is purely expedient.

"Cynic that I am, sometimes I think the desire to lead a nation is a character flaw. I find George and Fidel fascinating, both admirable and astonishingly obtuse. It was interesting to try to get into their heads; I can't claim any great insight, but this is the closest I'll ever come to either the White House or the majors."

Whoever wants to know the heart and mind of America had better learn baseball.

—Jacques Barzun

ONE

When George Herbert Walker Bush strode into the batter's box to face the pitcher they called the Franchise, it was the bottom of the second, and the Senators were already a run behind.

But Killebrew had managed a bloop double down the right-field line and two outs later still stood on second in the bright October sunlight, waiting to be driven in. The bleachers were crammed full

of restless fans in colorful shirts. Far behind Killebrew, Griffith Stadium's green center-field wall zigzagged to avoid the towering oak
in Mrs. Mahan's backyard, lending the stadium its crazy dimensions.
They said the only players ever to homer into that tree were Mantle
and Ruth. George imagined how the stadium would erupt if he did
it, drove the first pitch right out of the old ball yard, putting the
Senators ahead in the first game of the 1959 World Series. If wishes
were horses, his father had told him more than once, then beggars
would ride.

George stepped into the box, ground in his back foot, squinted
at the pitcher. The first pitch, a fastball, so surprised him that he
didn't get his bat off his shoulder. Belt high, it split the middle of
the plate, but the umpire called, "Ball!"

"Ball?" Schmidt, the Giants' catcher, grumbled.

"You got a problem?" the umpire said.

"Me? I got no problem." Schmidt tossed the ball back to the
pitcher, who shook his head in histrionic Latin American dismay, as
if bemoaning the sins of the world that he'd seen only too much of
since he'd left Havana eleven years before. "But the Franchise, he
no like."

George ignored them and set himself for the next pitch. The big
Cuban went into his herky-jerky windup, deceptively slow, then
kicked and threw. George was barely into his swing when the ball
thwacked into the catcher's glove. "Steerike one!" the umpire
called.

He was going to have to get around faster. The next pitch was
another fastball, outside and high, but George had already triggered
before the release and missed it by a foot, twisting himself around
so that he almost fell over.

Schmidt took the ball out of his glove, showed it to George, and
threw it back to the mound.

The next was a curve, outside by an inch. Ball two.

The next a fastball that somehow George managed to foul into
the dirt.

The next a fastball up under his chin that had him diving into
the dirt himself. Ball three. Full count.

An expectant murmur rose in the crowd, then fell to a profound
silence, the silence of a church, of heaven, of a lover's secret heart.

Was his father among them, breathless, hoping? Thousands awaited the next pitch. Millions more watched on television. Killebrew took a three-step lead off second. The Giants made no attempt to hold him on. The chatter from the Senators' dugout lit up. "Come on, George Herbert Walker Bush, bear down! Come on, Professor, grit up!"

George set himself, weight on his back foot. He cocked his bat, squinted out at the pitcher. The vainglorious Latino gave him a piratical grin, shook off Schmidt's sign. George felt his shoulders tense. Calm, boy, calm, he told himself. You've been shot at, you've faced Prescott Bush across a dining-room table—this is nothing but baseball. But instead of calm he felt panic, and as the Franchise went into his windup his mind stood blank as a stone.

The ball started out right for his head. George jerked back in a desperate effort to get out of the way as the pitch, a curve of prodigious sweep, dropped through the heart of the plate. "Steerike!" the umpire called.

Instantly the scene changed from hushed expectation to sudden movement. The crowd groaned. The players relaxed and began jogging off the field. Killebrew kicked the dirt and walked back to the dugout to get his glove. The organist started up. Behind the big Chesterfield sign in right, the scorekeeper slid another goose egg onto the board for the Senators. Though the whole thing was similar to moments he had experienced more times than he would care to admit during his ten years in the minors, the simple volume of thirty thousand voices sighing in disappointment because he, George Herbert Walker Bush, had failed, left him standing stunned at the plate with the bat limp in his clammy hands. They didn't get thirty thousand fans in Chattanooga.

Schmidt flipped the ball toward the mound. As the Franchise jogged past him, he flashed George that superior smile. "A magnificent swing," he said.

George stumbled back to the dugout. Lemon, heading out to left, shook his head. "Nice try, Professor," the shortstop Consolo said.

"Pull your jock up and get out to first," said Lavagetto, the manager. He spat a stream of tobacco juice onto the sod next to the end of the dugout. "Señor Fidel Castro welcomes you to the bigs."

TWO

The Senators lost 7–1. Castro pitched nine innings, allowed four hits, struck out ten. George fanned three times. In the sixth, he let a low throw get by him; the runner ended up on third, and the Giants followed with four unearned runs.

In the locker room his teammates avoided him. Nobody had played well, but George knew they had him pegged as a choker. Lavagetto came through with a few words of encouragement. "We'll get 'em tomorrow," he said. George expected the manager to yank him for somebody who at least wouldn't cost them runs on defense. When he left without saying anything, George was grateful to him for at least letting him go another night before benching him.

Barbara and the boys had been in the stands, but had gone home. They would be waiting for him. He didn't want to go. The place was empty by the time he walked out through the tunnels to the street. His head was filled with images from the game. Castro had toyed with him; he no doubt enjoyed humiliating the son of a U.S. senator. The Cuban's look of heavy-lidded disdain sparked an unaccustomed rage in George. It wasn't good sportsmanship. You played hard, and you won or lost, but you didn't rub the other guy's nose in it. That was bush league, and George, despite his unfortunate name, was anything but bush.

That George Bush should end up playing first base for the Washington Senators in the 1959 World Series was the result of as improbable a sequence of events as had ever conspired to make a man of a rich boy. The key moment had come on a May Saturday in 1948 when he had shaken the hand of Babe Ruth.

That May morning the Yale baseball team was to play Brown, but before the game a ceremony was held to honor Ruth, donating the manuscript of his autobiography to the university library. George, captain of the Yale squad, would accept the manuscript. As he stood before the microphone set up between the pitcher's mound and second base, he was stunned by the gulf between the pale hulk standing before him and the legend he represented. Ruth, only fifty-three on that spring morning, could hardly speak for the throat cancer that was killing him. He gasped out a few words, stooped over, rail thin, no longer the giant he had been in the twenties. George took his hand. It was dry and papery and brown as a leaf in fall. Through his grip George felt the contact with glorious history, with feats of heroism that would never be matched, with 714 home runs and 1,356 extra-base hits, with a lifetime slugging percentage of .690, with the called shot and the sixty-homer season and the 1927 Yankees and the curse of the Red Sox. An electricity surged up his arm and directly into his soul. Ruth had accomplished as much, in his way, as a man could accomplish in a life, more, even, George realized to his astonishment, than had his father, Prescott Bush. He stood there stunned, charged with an unexpected, unasked-for purpose.

He had seen death in the war, had tasted it in the blood that streamed from his forehead when he'd struck it against the tail of the TBM Avenger as he parachuted out of the flaming bomber over the Pacific in 1943. He had felt death's hot breath on his back as he frantically paddled the yellow rubber raft away from Chichi Jima against waves pushing him back into the arms of the Japanese, had felt death draw away and offered up a silent prayer when the conning tower of the U.S.S. *Finback* broke through the agitated seas to save him from a savage fate—to, he always knew, some higher purpose. He had imagined that purpose to be business or public service. Now he recognized that he had been seeing it through his father's eyes, that in fact his fate lay elsewhere. It lay between the chalk lines of a playing field, on the greensward of the infield, within the smells of pine tar and sawdust and chewing tobacco and liniment. He could feel it through the tendons of the fleshless hand of Babe Ruth that he held in his own at that very instant.

The day after he graduated from Yale he signed, for no bonus, with the Cleveland Indians. Ten years later, George had little to show for his bold choice. He wasn't the best first baseman you ever saw. Nobody ever stopped him on the street to ask for his autograph. He never made the Indians, got traded to the Browns. He hung on, bouncing up and down the farm systems of seventh- and eighth-place teams. Every spring he went to Florida with high expectations, every April he started the season in Richmond, in Rochester, in Chattanooga. Just two months earlier he had considered packing it in and looking for another career. Then a series of miracles happened.

Chattanooga was the farm team for the Senators, who hadn't won a pennant since 1933. For fifteen years, under their notoriously cheap owner, Clark Griffith, they'd been as bad as you could get. But in 1959 their young third baseman, Harmon Killebrew, hit forty-two home runs. Sluggers Jim Lemon and Roy Sievers had career years. A big Kansas boy named Bob Allison won rookie of the year in center field. Camilo Pascual won twenty-two games, struck out 215 men. A kid named Jim Kaat won seventeen. Everything broke right, including Mickey Mantle's leg. After hovering a couple of games over .500 through the All Star break, the Senators got hot in August, won ninety games, and finished one ahead of the Yankees.

When, late in August, right fielder Albie Pearson got hurt, Lavagetto switched Sievers to right, and there was George Bush, thirty-five years old, starting at first base for the American League champions in the 1959 World Series against the New York Giants.

The Giants were heavy favorites. Who would bet against a team that fielded Willie Mays, Orlando Cepeda, Willie McCovey, Felipe Alou, and pitchers like Johnny Antonelli, the fireballer Toothpick Sam Jones, and the Franchise, Fidel Castro? If, prior to the series, you'd told George Herbert Walker Bush the Senators were doomed, he would not have disagreed with you. After game one he had no reason to think otherwise.

He stood outside the stadium looking for a cab, contemplating his series record—one game, 0 for 4, one error—when a pale old man in a loud sports coat spoke to him. "Just be glad you're here," the man said.

The man had watery blue eyes, a sharp face. He was thin enough to look ill. "I beg your pardon?"

"You're the fellow the Nats called up in September, right? Remember, even if you never play another inning, at least you were there. You felt the sun on your back, got dirt on your hands, saw the stands full of people from down on the field. Not many get even that much."

"The Franchise made me look pretty sick."

"You have to face him down."

"Easier said than done."

"Don't say—do."

"Who are you, old man?"

The man hesitated. "Name's Weaver. I'm a—a fan. Yes, I'm a baseball fan." He touched the brim of his hat and walked away.

George thought about it on the cab ride home. It did not make him feel much better. When he got back to the cheap furnished apartment they were renting, Barbara tried to console him.

"My father wasn't there, was he?" George said.

"No. But he called after the game. He wants to see you."

"Probably wants to give me a few tips on how to comport myself. Or maybe just gloat."

Bar came around behind his chair, rubbed his tired shoulders. George got up and switched on the television. While he waited for it to warm up, the silence stretched. He faced Barbara. She had put on a few pounds over the years, but he remembered the first time he'd seen her across the dance floor in the red dress. He was seventeen. "What do you think he wants?"

"I don't know, George."

"I haven't seen him around in the last ten years. Have you?"

The TV had warmed up, and Prescott Bush's voice blared out from behind George. "I hope the baseball Senators win," he was saying. "They've had a better year than the Democratic ones."

George twisted down the volume, stared for a moment at his father's handsome face, then snapped it off. "Give me a drink," he told Barbara. He noticed the boys standing in the doorway, afraid. Barbara hesitated, poured a scotch and water.

"And don't stint on the scotch!" George yelled. He turned to Neil. "What are you looking at, you little weasel! Go to bed."

Barbara slammed down the glass so hard the scotch splashed the counter. "What's got into you, George? You're acting like a crazy man."

George took the half-empty glass from her hand. "My father's got into me, that's what. He got into me thirty years ago, and I can't get him out."

Barbara shot him a look in which disgust outweighed pity and went back to the boys' room. George slumped in the armchair and stared at the sports page of the *Post* lying on the ottoman. CASTRO TO START SERIES, the headline read.

Castro. What did he know about struggle? Yet the egomaniac lout was considered a hero, while he, George Herbert Walker Bush, who at twenty-four had been at the head of every list of the young men most likely to succeed, had accomplished precisely nothing.

People who didn't know any better had assumed that because of his background, money, and education he would grow to be one of the ones who told others what it was necessary for them to do, but George was coming to realize, with a surge of panic, that he was not special. His moment of communion with Babe Ruth had been a delusion, because Ruth was another type of man. Perhaps Ruth was used by the teams that bought and sold him, but inside Ruth was some compulsion that drove him to be larger than the uses to which he was put, so that in the end he deformed those uses, remade the game itself.

George, talented though he had seemed, had no such *size*. The vital force that had animated his grandfather George Herbert Walker, after whom he was named, the longing after mystery that had impelled the metaphysical poet George Herbert, after whom that grandfather had been named, had diminished into a pitiful trickle in George Herbert Walker Bush. No volcanic forces surged inside him. When he listened late in the night, all he could hear of his soul was a thin keening, a buzz like a bug trapped in a jar. *Let me go, let me go,* it whined. Love me. Admire me. I pray to God and dad and the president and Mr. Griffith to make me a success.

That old man at the ball park was wrong. It was not enough, not nearly enough, just to be there. He wanted to *be* somebody. What good was it just to stand on first base in the World Series if you came away from it a laughingstock? To have your father call you not because you were a hero but only to remind you once again what a failure you are.

"I'll be damned if I go see him," George muttered to the empty room.

THREE

President Nixon called Lavagetto in the middle of the night with a suggestion for the batting order in the second game. "Put Bush in the number-five slot," Nixon said.

Lavagetto wondered how he was supposed to tell the President of the United States that he was out of his mind. "Yessir, Mr. President."

"See, that way you get another right-handed batter at the top of the order."

Lavagetto considered pointing out to the president that the Giants were pitching a right hander in game two. "Yessir, Mr. President," Lavagetto said. His wife was awake now, looking at him with irritation from her side of the bed. He put his hand over the mouthpiece and said, "Go to sleep."

"Who is it at this hour?"

"The President of the United States."

"Uh-huh."

Nixon had some observations about one-run strategies. Lavagetto agreed with him until he could get him off the line. He looked at his alarm clock. It was half past two.

Nixon had sounded full of manic energy. His voice dripped dogmatic assurance. He wondered if Nixon was a drinking man. Walter Winchell said that Eisenhower's death had shoved the veep into an office he was unprepared to hold.

Lavagetto shut off the light and lay back down, but he couldn't sleep. What about Bush? Damn Pearson for getting himself hurt. Bush should be down in the minors where he belonged. He looked to be cracking under the pressure like a ripe melon.

But maybe the guy could come through, prove himself. He was no kid. Lavagetto knew from personal experience the pressures of the Series, how the unexpected could turn on the swing of the bat. He recalled that fourth game of the '47 series, his double to right field that cost Floyd Bevens his no-hitter, and the game. Lavagetto had been a thirty-four-year-old utility infielder for the luckless Dodgers, an aging substitute playing out the string at the end of his career. In that whole season he'd hit only one other double. When he'd seen that ball twist past the right fielder, the joy had shot through his chest like lightning. The Dodger fans had gone crazy; his teammates had leapt all over him laughing and shouting and swearing like Durocher himself.

He remembered that, despite the miracle, the Dodgers had lost the Series to the Yankees in seven.

Lavagetto turned over. First in War, First in Peace, Last in the American League . . . that was the Washington Senators. He hoped young Kaat was getting more sleep than he was.

FOUR

Tuesday afternoon, in front of a wild capacity crowd, young Jim Kaat pitched one of the best games by a rookie in the history of the Series. The twenty-year-old left-hander battled Toothpick Sam Jones pitch for pitch, inning for inning. Jones struggled with his control, walking six in the first seven innings, throwing two wild pitches. If it weren't for the overeagerness of the Senators, swinging at balls a foot out of the strike zone, they would surely have scored; instead they squandered opportunity after opportunity. The fans grew restless. They could see it happening, in sour expectation of disaster built up over twenty-five frustrated years: Kaat would pitch brilliantly, and it would be wasted because the Giants would score on some bloop single.

Through seven the game stayed a scoreless tie. By some fluke George could not fathom, Lavagetto, instead of benching him, had moved him up in the batting order. Though he was still without a hit, he had been playing superior defense. In the seventh he snuffed a Giant uprising when he dove to snag a screamer off the bat of Schmidt for the third out, leaving runners at second and third.

Then, with two down in the top of the eighth, Cepeda singled. George moved in to hold him on. Kaat threw over a couple of times to keep the runner honest, with Cepeda trying to judge Kaat's move. Mays took a strike, then a ball. Cepeda edged a couple of strides away from first.

Kaat went into his stretch, paused, and whipped the ball to first, catching Cepeda leaning the wrong way. Picked off! But Cepeda, instead of diving back, took off for second. George whirled and threw hurriedly. The ball sailed over Consolo's head into left field, and Cepeda went to third. E-3.

Kaat was shaken. Mays hit a screamer between first and second. George dove, but it was by him, and Cepeda jogged home with the lead.

Kaat struck out McCovey, but the damage was done. "You bush-league clown!" a fan yelled. George's face burned. As he trotted off the field, from the Giants' dugout came Castro's shout: "A heroic play, Mr. Rabbit!"

George wanted to keep going through the dugout and into the

clubhouse. On the bench his teammates were conspicuously silent. Consolo sat down next to him. "Shake it off," he said. "You're up this inning."

George grabbed his bat and moved to the end of the dugout. First up in the bottom of the eighth was Sievers. He got behind 0–2, battled back as Jones wasted a couple, then fouled off four straight strikes until he'd worked Jones for a walk. The organist played charge lines and the crowd started chanting. Lemon sacrificed Sievers to second. Killebrew hit a drive that brought the people to their feet screaming before it curved just outside the left-field foul pole, then popped out to short. He threw down his bat and stalked back toward the dugout.

"C'mon, professor," Killebrew said as he passed Bush in the on-deck circle. "Give yourself a reason for being here."

Jones was a scary right hander with one pitch: the heater. In his first three at-bats George had been overpowered; by the last he'd managed a walk. This time he went up with a plan: he was going to take the first pitch, get ahead in the count, then drive the ball.

The first pitch was a fastball just high. Ball one.

Make contact. Don't force it. Go with the pitch.

The next was another fastball; George swung as soon as Jones let it go and sent a screaming line drive over the third baseman's head. The crowd roared, and he was halfway down the first-base line when the third-base umpire threw up his hands and yelled, "Foul ball!"

He caught his breath, picked up his bat, and returned to the box. Sievers jogged back to second. Schmidt, standing with his hands on his hips, didn't look at George. From the Giants' dugout George heard, "Kiss your luck good-bye, you effeminate rabbit! You rich man's table leavings! You are devoid of even the makings of guts!"

George stepped out of the box. Castro had come down the dugout to the near end and was leaning out, arms braced on the field, hurling his abuse purple faced. Rigney and the pitching coach had him by the shoulders, tugging him back. George turned away, feeling a cold fury in his belly.

He would show them all. He forgot to calculate, swept by rage. He set himself as far back in the box as possible. Jones took off his cap, wiped his forearm across his brow, and leaned over to check the signs. He shook off the first, then nodded and went into his windup.

As soon as he released George swung, and was caught completely off balance by a change-up. "Strike two, you shadow of a man!" Castro shouted. "Unnatural offspring of a snail and a worm! Strike two!"

Jones tempted him with an outside pitch; George didn't bite. The next was another high fastball; George started, then checked his swing. "Ball!" the home-plate ump called. Fidel booed. Schmidt argued, the ump shook his head. Full count.

George knew he should look for a particular pitch, in a particular part of the plate. After ten years of professional ball, this ought to be second nature, but Jones was so wild he didn't have a clue. George stepped out of the box, rubbed his hands on his pants. "Yes, wipe your sweaty hands, mama's boy! You have all the machismo of a bankbook!"

The rage came to his defense. He picked a decision out of the air, arbitrary as the breeze: fastball, outside.

Jones went into his windup. He threw his body forward, whipped his arm high over his shoulder. Fastball, outside. George swiveled his hips through the box, kept his head down, extended his arms. The contact of the bat with the ball was so slight he wasn't sure he'd hit it at all. A line drive down the right-field line, hooking as it rose, hooking, hooking . . . curling just inside the foul pole into the stands 320 feet away.

The fans exploded. George, feeling rubbery, jogged around first, toward second. Sievers pumped his fist as he rounded third; the Senators were up on their feet in the dugout shouting and slapping each other. Jones had his hands on his hips, head down and back to the plate. George rounded third and jogged across home, where he was met by Sievers, who slugged him in the shoulder, and the rest of his teammates in the dugout, who laughed and slapped his butt.

The crowd began to chant, "SEN-a-TOR, SEN-a-TOR." After a moment George realized they were chanting for him. He climbed out of the dugout again and tipped his hat, scanning the stands for Barbara and the boys. As he did he saw his father in the presidential box, leaning over to speak into the ear of the cheering President Nixon. He felt a rush of hope, ducked his head, and got back into the dugout.

Kaat held the Giants in the ninth, and the Senators won, 2–1.

In the locker room after the game, George's teammates whooped and slapped him on the back. Chuck Stobbs, the clubhouse comic, called him "the Bambino." For a while George hoped that his father might come down to congratulate him. Instead, for the first time in his career, reporters swarmed around him. They fired flashbulbs in salvoes. They pushed back their hats, flipped open their notebooks, and asked him questions.

"What's it feel like to win a big game like this?"

"I'm just glad to be here. I'm not one of these winning-is-everything guys."

"They're calling you the senator. Your father is a senator. How do you feel about that?"

"I guess we're both senators," George said. "He just got to Washington a little sooner than I did."

They liked that a lot. George felt the smile on his face like a frozen mask. For the first time in his life he was aware of the muscles it took to smile, as tense as if they were lifting a weight.

After the reporters left he showered. George wondered what his father had been whispering into the president's ear, while everyone around him cheered. Some sarcastic comment? Some irrelevant political advice?

When he got back to his locker, toweling himself dry, he found a note lying on the bench. He opened it eagerly. It read:

> To the Effeminate Rabbit:
> Even the rodent has his day. But not when the eagle pitches.
> Sincerely,
> Fidel Alejandro Castro Ruz

FIVE

That Fidel Castro would go so far out of his way to insult George Herbert Walker Bush would come as no surprise to anyone who knew him. Early in Castro's first season in the majors, a veteran Phillies reliever, after watching Fidel warm up, approached the young Cuban. "Where did you get that curve?" he asked incredulously.

"From you," said Fidel. "That's why you don't have one."

But sparking his reaction to Bush was more than simple egotism. Fidel's antipathy grew from circumstances of background and character that made such animosity as inevitable as the rising of the sun in the east of Oriente province where he had been born thirty-two years before.

Like George Herbert Walker Bush, Fidel was the son of privilege, but a peculiarly Cuban form of privilege, as different from the blue-blooded Bush variety as the hot and breathless climate of Oriente was from chilly New England. Like Bush, Fidel endured a father as parsimonious with his warmth as those New England winters. Young Fidelito grew up well acquainted with the back of Angel Castro's hand, the jeers of classmates who tormented him and his brother Raul for their illegitimacy. Though Angel Castro owned two thousand acres and had risen from common sugarcane laborer to local caudillo, he did not possess the easy assurance of the rich of Havana, for whom Oriente was the Cuban equivalent of Alabama. The Castros were peasants. Fidel's father was illiterate, his mother a maid. No amount of money could erase Fidel's bastardy.

This history raged in Fidelito. Always in a fight, alternating boasts with moody silences, he longed for accomplishment in a fiery way that cast the longing of Bush to impress his own father into a sickly shadow. At boarding school in Santiago, he sought the praise of his teachers and admiration of his schoolmates. At Belén, Havana's exclusive Jesuit preparatory school, he became the champion athlete of all of Cuba. "El Loco Fidel," his classmates called him as, late into the night, at an outdoor court under a light swarming with insects, he would practice basketball shots until his feet were torn bloody and his head swam with forlorn images of the ball glancing off the iron rim.

At the University of Havana, between the scorching expanses of the baseball and basketball seasons, Fidel toiled over the scorching expanse of the law books. He sought triumph in student politics as he did in sports. In the evenings he met in tiny rooms with his comrades and talked about junk pitches and electoral strategy, about the reforms that were only a matter of time because the people's will could not be forever thwarted. They were on the side of history. Larger than even the largest of men, history would overpower anyone unless, like Fidel, he aligned himself with it so as not to be swept under by the tidal force of its inescapable currents.

In the spring of 1948, at the same time George Herbert Walker Bush was shaking the hand of Babe Ruth, these currents transformed Fidel's life. He was being scouted by several major-league teams. In the university he had gained control of his fastball and given birth to a curve of so monstrous an arc that Alex Pompez, the Giants' scout, reported that the well-spoken law student owned "a hook like Bo-Peep." More significantly, Pirates' scout Howie Haak observed that Fidel "could throw and think at the same time."

Indeed Fidel could think, though no one could come close to guessing the content of his furious thought. A war between glory and doom raged within him. Fidel's fury to accomplish things threatened to keep him from accomplishing anything at all. He had made enemies. In the late forties, student groups punctuated elections for head of the law-school class with assassinations. Rival political gangs fought in the streets. Events conspired to drive Fidel toward a crisis. And so, on a single day in 1948, he abandoned his political aspirations, quit school, married his lover, the fair Mirta Diaz Balart, and signed a contract with the New York Giants.

It seemed a fortunate choice. In his rookie year he won fifteen games. After he took the Cy Young Award and was named MVP of the 1951 Series, the sportswriters dubbed him "the Franchise." This past season he had won twenty-nine. He earned, and squandered, a fortune. Controversy dogged him, politics would not let him go, the uniform of a baseball player at times felt much too small. His brother Raul was imprisoned when Batista overthrew the government to avoid defeat in the election of 1952. Fidel made friends among the expatriates in Miami. He protested U.S. policies. His alternative nickname became "the Mouth."

But all along Fidel knew his politics was mere pose. His spouting off to sports reporters did nothing compared to what money might do to help the guerrillas in the Sierra Maestra. Yet he had no money.

After the second game of the Series, instead of returning to the hotel Fidel took a cab down to the Mall. He needed to be alone. It was early evening when he got out at the Washington Monument. The sky beyond the Lincoln Memorial shone orange and purple. The air still held some of the sultry heat of summer, like an evening in Havana. But this was a different sort of capital. These North Americans liked to think of themselves as clean, rational men of law instead of passion, a land of Washingtons and Lincolns, but away from the public buildings it was still a southern city full of ex-slaves. Fidel looked down the Mall toward the bright Capitol, white and towering as a wedding cake, and wondered what he might have become had he continued law school. At one time he had imagined himself the Washington of his own country, a liberating warrior. The true heir of José Martí, scholar, poet, and revolutionary. Like Martí he admired the idealism of the United States, but like him he saw its dark side. Here at the Mall, however, you could almost forget about that in an atmosphere of bogus Greek democracy, of liberty and justice for all. You might even forget that this liberty could be bought and sold, a franchise purchasable for cold cash.

Fidel walked along the pool toward the Lincoln Memorial. The floodlights lit up the white columns, and inside shone upon the brooding figure of Lincoln. Despite his cynicism, Fidel was caught by the sight of it. He had been to Washington only once before, for the All Star Game in 1956. He remembered walking through Georgetown with Mirta on his arm, feeling tall and handsome, ignoring the scowl of the maître d' in the restaurant who clearly disapproved of two such dark ones in his establishment.

He'd triumphed but was not satisfied. He had forced others to admit his primacy through the power of his will. He had shown them, with his strong arm, the difference between right and wrong. He was the Franchise. He climbed up the steps into the Memorial, read the words of Lincoln's Second Inaugural address engraved on the wall. THE PROGRESS OF OUR ARMS UPON WHICH ALL ELSE CHIEFLY DEPENDS IS AS WELL KNOWN TO THE PUBLIC AS TO MYSELF . . . But he was still the crazy Cuban, taken little more seriously than Desi Arnaz, and the minute that arm that made him a useful commodity should begin to show signs of weakening—in that same minute he would be undone. IT MAY SEEM STRANGE THAT ANY MEN SHOULD DARE TO ASK A JUST GOD'S ASSISTANCE IN WRINGING THEIR BREAD FROM THE SWEAT OF OTHER MEN'S FACES BUT LET US JUDGE NOT THAT WE BE NOT JUDGED.

Judge not? Perhaps Lincoln could manage it, but Fidel was a different sort of man.

In the secrecy of his mind Fidel could picture another world than the one he lived in. The marriage of love to Mirta had long since gone sour, torn apart by Fidel's lust for renown on the ball field and his lust for the astonishing women who fell like fruit from the trees into the laps of players such as he. More than once he felt grief over his faithlessness. He knew his solitude to be just punishment. That was the price of greatness, for, after all, greatness was a crime and deserved punishment.

Mirta was gone now, and their son with her. She worked for the hated Batista. He thought of Raul languishing in Batista's prison on the Isle of Pines. Batista, embraced by this United States that ran Latin America like a company store. Raul suffered for the people, while Fidel ate in four-star restaurants and slept with a different woman in every city, throwing away his youth, and the money he earned with it, on excrement.

He looked up into the great sad face of Lincoln. He turned from the monument to stare out across the Mall toward the gleaming white shaft of the Washington obelisk. It was full night now. Time to amend his life.

SIX

The headline in the *Post* the next morning read, SENATOR BUSH EVENS SERIES. The story mentioned that Prescott Bush had shown up in the sixth inning and sat beside Nixon in the presidential box. But nothing more.

Bar decided not to go up to New York for the middle games of the Series. George traveled with the team to the Roosevelt Hotel. The home run had done something for him. He felt a new confidence.

The game-three starters were the veteran southpaw Johnny Antonelli for the Giants and Pedro Ramos for the Senators. The echoes of the national anthem had hardly faded when Allison led off for the Senators with a home run into the short porch in left field. The Polo Grounds fell dead silent. The Senators scored three runs in the first; George did his part, hitting a change-up into right center for a double, scoring the third run of the inning.

In the bottom half of the first the Giants came right back, tying it up on Mays's three-run homer.

After that the Giants gradually wore Ramos down, scoring a single run in the third and two in the fifth. Lavagetto pulled him for a pinch hitter in the sixth with George on third and Consolo at first, two outs. But Aspromonte struck out, ending the inning.

Though Castro heckled George mercilessly throughout the game and the brash New York fans joined in, he played above himself. The Giants eventually won, 8–3, but George went three for five. Despite his miserable first game he was batting .307 for the Series. Down two games to one, the Washington players felt the loss, but had stopped calling him "George Herbert Walker Bush" and started calling him "the Senator."

SEVEN

Lavagetto had set an eleven o'clock curfew, but Billy Consolo persuaded George to go out on the town. The Hot Corner was a dive on Seventh Avenue with decent Italian food and cheap drinks. George ordered a club soda and tried to get into the mood. Ramos moaned about the plate umpire's strike zone, and Consolo changed the subject.

Consolo had been a bonus boy; in 1953 the Red Sox had signed him right out of high school for $50,000. He had never panned out. George wondered if Consolo's career had been any easier to take than his own. At least nobody had hung enough expectations on George for him to be called a flop.

Stobbs was telling a story. "So the Baseball Annie says to him, 'But will you respect me in the morning?' and the shortstop says, 'Oh baby, I'll respect you like crazy!' "

While the others were laughing, George headed for the men's room. Passing the bar, he saw, in a corner booth, Fidel Castro talking to a couple of men in slick suits. Castro's eyes flicked over him but registered no recognition.

When George came out the men in suits were in heated conversation with Castro. In the back of the room somebody dropped a quarter into the jukebox, and Elvis Presley's slinky "Money Honey" blared out. Bush had no use for rock and roll. He sat at the table, ignored his teammates' conversation, and kept an eye on Castro. The Cuban was strenuously making some point, stabbing the tabletop with his index finger. After a minute George noticed that someone

at the bar was watching them, too. It was the pale old man he had
seen at Griffith Stadium.

On impulse, George went up to him. "Hello, old-timer. You
really must be a fan, if you followed the Series up here. Can I buy
you a drink?"

The man turned decisively from watching Castro, as if deliber-
ately putting aside some thought. He seemed about to smile but did
not. Small red splotches colored his face. "Buy me a ginger ale."

George ordered a ginger ale and another club soda and sat on
the next stool. "Money honey, if you want to get along with me,"
Elvis sang.

The old man sipped his drink. "You had yourself a couple of
good games," he said. "You're in the groove."

"I just got some lucky breaks."

"Don't kid me. I know how it feels when it's going right. You
know just where the next pitch is going to be, and there it is. Somebody hits a line drive right at you, you throw out your glove and snag
it without even thinking. You're in the groove."

"It comes from playing the game a long time."

The old man snorted. "Do you really believe this guff you spout?
Or are you just trying to hide something?"

"What do you mean? I've spent ten years playing baseball."

"And you expect me to believe you still don't know anything
about it? Experience doesn't explain the groove." The man looked
as if he were watching something far away. "When you're in that
groove you're not playing the game, the game is playing you."

"But you have to plan your moves."

The old man looked at him as if he were from Mars. "Do you
plan your moves when you're making love to your wife?" He finished
his ginger ale, took another look back at Castro, then left.

Everyone, it seemed, knew what was wrong with him. George
felt steamed. As if that wasn't enough, as soon as he returned to the
table Castro's pals left and the Cuban swaggered over to George,
leaned into him, and blew cigar smoke into his face. "I know you,
George Herbert Walker Bush," he said, "Sen-a-tor Rabbit. The rich
man's son."

George pushed him away. "You know, I'm beginning to find your
behavior darned unconscionable, compadre."

"I stand here quaking with fear," Castro said. He poked George in the chest. "Back home in Biran we had a pen for the pigs. The gate of this pen was in disrepair. But it is still a fact, Senator Rabbit, that the splintered wooden gate of that pigpen, squealing on its rusted hinges, swung better than you."

Consolo started to get up, but George put a hand on his arm. "Say, Billy, our Cuban friend here didn't by any chance help you pick out this restaurant tonight, did he?"

"What, are you crazy? Of course not."

"Too bad. I thought if he did, we could get some good Communist food here."

The guys laughed. Castro leaned over.

"Very funny, Machismo Zero." His breath reeked of cigar smoke, rum, and garlic. "I guarantee that after tomorrow's game you will be even funnier."

EIGHT

Fidel had never felt sharper than he did during his warmups the afternoon of the fourth game. It was a cool fall day, partial overcast with a threat of rain, a breeze blowing out to right. The chill air only invigorated him. Never had his curve had more bite, his screwball more movement. His arm felt supple, his legs strong. As he strode in from the bull pen to the dugout, squinting out at the apartment buildings on Coogan's Bluff towering over the stands, a great cheer rose from the crowd.

Before the echoes of the national anthem had died he walked the first two batters, on eight pitches. The fans murmured. Schmidt came out to talk with him. "What's wrong?"

"Nothing is wrong," Fidel said, sending him back.

He retired Lemon on a pop fly and Killebrew on a fielder's choice. Bush came to the plate with two outs and men on first and second. The few Washington fans who had braved the Polo Grounds set up a chant: "SEN-a-TOR, SEN-a-TOR!"

Fidel studied Bush. Beneath Bush's bravado he could see panic in every motion of the body he wore like an ill-fitting suit. Fidel struck him out on three pitches.

Kralick held the Giants scoreless through three innings.

As the game progressed Fidel's own personal game, the game of pitcher and batter, settled into a pattern. Fidel mowed down the batters after Bush in the order with predictable dispatch, but fell into trouble each time he faced the top of the order, getting just enough outs to bring Bush up with men on base and the game in the balance. He did this four times in the first seven innings.

Each time Bush struck out.

In the middle of the seventh, after Bush fanned to end the inning, Mays sat down next to Fidel on the bench. "What the hell do you think you're doing?"

Mays was the only player on the Giants whose stature rivaled that of the Franchise. Fidel, whose success came as much from craft as physical prowess, could not but admit that Mays was the most beautiful ball player he had ever seen. "I'm shutting out the Washington Senators in the fourth game of the World Series," Fidel said.

"What's this mickey mouse with Bush? You trying to make him look bad?"

"One does not have to try very hard."

"Well, cut it out—before you make a mistake with Killebrew or Sievers."

Fidel looked him dead in the eyes. "I do not make mistakes."

The Giants entered the ninth with a 3–0 lead. Fidel got two quick outs, then gave up a single to Sievers and walked Lemon and Killebrew to load the bases. Bush, at bat, represented the lead run. Schmidt called time and came out again. Rigney hurried out from the dugout, and Mays, to the astonishment of the crowd, came all the way in from center. "Yank him," he told Rigney.

Rigney looked exasperated. "Who's managing this team, Willie?"

"He's setting Bush up to be the goat."

Rigney looked at Fidel. Fidel looked at him. "Just strike him out," the manager said.

Fidel rubbed up the ball and threw three fastballs through the heart of the plate. Bush missed them all. By the last strike the New York fans were screaming, rocking the Polo Grounds with a parody of the Washington chant: "Sen-a-TOR, Sen-a-TOR, BUSH, BUSH, BUSH!" and exploding into fits of laughter. The Giants led the series, 3–1.

NINE

George made the cabbie drop him off at the corner of Broadway and Pine, in front of the old Trinity Church. He walked down Wall Street through crowds of men in dark suits, past the Stock Exchange to the offices of Brown Brothers, Harriman. In the shadows of the buildings the fall air felt wintry. He had not been down here in more years than he cared to remember.

The secretary, Miss Goode, greeted him warmly; she still remembered him from his days at Yale. Despite Prescott Bush's move to the Senate, they still kept his inner office for him, and as George stood outside the door he heard a piano. His father was singing. He had a wonderful singing voice, of which he was too proud.

George entered. Prescott Bush sat at an upright piano, playing Gilbert and Sullivan:

> "Go, ye heroes, go to glory
> Though you die in combat gory,
> Ye shall live in song and story.
> Go to immortality!"

Still playing, he glanced over his shoulder at George, then turned back and finished the verse:

> "Go to death, and go to slaughter;
> Die, and every Cornish daughter
> With her tears your grave shall water.
> Go, ye heroes, go and die!"

George was all too familiar with his father's theatricality. Six feet four inches tall, with thick salt-and-pepper hair and a handsome, craggy face, he carried off his Douglas Fairbanks imitation without any hint of self-consciousness. It was a quality George had tried to emulate his whole life.

Prescott adjusted the sheet music and swiveled his piano stool around. He waved at the sofa against the wall beneath his shelf of golfing trophies and photos of the Yale Glee Club. "Sit down, son.

I'm glad you could make it. I know you must have a lot on your mind."

George remained standing. "What did you want to see me about?"

"Relax, George. This isn't the dentist's office."

"If it were I would know what to expect."

"Well, one thing you can expect is to hear me tell you how proud I am."

"Proud? Did you see that game yesterday?"

Prescott Bush waved a hand. "Temporary setback. I'm sure you'll get them back this afternoon."

"Isn't it a little late for compliments?"

Prescott looked at him as calmly as if he were appraising some stock portfolio. His bushy eyebrows quirked a little higher. "George, I want you to sit down and shut up."

Despite himself, George sat. Prescott got up and paced to the window, looked down at the street, then started pacing again, his big hands knotted behind his back. George began to dread what was coming.

"George, I have been indulgent of you. Your entire life, despite my misgivings, I have treated you with kid gloves. You are not a stupid boy; at least your grades in school suggested you weren't. You've got that Phi Beta Kappa key, too—which only goes to show you what they are worth." He held himself very erect. "How old are you now?"

"Thirty-five."

Prescott shook his head. "Thirty-five? Lord. At *thirty-five* you show no more sense than you did at seventeen, when you told me that you intended to enlist in the Navy. Despite the fact that the Secretary of War himself, God-forbid-me *Franklin D. Roosevelt's* Secretary of War, had just told the graduating class that you, the cream of the nation's youth, could best serve your country by going to college instead of getting shot up on some Pacific island."

He strolled over to the piano, flipped pensively through the sheet music on top. "I remember saying to myself that day that maybe you knew something I didn't. You were young. I recalled my own reck-lessness in the first war. God knew we needed to lick the Japanese. But that didn't mean a boy of your parts and prospects should do the fighting. I prayed you'd survive and that by the time you came back you'd have grown some sense." Prescott closed the folder of music and faced him.

George, as he had many times before, instead of looking into his father's eyes looked at a point beyond his left ear. At the moment, just past that ear he could see half of a framed photograph of one of his father's singing groups. Probably the Silver Dollar Quartet. He could not make out the face of the man on the end of the photo. Some notable businessman, no doubt. A man who sat on four boards of directors making decisions that could topple the economies of six banana republics while he went to the club to shoot eight-handicap golf. Someone like Prescott Bush.

"When you chose this baseball career," his father said, "I finally realized you had serious problems facing reality. I would think the dismal history of your involvement in this sport might have taught you something. Now, by the grace of God and sheer luck you find yourself, on the verge of your middle years, in the spotlight. I can't imagine how it happened. But I know one thing: you must take advantage of this situation. You must seize the brass ring before the carousel stops. As soon as the Series is over I want you to take up a career in politics."

George stopped looking at the photo. His father's eyes were on his. "Politics? But, dad, I thought I could become a coach."

"A coach?"

"A coach. I don't know anything about politics. I'm a baseball player. Nobody is going to elect a baseball player."

Prescott Bush stepped closer. He made a fist, beginning to be carried away by his own rhetoric. "Twenty years ago, maybe, you would be right. But, George, times are changing. People want an attractive face. They want somebody famous. It doesn't matter so much what they've done before. Look at Eisenhower. He had no experience of government. The only reason he got elected was because he was a war hero. Now you're a war hero, or at least we can dress you up into a reasonable facsimile of one. You're Yale educated, a brainy boy. You've got breeding and class. You're not bad looking. And thanks to this children's game, you're famous—for the next two weeks, anyway. So after the Series we strike while the iron's hot. You retire from baseball. File for Congress on the Republican ticket in the third Connecticut district."

"But I don't even live in Connecticut."

"Don't be contrary, George. You're a baseball player; you live on the road. Your last stable residence before you took up this, this—baseball—was New Haven. I've held an apartment there for years in your name. That's good enough for the people we're going to convince."

His father towered over him. George got up, retreated toward the window. "But I don't know anything about politics!"

"So? You'll learn. Despite the fact I've been against your playing baseball, I have to say that it will work well for you. It's the national game. Every kid in the country wants to be a ball player, most of the adults do, too. It's hard enough for people from our class to overcome the prejudice against money, George. Baseball gives you the common touch. Why, you'll probably be the only Republican in the Congress ever to have showered with a Negro. On a regular basis, I mean."

"I don't even like politics."

"George, there are only two kinds of people in the world, the employers and the employees. You were born and bred to the former. I will not allow you to persist in degrading yourself into one of the latter."

"Dad, really, I appreciate your trying to look out for me. Don't get me wrong, gratitude's my middle name. But I love baseball. There's some big opportunities there, I think. Down in Chattanooga I made some friends. I think I can be a good coach, and eventually I'll wear a manager's uniform."

Prescott Bush stared at him. George remembered that look when he'd forgotten to tie off the sailboat one summer up in Kennebunkport. He began to wilt. Eventually his father shook his head. "It comes to me at last that you do not possess the wits that God gave a Newfoundland retriever."

George felt his face flush. He looked away. "You're just jealous because I did what you never had the guts to do. What about you and your golf? You, you—dilettante! I'm going to be a manager!"

"George, if I want to I can step into that outer office, pick up the telephone, and in fifteen minutes set in motion a chain of events that will guarantee you won't get a job mopping toilets in the clubhouse."

George retreated to the window. "You think you can run my

life? You just want me to be another appendage of Senator Bush. Well, you can forget it! I'm not your boy anymore."

"You'd rather spend the rest of your life letting men like this Communist Castro make a fool of you?"

George caught himself before he could completely lose his temper. Feeling hopeless, he drummed his knuckles on the windowsill, staring down into the narrow street. Down below them brokers and bankers hustled from meeting to meeting trying to make a buck. He might have been one of them. Would his father have been any happier?

He turned. "Dad, you don't know anything. Try for once to understand. I've never been so alive as I've been for moments—just moments out of eleven years—on the ball field. It's truly American."

"I agree with you, George—it's as American as General Motors. Baseball is a product. You players are the assembly-line workers who make it. But you refuse to understand that, and that's your undoing. Time eats you up, and you end up in the dustbin, a wasted husk."

George felt the helpless fury again. "Dad, you've got to—"

"Are you going to tell me I *have to* do something, George?" Prescott Bush sat back down at the piano, tried a few notes. He peeked over his shoulder at George, unsmiling, and began again to sing:

> "Go and do your best endeavor,
> And before all links we sever,
> We will say farewell for ever.
> Go to glory and the grave!

> "For your foes are fierce and ruthless,
> False, unmerciful and truthless.
> Young and tender, old and toothless,
> All in vain their mercy crave."

George stalked out of the room, through the secretary's office, and down the corridor toward the elevators. It was all he could do to keep from punching his fist through the rosewood paneling. He felt his pulse thrumming in his temples, slowing as he waited for the dilatory elevator to arrive, rage turning to depression.

Riding down he remembered something his mother had said to

him twenty years before. He'd been one of the best tennis players at the River Club in Kennebunkport. One summer, in front of the whole family, he lost a championship match. He knew he'd let them down, and tried to explain to his mother that he'd only been off his game.

"You don't have a game," she'd said.

The elevator let him out into the lobby. On Seventh Avenue he stepped into a bar and ordered a beer. On the TV in the corner, sound turned low, an announcer was going over the highlights of the Series. The TV switched to an image of some play in the field. George heard a reference to "Senator Bush," but he couldn't tell which one of them they were talking about.

TEN

A few of the pitchers, including Camilo Pascual, the young right-hander who was to start game five, were the only others in the club-house when George showed up. The tone was grim. Nobody wanted to talk about how their season might be over in a few hours. Instead they talked fishing.

Pascual was nervous; George was keyed tighter than a Christmas toy. Ten years of obscurity, and now hero one day, goat the next. The memory of his teammates' hollow words of encouragement as he'd slumped back into the dugout each time Castro struck him out made George want to crawl into his locker and hide. The supercilious brown bastard. What kind of man would go out of his way to humiliate him?

Stobbs sauntered in, whistling. He crouched into a batting stance, swung an imaginary Louisville Slugger through Kralick's head, then watched it sail out into the imaginary bleachers. "Hey, guys, I got an idea," he said. "If we get the lead today, let's call time out."

But they didn't get the lead. By the top of the second, they were down 3–0. But Pascual, on the verge of being yanked, settled down. The score stayed frozen through six. The Senators finally got to Jones in the seventh when Allison doubled and Killebrew hit a towering home run into the bull pen in left center: 3–2, Giants. Meanwhile the Senators' shaky relief pitching held, as the Giants stranded runners in the sixth and eighth and hit into three double plays.

By the top of the ninth the Giants still clung to the 3–2 lead, three outs away from winning the Series, and the rowdy New York fans were gearing up for a celebration. The Senators' dugout was grim, but they had the heart of the order up: Sievers, Lemon, Killebrew. Between them they had hit ninety-four home runs that season. They had also struck out almost three hundred times.

Rigney went out to talk to Jones, then left him in, though he had Stu Miller up and throwing in the bull pen. Sievers took the first pitch for a strike, fouled off the second, and went down swinging at a high fastball. The crowd roared.

Lemon went into the hole 0–2, worked the count even, and grounded out to second.

The crowd, on their feet, chanted continuously now. Fans pounded on the dugout roof, and the din was deafening. Killebrew stepped into the batter's box, and George moved up to the on-deck circle. On one knee in the dirt, he bowed his head and prayed that Killer would get on base.

"He's praying!" Castro shouted from the Giants' dugout. "Well might you pray, Sen-a-tor Bush!"

Killebrew called time and spat toward the Giants. The crowd screamed abuse at him. He stepped back into the box. Jones went into his windup. Killebrew took a tremendous cut and missed. The next pitch was a change-up that Killebrew mistimed and slammed five hundred feet down the left-field line into the upper deck—foul. The crowd quieted. Jones stepped off the mound, wiped his brow, shook off a couple of signs, and threw another fastball that Killebrew slapped into right for a single.

That was it for Jones. Rigney called in Miller. Lavagetto came out and spoke to George. "All right. He won't try anything tricky. Look for the fastball."

George nodded, and Lavagetto bounced back into the dugout. "Come on, George Herbert Walker Bush!" Consolo yelled. George tried to ignore the crowd and the Giants heckling while Miller warmed up. His stomach was tied into twelve knots. He avoided looking into the box seats where he knew his father sat. Politics. What the blazes did he want with politics?

Finally Miller was ready. "Play ball!" the ump yelled. George stepped into the box.

He didn't wait. The first pitch was a fastball. He turned on it, made contact, but got too far under it. The ball soared out into left, a high, lazy fly. George slammed down his bat and, heart sinking, legged it out. The crowd cheered, and Alou was circling back to make the catch. George was rounding first, his head down, when he heard a stunned groan from fifty thousand throats at once. He looked up to see Alou slam his glove to the ground. Miller, on the mound, did the same. The Senators' dugout was leaping insanity. Somehow, the ball had carried far enough to drop into the overhanging upper deck, 250 feet away. Home run. Senators lead, 4–3.

"Lucky bastard!" Castro shouted as Bush rounded third.

Stobbs shut them down in the ninth, and the Senators won.

ELEVEN

SENATOR BUSH SAVES WASHINGTON! the headlines screamed. MAKES CASTRO SEE RED. They were comparing it to the 1923 Series, held in these same Polo Grounds, where Casey Stengel, a thirty-two-year-old outfielder who'd spent twelve years in the majors without doing anything that might cause anyone to remember him, batted .417 and hit home runs to win two games.

Reporters stuck to him like flies on sugar. The pressure of released humiliation loosened George's tongue. "I know Castro's type," he said, snarling what he hoped was a good imitation of a manly snarl. "At the wedding he's the bride, at the funeral he's the dead person. You know, the corpse. That kind of poor sportsmanship just burns me up. But I've been around. He can't get my goat because of where I've got it in the guts department."

The papers ate it up. Smart money had said the Series would never go back to Washington. Now they were on the train to Griffith Stadium, and if the Senators were going to lose, at least the home fans would have the pleasure of going through the agony in person.

Game six was a slugfest. Five homers: McCovey, Mays, and Cepeda for the Giants; Naragon and Lemon for the Senators. Kaat and Antonelli were both knocked out early. The lead changed back and forth three times.

George hit three singles, a sacrifice fly, and drew a walk. He scored twice. The Senators came from behind to win, 10–8. In the ninth, George sprained his ankle sliding into third. It was all he could do to hobble into the locker room after the game.

"It doesn't hurt," George told the reporters. "Bar always says, and she knows me better than anybody, go ahead and ask around, 'You're the game one, George.' Not the gamy one, mind you!" He laughed, smiled a crooked smile.

"A man's gotta do what a man's gotta do," he told them. "That strong but silent type of thing. My father said so."

TWELVE

Fonseca waited until Fidel emerged into the twilight outside the Fifth Street stadium exit. As Fonseca approached, his hand on the slick automatic in his overcoat pocket, his mind cast back to their political years in Havana, where young men such as they, determined to seek prominence, would be as likely to face the barrel of a pistol as an electoral challenge. Ah, nostalgia.

"Pretty funny, that Sen-a-TOR Bush," Fonseca said. He shoved Fidel back toward the exit. Nobody was around.

If Fidel was scared, a slight narrowing of his eyes was the only sign. "What is this about?"

"Not a thing. Raul says hello."

"Hello to Raul."

"Mirta says hello, too."

"You haven't spoken to her." Fidel took a cigar from his mohair jacket, fished a knife from a pocket, trimmed off the end, and lit it with a battered Zippo. "She doesn't speak with exiled radicals. Or mobsters."

Fonseca was impressed by the performance. "Are you going to do this job, finally?"

"I can only do my half. One cannot make a sow look like a ballet dancer."

"It is not apparent to our friends that you're doing your half."

"Tell them I am truly frightened, Luis." He blew a plume of smoke. It was dark now, almost full night. "Meanwhile, I am hungry. Let me buy you a Washington dinner."

The attitude was all too typical of Fidel, and Fonseca was sick of it. He had fallen under Fidel's spell back in the university, thought him some sort of great man. In 1948 his self-regard could be justified as necessary boldness. But when the head of the National Sports Directory was shot dead in the street, Fonseca had not been the only one to think Fidel was the killer. It was a gesture of suicidal machismo of the sort that Fidel admired. Gunmen scoured the streets for them. While Fonseca hid in a series of airless apartments, Fidel got a quick tryout with the Giants, married Mirta, and abandoned Havana, leaving Fonseca and their friends to deal with the consequences.

"If you don't take care, Fidel, our friends will buy you a Washington grave."

"They are not my friends—or yours."

"No, they aren't. But this was our choice, and you have to go through with it." Fonseca watched a beat cop stop at the corner, then turn away down the street. He moved closer, stuck the pistol into Fidel's ribs. "You know, Fidel, I have a strong desire to shoot you right now. Who cares about the World Series? It would be pleasant just to see you bleed."

The tip of Fidel's cigar glowed in the dark. "This Bush would be no hero then."

"But I would be."

"You would be a traitor."

Fonseca laughed. "Don't say that word again. It evokes too many memories." He plucked the cigar from Fidel's hand, threw it onto the sidewalk. "Athletes should not smoke."

He pulled the gun back, drew his hand from his overcoat, and crossed the street.

THIRTEEN

The night before, the Russians announced they had shot down a U.S. spy plane over the Soviet Union. A pack of lies, President Nixon said. No such planes existed.

Meanwhile, on the clubhouse radio, a feverish announcer was discussing strategy for game seven. A flock of telegrams had arrived to urge the Senators on. Tacked on the bulletin board in the locker room, they gave pathetic glimpses into the hearts of the thousands who had for years tied their sense of well-being to the fate of a punk team like the Senators.

Show those racially polluted commie-symps what Americans stand for.

My eight year old son, crippled by polio, sits up in his wheelchair so that he can watch the games on TV.

Jesus Christ, creator of the heavens and earth, is with you.

As George laced up his spikes over his aching ankle in preparation for the game, thinking about facing Castro one last time, it came to him that he was terrified.

In the last week he had entered an atmosphere he had not lived in since Yale. He was a hero. People had expectations of him. He was admired and courted. If he had received any respect before, it was the respect given to someone who refused to quit when every indication shouted he ought to try something else. He did not have the braggadocio of a Castro. Yet here, miraculously, he was shining.

Except he *knew* that Castro was better than he was, and he knew that anybody who really knew the game knew it, too. He knew that this week was a fluke, a strange conjunction of the stars that had knocked him into the "groove," as the old man in the bar had said. It could evaporate at any instant. It could already have evaporated.

Lavagetto and Mr. Griffith came in and turned off the radio. "Okay, boys," Lavagetto said. "People in this city been waiting a long time for this game. A lot of you been waiting your whole careers for it, and you younger ones might not get a lot of chances to play in the seventh game of the World Series. Nobody gave us a chance to be here today, but here we are. Let's make the most of it, go out there and kick the blazes out of them, then come back in and drink some champagne!"

The team whooped and headed out to the field.

Coming up the tunnel, the sound of cleats scraping damp concrete, the smell of stale beer and mildew, Bush could see a sliver of the bright grass and white baselines, the outfield fence and crowds in the bleachers, sunlight so bright it hurt his eyes. When the team climbed the dugout steps onto the field, a great roar rose from the throats of the thirty thousand fans. He had never heard anything so beautiful, or frightening. The concentrated focus of their hope swelled George's chest with unnameable emotion, brought tears to his eyes, and he ducked his head and slammed his fist into his worn first baseman's glove.

The teams lined up on the first- and third-base lines for the National Anthem. The fans began cheering even before the last line of the song faded away, and George jogged to first, stepping on the bag for good luck. His ankle twinged; his whole leg felt hot. Ramos finished his warmups, the umpire yelled "Play ball!" and they began.

Ramos set the Giants down in order in the top of the first. In the home half Castro gave up a single to Allison, who advanced to third on a single by Lemon. Killebrew walked. Bush came up with bases loaded, one out. He managed a fly ball to right, and Allison beat the throw to the plate. Castro stuck out Bertoia to end the inning. 1–0, Senators.

Ramos retired the Giants in order in the second. In the third, Lemon homered to make it 2–0.

Castro had terrific stuff, but seemed to be struggling with his control. Or else he was playing games again. By the fourth inning he had seven strikeouts to go along with the two runs he'd given up. He shook off pitch after pitch, and Schmidt went out to argue with him. Rigney talked to him in the dugout, and the big Cuban waved his arms as if emphatically arguing his case.

Schmidt homered for the Giants in the fourth, but Ramos was able to get out of the inning without further damage. Senators, 2–1.

In the bottom of the fourth, George came up with a man on first. Castro struck him out on a high fastball that George missed by a foot.

In the Giants' fifth, Spencer doubled off the wall in right. Alou singled him home to tie the game, and one out later Mays launched a triple over Allison's head into the deepest corner of center field, just shy of the crazy wall protecting Mrs. Mahan's backyard. Giants up, 3–2. The crowd groaned. As he walked out to the mound, Lavagetto was already calling for a left-hander to face McCovey. Ramos kicked the dirt, handed him the ball, and headed to the showers, and Stobbs came on to pitch to McCovey. He got McCovey on a weak grounder to George at first, and Davenport on a pop fly.

The Senators failed to score in the bottom of the fifth and sixth, but in the seventh George, limping for real now, doubled in Killer to tie the game, and was driven home, wincing as he forced weight down on his ankle, on a single by Naragon. Senators 4–3. The crowd roared.

Rigney came out to talk to Castro, but Castro convinced him to let him stay in. He'd struck out twelve already, and the Giants' bull pen was depleted after the free-for-all in game six.

The score stayed that way through the eighth. By the top of the ninth the crowd was going wild in the expectation of a world championship. Lavagetto had pulled Stobbs, who sat next to Bush in his warmup jacket, and put in the right-hander Hyde, who'd led the team in saves.

The Giants mounted another rally. On the first pitch, Spencer laid a bunt down the first-base line. Hyde stumbled coming off the mound, and George, taken completely by surprise, couldn't get to it on his bad foot. He got up limping, and the trainer came out to ask him if he could play. George was damned if he would let it end so pitifully, and shook him off. Alou grounded to first, Spencer advancing. Cepeda battled the count full, then walked.

Mays stepped into the box. Hyde picked up the rosin bag, walked off the mound, and rubbed up the ball. George could see he was sweating. He stepped back onto the rubber, took the sign, and threw a high fastball that Mays hit four hundred feet, high into the bleachers in left. The Giants leapt out of the dugout, slapping Mays on the back, congratulating each other. The fans tore their clothing in despair, slumped into their seats, cursed and moaned. The proper order had been restored to the universe. George looked over at Castro, who sat in the dugout impassively. Lavagetto came out to talk to Hyde; the crowd booed when the manager left him in, but Hyde managed to get them out of the inning without further damage. As the Senators left the field the organist tried to stir the crowd, but despair had settled over them like a lead blanket. Giants, 6–4.

In the dugout Lavagetto tried to get them up for the inning. "This is it, gentlemen. Time to prove we belong here."

Allison had his bat out and was ready to go to work before the umpire had finished sweeping off the plate. Castro threw three warmups and waved him into the box. When Allison lined a single between short and third, the crowd cheered and rose to their feet.

Sievers, swinging for the fences, hit a nubbler to the mound, a sure double play. Castro pounced on it in good time, but fumbled the ball, double-clutched, and settled for the out at first. The fans cheered.

Rigney came out to talk it over. He and Schmidt stayed on the mound a long time, Castro gesturing wildly, insisting he wasn't tired. He had struck out the side in the eighth.

Rigney left him in, and Castro rewarded him by striking out Lemon for his seventeenth of the game, a new World Series record. Two down. Killebrew was up. The fans hovered on the brink of nervous collapse. The Senators were torturing them; they were going to drag this out to the last fatal out, not give them a clean killing or a swan-dive fade—no, they would hold out the chance of victory to the last moment, then crush them dead.

Castro rubbed up the ball, checked Allison over his shoulder, shook off a couple of Schmidt's signs, and threw. He got Killebrew in an 0–2 hole, then threw four straight balls to walk him. The crowd noise reached a frenzy.

And so, as he stepped to the plate in the bottom of the ninth, two outs, George Herbert Walker Bush represented the winning run, the potential end to twenty-seven years of Washington frustration, the apotheosis of his life in baseball, or the ignominious end of it. Castro had him set up again, to be the glorious goat for the entire Series. His ankle throbbed. "C'mon, Senator!" Lavagetto shouted. "Make me a genius!"

Castro threw a fat hanging curve. George swung. As he did, he felt the last remaining strength of the dying Babe Ruth course down his arms. The ball kissed off the sweet spot of the bat and soared, pure and white as a six-year-old's prayer, into the left-field bleachers.

The stands exploded. Fans boiled onto the field even before George touched second. Allison did a kind of hopping balletic dance around the bases ahead of him, a cross between Nureyev and a man on a pogo stick. The Senators ran out of the dugout and bear-hugged George as he staggered around third; like a broken-field runner he struggled through the fans toward home. A weeping fat man in a plaid shirt, face contorted by ecstasy, blocked his way to the plate, and it was all he could do to keep from knocking him over.

As his teammates pulled him toward the dugout, he caught a glimpse over his shoulder of the Franchise standing on the mound, watching the melee and George at the center of it with an inscrutable expression on his face. Then George was pulled back into the happy maelstrom and surrendered to his bemused joy.

FOURTEEN

Long after everyone had left and the clubhouse was deserted, Fidel dressed, and instead of leaving walked back out to the field. The stadium was dark, but in the light of the moon he could make out the trampled infield and the obliterated base paths. He stood on the mound and looked around at the empty stands. He was about to leave when someone called him from the dugout. "Beautiful, isn't it?"

Fidel approached. It was a thin man in his sixties. He wore a sporty coat and a white dress shirt open at the collar. "Yes?" Fidel asked.

"The field is beautiful."

Fidel sat next to him on the bench. They stared across the diamond. The wind rustled the trees beyond the outfield walls. "Some people think so," Fidel said.

"I thought we might have a talk," the man said. "I've been waiting around the ball park before the last few games trying to get hold of you."

"I don't think we have anything to talk about, Mr. . . . ."

"Weaver. Buck Weaver."

"Mr. Weaver. I don't know you, and you don't know me."

The man came close to smiling. "I know about winning the World Series. And losing it. I was on the winning team in 1917, and the losing one in 1919."

"You would not be kidding me, old man?"

"No. For a long time after the second one, I couldn't face a ball park. Especially during the Series. I might have gone to quite a few, but I couldn't make myself do it. Now I go to the games every chance I get."

"You still enjoy baseball."

"I love the game. It reminds me where my body is buried." As he said all of this the man kept smiling, as if it were a funny story he was telling, and a punch line waited in the near future.

"You should quit teasing me, old man," Fidel said. "You're still alive."

"To all outward indications I'm alive, most of the year now. For a long time I was dead the year round. Eventually I was dead only during the summer, and now it's come down to just the Series."

"You are the mysterious one. Why do you not simply tell me what you want with me?"

"I want to know why you did what you just did."

"What did I do?"

"You threw the game."

Fidel watched him. "You cannot prove that."

"I don't have to prove it. I know it, though."

"How do you know it?"

"Because I've seen it done before."

From somewhere in his boyhood, Fidel recalled the name now. Buck Weaver. The 1919 Series. "The Black Sox. You were one of them."

That appeared to be the punch line. The man smiled. His eyes were set in painful nets of wrinkles. "I was never one of them. But I knew about it, and that was enough for that bastard Landis to kick me out of the game."

"What does that have to do with me?"

"At first I wanted to stop you. Now I just want to know why you did it. Are you so blind to what you've got that you could throw it away? You're not a fool. Why?"

"I have my reasons, old man. Eighty thousand dollars, for one."

"You don't need the money."

"My brother, in prison, does. The people in my home do."

"Don't give me that. You don't really care about them."

Fidel let the moment stretch, listening to the rustling of the wind through the trees, the traffic in the distant street. "No? Well, perhaps. Perhaps I did it just because I *could*. Because the game betrayed me, because I wanted to show it is as corrupt as the *mierda* around it. It's not any different from the world. You know how it works. How every team has two black ball players—the star and the star's roommate." He laughed. "It's not a religion, and this place"— he gestured at Griffith Stadium looming in the night before them— "is not a cathedral."

"I thought that way, when I was angry," Weaver said. "I was a young man. I didn't know how much it meant to me until they took it away."

"Old man, you would have lost it regardless. How old were you? Twenty-five? Thirty? In ten years it would have been taken from you anyway, and you'd be in the same place you are now."

"But I'd have my honor. I wouldn't be a disgrace."

"That's only what other people say. Why should you let their ignorance affect who you are?"

"Brave words. But I've lived it. You haven't—yet." Plainly upset, Weaver walked out onto the field to stand at third base. He crouched; he looked in toward the plate. After a while he straightened, a frail old man, and called in toward Fidel: "When I was twenty-five, I stood out here; I thought I had hold of a baseball in my hand. It turned out it had hold of me."

He came back and stood at the top of the dugout steps. "Don't worry, I'm not going to tell. I didn't then, and I won't now."

Weaver left, and Fidel sat in the dugout.

FIFTEEN

They used the photo of George's painfully shy, crooked smile, a photograph taken in the locker room after he'd been named MVP of the 1959 World Series, on his first campaign poster.

In front of the photographers and reporters, George was greeted by Mr. Griffith. And his father. Prescott Bush wore a political smile as broad as his experience of what was necessary to impress the world. He put his arm around his son's shoulders, and although George was a tall man, it was apparent that his father was still a taller one.

"I'm proud of you, son," Prescott said, in a voice loud enough to be heard by everyone. "You've shown the power of decency and persistence in the face of hollow boasts."

Guys were spraying champagne, running around with their hair sticky and their shirts off, whooping and shouting and slapping each other on the back. Even his father's presence couldn't entirely deflect George's satisfaction. He had done it. Proved himself for once and for all. He wished Bar and the boys could be there. He wanted to shout in the streets, to stay up all night, be pursued by beautiful women. He sat in front of his locker and patiently answered the reporters' questions at length, repeatedly. Only gradually did the furor settle down. George glanced across the room to the brightly lit corner where Prescott was talking, on camera, with a television reporter.

It was clear that his father was setting him up for this planned political career. It infuriated him that he assumed he could control George so easily, but at the same time George felt confused about what he really wanted for himself. As he sat there in the diminishing chaos, Lavagetto came over and sat down beside him. The manager was still high from the victory.

"I don't believe it!" Lavagetto said. "I thought he was crazy, but old Tricky Dick must have known something I didn't!"

"What do you mean?"

"Mean?—nothing. Just that the president called after the first game and told me to bat you behind Killebrew. I thought he was crazy. But it paid off."

George remembered Prescott Bush whispering into Nixon's ear. He felt a crushing weight on his chest. He stared over at his father in the TV lights, not hearing Lavagetto.

But as he watched, he wondered. If his father had indeed fixed the Series, then everything he'd accomplished came to nothing. But his father was an honorable man. Besides, Nixon was noted for his sports obsession, full of fantasies because he hadn't succeeded himself. His calling Lavagetto was the kind of thing he would do anyway. Winning had been too hard for it to be a setup. No, Castro had wanted to humiliate George, and George had stood up to him.

The reporter finished talking to his father; the TV lights snapped off. George thanked Lavagetto for the faith the manager had shown in him, and limped over to Prescott Bush.

"Feeling pretty good, George?"

"It was a miracle we won. I played above myself."

"Now, don't take what I said back in New York so much to heart. You proved yourself equal to the challenge, that's what." Prescott lowered his voice. "Have you thought any more about the proposition I put to you?"

George looked his father in the eye. If Prescott Bush felt any discomfort, there was no trace of it in his patrician's gaze.

"I guess maybe I've played enough baseball," George said.

His father put his hand on George's shoulder; it felt like a burden. George shrugged it off and headed for the showers.

Many years later, as he faced the Washington press corps in the East Room of the White House, George Herbert Walker Bush was to remember that distant afternoon, in the ninth inning of the seventh game of the World Series, when he'd stood in the batter's box against the Franchise. He had not known then what he now understood: that, like his father, he would do anything to win.

THE NIGHT WE BURIED ROAD DOG

Jack Cady

Jack Cady's many honors include a World Fantasy Award, the Iowa Prize for Short Fiction, the Atlantic Monthly First Award, and now a Nebula Award. His short fiction has been reprinted in *The Best American Short Stories*, and he recently received a National Endowment for the Arts fellowship. Among his novels are *The Well*, *Singleton*, *The Jonah Watch*, *The Man Who Could Make Things Vanish*, and, most recently, *Inagehi* and *Street*. A short-story collection, *The Night We Buried Road Dog and Other Gentle Spirits*, is forthcoming.

His Nebula Award–winning novella, which was also honored with a Bram Stoker Award, is a compellingly written fantasy of highways and cars, a technology with a special place in the American heart. About "The Night We Buried Road Dog," Jack Cady writes:

"When a child, I knew graveled two-lane roads, and main highways of two-lane concrete or macadam. The cars and trucks of those days were mostly bare-bones functional, but some of them would run like the hammers of hell. I grew up in the company of Terraplanes and Hudsons and LaSalles, together with the hot Lincolns, cold Chevvies, and lukewarm Plymouths. After World War II all of this changed.

"In the fifties cars improved, and in '57 suspensions began to improve, with torsion bars on the Chrysler products. The road blossomed. Wider two-lanes opened, and the freeway system was just beginning to be constructed. It was a great time to be a young man with a head full of engines and a heart full of love for life and land and ladies. And what was even nicer in a historic way—some of those old scorching cars from the thirties were still around.

"This story grew out of a trip through Montana, a trip that reminded me of many years spent on the road, reminded me of the power of the American land, and recalled the passions of youth. As the story grew I knew that it carried a sort of magic that very lucky writers get to deal with perhaps once or twice in their lives."

I

Brother Jesse buried his '47 Hudson back in '61, and the roads got just that much more lonesome. Highway 2 across north Montana still wailed with engines as reservation cars blew past; and it lay like a tunnel of darkness before headlights of big rigs. Tandems pounded, and the smart crack of downshifts rapped across grassland as trucks swept past the bars at every crossroad. The state put up metal crosses to mark the sites of fatal accidents. Around the bars, those crosses sprouted like thickets.

That Hudson was named Miss Molly, and it logged 220,000 miles while never burning a clutch. Through the years, it wore into the respectable look that comes to old machinery. It was rough as a cob, cracked glass on one side, and primer over dents. It had the tough-and-ready look of a hunting hound about its business. I was a good deal younger then, but not so young that I was fearless. The burial had something to do with mystery, and Brother Jesse did his burying at midnight.

Through fluke or foresight, Brother Jesse had got hold of eighty acres of rangeland that wasn't worth a shake. There wasn't enough of it to run stock, and you couldn't raise anything on it except a little hell. Jesse stuck an old house trailer out there, stacked hay around it for insulation in Montana winters, and hauled in just enough water to suit him. By the time his Hudson died, he was ready to go into trade.

"Jed," he told me the night of the burial, "I'm gonna make myself some history, despite this damn Democrat administration." Over beside the house trailer, the Hudson sat looking like it was about ready to get off the mark in a road race, but the poor thing was a goner. Moonlight sprang from between spring clouds, and to the westward the peaks of mountains glowed from snow and moonlight. Along Highway 2, some hot rock wound second gear on an old flathead Ford. You could hear the valves begin to float.

"Some little darlin' done stepped on that boy's balls," Jesse said about the driver. "I reckon that's why he's looking for a ditch." Jesse sighed and sounded sad. "At least we got a nice night. I couldn't stand a winter funeral."

"Road Dog?" I said about the driver of the Ford, which shows just how young I was at the time.

"It ain't The Dog," Jesse told me. "The Dog's a damn survivor."

You never knew where Brother Jesse got his stuff, and you never really knew if he was anybody's brother. The only time I asked, he said, "I come from a close-knit family such as your own," and that made no sense. My own father died when I was twelve, and my mother married again when I turned seventeen. She picked up and moved to Wisconsin.

No one even knew when, or how, Jesse got to Montana territory. We just looked up one day, and there he was, as natural as if he'd always been here, and maybe he always had.

His eighty acres began to fill up. Old printing presses stood gap mouthed like spinsters holding conversation. A salvaged greenhouse served for storing dog food, engine parts, chromium hair dryers from 1930s beauty shops, dime-store pottery, blades for hay cutters, binder twine, an old gas-powered crosscut saw, seats from a school bus, and a bunch of other stuff not near as useful.

A couple of tabbies lived in that greenhouse, but the Big Cat stood outside. It was an old D6 bulldozer with a shovel, and Jesse stoked it up from time to time. Mostly it just sat there. In summers, it provided shade for Jesse's dogs: Potato was brown and fat and not too bright, while Chip was little and fuzzy. Sometimes they rode with Jesse, and sometimes stayed home. Me or Mike Tarbush fed them. When anything big happened, you could count on those two dogs to get underfoot. Except for me, they were the only ones who attended the funeral.

"If we gotta do it," Jesse said mournfully, "we gotta." He wound up the Cat, turned on the headlights, and headed for the grave site, which was an embankment overlooking Highway 2. Back in those days, Jesse's hair still shone black, and it was even blacker in the darkness. It dangled around a face that carried an Indian forehead and a Scotsman's nose. Denim stretched across most of the six feet of him, and he wasn't rangy; he was thin. He had feet to match his height, and his hands seemed bigger than his feet; but the man could skin a Cat.

I stood in moonlight and watched him work. A little puff of flame dwelt in the stack of the bulldozer. It flashed against the darkness of those distant mountains. It burbled hot in the cold spring moonlight. Jesse made rough cuts pretty quick, moved a lot of soil, then started getting delicate. He shaped and reshaped that grave. He carved a little from one side, backed the dozer, found his cut not satisfactory. He took a spoonful of earth to straighten things, then fussed with the grade leading into the grave. You could tell he wanted a slight elevation, so the Hudson's nose would be sniffing toward the road. Old Potato dog had a hound's ears but not a hound's good sense. He started baying at the moon.

It came to me that I was scared. Then it came to me that I was scared most of the time anyway. I was nineteen, and folks talked about having a war across the sea. I didn't want to hear about it. On top of the war talk, women were driving me crazy: the ones who said "no" and the ones who said "yes." It got down-right mystifying just trying to figure out which was worse. At nineteen, it's hard to know how to act. There were whole weeks when I could pass myself off as a hellion, then something would go sour. I'd get hit by a streak of conscience and start acting like a missionary.

"Jed," Jesse told me from the seat of the dozer, "go rig a tow on Miss Molly." In the headlights the grave now looked like a garage dug into the side of that little slope. Brother Jesse eased the Cat back in there to fuss with the grade. I stepped slow toward the Hudson, wiggled under, and fetched the towing cable around the frame. Potato howled. Chip danced like a fuzzy fury, and started chewing on my boot like he was trying to drag me from under the Hudson. I was on my back trying to kick Chip away and secure the cable. Then I like to died from fright.

Nothing else in the world sounds anywhere near like a Hudson starter. It's a combination of whine and clatter and growl. If I'd been dead a thousand years, you could stand me right up with a Hudson starter. There's threat in that sound. There's also the promise that things can get pretty rowdy, pretty quick.

The starter went off. The Hudson jiggled. In the one-half second it took to get from under that car, I thought of every bad thing I ever did in my life. I was headed for Hell, certain sure. By the time I was on my feet, there wasn't an ounce of blood showing anywhere on me. When the old folks say "white as a sheet," they're talking about a guy under a Hudson.

Brother Jesse climbed from the Cat and gave me a couple of shakes.

"She ain't dead," I stuttered. "The engine turned over. Miss Molly's still thinking speedy." From Highway 2 came the wail of Mike Tarbush's '48 Roadmaster. Mike loved and cussed that car. It always flattened out at around eighty.

"There's still some sap left in the batt'ry," Jesse said about the Hudson. "You probably caused a short." He dropped the cable around the hitch on the dozer. "Steer her," he said.

The steering wheel still felt alive, despite what Jesse said. I crouched behind the wheel as the Hudson got dragged toward the grave. Its brakes locked twice, but the towing cable held. The locked brakes caused the car to sideslip. Each time, Jesse cussed. Cold spring moonlight made the shadowed grave look like a cave of darkness.

The Hudson bided its time. We got it lined up, then pushed it backward into the grave. The hunched front fenders spread beside the snarly grille. The front bumper was the only thing about that car that still showed clean and uncluttered. I could swear Miss Molly moved in the darkness of the grave, about to come charging onto Highway 2. Then she seemed to make some kind of decision, and sort of settled down. Jesse gave the eulogy.

"This here car never did nothing bad," he said. "I must have seen a million crap crates, but this car wasn't one of them. She had a second gear like Hydra-Matic, and you could wind to seventy before you dropped to third. There wasn't no top end to her—at least I never had the guts to find it. This here was a hundred-mile-an-hour car on a bad night, and God knows what on a good'n." From Highway 2, you could hear the purr of Matt Simons's '56 Dodge, five speeds, what with the overdrive, and Matt was scorching.

Potato howled long and mournful. Chip whined. Jesse scratched his head, trying to figure a way to end the eulogy. It came to him like a blessing. "I can't prove it," he said, " 'cause no one could. But I expect this car has passed The Road Dog maybe a couple of hundred times." He made like he was going to cross himself, then remembered he was Methodist. "Rest in peace," he said, and he said

it with eyes full of tears. "There ain't that many who can comprehend
The Dog." He climbed back on the Cat and began to fill the grave.

Next day, Jesse mounded the grave with real care. He erected a
marker, although the marker was more like a little signboard:

1947–1961
Hudson coupe—"Molly"
220,023 miles on straight eight cylinder
Died of busted crankshaft
Beloved in the memory of
Jesse Still

Montana roads are long and lonesome, and Highway 2 is lonesomest. You pick it up over on the Idaho border where the land is
mountains. Bear and cougar still live pretty good, and beaver still
build dams. The highway runs beside some pretty lakes. Canada is
no more than a jump away; it hangs at your left shoulder when you're
headed east.

And can you roll those mountains? Yes, oh yes. It's two-lane all
the way across, and twisty in the hills. From Libby, you ride down
to Kalispell, then pop back north. The hills last till the Blackfoot
reservation. It's rangeland into Cut Bank, then to Havre. That's just
about the center of the state.

Just let the engine howl from town to town. The road goes
through a dozen, then swings south. And there you are at Glasgow
and the river. By Wolf Point, you're in cropland, and it's flat from
there until Chicago.

I almost hate to tell about this road, because easterners may want
to come and visit. Then they'll do something dumb at a blind entry.
The state will erect more metal crosses. Enough folks die up here
already. And it's sure no place for rice grinders, or tacky Swedish
station wagons, or high-priced German crap crates. This was always
a V-8 road, and V-12 if you had 'em. In the old, old days there were
even a few V-16s up here. The top end on those things came when
friction stripped the tires from too much speed.

Speed or not, brakes sure sounded as cars passed Miss Molly's grave.
Pickup trucks fishtailed as men snapped them to the shoulder. The

men would sit in their trucks for a minute, scratching their heads like they couldn't believe what they'd just seen. Then they'd climb from the truck, walk back to the grave, and read the marker. About half of them would start holding their sides. One guy even rolled around on the ground, he was laughing so much.

"These old boys are laughing now," Brother Jesse told me, "but I predict a change in attitude. I reckon they'll come around before first snowfall."

With his car dead, Jesse had to find a set of wheels. He swapped an old hay rake and a gang of discs for a '49 Chevrolet.

"It wouldn't pull the doorknob off a cathouse," he told me. "It's just to get around in while I shop."

The whole deal was going to take some time. Knowing Jesse, I figured he'd go through half a dozen trades before finding something comfortable. And I was right.

He first showed up in an old Packard hearse that once belonged to a funeral home in Billings. He'd swapped the Chev for the hearse, plus a gilt-covered coffin so gaudy it wouldn't fit anybody but a radio preacher. He swapped the hearse to Sam Winder, who aimed to use it for hunting trips. Sam's dogs wouldn't go anywhere near the thing. Sam opened all the windows and the back door, then took the hearse up to speed trying to blow out all the ghosts. The dogs still wouldn't go near it. Sam said, "To hell with it," and pushed it into a ravine. Every rabbit and fox and varmint in that ravine came bailing out, and nobody has gone in there ever since.

Jesse traded the coffin to Old Man Jefferson, who parked the thing in his woodshed. Jefferson was supposed to be on his last legs, but figured he wasn't ever, never, going to die if his poor body knew it would be buried in that monstrosity. It worked for several years, too, until a bad winter came along, and he split it up for firewood. But we still remember him.

Jesse came out of those trades with a '47 Pontiac and a Model T. He sold the Model T to a collector, then traded the Pontiac and forty bales of hay for a '53 Studebaker. He swapped the Studebaker for a ratty pickup and all the equipment in a restaurant that went bust. He peddled the equipment to some other poor fellow who was hell-bent to go bust in the restaurant business. Then he traded the pickup for a motorcycle, plus a '51 Plymouth that would just about get out of its own way. By the time he peddled both of them, he had his pockets full of cash and was riding shanks' mare.

"Jed," he told me, "let's you and me go to the big city." He was pretty happy, but I remembered how scared I'd been at the funeral. I admit to being skittish.

From the center of north Montana, there weren't a championship lot of big cities. West was Seattle, which was sort of rainy and mythological. North was Winnipeg, a cow town. South was Salt Lake City. To the east . . .

"The hell with it," Brother Jesse said. "We'll go to Minneapolis."

It was about a thousand miles. Maybe fifteen hours, what with the roads. You could sail Montana and North Dakota, but those Minnesota cops were humorless.

I was shoving a sweet old '53 Desoto. It had a good bit under the bonnet, but the suspension would make a grown man cry. It was a beautiful beast, though. Once you got up to speed, that front end would track like a cat. The upholstery was like brand-new. The radio worked. There wasn't a scratch or ding on it. I had myself a banker's car, and there I was, only nineteen.

"We may want to loiter," Jesse told me. "Plan on a couple of overnights."

I had a job, but told myself that I was due for a vacation; and so screw it. Brother Jesse put down food for the tabbies and whistled up the dogs. Potato hopped into the backseat in his large, dumb way. He looked expectant. Chip sort of hesitated. He made a couple of jumps straight up, then backed down and started barking. Jesse scooped him up and shoved him in with old Potato dog.

"The upholstery," I hollered. It was the first time I ever stood up to Jesse.

Jesse got an old piece of tarp to put under the dogs. "Pee, and you're a goner," he told Potato.

We drove steady through the early-summer morning. The Desoto hung in around eighty, which was no more than you'd want, considering the suspension. Rangeland gave way to cropland. The radio plugged away with western music, beef prices, and an occasional preacher saying, "Grace" and "Gimmie." Highway 2 rolled straight ahead, sometimes rising gradual, so that cars appeared like rapid-running spooks out of the blind entries. There'd be a little flash of sunlight from a windshield. Then a car would appear over the rise, and usually it was wailing.

We came across a hell of a wreck just beyond Havre. A new Mercury station wagon rolled about fifteen times across the landscape. There were two nice-dressed people and two children. Not one of them ever stood a chance. They rattled like dice in a drum. I didn't want to see what I was looking at.

Bad wrecks always made me sick, but not sick to puking. That would not have been manly. I prayed for those people under my breath and got all shaky. We pulled into a crossroads bar for a sandwich and a beer. The dogs hopped out. Plenty of hubcaps were nailed on the wall of the bar. We took a couple of them down and filled them with water from an outside tap. The dogs drank and peed.

"I've attended a couple myself," Brother Jesse said about the wreck. "Drove a Terraplane off a bridge back in '53. Damn near drownded." Jesse wasn't about to admit to feeling bad. He just turned thoughtful.

"This here is a big territory," he said to no one in particular. "But you can get across her if you hustle. I reckon that Merc was loaded wrong, or blew a tire." Beyond the windows of the bar, eight metal crosses lined the highway. Somebody had tied red plastic roses on one of them. Another one had plastic violets and forget-me-nots.

We lingered a little. Jesse talked to the guy at the bar, and I ran a rack at the pool table. Then Jesse bought a six-pack while I headed for the can. Since it was still early in the day, the can was clean; all the last night's pee and spit mopped from the floor. Somebody had just painted the walls. There wasn't a thing written on them, except that Road Dog had signed in.

Road Dog
How are things in Glocca Mora?

His script was spidery and perfect, like an artist who drew a signature. I touched the paint, and it was still tacky. We had missed The Dog by only a few minutes.

Road Dog was like Jesse in a way. Nobody could say exactly when he first showed up, but one day he was there. We started seeing the name "Road Dog" written in what Matt Simons called "a fine Spencerian hand." There was always a message attached, and Matt called them "cryptic." The signature and messages flashed from the walls of cans in bars, truck stops, and roadside cafés through four states.

We didn't know Road Dog's route at first. Most guys were tied to work or home or laziness. In a year or two, though, Road Dog's trail got mapped. His fine hand showed up all along Highway 2, trailed east into North Dakota, dropped south through South Dakota, then ran back west across Wyoming. He popped north through Missoula and climbed the state until he connected with Highway 2 again. Road Dog, whoever he was, ran a constant square of road that covered roughly two thousand miles.

Sam Winder claimed Road Dog was a Communist who taught social studies at U. of Montana. "Because," Sam claimed, "that kind of writing comes from Europe. That writing ain't U.S.A."

Mike Tarbush figured Road Dog was a retired cartoonist from a newspaper. He figured nobody could spot The Dog because The Dog slipped past us in a Nash, or some other old-granny car.

Brother Jesse suggested that Road Dog was a truck driver, or maybe a gypsy, but sounded like he knew better.

Matt Simons supposed Road Dog was a traveling salesman with a flair for advertising. Matt based his notion on one of the cryptic messages:

Road Dog
Ringling Bros. Barnum and Toothpaste

I didn't figure anything. Road Dog stood in my imagination as the heart and soul of Highway 2. When night was deep and engines blazed, I could hang over the wheel and run down that tunnel of two-lane into the night.

The nighttime road is different than any other thing. Ghosts rise around the metal crosses, and ghosts hitchhike along the wide berm. All the mysteries of the world seem normal after dark. If imagination shows dead thumbs aching for a ride, those dead folk only prove the hot and spermy goodness of life. I'd overtake some taillights, grab the other lane, and blow doors off some party goer who tried to stay out of the ditches. A man can sing and cuss and pray. The miles fill with dreams of power, and women, and happy, happy times.

Road Dog seemed part of that romance. He was the very soul of mystery, a guy who looked at the dark heart of the road and still flew free enough to make jokes and write that fine hand.

In daytime it was different, though. When I saw Road Dog signed in on the wall of that can, it just seemed like a real bad sign.

The guy who owned the bar had seen no one. He claimed he'd been in the back room putting bottles in his cold case. The Dog had come and gone like a spirit.

Jesse and I stood in the parking lot outside the bar. Sunlight lay earthy and hot across the new crops. A little puff of dust rose from a side road. It advanced real slow, so you could tell it was a farm tractor. All around us meadowlarks and tanagers were whooping it up.

"We'll likely pass him," Jesse said, "if we crowd a little." Jesse pretended he didn't care, but anyone would. We loaded the dogs, and even hung the hubcaps back up where we got them, because it was what a gentleman would do. The Desoto acted as eager as any Desoto could. We pushed the top end, which was eighty-nine, and maybe ninety-two downhill. At that speed, brakes don't give you much, so you'd better trust your steering and your tires.

If we passed The Dog we didn't know it. He might have parked in one of the towns, and of course we dropped a lot of revs passing through towns, that being neighborly. What with a little loafing, some pee stops, and general fooling around, we did not hit Minneapolis until a little after midnight. When we checked into a motel on the strip, Potato was sleepy and grumpy. Chip looked relieved.

"Don't fall in love with that bed," Jesse told me. "Some damn salesman is out there waitin' to do us in. It pays to start early."

Car shopping with Jesse turned out as fascinating as anybody could expect. At 7:00 A.M. we cruised the lots. Cars stood in silent rows like advertising men lined up for group pictures. It being Minneapolis, we saw a lot of high-priced iron. Cadillacs and Packards and Lincolns sat beside Buick convertibles, hemi Chryslers, and Corvettes ("Nice c'hars," Jesse said about the Corvettes, "but no room to 'em. You couldn't carry more than one sack of feed."). Hudsons and Studebakers hunched along the back rows. On one lot was something called "Classic Lane." A Model A stood beside a '37 International pickup. An L29 Cord sat like a tombstone, which it was, because it had no engine. But, glory be, beside the Cord nestled a '39 LaSalle coupe just sparkling with threat. That LaSalle might have snookered Jesse, except something highly talented sat buried deep in the lot.

It was the last of the fast and elegant Lincolns, a '54 coupe as snarly as any man could want. The '53 model had taken the Mexican Road Race. The '54 was a refinement. After that the marque went downhill. It started building cars for businessmen and rich grannies.

Jesse walked round and round the Lincoln, which looked like it was used to being cherished. Matchless and scratchless. It was a little less than fire-engine red, with a white roof and a grille that could shrug off a cow. That Linc was a solid set of fixings. Jesse got soft lights in his eyes. This was no Miss Molly, but this was Miss somebody. There were a lot of crap crates running out there, but this Linc wasn't one of them.

"You prob'ly can't even get parts for the damn thing," Jesse murmured, and you could tell he was already scrapping with a salesman. He turned his back on the Lincoln. "We'll catch a bite to eat," he said. "This may take a couple days."

I felt sort of bubbly. "The Dog ain't gonna like this," I told Jesse.

"The Dog is gonna love it," he said. "Me and The Dog *knows* that road."

By the time the car lots opened at 9:00 A.M., Jesse had a trader's light in his eyes. About all that needs saying is that never before or since did I ever see a used-car salesman cry.

The poor fellow never had a chance. He stood in his car lot most of the day while me and Jesse went through every car lot on the strip. We waved to him from a sweet little '57 Cad, and we cruised past real smooth in a mama-san '56 Imperial. We kicked tires on anything sturdy while he was watching, and we never even got to his lot until fifteen minutes before closing. Jesse and I climbed from my Desoto. Potato and Chip tailed after us.

"I always know when I get to Minneapolis," Jesse said to me, but loud enough the salesman could just about hear. "My woman wants to lay a farmer, and my dogs start pukin'." When we got within easy hearing range, Jesse's voice got humble. "I expect this fella can help a cowboy in a fix."

I followed, experiencing considerable admiration. In two sentences, Jesse had his man confused.

Potato was dumb enough that he trotted right up to the Lincoln. Chip sat and panted, pretending indifference. Then he ambled over to a ragged-out Pontiac and peed on the tire. "I must be missing something," Jesse said to the salesman, "because that dog has himself a dandy nose." He looked at the Pontiac. "This thing got an engine?"

We all conversed for the best part of an hour. Jesse refused to even look at the Lincoln. He sounded real serious about the LaSalle, to the point of running it around a couple of blocks. It was a darling. It had ceramic-covered manifolds to protect against heat and rust. It packed a long-stroke V-8 with enough torque to bite rubber in second gear. My Desoto was a pretty thing, but until that LaSalle I never realized that my car was a total pussycat. When we left the lot, the salesman looked sad. He was late for supper.

"Stay with what you've got," Jesse told me as he climbed in my Desoto. "The clock has run out on that LaSalle. Let a collector have it. I hate it when something good dies for lack of parts."

I wondered if he was thinking of Miss Molly.

"Because," Jesse said, and kicked the tire on a silly little Volkswagen, "the great, good cars are dying. I blame it on the Germans."

Next day we bought the Lincoln and made the salesman feel like one proud pup. He figured he foisted something off on Jesse that Jesse didn't want. He was so stuck on himself that he forgot that he had asked a thousand dollars, and come away with $550. He even forgot that his eyes were swollen, and that maybe he crapped his pants.

We went for a test drive, but only after Jesse and I crawled around under the Linc. A little body lead lumped in the left rear fender, but the front end stood sound. Nobody had pumped any sawdust into the differential. We found no water in the oil, or oil in the water. The salesman stood around, admiring his shoeshine. He was one of those easterners who can't help talking down to people, especially when he's trying to be nice. I swear he wore a white tie with little red ducks on it. That Minnesota sunlight made his red hair blond and his face pop with freckles.

Jesse drove real quiet until he found an interesting stretch of road. The salesman sat beside him. Me and Potato and Chip hunkered in the backseat. Chip looked sort of nauseated, but Potato was pretty happy.

"I'm afraid," Jesse said, regretful, "that this thing is gonna turn out to be a howler. A fella gets a few years on him, and he don't want a screamy car." Brother Jesse couldn't have been much more than thirty, but he tugged on his nose and ears like he was ancient. "I sure hope," he said, real mournful, "that nobody stuck a boot in any of these here tires." Then he poured on some coal.

There was a most satisfying screech. That Linc took out like a roadrunner in heat. The salesman's head snapped backward, and his shoulders dug into the seat. Potato gave a happy, happy woof and stuck his nose out the open window. I felt like yelling, "Hosanna," but knew enough to keep my big mouth shut. The Linc shrugged off a couple of cars that were conservatively motoring. It wheeled past a hay truck as the tires started humming. The salesman's freckles began to stand up like warts while the airstream howled. Old Potato kept his nose sticking through the open window, and the wind kept drying it. Potato was so damn dumb he tried to lick it wet while his nose stayed in the airstream. His tongue blew sideways.

"It ain't nothing but speed," Jesse complained. "Look at this here steering." He joggled the wheel considerable, which at ninety got even more considerable. The salesman's tie blew straight backward. The little red ducks matched his freckles. "Jee-sus-Chee-sus," he said. "Eight hundred, and slow down." He braced himself against the dash.

When it hit the century mark, the Linc developed a little float in the front end. I expect all of us were thinking about the tires.

You could tell Jesse was jubilant. The Linc still had some pedal left.

"I'm gettin' old," Jesse hollered above the wind. "This ain't no car for an old man."

"Seven hundred," the salesman said. "And Mother of God, slow it down."

"Five-fifty," Jesse told him, and dug the pedal down one more notch.

"You got it," the salesman hollered. His face twisted up real teary. Then Potato got all grateful and started licking the guy on the back of the neck.

So Jesse cut the speed and bought the Linc. He did it diplomatic, pretending he was sorry he'd made the offer. That was kind of him. After all, the guy was nothing but a used-car salesman.

We did a second night in that motel. The Linc and Desoto sat in an all-night filling station. Lube, oil change, and wash, because we were riding high. Jesse had a heap of money left over. In the morning, we got new jeans and shirts, so as to ride along like gentlemen.

"We'll go back through South Dakota," Jesse told me. "There's a place I've heard about."

"What are we looking for?"

"We're checking on The Dog," Jesse told me, and would say no more.

We eased west to Bowman, just under the North Dakota line. Jesse sort of leaned into it, just taking joy from the whole occasion. I flowed along as best the Desoto could. Potato rode with Jesse, and Chip sat on the front seat beside me. Chip seemed rather easier in his mind.

A roadside café hunkered among tall trees. It didn't even have a neon sign. Real old-fashioned.

"I heard of this place all my life," Jesse said as he climbed from the Linc. "This here is the only outhouse in the world with a guest registry." He headed toward the rear of the café.

I tailed along, and Jesse, he was right. It was a palatial privy built like a little cottage. The men's side was a three-holer. There was enough room for a stand-up desk. On the desk was one of those old-fashioned business ledgers like you used to see in banks.

"They're supposed to have a slew of these inside," Jesse said about the register as he flipped pages. "All the way back to the early days."

Some spirit of politeness seemed to take over when you picked up that register. There was hardly any bad talk. I read a few entries:

On this site, May 16th, 1971, James John Johnson (John-John)
cussed hell out of his truck.

I came, I saw, I kinda liked it. —Bill Samuels, Tulsa

This place does know squat. —Pauley Smith, Ogden

This South Dakota ain't so bad,
but I sure got the blues,
I'm working in Tacoma,
'cause my kids all need new shoes. —Sad George

Brother Jesse flipped through the pages. "I'm even told," he said, "that Teddy Roosevelt crapped here. This is a fine old place." He sort of hummed as he flipped. "Uh, huh," he said, "The Dog done made his pee spot." He pointed to a page:

Road Dog
Run and run as fast as you can
you can't catch me—I'm the Gingerbread Man.

Jesse just grinned. "He's sorta upping the ante, ain't he? You reckon this is getting serious?" Jesse acted like he knew what he was talking about, but I sure didn't.

II

We didn't know, as we headed home, that Jesse's graveyard business was about to take off. That wouldn't change him, though. He'd almost always had a hundred dollars in his jeans anyway, and was usually a happy man. What changed him was Road Dog and Miss Molly.

The trouble started awhile after we crossed the Montana line. Jesse ran ahead in the Lincoln, and I tagged behind in my Desoto. We drove Highway 2 into a western sunset. It was one of those magic summers where rain sweeps in from British Columbia just regular enough to keep things growing. Rabbits get fat and foolish, and foxes put on weight. Rattlesnakes come out of ditches to cross the sun-hot road. It's not sporting to run over their middles. You have to take them in the head. Redwings perch on fence posts, and magpies flash black and white from the berm, where they scavenge road kills.

We saw a hell of a wreck just after Wolf Point. A guy in an old Kaiser came over the back of a rise and ran under a tanker truck that burned. Smoke rose black as a plume of crows, and we saw it five miles away. By the time we got there, the truck driver stood in the middle of the road, all white and shaking. The guy in the Kaiser sat behind the wheel. It was fearful to see how fast fire can work, and just terrifying to see bones hanging over a steering wheel. I remember thinking the guy no doubt died before any fire started, and we were feeling more than he was.

That didn't help. I said a prayer under my breath. The truck driver wasn't to blame, but he took it hard as a Presbyterian. Jesse tried to comfort him, without much luck. The road melted and stank and began to burn. Nobody was drinking, but it was certain sure we were all more sober than we'd ever been in our lives. Two deputies showed up. Cars drifted in easy, because of the smoke. In a couple of hours there were probably twenty cars lined up on either side of the wreck.

"He must of been asleep or drunk," Jesse said about the driver of the Kaiser. "How in hell can a man run under a tanker truck?"

When the cops reopened the road, night hovered over the plains. Nobody cared to run much over sixty, even beneath a bright moon. It seemed like a night to be superstitious, a night when there was a deer or pronghorn out there just ready to jump into your headlights. It wasn't a good night to drink, or shoot pool, or mess around in strange bars. It was a time for being home with your woman, if you had one.

On most nights, ghosts do not show up beside the metal crosses, and they sure don't show up in owl light. Ghosts stand out on the darkest, moonless nights, and only then when bars are closed and the only thing open is the road.

I never gave it a thought. I chased Jesse's taillights, which on that Lincoln were broad, up-and-down slashes in the dark. Chip sat beside me, sad and solemn. I rubbed his ears to perk him, but he just laid down and snuffled. Chip was sensitive. He knew I felt bad over that wreck.

The first ghost showed up on the left berm and fizzled before the headlights. It was a lady ghost, and a pretty old one, judging from her long white hair and long white dress. She flicked on and off in just a flash, so maybe it was a road dream. Chip was so depressed he didn't even notice, and Jesse didn't, either. His steering and his brakes didn't wave to me.

Everything stayed straight for another ten miles, then a whole peck of ghosts stood on the right berm. A bundle of crosses shone all silvery white in the headlights. The ghosts melted into each other. You couldn't tell how many, but you could tell they were expectant. They looked like people lined up for a picture show. Jesse never gave a sign he saw them. I told myself to get straight. We hadn't had much sleep in the past two nights, and did some drinking the night before. We'd rolled near two thousand miles.

Admonishing seemed to work. Another twenty minutes passed, maybe thirty, and nothing happened. Wind chased through the open windows of the Desoto, and the radio gave mostly static. I kicked off my boots because that helps you stay awake, the bottoms of the feet being sensitive. Then a single ghost showed up on the right-hand berm, and boy-howdy.

Why anybody would laugh while being dead has got to be a puzzle. This ghost was tall, with Indian hair like Jesse's, and I could swear he looked like Jesse, the spitting image. This ghost was jolly. He clapped his hands and danced. Then he gave me the old road sign for "roll 'em," his hand circling in the air as he danced. The headlights penetrated him, showed tall grass solid at the roadside, and instead of legs he stood on a column of mist. Still, he was dancing.

It wasn't road dreams. It was hallucination. The nighttime road just fills with things seen or partly seen. When too much scary stuff happens, it's time to pull her over.

I couldn't do it, though. Suppose I pulled over, and suppose it wasn't hallucination? I recall thinking that a man don't ordinarily care for preachers until he needs one. It seemed like me and Jesse were riding through the Book of Revelations. I dropped my speed, then flicked my lights a couple times. Jesse paid it no attention, and then Chip got peculiar.

He didn't bark; he chirped. He stood up on the front seat, looking out the back window, and his paws trembled. He shivered, chirped, shivered, and went chirp, chirp, chirp. Headlights in back of us were closing fast.

I've been closed on plenty of times by guys looking for a ditch. Headlights have jumped out of night and fog and mist when nobody should be pushing forty. I've been overtaken by drunks and suiciders.

No set of headlights ever came as fast as the ones that began to wink in the mirrors. This Highway 2 is a quick, quick road, but it's not the salt flats of Utah. The crazy man behind me was trying to set a new land speed record.

Never confuse an idiot. I stayed off the brakes and coasted, taking off speed and signaling my way onto the berm. The racer could have my share of the road. I didn't want any part of that boy's troubles. Jesse kept pulling away as I slowed. It seemed like he didn't even see the lights. Chip chirped, then sort of rolled down on the floorboards and cried.

For ninety seconds, I feared being dead. For one second, I figured it already happened. Wind banged the Desoto sideways. Wind whooped, the way it does in winter. The headlights blew past. What showed was the curve of a Hudson fender—the kind of curve you'd recognize if you'd been dead a million years—and what showed was the little, squinchy shapes of a Hudson's taillights; and what showed was the slanty doorpost like a nail running kitty-corner; and what showed was slivers of reflection from cracked glass on the rider's side; and what sounded was the drumbeat of a straight-eight engine whanging like a locomotive gone wild; the thrump, bumpa, thrum of a crankshaft whipping in its bed. The slaunch-forward form of Miss Molly wailed, and showers of sparks blew from the tailpipe as Miss Molly rocketed.

Chip was not the only one howling. My voice rose high as the howl of Miss Molly. We all sang it out together, while Jesse cruised three, maybe four miles ahead. It wasn't two minutes before Miss Molly swept past that Linc like it was foundationed in cement. Sparks showered like the Fourth of July, and Jesse's brake lights looked pale beside the fireworks. The Linc staggered against wind as Jesse headed for the berm. Wind smashed against my Desoto.

Miss Molly's taillights danced as she did a jig up the road, and then they winked into darkness as Miss Molly topped a rise, or disappeared. The night went darker than dark. A cloud scudded out of nowhere and blocked the moon.

Alongside the road the dancing ghost showed up in my headlights, and I could swear it was Jesse. He laughed like at a good joke, but he gave the old road sign for "slow it down," his hand palm down like he was patting an invisible pup. It seemed sound advice, and I blamed near liked him. After Miss Molly, a happy ghost seemed downright companionable.

"Shitfire," said Jesse, and that's all he said for the first five minutes after I pulled in behind him. I climbed from the Desoto and walked to the Linc. Old Potato dog sprawled on the seat in a dead faint, and Jesse rubbed his ears trying to warm him back to consciousness. Jesse sat over the wheel like a man who had just met Jesus. His hand touched gentle on Potato's ears, and his voice sounded reverent. Brother Jesse's conversion wasn't going to last, but at the time it was just beautiful. He had the lights of salvation in his eyes, and his skinny shoulders weren't shaking too much. "I miss my c'har," he muttered finally, and blinked. He wasn't going to cry if he could help. "She's trying to tell me something," he whispered. "Let's find a bar. Miss Molly's in car heaven, certain sure."

We pulled away, found a bar, and parked. We drank some beer and slept across the car seats. Nobody wanted to go back on that road.

When we woke to a morning hot and clear, Potato's fur had turned white. It didn't seem to bother him much, but, for the rest of his life, he was a lot more thoughtful.

"Looks like mashed Potato," Jesse said, but he wasn't talking a whole lot. We drove home like a couple of old ladies. Guys came scorching past, cussing at our granny speed. We figured they could get mad and stay mad, or get mad and get over it. We made it back to Jesse's place about two in the afternoon.

A couple of things happened quick. Jesse parked beside his house trailer, and the front end fell out of the Lincoln. The right side went down, thump, and the right front tire sagged. Jesse turned even whiter than me, and I was bloodless. We had posted over a hundred miles an hour in that thing. Somehow, when we crawled around underneath inspecting it, we missed something. My shoulders and legs shook so hard I could barely get out of the Desoto. Chip was polite. He just yelped with happiness about being home, but he didn't trot across my lap as we climbed from the car.

Nobody could trust their legs. Jesse climbed out of the Linc and leaned against it. You could see him chewing over all the possibilities, then arriving at the only one that made sense. Some hammer mechanic bolted that front end together with no locknut, no cotter pin, no lock washer, no lock nothin'. He just wrenched down a plain old nut, and the nut worked loose.

"Miss Molly knew," Jesse whispered. "That's what she was trying to tell." He felt a lot better the minute he said it. Color came back to his face. He peered around the corner of the house trailer, looking toward Miss Molly's grave.

Mike Tarbush was over there with his '48 Roadmaster. Matt Simons stood beside him, and Matt's '56 Dodge sat beside the Roadmaster, looking smug; which that model Dodge always did.

"I figger," Brother Jesse whispered, "that we should keep shut about last night. Word would just get around that we were alkies." He pulled himself together, arranged his face like a horse trying to grin, and walked toward the Roadmaster.

Mike Tarbush was a man in mourning. He sat on the fat trunk of that Buick and gazed off toward the mountains. Mike wore extra large of everything, and still looked stout. He sported a thick red mustache to make up for his bald head. From time to time he bragged about his criminal record, which amounted to three days in jail for assaulting a pool table. He threw it through a bar window.

Now his mustache drooped, and Mike seemed small inside his clothes. The hood of the Roadmaster gaped open. Under that hood things couldn't be worse. The poor thing had thrown a rod into the next county.

Jesse looked under the hood and tsked. "I know what you're going through," he said to Mike. He kind of petted the Roadmaster. "I always figured Betty Lou would last a century. What happened?"

There's no call to tell about a grown man blubbering, and especially not one who can heave pool tables. Mike finally got straight enough to tell the story.

"We was chasing the Dog," he said. "At least I think so. Three nights ago over to Kalispell. This Golden Hawk blew past me sittin'." Mike watched the distant mountains like he'd seen a miracle, or else like he was expecting one to happen. "That sonovabitch shore can drive," he whispered in disbelief. "Blown out by a damn Studebaker."

"But a very swift Studebaker," Matt Simons said. Matt is as small as Mike is large, and Matt is educated. Even so, he's set his share of fence posts. He looks like an algebra teacher, but not as delicate.

"Betty Lou went on up past her flat spot," Mike whispered. "She was tryin'. We had ninety on the clock, and The Dog left us sitting." He patted the Roadmaster. "I reckon she died of a broken heart."

"We got three kinds of funerals," Jesse said, and he was sympathetic. "We got the no-frills type, the regular type, and the extra special. The extra special comes with flowers." He said it with a straight face, and Mike took it that way. He bought the extra special, and that was sixty-five dollars.

Mike put up a nice marker:

1948–1961
Roadmaster two-door—Betty Lou
Gone to Glory while chasing The Dog
She was the best friend of Mike Tarbush

Brother Jesse worked on the Lincoln until the front end tracked rock solid. He named it Sue Ellen, but not *Miss* Sue Ellen, there being no way to know if Miss Molly was jealous. When we examined Miss Molly's grave, the soil seemed rumpled. Wildflowers, which Jesse sowed on the grave, bloomed in midsummer. I couldn't get it out of my head that Miss Molly was still alive, and maybe Jesse couldn't either.

Jesse explained about the Lincoln's name. "Sue Ellen is a lady I knew in Pocatello. I expect she misses me." He said it hopeful, like he didn't really believe it.

It looked to me like Jesse was brooding. Night usually found him in town, but sometimes he disappeared. When he was around, he drove real calm and always got home before midnight. The wildness hadn't come out of Jesse, but he had it on a tight rein. He claimed he dreamed of Miss Molly. Jesse was working something out.

And so was I, awake or dreaming. Thoughts of the Road Dog filled my nights, and so did thoughts of the dancing ghost. As summer deepened, restlessness took me wailing under moonlight. The road unreeled before my headlights like a magic line that pointed to places under a warm sun where ladies laughed and fell in love. Something went wrong, though. During that summer the ladies stopped being dreams and became only imagination. When I told Jesse, he claimed

I was just growing up. I wished for once Jesse was wrong. I wished for a lot of things, and one of the wishes came true. It was Mike Tarbush, not me, who got in the next tangle with Miss Molly.

Mike rode in from Billings, where he'd been car shopping. He showed up at Jesse's place on Sunday afternoon. Montana lay restful. Birds hunkered on wires, or called from high grass. Highway 2 ran watery with sunlight, deserted as a road ever could be. When Mike rolled a '56 Merc up beside the Linc, it looked like Old Home Week at a Ford dealership.

"I got to look at something," Mike said when he climbed from the Mercury. He sort of plodded over to Miss Molly's grave and hovered. Light breezes blew the wildflowers sideways. Mike looked like a bear trying to shake confusion from its head. He walked to the Roadmaster's grave. New grass sprouted reddish green. "I was sober," Mike said. "Most Saturday nights, maybe I ain't, but I was sober as a deputy."

For a while nobody said anything. Potato sat glowing and white and thoughtful. Chip slept in the sun beside one of the tabbies. Then Chip woke up. He turned around three times and dashed to hide under the bulldozer.

"Now, tell me I ain't crazy," Mike said. He perched on the front fender of the Merc, which was blue and white and adventuresome. "Name of Judith," he said about the Merc. "A real lady." He swabbed sweat from his bald head. "I got blown out by Betty Lou and Miss Molly. That sound reasonable?" He swabbed some more sweat and looked at the graves, which looked like little speed bumps on the prairie. "Nope," he answered himself, "that don't sound reasonable a-tall."

"Something's wrong with your Mercury," Jesse said, real quiet. "You got a bad tire, or a hydraulic line about to blow, or something screwy in the steering."

He made Mike swear not to breathe a word. Then he told about Miss Molly and about the front end of the Lincoln. When the story got over, Mike looked like a halfback hit by a twelve-man line.

"Don't drive another inch," Jesse said. "Not until we find what's wrong."

"That car already cracked a hundred," Mike whispered. "I bought it special to chase one sumbitch in a Studebaker." He looked toward Betty Lou's grave. "The Dog did that."

The three of us went through that Merc like men panning gold. The trouble was so obvious we missed it for two hours while the engine cooled. Then Jesse caught it. The fuel filter rubbed its underside against the valve cover. When Jesse touched it, the filter collapsed. Gasoline spilled on the engine and the spark plugs. That Merc was getting set to catch on fire.

"I got to wonder if The Dog did it," Jesse said about Betty Lou after Mike drove away. "I wonder if the Road Dog is the Studebaker type."

Nights started to get serious, but any lonesomeness on that road was only in a man's head. As summer stretched past its longest days, and sunsets started earlier, ghosts rose beside crosses before daylight hardly left the land. We drove to work and back, drove to town and back. My job was steady at a filling station, but it asked day after day of the same old thing. We never did any serious wrenching; no engine rebuilds or transmissions, just tune-ups and flat tires. I dearly wanted to meet a nice lady, but no woman in her right mind would mess with a pump jockey.

Nights were different, though. I figured I was going crazy, and Jesse and Mike were worse. Jesse finally got his situation worked out. He claimed Miss Molly was protecting him. Jesse and Mike took the Linc and the Merc on long runs, just wringing the howl out of those cars. Some nights, they'd flash past me at speed no sane man would try in darkness. Jesse was never a real big drinker, and Mike stopped altogether. They were too busy playing road games. It got so the state cop never tried to chase them. He just dropped past Jesse's place next day and passed out tickets.

The dancing ghost danced in my dreams, both asleep and driving. When daylight left the land, I passed metal crosses and remembered some of the wrecks.

Three crosses stood on one side of the railroad track, and four crosses on the other side. The three happened when some Canadian cowboys lost a race with a train. It was too awful to remember, but on most nights those guys stood looking down the tracks with startled eyes.

The four crosses happened when one-third of the senior class of '59 hit that grade too fast on prom night. They rolled a damned old Chevrolet. More bodies by Fisher. Now the two girls stood in their long dresses, looking wistful. The two boys pretended that none of it meant nothin'.

Farther out the road, things had happened before my time. An Indian ghost most often stood beside the ghost of a deer. In another place a chubby old rancher looked real picky and angry.

The dancing ghost continued unpredictable. All the other ghosts stood beside their crosses, but the dancing ghost showed up anywhere he wanted, anytime he wanted. I'd slow the Desoto as he came into my lights, and he was the spitting image of Jesse.

"I don't want to hear about it," Jesse said when I tried to tell him. "I'm on a roll. I'm even gettin' famous."

He was right about that. People up and down the line joked about Jesse and his graveyard business.

"It's the very best kind of advertising," he told me. "We'll see more action before snow flies."

"You won't see snow fly," I told him, standing up to him a second time. "Unless you slow down and pay attention."

"I've looked at heaps more road than you," he told me, "and seeing things is just part of the night. That nighttime road is different."

"This is starting to happen at last light."

"I don't see no ghosts," he told me, and he was lying. "Except Miss Molly once or twice." He wouldn't say anything more.

And Jesse was right. As summer ran on, more graves showed up near Miss Molly. A man named Mcguire turned up with a '41 Cad.

1941–1961
Fleetwood Coupe—Annie
304,018 miles on flathead V-8
She was the luck of the Irishman
Pat Mcguire

And Sam Winder buried his '47 Packard.

1947–1961
Packard 2-door—Lois Lane
Super Buddy of Sam Winder
Up Up and Away

And Pete Johansen buried his pickup.

1946–1961
Ford pickup—Gertrude
211,000 miles give or take
Never a screamer
but a good pulling truck.
Pete Johansen put up many a day's work with her.

Montana roads are long and lonesome, and along the high line is lonesomest of all. From Saskatchewan to Texas, nothing stands tall enough to break the wind that begins to blow cold and clear toward late October. Rains sob away toward the Middle West, and grass turns goldish amber. Rattlesnakes move to high ground, where they will winter. Every creature on God's plains begins to fat up against the winter. Soon it's going to be thirty below and the wind blowing.

Four-wheel-drive weather. Internationals and Fords, with Dodge crummy wagons in the hills; cars and trucks will line up beside houses, garages, sheds, with electric wires leading from plugs to radiators and blocks. They look like packs of nursing pups. Work will slow, then stop. New work turns to accounting for the weather. Fuel, emergency generators, hay-bale insulation. Horses and cattle and deer look fuzzy beneath thick coats. Check your battery. If your rig won't start, and you're two miles from home, she won't die—but you might.

School buses creep from stop to stop, and bundled kids look like colorful little bears trotting through late-afternoon light. Snowy owls come floating in from northward, while folks go to church on Sunday against the time when there's some better amusement. Men hang around town, because home is either empty or crowded, depending on if you're married. Folks sit before television, watching the funny, goofy, unreal world where everybody plays at being sexy and naked, even when they're not.

And nineteen years old is lonesome, too. And work is lonesome when nobody much cares for you.

Before winter set in, I got it in my head to run the Road Dog's route. It was September. Winter would close us down pretty quick. The trip would be a luxury. What with room rent, and gas, and eating out, it was payday to payday with me. Still, one payday would account for gas and sandwiches. I could sleep across the seat. I hocked a Marlin .30-30 to Jesse for twenty bucks. He seemed happy with my notion. He even went into the greenhouse and came out with an arctic sleeping bag.

"In case things get vigorous," he said, and grinned. "Now get on out there and bite The Dog."

It was a happy time. Dreams of ladies sort of set themselves to one side as I cruised across the eternal land. I came to love the land that autumn, in a way that maybe ranchers do. The land stopped being something that a road ran across. Canadian honkers came winging in vees from the north. The great Montana sky stood easy as eagles. When I'd pull over and cut the engine, sounds of grass-hoppers mixed with birdcalls. Once, a wild turkey, as smart as any domestic turkey is dumb, talked to himself and paid me not the least mind.

The Dog showed up right away. In a café in Malta:

> Road Dog
> *"It was all a hideous mistake."*
> *Christopher Columbus*

In a bar in Tampico:

> Road Dog
> *Who's afraid of the big bad Woof?*

In another bar in Culbertson:

> Road Dog
> *Go East, young man, go East*

I rolled Williston and dropped south through North Dakota. The Dog's trail disappeared until Watford City, where it showed up in the can of a filling station:

Road Dog
Atlantis and Sargasso
Full fathom five thy brother lies

And in a joint in Grassy Butte:

Road Dog
Ain't Misbehavin'

That morning in Grassy Butte, I woke to a sunrise where the land lay bathed in rose and blue. Silhouettes of grazing deer mixed with silhouettes of cattle. They herded together peaceful as a dream of having your own place, your own woman, and you working hard; and her glad to see you coming home.

In Bowman, The Dog showed up in a nice restaurant:

Road Dog
The Katzenjammer Kids minus one

Ghosts did not show up along the road, but the road stayed the same. I tangled with a bathtub Hudson, a '53, outside of Spearfish in South Dakota. I chased him into Wyoming like being dragged on a string. The guy played with me for twenty miles, then got bored. He shoved more coal in the stoker and purely flew out of sight.

Sheridan was a nice town back in those days, just nice and friendly; plus, I started to get sick of the way I smelled. In early afternoon, I found a five-dollar motel with a shower. That gave me the afternoon, the evening, and next morning if it seemed right. I spiffed up, put on a good shirt, slicked down my hair, and felt just fine.

The streets lay dusty and lazy. Ranchers' pickups stood all dented and work worn before bars, and an old Indian sat on hay bales in the back of one of them. He wore a flop hat, and he seemed like the eyes and heart of the prairie. He looked at me like I was a splendid puppy that might someday amount to something. It seemed okay when he did it.

I hung around a soda fountain at the five-and-dime because a girl smiled. She was just beautiful. A little horsey faced, but with sun blond hair, and with hands long fingered and gentle. There wasn't a chance of talking, because she stood behind the counter for ladies' underwear. I pretended to myself that she looked sad when I left.

It got on to late afternoon. Sunlight drifted in between buildings, and shadows overreached the streets. Everything was normal, and then everything got scary.

I was just poking along, looking in store windows, checking the show at the movie house, when, ahead of me, Jesse walked toward a Golden Hawk. He was maybe a block and a half away, but it was Jesse, sure as God made sunshine. It was a Golden Hawk. There was no way of mistaking that car. Hawks were high-priced sets of wheels, and Studebaker never sold that many.

I yelled and ran. Jesse waited beside the car, looking sort of puzzled. When I pulled up beside him, he grinned.

"It's happening again," he said, and his voice sounded amused, but not mean. Sunlight made his face reddish, but shadow put his legs and feet in darkness. "You believe me to be a gentleman named Jesse Still." Behind him, shadows of buildings told that night was on its way. Sunset happens quick on the prairies.

And I said, "Jesse, what in the hell are you doing in Sheridan?"

And he said, "Young man, you are not looking at Jesse Still." He said it quiet and polite, and he thought he had a point. His voice was smooth and cultured, so he sure didn't sound like Jesse. His hair hung combed out, and he wore clothes that never came from a dry-goods. His jeans were soft looking and expensive. His boots were tooled. They kind of glowed in the dusk. The Golden Hawk didn't have a dust speck on it, and the interior had never carried a tool, or a car part, or a sack of feed. It just sparkled. I almost believed him, and then I didn't.

"You're fooling with me."

"On the contrary," he said, real soft. "Jesse Still is fooling with *me*, although he doesn't mean to. We've never met." He didn't exactly look nervous, but he looked impatient. He climbed in the Stude and started the engine. It purred like racing tune. "This is a large and awfully complex world," he said, "and Mr. Still will probably tell you the same. I've been told we look like brothers."

I wanted to say more, but he waved real friendly and pulled away. The flat and racy back end of the Hawk reflected one slash of sunlight, then rolled into shadow. If I'd had a hot car, I'd have gone out hunting him. It wouldn't have done a lick of good, but doing something would be better than doing nothing.

I stood sort of shaking and amazed. Life had just changed somehow, and it wasn't going to change back. There wasn't a thing in the world to do, so I went to get some supper.

The Dog had signed in at the café:

Road Dog
The Bobbsey Twins Attend The Motor Races

And—I sat chewing roast beef and mashed potatoes.

And—I saw how the guy in the Hawk might be lying, and that Jesse was a twin.

And—I finally saw what a chancy, dicey world this was, because without meaning to, exactly, and without even knowing it was happening, I had just run up against The Road Dog.

It was a night of dreams. Dreams wouldn't let me go. The dancing ghost tried to tell me Jesse was triplets. The ghosts among the crosses begged rides into nowhere, rides down the long tunnel of night that ran past lands of dreams, but never turned off to those lands. It all came back: the crazy summer, the running, running, running behind the howl of engines. The Road Dog drawled with Jesse's voice, and then The Dog spoke cultured. The girl at the five-and-dime held out a gentle hand, then pulled it back. I dreamed of a hundred roadside joints, bars, cafés, old-fashioned filling stations with grease pits. I dreamed of winter wind, and the dark, dark days of winter; and of nights when you hunch in your room because it's a chore too big to bundle up and go outside.

I woke to an early dawn and slurped coffee at the bakery, which kept open because they had to make morning doughnuts. The land lay all around me, but it had nothing to say. I counted my money and figured miles.

I climbed in the Desoto, thinking I had never got around to giving it a name. The road unreeled toward the west. It ended in Seattle, where I sold my car. Everybody said there was going to be a war, and I wasn't doing anything anyway. I joined the Navy.

III

What with him burying cars and raising hell, Jesse never wrote to me in summer. He was surely faithful in winter, though. He wrote long letters printed in a clumsy hand. He tried to cheer me up, and so did Matt Simons.

The Navy sent me to boot camp and diesel school, then to a motor pool in San Diego. I worked there three and a half years, sometimes even working on ships if the ships weren't going any-where. A sunny land and smiling ladies lay all about, but the ladies mostly fell in love by ten at night and got over it by dawn. Women in the bars were younger and prettier than back home. There was enough clap to go around.

"The business is growing like jimsonweed," Jesse wrote toward Christmas of '62. "I buried fourteen cars this summer, and one of them was a Kraut." He wrote a whole page about his morals. It didn't seem right to stick a crap crate in the ground beside real cars. At the same time, it was bad business not to. He opened a special corner of the cemetery, and pretended it was exclusive for foreign iron.

"And Mike Tarbush got to drinking," he wrote. "I'm sad to say we planted Judith."

Mike never had a minute's trouble with that Merc. Judith be-haved like a perfect lady until Mike turned upside down. He backed across a parking lot at night, rather hasty, and drove backward up the guy wire of a power pole. It was the only rollover wreck in history that happened at twenty miles an hour.

"Mike can't stop discussing it," Jesse wrote. "He's never caught The Dog, neither, but he ain't stopped trying. He wheeled in here in a beefed-up '57 Olds called Sally. It goes like stink and looks like a Hereford."

Home seemed far away, though it couldn't have been more than thirty-six hours by road for a man willing to hang over the wheel. I wanted to take a leave and drive home, but knew it better not hap-pen. Once I got there, I'd likely stay.

"George Pierson at the feed store says he's going to file a pater-nity suit against Potato," Jesse wrote. "The pups are cute, and there's a family resemblance."

It came to me then why I was homesick. I surely missed the

land, but even more I missed the people. Back home, folks were important enough that you knew their names. When somebody got messed up or killed, you felt sorry. In California, nobody knew nobody. They just swept up broken glass and moved right along. I should have meshed right in. I had made my rating and was pushing a rich man's car, a '57 hemi Chrysler, but never felt it fit.

"Don't pay it any mind," Jesse wrote when I told about meeting Road Dog. "I've heard about a guy who looks the same as me. Sometimes stuff like that happens."

And that was all he ever did say.

Nineteen sixty-three ended happy and hopeful. Matt Simons wrote a letter. Sam Winder bought a big Christmas card, and everybody signed it with little messages. Even my old boss at the filling station signed, "Merry Xmas, Jed—Keep It Between The Fence Posts." My boss didn't hold it against me that I left. In Montana a guy is supposed to be free to find out what he's all about.

Christmas of '63 saw Jesse pleased as a bee in clover. A lady named Sarah moved in with him. She waitressed at the café, and Jesse's letter ran pretty short. He'd put twenty-three cars under that year, and bought more acreage. He ordered a genuine marble gravestone for Miss Molly. "Sue Ellen is a real darling," Jesse wrote about the Linc. "That marker like to weighed a ton. We just about bent a back axle bringing it from the railroad."

From Christmas of '63 to January of '64 was just a few days, but they marked an awful downturn for Jesse. His letter was more real to me than all the diesels in San Diego.

He drew black borders all around the pages. The letter started out okay, but went downhill. "Sarah moved out and into a rented room," he wrote. "I reckon I was just too much to handle." He didn't explain, but I did my own reckoning. I could imagine that it was Jesse, plus two cats and two dogs, trying to get into a ten-wide-fifty trailer, that got to Sarah. "I think she misses me," he wrote, "but I expect she'll have to bear it."

Then the letter got just awful.

"A pack of wolves came through from Canada," Jesse wrote. "They picked off old Potato like a berry from a bush. Me and Mike found tracks, and a little blood in the snow."

I sat in the summery dayroom surrounded by sailors shooting

pool and playing Ping-Pong. I imagined the snow and ice of home. I imagined old Potato nosing around in his dumb and happy way, looking for rabbits or lifting his leg. Maybe he even wagged his tail when that first wolf came into view. I sat blinking tears, ready to bawl over a dog, and then I did, and to hell with it.

The world was changing, and it wouldn't change back. I put in for sea duty one more time, and the chief warrant who ramrodded that motor pool turned it down again. He claimed we kept the world safe by wrenching engines.

"The '62 Dodge is emerging as the car of choice for people in a hurry." Matt Simons wrote that in February '64, knowing I'd understand that nobody could tell which cars would be treasured until they had a year or two on them. "It's an extreme winter," he wrote, "and it's taking its toll on many of us. Mike has now learned not to punch a policeman. He's doing ten days. Sam Winder managed to roll a Jeep, and neither he nor I can figure out how a man can roll a Jeep. Sam has a broken arm, and lost two toes to frost. He was trapped under the wreck. It took awhile to pull him out. Brother Jesse is in the darkest sort of mood. He comes and goes in an irregular manner, but the Linc sits outside the pool hall on most days.

"And for myself," Matt wrote, "I think, come summer, I'll drop some revs. My flaming youth seems to be giving way to other interests. A young woman named Nancy started teaching at the school. Until now, I thought I was a confirmed bachelor."

A postcard came the end of February. The postmark said "Cheyenne, Wyoming," way down in the southeast corner of the state. It was written fancy. Nobody could mistake that fine, spidery hand. It read:

> Road Dog
> *Run and run as fast as he can,*
> *He can't find who is the Gingerbread Man*

The picture on the card had been taken from an airplane. It showed an oval racetrack where cars chased each other round and round. I couldn't figure why Jesse sent it, but it had to be Jesse. Then it came to me that Jesse was The Road Dog. Then it came to

me that he wasn't. The Road Dog was too slick. He wrote real delicate, and Jesse only printed real clumsy. On the other hand, The
Road Dog didn't know me from Adam's off ox. Somehow it *had* to
be Jesse.

"We got snow nut deep to a tall palm tree," Jesse wrote at about
the same time, "and Chip is failing. He's off his feed. He don't even
tease the kitties. Chip just can't seem to stop mourning."

I had bad premonitions. Chip was sensitive. I feared he wouldn't
be around by the time I got back home, and my fear proved right.
Chip held off until the first warm sun of spring, and then he died
while napping in the shade of the bulldozer. When Jesse sent a quick
note telling me, I felt pretty bad, but had been expecting it. Chip
had a good heart. I figured now he was with Potato, romping in the
hills somewhere. I knew that was a bunch of crap, but that's just the
way I chose to figure it.

They say a man can get used to anything, but maybe some can't.
Day after day, and week after week, California weather nagged.
Sometimes a puny little dab of weather dribbled in from the Pacific,
and people hollered it was storming. Sometimes temperatures
dropped toward the fifties, and people trotted around in thick sweat-
ers and coats. It was almost a relief when that happened, because
everybody put on their shirts. In three years, I'd seen more woman
skin than a normal man sees in a lifetime, and more tattoos on men.
The chief warrant at the motor pool had the only tattoo in the world
called "worm's-eye view of a pig's butt in the moonlight."

In autumn '64, with one more year to pull, I took a two-week
leave and headed north just chasing weather. It showed up first in
Oregon with rain, and more in Washington. I got hassled on the
Canadian border by a distressful little guy who thought, what with
the war, that I wanted political asylum.

I chased on up to Calgary, where matters got chill and whole-
some. Wind worked through the mountains like it wanted to drive
me south toward home. Elk and moose and porcupines went about
their business. Red-tailed hawks circled. I slid on over to Edmonton,
chased on east to Saskatoon, then dropped south through the Da-
kotas. In Williston, I had a terrible want to cut and run for home,
but didn't dare.

The Road Dog showed up all over the place, but the messages were getting strange. At a bar in Amidon:

>*Road Dog*
>*Taking Kentucky Windage*

At a hamburger joint in Belle Fourche:

>*Road Dog*
>*Chasing his tail*

At a restaurant in Redbird:

>*Road Dog*
>*Flea and flee as much as we can*
>*We'll soon find who is the Gingerbread Man*

In a poolroom in Fort Collins:

>*Road Dog*
>*Home home on derange*

Road Dog, or Jesse, was too far south. The Dog had never showed up in Colorado before. At least, nobody ever heard of such.

My leave was running out. There was nothing to do except sit over the wheel. I dropped on south to Albuquerque, hung a right, and headed back to the big city. All along the road, I chewed a dreadful fear for Jesse. Something bad was happening, and that didn't seem fair, because something good went on between me and the Chrysler. We reached an understanding. The Chrysler came alive and began to hum. All that poor car had ever needed was to look at road. It had been raised among traffic and poodles, but needed long sight distances and bears.

When I got back, there seemed no way out of writing a letter to Matt Simons, even if it was borrowing trouble. It took evening after evening of gnawing the end of a pencil. I hated to tell about Miss

Molly, and about the dancing ghost, and about my fears for Jesse. A man is supposed to keep his problems to himself.

At the same time, Matt was educated. Maybe he could give Jesse a hand if he knew all of it. The letter came out pretty thick. I mailed it thinking Matt wasn't likely to answer real soon. Autumn deepened to winter back home, and everybody would be busy.

So I worked and waited. There was an old White Mustang with a fifth wheel left over from the last war. It was a lean and hungry-looking animal, and slightly marvelous. I overhauled the engine, then dropped the tranny and adapted a ten-speed Roadranger. When I got that truck running smooth as a Baptist's mouth, the Navy surveyed it and sold it for scrap.

"Ghost cars are a tradition," Matt wrote toward the back of October, "and I'd be hard-pressed to say they are not real. I recall being passed by an Auburn boat tail about 3:00 A.M. on a summer day. That happened ten years ago. I was about your age, which means there was not an Auburn boat tail in all of Montana. That car died in the early thirties.

"And we all hear stories of huge old headlights overtaking in the mist, stories of Mercers and Duesenbergs and Bugattis. I try to believe the stories are true, because, in a way, it would be a shame if they were not.

"The same for road ghosts. I've never seen a ghost who looked like Jesse. The ghosts I've seen might not have been ghosts. To paraphrase an expert, they may have been a trapped beer belch, an undigested hamburger, or blowing mist. On the other hand, maybe not. They certainly seemed real at the time.

"As for Jesse—we have a problem here. In a way, we've had it for a long while, but only since last winter have matters become solemn. Then your letter arrives, and matters become mysterious. Jesse has—or had—a twin brother. One night when we were carousing, he told me that, but he also said his brother was dead. Then he swore me to a silence I must now break."

Matt went on to say that I must never, never say anything. He figured something was going on between brothers. He figured it must run deep.

"There is something uncanny about twins," Matt wrote. "What great matters are joined in the womb? When twins enter the world, they learn and grow the way all of us do; but some communication (or communion) surely happens before birth. A clash between brothers is a terrible thing. A clash between twins may spell tragedy."

Matt went on to tell how Jesse was going over the edge with road games, only the games stayed close to home. All during the summer, Jesse would head out, roll fifty or a hundred miles, and come home scorching like drawn by a string. Matt guessed the postcard I'd gotten from Jesse in February was part of the game, and it was the last time Jesse had been very far from home. Matt figured Jesse used tracing paper to imitate the Road Dog's writing. He also figured Road Dog had to be Jesse's brother.

"It's obvious," Matt wrote, "that Jesse's brother is still alive, and is only metaphorically dead to Jesse. There are look-alikes in this world, but you have reported identical twins."

Matt told how Jesse drove so crazy, even Mike would not run with him. That was bad enough, but it seemed the graveyard had sort of moved in on Jesse's mind. That graveyard was no longer just something to do. Jesse swapped around until he came up with a tractor and mower. Three times that summer, he trimmed the graveyard and straightened the markers. He dusted and polished Miss Molly's headstone.

"It's past being a joke," Matt wrote, "or a sentimental indulgence. Jesse no longer drinks, and no longer hells around in a general way. He either runs or tends the cemetery. I've seen other men search for a ditch, but never in such bizarre fashion."

Jesse had been seen on his knees, praying before Miss Molly's grave.

"Or perhaps he was praying for himself, or for Chip," Matt wrote. "Chip is buried beside Miss Molly. The graveyard has to be seen to be believed. Who would ever think so many machines would be so dear to so many men?"

Then Matt went on to say he was going to "inquire in various places" that winter. "There are ways to trace Jesse's brother," Matt wrote, "and I am very good at that sort of research." He said it was about the only thing he could still do for Jesse.

"Because," Matt wrote, "I seem to have fallen in love with a romantic. Nancy wants a June wedding. I look forward to another winter alone, but it will be an easy wait. Nancy is rather old-fashioned, and I find that I'm old-fashioned as well. I will never regret my years spent helling around, but am glad they are now in the past."

Back home, winter deepened. At Christmas a long letter came from Jesse, and some of it made sense. "I put eighteen cars under this summer. Business fell off because I lost my hustle. You got to scooch around a good bit, or you don't make contacts. I may start advertising.

"And the tabbies took off. I forgot to slop them regular, so now they're mousing in a barn on Jimmy Come Lately Road. Mike says I ought to get another dog, but my heart isn't in it."

Then the letter went into plans for the cemetery. Jesse talked some grand ideas. He thought a nice wrought-iron gate might be showy, and bring in business. He thought of finding a truck that would haul "deceased" cars. "On the other hand," he wrote, "if a guy don't care enough to find a tow, maybe I don't want to plant his iron." He went on for a good while about morals, but a lawyer couldn't understand it. He seemed to be saying something about respect for Miss Molly, and Betty Lou, and Judith. "Sue Ellen is a real hummer," he wrote about the Linc. "She's got two hundred thousand I know about, plus whatever went on before."

Which meant Jesse was piling up about seventy thousand miles a year, and that didn't seem too bad. Truck drivers put up a hundred thousand. Of course, they make a living at it.

Then the letter got so crazy it was hard to credit.

"I got The Road Dog figured out. There's two little kids. Their mama reads to them, and they play tag. The one that don't get caught gets to be the Gingerbread Man. This all come together because I ran across a bunch of kids down on the Colorado line. I was down that way to call on a lady I once knew, but she moved, and I said what the hell, and hung around a few days, and that's what clued me to The Dog. The kids were at a Sunday-school picnic, and I was napping across the car seat. Then a preacher's wife came over and saw I wasn't drunk, but the preacher was there, too, and they invited me. I eased over to the picnic, and everybody made me welcome. Anyway, those kids were playing, and I heard the gingerbread business, and I figured The Dog is from Colorado."

The last page of the letter was just as scary. Jesse took kids' crayons and drew the front ends of the Linc and Miss Molly. There was a tail that was probably Potato's sticking out from behind the picture of Miss Molly, and everything was centered around the picture of a marker that said "R.I.P. Road Dog."

But—there weren't any little kids. Jesse had not been to Colorado. Jesse had been tending that graveyard, and staying close to home. Jesse played make-believe, or else Matt Simons lied; and there was no reason for Matt to lie. Something bad, bad wrong was going on with Jesse.

There was no help for it. I did my time and wrote a letter every month or six weeks pretending everything was normal. I wrote about what we'd do when I got home, and about the Chrysler. Maybe that didn't make much sense, but Jesse was important to me. He was a big part of what I remembered about home.

At the end of April, a postcard came, this time from Havre. "The Dog is after me. I feel it." It was just a plain old postcard. No picture.

Matt wrote in May, mostly his own plans. He busied himself building a couple of rooms onto his place. "Nancy and I do not want a family right away," he wrote, "but someday we will." He wrote a bubbly letter with a feel of springtime to it.

"I almost forgot my main reason for writing," the letter said. "Jesse comes from around Boulder, Colorado. His parents are long dead, ironically in a car wreck. His mother was a schoolteacher, his father a librarian. Those people, who lived such quiet lives, somehow produced a hellion like Jesse, and Jesse's brother. That's the factual side of the matter.

"The human side is so complex it will not commit to paper. In fact, I do not trust what I know. When you get home next fall, we'll discuss it."

The letter made me sad and mad. Sad because I wasn't getting married, and mad because Matt didn't think I'd keep my mouth shut. Then I thought better of it. Matt didn't trust himself. I did what any gentleman would do, and sent him and Nancy a nice gravy boat for the wedding.

In late July, Jesse sent another postcard. "He's after me; I'm after him. If I ain't around when you get back, don't fret. Stuff happens. It's just a matter of chasing road."

Summer rolled on. The Navy released "nonessential personnel" in spite of the war. I put four years in the outfit and got called nonessential. Days choked past like a rig with fouled injectors. One good thing happened. My old boss moved his station to the outskirts of town and started an IH dealership. He straight out wrote how he needed a diesel mechanic. I felt hopeful thoughts, and dark ones.

In September, I became a veteran who qualified for an overseas ribbon, because of work on ships that later on went somewhere. Now I could join the Legion post back home, which was maybe the payoff. They had the best pool table in the county.

"Gents," I said to the boys at the motor pool, "it's been a distinct by-God pleasure enjoying your company, and don't never come to Montana, 'cause she's a heartbreaker." The Chrysler and me lit out like a kyoodle of pups.

It would have been easier to run to Salt Lake, then climb the map to Havre, but notions pushed. I slid east to Las Cruces, then popped north to Boulder with the idea of tracing Jesse. The Chrysler hummed and chewed up road. When I got to Boulder, the notion turned hopeless. There were too many people. I didn't even know where to start asking.

It's no big job to fool yourself. Above Boulder, it came to me how I'd been pointing for Sheridan all along, and not even Sheridan. I pointed toward a girl who smiled at me four years ago.

I found her working at a hardware, and she wasn't wearing any rings. I blushed around a little bit, then got out of there to catch my breath. I thought of how Jesse took whatever time was needed when he bought the Linc. It looked like this would take awhile.

My pockets were crowded with mustering-out pay and money for unused leave. I camped in a ten-dollar motel. It took three days to get acquainted, then we went to a show and supper afterward. Her name was Linda. Her father was a Mormon. That meant a year of courting, but it's not all that far from north Montana to Sheridan.

I had to get home and get employed, which would make the Mormon happy. On Saturday afternoon Linda and I went back to the same old movie, but this time we held hands. Before going home, she kissed me once, real gentle. That made up for those hard times in San Diego. It let me know I was back with my own people.

I drove downtown all fired up with visions. It was way too early for bed, and I cared nothing for a beer. A run-down café sat on the outskirts. I figured pie and coffee.

The Dog had signed in. His writing showed faint, like the wall had been scrubbed. Newer stuff scrabbled over it.

> *Road Dog*
> *Tweedledum and Tweedledee*
> *Lonely pups as pups can be*
> *For each other had to wait*
> *Down beside the churchyard gate.*

The café sort of slumbered. Several old men lined the counter. Four young gear heads sat at a table and talked fuel injection. The old men yawned and put up with it. Faded pictures of old racing cars hung along the walls. The young guys sat beneath a picture of the Bluebird. That car held the land speed record of 301.29 m.p.h. This was a racer's café, and had been for a long, long time.

The waitress was graying and motherly. She tsked and tished over the old men as much as she did the young ones. Her eyes held that long-distance prairie look, a look knowing wind and fire and hard times, stuff that either breaks people or leaves them wise. Matt Simons might get that look in another twenty years. I tried to imagine Linda when she became the waitress's age, and it wasn't bad imagining.

Pictures of quarter-mile cars hung back of the counter, and pictures of street machines hung on each side of the door. Fifties hot rods scorched beside worked-up stockers. Some mighty rowdy iron crowded that wall. One picture showed a Golden Hawk. I walked over, and in one corner was the name "Still"—written in The Road Dog's hand. It shouldn't have been scary.

I went back to the counter shaking. A nice-looking old gent nursed coffee. His hands wore knuckles busted by a thousand slipped wrenches. Grease was worked in deep around his eyes, the way it gets after years and years when no soap made will touch it. You could tell he'd been a steady man. His eyes were clear as a kid.

"Mister," I said, "and beg pardon for bothering you. Do you know anything about that Studebaker?" I pointed to the wall.

"You ain't bothering me," he said, "but I'll tell you when you do." He tapped the side of his head like trying to ease a gear in place, then he started talking engine specs on the Stude.

"I mean the man who owns it."

The old man probably liked my haircut, which was short. He liked it that I was raised right. Young guys don't always pay old men much mind.

"You still ain't bothering me." He turned to the waitress. "Sue," he said, "has Johnny Still been in?"

She turned from cleaning the pie case, and she looked toward the young guys like she feared for them. You could tell she was no big fan of engines. "It's been the better part of a year, maybe more." She looked down the line of old men. "I was fretting about him just the other day. . . ." She let it hang. Nobody said anything. "He comes and goes so quiet, you might miss him."

"I don't miss him a hell of a lot," one of the young guys said. The guy looked like a duck, and had a voice like a sparrow. His fingernails were too clean. That proved something.

"Because Johnny blew you out," another young guy said. "Johnny *always* blew you out."

"Because he's crazy," the first guy said. "There's noisy crazy and quiet crazy. The guy is a spook."

"He's going through something," the waitress said, and said it kind. "Johnny's taken a lot of loss. He's the type who grieves." She looked at me like she expected an explanation.

"I'm friends with his brother," I told her. "Maybe Johnny and his brother don't get along."

The old man looked at me rather strange. "You go back quite a ways," he told me. "Jesse's been dead a good long time."

I thought I'd pass out. My hands started shaking, and my legs felt too weak to stand. Beyond the window of the café, red light came from a neon sign, and inside the café everybody sat quiet, waiting to see if I was crazy, too. I sort of picked at my pie. One of the young guys moved real uneasy. He loafed toward the door, maybe figuring he'd need a shotgun. The other three young ones looked confused.

"No offense," I said to the old man, "but Jesse Still is alive. Up on the high line. We run together."

"Jesse Still drove a damn old Hudson Terraplane into the South Platte River in spring of '52, maybe '53." The old man said it real quiet. "He popped a tire when not real sober."

"Which is why Johnny doesn't drink," the waitress said. "At least, I expect that's the reason."

"And now you are bothering me." The old man looked to the waitress, and she was as full of questions as he was.

Nobody ever felt more hopeless or scared. These folks had no reason to tell this kind of yarn. "Jesse is sort of roughhouse." My voice was only whispering. It wouldn't make enough sound. "Jesse made his reputation helling around."

"You've got that part right," the old man told me, "and, youngster, I don't give a tinker's damn if you believe me or not, but Jesse Still is dead."

I saw what it had to be, but seeing isn't always believing. "Thank you, mister," I whispered to the old man, "and thank you, ma'am," to the waitress. Then I hauled out of there leaving them with something to discuss.

A terrible fear rolled with me, because of Jesse's last postcard. He said he might not be home, and now that could mean more than it said. The Chrysler bettered its reputation, and we just flew. From the Montana line to Shelby is eight hours on a clear day. You can wail it in seven, or maybe six and a half if a deer doesn't tangle with your front end. I was afraid, and confused, and getting mad. Me and Linda were just to the point of hoping for an understanding, and now I was going to get killed running over a porcupine or into a heifer. The Chrysler blazed like a hound on a hot scent. At eighty the pedal kept wanting to dig deep and really howl.

The nighttime road yells danger. Shadows crawl over everything. What jumps into your headlights may be real, and may be not. Metal crosses hold little clusters of dark flowers on their arms, and the land rolls out beneath the moon. Buttes stand like great ships anchored in the plains, and riverbeds run like dry ink. Come spring, they'll flow; but in September, all flow is in the road.

The dancing ghost picked me up on Highway 3 outside Comanche, but this time he wasn't dancing. He stood on the berm, and no mist tied him in place. He gave the old road sign for "roll 'em." Beyond Columbia, he showed up again. His mouth moved like he was yelling me along, and his face twisted with as much fear as my own.

That gave me reason to hope. I'd never known Jesse to be afraid like that, so maybe there was a mistake. Maybe the dancing ghost wasn't the ghost of Jesse. I hung over the wheel and forced myself to think of Linda. When I thought of her, I couldn't bring myself to get crazy. Highway 3 is not much of a road, but that's no bother. I can drive anything with wheels over any road ever made. The dancing ghost kept showing up and beckoning, telling me to scorch. I told myself the damn ghost had no judgment, or he wouldn't be a ghost in the first place.

That didn't keep me from pushing faster, but it wasn't fast enough to satisfy the roadside. They came out of the mist, or out of the ditches; crowds and clusters of ghosts standing pale beneath a weak moon. Some of them gossiped with each other. Some stood yelling me along. Maybe there was sense to it, but I had my hands full. If they were trying to help, they sure weren't doing it. They just made me get my back up, and think of dropping revs.

Maybe the ghosts held a meeting and studied out the problem. They could see a clear road, but I couldn't. The dancing ghost showed up on Highway 12 and gave me "thumbs up" for a clear road. I didn't believe a word of it, and then I really didn't believe what showed in my mirrors. Headlights closed like I was standing. My feelings said that all of this had happened before; except, last time, there was only one set of headlights.

It was Miss Molly and Betty Lou that brought me home. Miss Molly overtook, sweeping past with a lane change smooth and sober as an Adventist. The high, slaunch-forward form of Miss Molly thrummed with business. She wasn't blowing sparks or showing off. She wasn't playing Gingerbread Man or tag.

Betty Lou came alongside so I could see who she was, then Betty Lou laid back a half mile. If we ran into a claim-jumping deputy, he'd have to chase her first; and more luck to him. Her headlights hovered back there like angels.

Miss Molly settled down a mile ahead of the Chrysler and stayed at that distance, no matter how hard I pressed. Twice before Great Falls, she spotted trouble, and her squinchy little brake lights hauled me down. Once it was an animal, and once it was busted road surface. Miss Molly and Betty Lou dropped me off before Great Falls, and picked me back up the minute I cleared town.

We ran the night like rockets. The roadside lay deserted. The dancing ghost stayed out of it, and so did the others. That let me concentrate, which proved a blessing. At those speeds, a man don't have time to do deep thinking. The road rolls past, the hours roll, but you've got a racer's mind. No matter how tired you should be, you don't get tired until it's over.

I chased a ghost car northward while a fingernail moon moved across the sky. In deepest night the land turned silver. At speed, you don't think, but you do have time to feel. The farther north we pushed, the more my feelings went to despair. Maybe Miss Molly thought the same, but everybody did all they could.

The Chrysler was a howler, and Lord knows where the top end lay. I buried the needle. Even accounting for speedometer error, we burned along in the low half of the second century. We made Highway 2 and Shelby around three in the morning, then hung a left. In just about no time, I rolled home. Betty Lou dropped back and faded. Miss Molly blew sparks and purely flew out of sight. The sparks meant something. Maybe Miss Molly was still hopeful. Or maybe she knew we were too late.

Beneath that thin moon, mounded graves looked like dark surf across the acreage. No lights burned in the trailer, and the Linc showed nowhere. Even under the scant light, you could see snowy tops of mountains, and the perfectly straight markers standing at the head of each grave. A tent, big enough to hold a small revival, stood not far from the trailer. In my headlights a sign on the tent read "Chapel." I fetched a flashlight from the glove box.

A dozen folding chairs stood in the chapel, and a podium served as an altar. Jesse had rigged up two sets of candles, so I lit some. Matt Simons had written that the graveyard had to be seen to be believed. Hanging on one side of the tent was a sign reading "Shrine," and all along that side hung road maps, and pictures of cars, and pictures of men standing beside their cars. There was a special display of odometers, with little cards beneath them: "330,938 miles"; "407,000 miles"; "half a million miles, more or less." These were the championship cars, the all-time best at piling up road, and those odometers would make even a married man feel lonesome. You couldn't look at them without thinking of empty roads and empty nights.

Even with darkness spreading across the cemetery, nothing felt worse than the inside of the tent. I could believe that Jesse took it serious, and had tried to make it nice, but couldn't believe anyone else would buy it.

The night was not too late for owls, and nearly silent wings swept past as I left the tent. I walked to Miss Molly's grave, half-expecting ghostly headlights. Two small markers stood beside a real fine marble headstone.

Potato
Happy-go-sloppy and good
Rest in Peace Wherever You Are

Chip
A dandy little sidekicker
Running with Potato

From a distance, I could see piled dirt where the dozer had dug new graves. I stepped cautious toward the dozer, not knowing why, but knowing it had to happen.

Two graves stood open like little garages, and the front ends of the Linc and the Hawk poked out. The Linc's front bumper shone spotless, but the rest of the Linc looked tough and experienced. Dents and dings crowded the sides, and cracked glass starred the windows.

The Hawk stood sparkly, ready to come roaring from the grave. Its glass shone washed and clean before my flashlight. I thought of what I heard in Sheridan, and thought of the first time I'd seen the Hawk. It hadn't changed. The Hawk looked like it had just been driven off a showroom floor.

Nobody in his right mind would want to look in those two cars, but it wasn't a matter of "want." Jesse, or Johnny—if that's who it was—had to be here someplace. It was certain sure he needed help. When I looked, the Hawk sat empty. My flashlight poked against the glass of the Linc. Jesse lay there, taking his last nap across a car seat. His long black hair had turned gray. He had always been thin, but now he was skin and bones. Too many miles, and no time to eat. Creases around his eyes came from looking at road, but now the creases were deep like an old man's. His eyes showed that he was dead. They were open only a little bit, but open enough.

I couldn't stand to be alone with such a sight. In less than fifteen minutes, I stood banging on Matt Simons's door. Matt finally answered, and Nancy showed up behind him. She was in her robe. She stood taller than Matt, and sleepier. She looked blond and Swedish. Matt didn't know whether to be mad or glad. Then I got my story pieced together, and he really woke up.

"Dr. Jekyll has finally dealt with Mr. Hyde," he said in a low voice to Nancy. "Or maybe the other way around." To me, he said, "That may be a bad joke, but it's not ill meant." He went to get dressed. "Call Mike," he said to me. "Drunk or sober, I want him there."

Nancy showed me the phone. Then she went to the bedroom to talk with Matt. I could hear him soothing her fears. When Mike answered, he was sleepy and sober, but he woke up stampeding.

Deep night and a thin moon is a perfect time for ghosts, but none showed up as Matt rode with me back to the graveyard. The Chrysler loafed. There was no need for hurry.

I told Matt what I'd learned in Sheridan.

"That matches what I heard," he said, "and we have two mysteries. The first mystery is interesting, but it's no longer important. Was John Still pretending to be Jesse Still, or was Jesse pretending to be John?"

"If Jesse drove into a river in '53, then it has to be John." I didn't like what I said, because Jesse was real. The best actor in the world couldn't pretend that well. My sorrow choked me, but I wasn't ashamed.

Matt seemed to be thinking along the same lines. "We don't know how long the game went on," he said real quiet. "We never will know. John could have been playing at being Jesse way back in '53."

That got things tangled, and I felt resentful. Things were complicated enough. Me and Matt had just lost a friend, and now Matt was talking like that was the least interesting part.

"Makes no difference whether he was John or Jesse," I told Matt.

"He was Jesse when he died. He's laying across the seat in Jesse's car. Figure it any way you want, but we're talking about Jesse."

"You're right," Matt said. "Also, you're wrong. We're talking about someone who was both." Matt sat quiet for a minute, figuring things out. I told myself it was just as well that he'd married a school-teacher. "Assume, for the sake of argument," he said, "that John was playing Jesse in '53. John drove into the river, and people believed they were burying Jesse.

"Or, for the sake of argument, assume that it was Jesse in '53. In that case the game started with John's grief. Either way the game ran for many years." Matt was getting at something, but he always has to go roundabout.

"After years, John, or Jesse, disappeared. There was only a man who was both John and Jesse. That's the reason it makes no difference who died in '53."

Matt looked through the car window into the darkness like he expected to discover something important. "This is a long and lone-some country," he said. "The biggest mystery is: why? The answer may lie in the mystery of twins, or it may be as simple as a man reaching into the past for happy memories. At any rate, one brother dies, and the survivor keeps his brother alive by living his brother's life, as well as his own. Think of the planning, the elaborate schemes, the near self-deception. Think of how often the roles shifted. A time must have arrived when that lonely man could not even remember who he was."

The answer was easy, and I saw it. Jesse, or John, chased the road to find something they'd lost on the road. They lost their parents and each other. I didn't say a damn word. Matt was making me mad, but I worked at forgiving him. He was handling his own grief, and maybe he didn't have a better way.

"And so he invented The Road Dog," Matt said. "That kept the personalities separate. The Road Dog was a metaphor to make him proud. Perhaps it might confuse some of the ladies, but there isn't a man ever born who wouldn't understand it."

I remembered long nights and long roads. I couldn't fault his reasoning.

"At the same time," Matt said, "the metaphor served the twins. They could play road games with the innocence of children, maybe

even replay memories of a time when their parents were alive and
the world seemed warm. John played The Road Dog, and Jesse
chased; and, by God, so did the rest of us. It was a magnificent
metaphor."

"If it was that blamed snappy," I said, "how come it fell to
pieces? For the past year, it seems like Jesse's been running away
from The Dog."

"The metaphor began to take over. The twins began to defend
against each other," Matt said. "I've been watching it all along, but
couldn't understand what was happening. John Still was trying to take
over Jesse, and Jesse was trying to take over John."

"It worked for a long time," I said, "and then it didn't work.
What's the kicker?"

"Our own belief," Matt said. "We all believed in The Road Dog.
When all of us believed, John was forced to become stronger."

"And Jesse fought him off?"

"Successfully," Matt said. "All this year, when Jesse came firing
out of town, rolling fifty miles, and firing back, I thought it was Jesse's
problem. Now I see that John was trying to get free, get back on the
road, and Jesse was dragging him back. This was a struggle between
real men, maybe titans in the oldest sense, but certainly not imi-
tations."

"It was a guy handling his problems."

"That's an easy answer. We can't know what went on with John,"
Matt said, "but we know some of what went on with Jesse. He tried
to love a woman, Sarah, and failed. He lost his dogs—which doesn't
sound like much, unless your dogs are all you have. Jesse fought
defeat by building his other metaphor, which was that damned cemetery." Matt's voice got husky. He'd been holding in his sorrow,
but his sorrow started coming through. It made me feel better
about him.

"I think the cemetery was Jesse's way of answering John, or de-
nying that he was vulnerable. He needed a symbol. He tried to protect his loves and couldn't. He couldn't even protect his love for his
brother. That cemetery is the last bastion of Jesse's love." Matt
looked like he was going to cry, and I felt the same.

"Cars can't hurt you," Matt said. "Only bad driving hurts you.
The cemetery is a symbol for protecting one of the few loves you

can protect. That's not saying anything bad about Jesse. That's saying something with sadness for all of us."

I slowed to pull onto Jesse's place. Mike's Olds sat by the trailer. Lights were on in the trailer, but no other lights showed anywhere.

"Men build all kinds of worlds in order to defeat fear and loneliness," Matt said. "We give and take as we build those worlds. One must wonder how much Jesse, and John, gave in order to take the little that they got."

We climbed from the Chrysler as autumn wind moved across the graveyard and felt its way toward my bones. The moon lighted faces of grave markers, but not enough that you could read them. Mike had the bulldozer warming up. It stood and puttered, and darkness felt best, and Mike knew it. The headlights were off. Far away on Highway 2, an engine wound tight and squalling, and it seemed like echoes of engines whispered among the graves. Mike stood huge as a grizzly.

"I've shot horses that looked healthier than you two guys," he said, but said it sort of husky.

Matt motioned toward the bulldozer. "This is illegal."

"Nobody ever claimed it wasn't." Mike was ready to fight if a fight was needed. "Anybody who don't like it can turn around and walk."

"I like it," Matt said. "It's fitting and proper. But if we're caught, there's hell to pay."

"I like most everything and everybody," Mike said, "except the government. They paw a man to death while he's alive, then keep pawing his corpse. I'm saving Jesse a little trouble."

"They like to know that he's dead and what killed him."

"Sorrow killed him," Mike said. "Let it go at that."

Jesse killed himself, timing his tiredness and starvation just right, but I was willing to let it go, and Matt was, too.

"We'll go along with you," Matt said. "But they'll sell this place for taxes. Somebody will start digging sometime."

"Not for years and years. It's deeded to me. Jesse fixed up papers. They're on the kitchen table." Mike turned toward the trailer. "We're going to do this right, and there's not much time."

We found a blanket and a quilt in the trailer. Mike opened a kitchen drawer and pulled out snapshots. Some looked pretty new, and some were faded: a man and woman in old-fashioned clothes, a picture of two young boys in Sunday suits, pictures of cars and road signs, and pictures of two women who were maybe Sue Ellen and Sarah. Mike piled them like a deck of cards, snapped a rubber band around them, and checked the trailer. He picked up a pair of pale yellow sunglasses that some racers use for night driving. "You guys see anything else?"

"His dogs," Matt said. "He had pictures of his dogs."

We found them under a pillow, and it didn't pay to think why they were there. Then we went to the Linc and wrapped Jesse real careful in the blanket. We spread the quilt over him, and laid his stuff on the floor beside the accelerator. Then Mike remembered something. He half unwrapped Jesse, went through his pockets, then wrapped him back up. He took Jesse's keys and left them hanging in the ignition.

The three of us stood beside the Linc, and Matt cleared his throat.

"It's my place to say it," Mike told him. "This was my best friend." Mike took off his cap. Moonlight lay thin on his bald head.

"A lot of preachers will be glad this man is gone, and that's one good thing you can say for him. He drove nice people crazy. This man was a hellion, pure and simple; but what folks don't understand is, hellions have their place. They put everything on the line over nothing very much. Most guys worry so much about dying, they never do any living. Jesse was so alive with living, he never gave dying any thought. This man would roll ninety just to get to a bar before it closed." Mike kind of choked up and stopped to listen. From the graveyard came the echoes of engines, and from Highway 2 rose the thrum of a straight-eight crankshaft whipping in its bed. Dim light covered the graveyard, like a hundred sets of parking lights and not the moon.

"This man kept adventure alive, when, everyplace else, it's dying. There was nothing ever smug or safe about this man. If he had fears, he laughed. This man never hit a woman or crossed a friend. He did tie the can on Betty Lou one night, but can't be blamed. It was really The Dog who did that one. Jesse never had a problem until he climbed into that Studebaker."

So Mike had known all along. At least Mike knew something.

"I could always run even with Jesse," Mike said, "but I never could beat The Dog. The Dog could clear any track. And in a damn Studebaker."

"But a very swift Studebaker," Matt muttered, like a Holy Roller answering the preacher.

"Bored and stroked and rowdy," Mike said, "and you can say the same for Jesse. Let that be the final word. Amen."

IV

A little spark of flame dwelt at the stack of the dozer, and distant mountains lay white capped and prophesied winter. Mike filled the graves quick. Matt got rakes and a shovel. I helped him mound the graves with only moonlight to go on, while Mike went to the trailer. He made coffee.

"Drink up and git," Mike told us when he poured the coffee. "Jesse's got some friends who need to visit, and it will be morning pretty quick."

"Let them," Matt said. "We're no hindrance."

"You're a smart man," Mike told Matt, "but your smartness makes you dumb. You started to hinder the night you stopped driving beyond your headlights." Mike didn't know how to say it kind, so he said it rough. His red mustache and bald head made him look like a pirate in a picture.

"You're saying that I'm getting old." Matt has known Mike long enough not to take offense.

"Me, too," Mike said, "but not that old. When you get old, you stop seeing them. Then you want to stop seeing them. You get afraid for your hide."

"You stop imagining?"

"Shitfire," Mike said, "you stop seeing. Imagination is something you use when you don't have eyes." He pulled a cigar out of his shirt pocket and was chewing it before he ever got it lit. "Ghosts have lost it all. Maybe they're the ones the Lord didn't love well enough. If you see them, but ain't one, maybe you're important."

Matt mulled that, and so did I. We've both wailed a lot of road for some sort of reason.

"They're kind of rough," Matt said about ghosts. "They hitch rides, but don't want 'em. I've stopped for them and got laughed at. They fool themselves, or maybe they don't."

"It's a young man's game," Matt said.

"It's a game guys got to play. Jesse played the whole deck. He was who he was, whenever he was it. That's the key. That's the reason you slug cops when you gotta. It looks like Jesse died old, but he lived young longer than most. That's the real mystery. How does a fella keep going?"

"Before we leave," I said, "how long did you know that Jesse was The Dog?"

"Maybe a year and a half. About the time he started running crazy."

"And never said a word?"

Mike looked at me like something you'd wipe off your boot. "Learn to ride your own fence," he told me. "It was Jesse's business." Then he felt sorry for being rough. "Besides," he said, "we were having fun. I expect that's all over now."

Matt followed me to the Chrysler. We left the cemetery, feeling tired and mournful. I shoved the car onto Highway 2, heading toward Matt's place.

"Wring it out once for old times?"

"Putter along," Matt said. "I just entered the putter stage of life, and may as well practice doing it."

In my mirrors a stream of headlights showed, then vanished one by one as cars turned into the graveyard. The moon had left the sky. Over toward South Dakota was a suggestion of first faint morning light. Mounded graves lay at my elbow, and so did Canada. On my left the road south ran fine and fast as a man can go. Mist rose from the roadside ditches, and maybe there was movement in the mist, maybe not.

There's little more to tell. Through fall and winter and spring and summer, I drove to Sheridan. The Mormon turned out to be a pretty good man, for a Mormon. I kept at it, and drove through another autumn and another winter. Linda got convinced. We got married in the spring, and I expected trouble. Married people are supposed to fight, but nothing like that ever happened. We just worked hard, got our own place in a few years, and Linda birthed two girls. That disappointed the Mormon, but was a relief to me.

And in those seasons of driving, when the roads were good for twenty miles an hour in the snow, or eighty under sun, the road stood empty except for a couple times. Miss Molly showed up once early on to say a bridge was out. She might have showed up another time. Squinchy little taillights winked one night when it was late and I was highballing. Some guy jackknifed a Freightliner, and his trailer lay across the road.

But I saw no other ghosts. I'd like to say that I saw the twins, John and Jesse, standing by the road, giving the high sign or dancing, but it never happened.

I did think of Jesse, though, and thought of one more thing. If Matt was right, then I saw how Jesse had to die before I got home. He had to, because I believed in Road Dog. My belief would have been just enough to bring John forward, and that would have been fatal, too. If either one of them became too strong, they both of them lost. So Jesse had to do it.

The graveyard sank beneath the weather. Mike tended it for a while, but lost interest. Weather swept the mounds flat. Weed-covered markers tumbled to decay and dust, so that only one marble headstone stands solid beside Highway 2. The marker doesn't bend before the winter winds, nor does the little stone that me and Mike and Matt put there. It lays flat against the ground. You have to know where to look:

Road Dog
1931–1965
2 million miles, more or less
Run and run as fast as we can
We never can catch the Gingerbread Man

And now even the great good cars are dead, or most of them. What with gas prices and wars and rumors of wars, the cars these days are all suspensions. They'll corner like a cat, but don't have the scratch of a cat; and maybe that's a good thing. The state posts fewer crosses.

Still, there are some howlers left out there, and some guys are still howling. I lie in bed of nights and listen to the scorch of engines along Highway 2. I hear them claw the darkness, stretching lonesome at the sky, scatting across the eternal land; younger guys running as young guys must; chasing each other, or chasing the land of dreams, or chasing into ghost land while hoping it ain't true—guys running into darkness chasing each other, or chasing something—chasing road.

APPENDIXES

ABOUT THE NEBULA AWARDS

Throughout every calendar year, the members of the Science-fiction and Fantasy Writers of America read and recommend novels and stories for the annual Nebula Awards. The editor of the "Nebula Awards Report" collects the recommendations and publishes them in the *SFWA Forum*. Near the end of the year, the NAR editor tallies the endorsements, draws up the preliminary ballot, and sends it to all active SFWA members. Under the current rules, each novel and story enjoys a one-year eligibility period from its date of publication. If the work fails to make the preliminary ballot during that interval, it is dropped from further Nebula consideration.

The NAR editor processes the results of the preliminary ballot and then compiles a final ballot listing the five most popular novels, novellas, novelettes, and short stories. For purposes of the Nebula Award, a novel is 40,000 words or more; a novella is 17,500 to 39,999 words; a novelette is 7,500 to 17,499 words; and a short story is 7,499 words or fewer. At the present time, SFWA impanels both a novel jury and a short-fiction jury to oversee the voting process and, in cases where a presumably worthy title was neglected by the membership at large, to supplement the five nominees with a sixth choice. Thus, the appearance of extra finalists in any category bespeaks two distinct processes: jury discretion and ties.

Founded in 1965 by Damon Knight, the Science Fiction Writers of America began with a charter membership of seventy-eight authors. Today it boasts about a thousand members and an augmented name. Early in his tenure, Lloyd Biggle, Jr., SFWA's first secretary-treasurer, proposed that the organization periodically select and publish the year's best stories. This notion quickly evolved into the elaborate balloting process, an annual awards banquet, and a series of Nebula anthologies. Judith Ann Lawrence designed the trophy from a sketch by Kate Wilhelm. It is a block of Lucite containing a rock crystal and a spiral nebula made of metallic glitter. The prize is handmade, and no two are exactly alike.

The Grand Master Nebula Award goes to a living author for a lifetime of achievement. In accordance with SFWA's bylaws, the president nominates a candidate, normally after consulting with previous presidents and the board of directors. This nomination then goes before the officers; if a majority approves, the candidate becomes a Grand Master. Past recipients include Robert A. Heinlein (1974), Jack Williamson (1975), Clifford D. Simak (1976), L. Sprague de Camp (1978), Fritz Leiber (1981), Andre Norton (1983), Arthur C. Clarke (1985), Isaac Asimov (1986), Alfred Bester (1987), Ray Bradbury (1988), Lester del Rey (1990), and Frederik Pohl (1992).

The twenty-ninth annual Nebula Awards banquet was held at the Valley River Inn in Eugene, Oregon, on April 23, 1994, where Nebula Awards were given in the categories of novel, novella, novelette, and short story.

SELECTED TITLES FROM THE 1993 PRELIMINARY NEBULA BALLOT

The following lists provide an overview of those works, authors, and periodicals that particularly attracted SFWA's notice during 1993. Finalists and winners are excluded from this listing, as these are documented in the introduction.

Novels

Dark Sky Legion by William Barton (Bantam)

Count Geiger's Blues by Michael Bishop (Tor)

The Spirit Ring by Lois McMaster Bujold (Baen)

Fools by Pat Cadigan (Bantam)

Virtual Light by William Gibson (Bantam)

The Thread That Binds the Bones by Nina Kiriki Hoffman (AvoNova)

Exile by Michael Kube-McDowell (Ace)

Metaphase by Vonda N. McIntyre (Bantam)

Oracle by Mike Resnick (Ace)

Purgatory: A Chronicle of a Distant World by Mike Resnick (Tor)

Destroying Angel by Richard Paul Russo (Ace)

Fossil Hunter by Robert J. Sawyer (Ace)

Last Refuge by Elizabeth Ann Scarborough (Bantam)

The Hollow Man by Dan Simmons (Bantam)

Manhattan Transfer by John E. Stith (Tor)

Guns of the South by Harry Turtledove (Ballantine)

Steel Beach by John Varley (Putnam)

Aristoi by Walter Jon Williams (Tor)

Novellas

"The Young Person's Guide to the Organism" by James Alan
Gardner (*Amazing Stories*, April 1992)

"The Immediate Family" by Spider Robinson
(*Analog*, January 1993)

"Synthesis" by Mary Rosenblum
(*Asimov's Science Fiction*, March 1992)

Novelettes

"Jumping the Road" by Jack Dann
(*Asimov's Science Fiction*, October 1992)

"Monsters" by James Patrick Kelly
(*Asimov's Science Fiction*, June 1992)

"Beneath the Stars of Winter" by Geoffrey A. Landis
(*Asimov's Science Fiction*, January 1993)

"Embracing the Alien" by Geoffrey A. Landis
(*Analog*, November 1992)

"Vanilla Dunk" by Jonathan Lethem
(*Asimov's Science Fiction*, September 1992)

"Beast of the Heartland" by Lucius Shepard (*Playboy*, September
1992; *Asimov's Science Fiction*, April 1993)

"Suicidal Tendencies" by Dave Smeds (*Full Spectrum 4*, Bantam)

"Deep Eddy" by Bruce Sterling
(*Asimov's Science Fiction*, August 1993)

"Ice Covers the Hole" by Rick Wilber (*The Magazine of Fantasy & Science Fiction*, December 1992)

Short Stories

"The Winterberry" by Nick DiChario (*Alternate Kennedys*, Tor)

"Mwalimu in the Squared Circle" by Mike Resnick
(*Asimov's Science Fiction*, March 1993)

"The Pale Thin God" by Mike Resnick (*Xanadu 1*, Tor)

"A Little Night Music" by Lucius Shepard (*Omni*, March 1992)

"Reef Apes" by Dave Smeds
(*Asimov's Science Fiction*, August 1992)

"The Story So Far" by Martha Soukup (*Full Spectrum 4*, Bantam)

"The GooglePlex Comes and Goes" by Del Stone, Jr.
(*Full Spectrum 4*, Bantam)

"Change of Life" by L. A. Taylor (*Analog*, April 1992)

"Useful Phrases" by Gene Wolfe (*Tomorrow SF*)

PAST NEBULA AWARD WINNERS

1965

Best Novel: *Dune* by Frank Herbert

Best Novella: "The Saliva Tree" by Brian W. Aldiss
"He Who Shapes" by Roger Zelazny (tie)

Best Novelette: "The Doors of His Face, the Lamps of His Mouth" by Roger Zelazny

Best Short Story: " 'Repent, Harlequin!' Said the Ticktockman" by Harlan Ellison

1966

Best Novel: *Flowers for Algernon* by Daniel Keyes
Babel-17 by Samuel R. Delany (tie)
Best Novella: "The Last Castle" by Jack Vance
Best Novelette: "Call Him Lord" by Gordon R. Dickson
Best Short Story: "The Secret Place" by Richard McKenna

1967

Best Novel: *The Einstein Intersection* by Samuel R. Delany
Best Novella: "Behold the Man" by Michael Moorcock
Best Novelette: "Gonna Roll the Bones" by Fritz Leiber
Best Short Story: "Aye, and Gomorrah" by Samuel R. Delany

1968

Best Novel: *Rite of Passage* by Alexei Panshin
Best Novella: "Dragonrider" by Anne McCaffrey
Best Novelette: "Mother to the World" by Richard Wilson
Best Short Story: "The Planners" by Kate Wilhelm

1969

Best Novel: *The Left Hand of Darkness* by Ursula K. Le Guin
Best Novella: "A Boy and His Dog" by Harlan Ellison
Best Novelette: "Time Considered as a Helix of Semi-Precious
Stones" by Samuel R. Delany
Best Short Story: "Passengers" by Robert Silverberg

1970

Best Novel: *Ringworld* by Larry Niven
Best Novella: "Ill Met in Lankhmar" by Fritz Leiber
Best Novelette: "Slow Sculpture" by Theodore Sturgeon
Best Short Story: no award

1971

Best Novel: *A Time of Changes* by Robert Silverberg

Best Novella: "The Missing Man" by Katherine MacLean

Best Novelette: "The Queen of Air and Darkness"
by Poul Anderson

Best Short Story: "Good News from the Vatican"
by Robert Silverberg

1972

Best Novel: *The Gods Themselves* by Isaac Asimov

Best Novella: "A Meeting with Medusa" by Arthur C. Clarke

Best Novelette: "Goat Song" by Poul Anderson

Best Short Story: "When It Changed" by Joanna Russ

1973

Best Novel: *Rendezvous with Rama* by Arthur C. Clarke

Best Novella: "The Death of Doctor Island" by Gene Wolfe

Best Novelette: "Of Mist, and Grass, and Sand"
by Vonda N. McIntyre

Best Short Story: "Love Is the Plan, the Plan Is Death"
by James Tiptree, Jr.

Best Dramatic Presentation: *Soylent Green*
Stanley R. Greenberg for Screenplay
(based on the novel *Make Room! Make Room!*)
Harry Harrison for *Make Room! Make Room!*

1974

Best Novel: *The Dispossessed* by Ursula K. Le Guin

Best Novella: "Born with the Dead" by Robert Silverberg

Best Novelette: "If the Stars Are Gods" by Gordon Eklund and
Gregory Benford

Best Short Story: "The Day Before the Revolution"
by Ursula K. Le Guin
Best Dramatic Presentation: *Sleeper* by Woody Allen
Grand Master: Robert A. Heinlein

1975

Best Novel: *The Forever War* by Joe Haldeman
Best Novella: "Home Is the Hangman" by Roger Zelazny
Best Novelette: "San Diego Lightfoot Sue" by Tom Reamy
Best Short Story: "Catch That Zeppelin!" by Fritz Leiber
Best Dramatic Writing: Mel Brooks and Gene Wilder
for *Young Frankenstein*
Grand Master: Jack Williamson

1976

Best Novel: *Man Plus* by Frederik Pohl
Best Novella: "Houston, Houston, Do You Read?"
by James Tiptree, Jr.
Best Novelette: "The Bicentennial Man" by Isaac Asimov
Best Short Story: "A Crowd of Shadows" by Charles L. Grant
Grand Master: Clifford D. Simak

1977

Best Novel: *Gateway* by Frederik Pohl
Best Novella: "Stardance" by Spider and Jeanne Robinson
Best Novelette: "The Screwfly Solution" by Raccoona Sheldon
Best Short Story: "Jeffty Is Five" by Harlan Ellison
Special Award: *Star Wars*

1978

Best Novel: *Dreamsnake* by Vonda N. McIntyre

Best Novella: "The Persistence of Vision" by John Varley

Best Novelette: "A Glow of Candles, a Unicorn's Eye"
by Charles L. Grant

Best Short Story: "Stone" by Edward Bryant

Grand Master: L. Sprague de Camp

1979

Best Novel: *The Fountains of Paradise* by Arthur C. Clarke

Best Novella: "Enemy Mine" by Barry Longyear

Best Novelette: "Sandkings" by George R. R. Martin

Best Short Story: "giANTS" by Edward Bryant

1980

Best Novel: *Timescape* by Gregory Benford

Best Novella: "The Unicorn Tapestry" by Suzy McKee Charnas

Best Novelette: "The Ugly Chickens" by Howard Waldrop

Best Short Story: "Grotto of the Dancing Deer"
by Clifford D. Simak

1981

Best Novel: *The Claw of the Conciliator* by Gene Wolfe

Best Novella: "The Saturn Game" by Poul Anderson

Best Novelette: "The Quickening" by Michael Bishop

Best Short Story: "The Bone Flute" by Lisa Tuttle°

Grand Master: Fritz Leiber

°This Nebula Award was declined by the author.

1982

Best Novel: *No Enemy But Time* by Michael Bishop
Best Novella: "Another Orphan" by John Kessel
Best Novelette: "Fire Watch" by Connie Willis
Best Short Story: "A Letter from the Clearys" by Connie Willis

1983

Best Novel: *Startide Rising* by David Brin
Best Novella: "Hardfought" by Greg Bear
Best Novelette: "Blood Music" by Greg Bear
Best Short Story: "The Peacemaker" by Gardner Dozois
Grand Master: Andre Norton

1984

Best Novel: *Neuromancer* by William Gibson
Best Novella: "PRESS ENTER ■" by John Varley
Best Novelette: "Bloodchild" by Octavia E. Butler
Best Short Story: "Morning Child" by Gardner Dozois

1985

Best Novel: *Ender's Game* by Orson Scott Card
Best Novella: "Sailing to Byzantium" by Robert Silverberg
Best Novelette: "Portraits of His Children"
by George R. R. Martin
Best Short Story: "Out of All Them Bright Stars" by Nancy Kress
Grand Master: Arthur C. Clarke

1986

Best Novel: *Speaker for the Dead* by Orson Scott Card
Best Novella: "R & R" by Lucius Shepard
Best Novelette: "The Girl Who Fell into the Sky" by Kate Wilhelm
Best Short Story: "Tangents" by Greg Bear
Grand Master: Isaac Asimov

1987

Best Novel: *The Falling Woman* by Pat Murphy
Best Novella: "The Blind Geometer" by Kim Stanley Robinson
Best Novelette: "Rachel in Love" by Pat Murphy
Best Short Story: "Forever Yours, Anna" by Kate Wilhelm
Grand Master: Alfred Bester

1988

Best Novel: *Falling Free* by Lois McMaster Bujold
Best Novella: "The Last of the Winnebagos" by Connie Willis
Best Novelette: "Schrödinger's Kitten" by George Alec Effinger
Best Short Story: "Bible Stories for Adults, No. 17: The Deluge"
by James Morrow
Grand Master: Ray Bradbury

1989

Best Novel: *The Healer's War* by Elizabeth Ann Scarborough
Best Novella: "The Mountains of Mourning"
by Lois McMaster Bujold
Best Novelette: "At the Rialto" by Connie Willis
Best Short Story: "Ripples in the Dirac Sea" by Geoffrey Landis

1990

Best Novel: *Tehanu: The Last Book of Earthsea*
by Ursula K. Le Guin
Best Novella: "The Hemingway Hoax" by Joe Haldeman
Best Novelette: "Tower of Babylon" by Ted Chiang
Best Short Story: "Bears Discover Fire" by Terry Bisson
Grand Master: Lester del Rey

1991

Best Novel: *Stations of the Tide* by Michael Swanwick
Best Novella: "Beggars in Spain" by Nancy Kress
Best Novelette: "Guide Dog" by Mike Conner
Best Short Story: "Ma Qui" by Alan Brennert

1992

Best Novel: *Doomsday Book* by Connie Willis
Best Novella: "City of Truth" by James Morrow
Best Novelette: "Danny Goes to Mars" by Pamela Sargent
Best Short Story: "Even the Queen" by Connie Willis
Grand Master: Frederik Pohl

Those who are interested in category-related awards should also consult *A History of the Hugo, Nebula, and International Fantasy Awards* by Donald Franson and Howard DeVore (Misfit Press, 1987). Periodically updated, the book is available from Howard DeVore, 4705 Weddel, Dearborn, Michigan 48125.

Permissions Acknowledgments